Elias John W. Gibb, Shaikh S. Ali

The History of the Forty Vezirs

The story of the forty morns and eves

Elias John W. Gibb, Shaikh S. Ali

The History of the Forty Vezirs
The story of the forty morns and eves

ISBN/EAN: 9783337267704

Printed in Europe, USA, Canada, Australia, Japan

Cover: Foto ©Andreas Hilbeck / pixelio.de

More available books at **www.hansebooks.com**

THE HISTORY

OF

THE FORTY VEZIRS

OR

THE STORY OF THE FORTY MORNS AND EVES

WRITTEN IN TURKISH

By SHEYKH-ZĀDA

DONE INTO ENGLISH

By E. J. W. GIBB M. R. A. S.

Membre de la Société Asiatique de Paris, Author of "Ottoman Poems,"
Translator of "The Story of Jewād," &c.

LONDON

GEORGE REDWAY

MDCCCLXXXVI

PREFACE.

HE following translation of the celebrated Turkish Romance generally known as the History of the Forty Vezirs, has been made from a printed but undated text procured a few years ago in Constantinople. The MS. version, of which this copy, which I shall call the Const. Text, is an impression, has been dedicated to a Sultan Mustafà; but there is nothing to indicate which of the four Ottoman monarchs who bore that name is intended. The fact of him being styled simply Sultan Mustafà would lead us to imagine that the first Emperor so called must be meant; as in the

case of any of the others, some such addition as
his father's name or one of the words, Second,
Third or Fourth, would be absolutely necessary to
distinguish him from his predecessor or predeces-
sors of the same name. Sultan Mustafà I reigned
from 1617 to 1618, and again from 1622 to
1623. It will thus be seen that this edition of
the text is, even at the earliest, by no means an
old one. That from which extracts were published by Belletête about the beginning of the
present century, is clearly much older, and
appears to represent a very early, if not the
original, Turkish version of the work.* The
style in which it is written is very antiquated,
obsolete words and archaic expressions meeting
us at every turn. It is dedicated to Sultan
Murād, the son of Muhammed, the son of
Bayezid, *i. e.* Murād II (the father of Muhammed II, the conqueror of Constantinople), whose
reign extended from 1421 to 1451.

---

* Contes Turcs en langue turque, extraits du Roman intitulé
Les Quarante Vizirs, par feu M. Belletête, Paris, 1812. The
extracts consist of the Dedication or Preface, the prefatory Story
of Sultan Mahmud, the Introduction, forty out of the eighty
subordinate Stories, and the Conclusion.

Of the Ottoman author or compiler, who
calls himself simply Sheykh-zāda (=Sheykh-
born, *i.e.* Child of the Sheykh), nothing appears
to be known.   He states in his Dedication that
the work is a translation from the Arabic; but
it is not very clear from his words, as published
by Belletête, whether the title which he there
mentions is that of the Arab original or of the
Turkish translation : probably it is intended for
both.   He says, " Now, by reason of this,
Sheykh-zāda hath written out (lit. made a fair
copy of) this book, named *Hikāyetu-Erba'ina-
Sabāhin we Mesā* (=The Story of the Forty
Morns and Eves), for the Sultan of the age."[*]
The popular Turkish title of the work, *Qirq
Vezīr Tārīkhi* (= he History of the Forty
Vezirs), which alone is given as the name of the
Romance in the Const. Text, nowhere occurs
in the Paris edition.[†]   According to Dr. Behr-

---

[*] *Bu sebebden Sheykh-zāda Sultān-i ' asr ichun bu Hikāyetu-
Erba'ina Sabāhin we Mesā adlu kitāb beyāza geturdi.*   For
' *asr*=age, Belletête has *Misr*=Egypt, which makes nonsense.

[†] It appears, however, on the title-page, the work of the
French editor, travestied thus : *Qirq Vezīrin ve Qirq Khatunin
Hikāyetleri*=The Stories of the Forty Vezirs and of the Forty
Ladies.

nauer, who five-and-thirty years ago published
an excellent German version from a MS. preserved in the Royal Library at Dresden,* a
certain Ahmed the Egyptian made an inde-
pendent but abridged Turkish translation of
the Romance, a MS. of which is to be seen in
the Municipal Library of Leipzig.

By the courtesy of Dr. Rost I have been
favoured with the loan of a manuscript of
the Forty Vezirs belonging to the Library
of the India Office (No. 3,211). Unhappily,
this copy, which begins with the prefatory
Story of Sultan Mahmūd,† contains no
Dedication whatever, and, consequently, affords
no information as to the origin and title of
the book, the name of the author or that of
his patron. The copyist has, moreover, omitted
to mention the year in which he transcribed the
work ; so that it is impossible to ascertain the
date of the volume. Its style is pretty much

---

* Die Vierzig Veziere oder Weisen Meister, ein altmorgen-
ländischer Sittenroman aus dem Türkischen übertragen von
Dr. Walter Fr. Adolf Behrnauer, Leipzig, 1851.

† This prefatory Story of Sultan Mahmūd of Ghazni, which
forms no part of the Romance of the Forty Vezirs, properly so-
called, seems nevertheless to occur in every edition.

the same as that of the Const. Text; but it deals somewhat less in detail than the latter. Belletête's volume is fuller than either; but it is extremely carelessly printed, teeming with typographical errors, doubly vexatious in an edition of an archaic text.*

While there is little difference, save in minor details, such as the names of towns, the professions of the characters, and so forth, between the several versions of those among the subordinate stories that are common to two or more of these texts (including Behrnauer's Translation, which may be taken as correctly representing the Dresden MS.), there is a vast difference in the selection of such stories given

---

* While these pages were passing through the press I examined two MSS. of the Forty Vezirs preserved in the British Museum (Add. 7882 and Or. 20). Both are dedicated to Murād II, but in the first-mentioned the name of Ahmed-i Misrī=Ahmed the Egyptian is substituted for that of Sheykh-zāda. While it shows no variations of any moment, this MS., far from being an abridgment, is fuller in point of detail than any other text of the work that has come under my notice. Neither MS. yields any story that is not to be found in the present volume. It is possible that Sheykh-zāda and Ahmed-i Misrī may be one and the same person, whose full name would then be Sheykh-zāda Ahmed-i Misrī=Ahmed Sheykh-son of Egypt (or Cairo).

in each. Indeed, the Forty Vezirs may be
called, as the Thousand and One Nights has
been, "rather a vehicle for stories, partly fixed
and partly arbitrary, than a collection fairly
deserving from its constant identity with itself
the name of a distinct work." Thus the total
number of subordinate stories in a complete
text ought to be eighty (one for each of the
Vezirs, and a corresponding, or rather counter-
acting, one each night for the Lady), but of
those that I have seen, the Const. Text alone
has this number; Belletête's edition, being but
a selection, has only the half; while the India
Office MS. omits four, and the Dresden MS.
two, for no very palpable reason.* These four
texts yield a total of one hundred and ten distinct stories, of which I have translated all save
three (whereof more anon), placing in an Appendix such as do not occur in the Const. Text,
which, as already stated, serves as the ground-
work of my Translation. I have, however,
given Belletête's Dedication, as representing

---

* Details are shown in the Comparative Table in Appendix C.

that of the original work, instead of the one in
which occurs the name of Sultan Mustafà, and
in which, I should add, nothing is said as to the
work being a translation from the Arabic, and
no mention is made of Sheykh-zāda or any
other writer. As the order, even of those
stories that are common to all the texts, varies
greatly in each, such titles as the First Vezir's
Story, the Lady's Second Story, &c., are in-
sufficient to particularize the several tales. I
have therefore, in the Table of Contents,
labelled each story with a number, and so
obtained a clear and simple means of reference.
By this plan I have been enabled to show at a
glance in the Comparative Table in Appendix C,
not only the stories that are found in the several
texts, but the order in which they occur in each.

An incomplete translation of the History of
the Forty Vezirs made by Petis de la Croix, a
French orientalist who died in 1713, was found
among that author's papers and published in
1722, under the title of *L'Histoire de la Sultane
de Perse et des Visirs.* This fragment, which
first brought our Romance under the notice of

European scholars, omitting the Dedication and the prefatory Story of Sultan Mahmūd, begins with the Introduction, and contains nineteen of the subordinate stories. All the nineteen occur in the Const. Text ; but so great are the variations that appear in many of them in De la Croix that I have thought it advisable to discuss them elsewhere.* As far as translation goes, this French version represents the Turkish original (such as I have seen it) about as faithfully as Galland's celebrated production does the Arabic Thousand and One Nights. Turned into English, and published in 1809, it forms the " Turkish Tales " to which Dunlop refers in his History of Fiction, and which, up till now, has remained the sole representative of the History of the Forty Vezirs in our language. It is rather unfortunate that De la Croix has not translated the Dedication of his text ; but, as he says that the Romance is the work of Chéc Zadé (*i. e.* Sheykh-zäda), preceptor† to Amurath II (*i. e.*

---

* In Appendix B.

† There seems to be no authority for the statement that Sheykh-zäda held the office of preceptor to Murād II.

Murād II), and that the book is ene, ary to the Nasa (*i. e.* [Hikāyetu] Erba'ina [Sa.y wever, Mesā), it does not appear to have .] in-ase essentially from that printed by Belletêtes] 're now translated. °s ;

Of Dr. Behrnauer's Translation I have already spoken, and need only add that it is a most scholarly piece of work, and, so far as it goes, leaves nothing to be desired ; but being simply a German version of the Dresden MS. it contains only seventy-eight of the hundred and ten stories which I have collected from various texts and printed in the present volume.

The frame of the History of the Forty Vezirs —the story of the King who, misled by the false accusations of his baffled and revengeful wife, orders the execution of his innocent son, a crime from committing which he is diverted by the wise advice of his chief councillor, only to be urged to it again at night by the Queen, to be restrained again by the words of his second councillor, to be incited to it once more by the Queen, and so on, tossed to and fro, till each of his councillors has in turn done his duty and the

guilt of the
—this ha~wicked Queen is at last made clear
in the ~been shown by Mr. W. A. Clouston,
have .troduction to his Book of Sindibād, to
     .een among the best known and most
p⸵lar of romances during many ages and in
any widely separated lands. Judging from
the present state of our knowledge, it would
appear that this story arose in early times in
India, whence in the sixth century it passed to
Persia, thence to be spread over all the West.
Thus we have Syriac Sindban, Greek Syntipas,
Hebrew Sandabar, Neo-Persian Sindibād,
French Dolopathos, English Seven Wise
Masters, and a host of others. But in all these
the number of vezirs, sages, masters, or whatever local usage has caused the advisers of the
king to be termed, is limited to seven. In the
Turkish version alone, so far as we know, are
there forty councillors; for, if any copies of the
Arabic original, from which the Ottoman writers
profess to have made their translations are still
extant, these copies have hitherto eluded the
search of European scholars.*

---

* Those readers who are desirous of going into the question

Of the hundred and ten subordin, ary to the
have collected, some possess consider;y wever,
others again have little or none, while ,l incase
both classes are inappropriate enough t8] 're
occasion on which they are supposed to es ;
related ; several, indeed, being in one text pu:
into the mouth of a Vezir, which are, in another,
attributed to the Lady. Probably not one
among them is original; many are quite familiar
to us in other dresses, and the student of fiction
will be able to point out several variants of the
greater number. Considering my task as simply
that of a collector and translator, I have made
no attempt to trace these stories, through
the many lands where they have become local-
ized, back to the fountain-head in India, or
wherever else it may be. To do this work as it
ought to be done would demand a far more
intimate and extensive acquaintance with popular fiction than I can pretend to, and may safely

---

of the origin of this cycle of romance are referred to Mr. Clouston's Book of Sindibād (1884), where they will find the subject
fully discussed ; also to the same scholar's forthcoming work on
"Popular Tales and Fictions : their Migrations and Transforma-
tions," in which the most recent information will be embodied.

guilt of the
—this hae hands of those eminent scholars
in the now making a special study of the
hav id spread of "old world tales." I may,
r ver, be permitted to mention a few variants
have occured to me during the course of
iy work : [3]* finds a parallel in the Thousand
and One Nights, and in the Book of Sindibād;
[7] in the Talmud ; [8] in Poggio ; [16] in the
Baytāl Pachīsī ; [18*b*] in Rabelais ; [22] in the
Contes Devots ; part of [25] in the Voyages of
Sindbad the Sailor ; [28] in Straparola ; [34] in
the Fabliau des Trois Larrons by Jehan de
Boves, and in Straparola ; [35*a*] in the Thousand
and One Nights ; [37] in Galland's Story of
Prince Codadad (for Khudā-dād=God-given :
Theodore, Nathanael, &c.) ; [38] in Poggio
and Æsop ; [39] in the Gesta Romanorum; [44]
in the Kathā-Sarit-Sāgara, the Book of Sindibād,
the Cento Novelle Antiche, the Contes Devots,
and the Gesta Romanorum ; part of [45] in
Cinthio, and the Ballad of the Heir of Linne;
part of [46] in the Story of the Second Calender

---

* The figures in brackets indicate the stories as numbered in
the Table of Contents.

in the Thousand and One Nights, airy to the Mabinogion; [53] in Machiavelli's Story wever, phegor, in Straparola, and Brevio; [57] in case Decameron, and the Bahār-i Dānish; [58] 're the Gesta Romanorum, and the Vies des Pères; [60] in the Story of Vikram, King of Ujjayn; [74] in the Bakhtyār-Nāma; [77] in Straparola; [87] in the Book of Sindibād; [93] in Æsop and the Anvār-i Suhaylī; [94] in the Hitopadesha, and the Anvār-i Suhaylī; [108] in the Gulistān; and so on.

Some of these tales are still current in Turkey; thus [18a], that of the three youths who misunderstood the enigmatic counsels of their father, is given, very slightly modified, as a popular story in the Memoirs of Mr. Barker, who was for many years British Consul at Aleppo. But there is nothing peculiarly Turkish in any of them; indeed, many of the incidents narrated would have been impossible in the Turkish society of any period.

The Romance of the Forty Vezirs is, like all the other members of the same family, Eastern and Western, Hindu, Muhammedan and Christian,

guilt of
—this satire on the fair sex. Stories that told
in women were very popular everywhere
ing the Middle Ages, though, perhaps, they
joyed a yet greater share of public favour in
Europe than in Asia. We all recollect how
Jankyn, clerk of Oxenford and fifth husband to
the immortal Wyf of Bath, used to gloat over
his book of tales of the wickedness of wives.
The most striking characteristic of the old
French Fabliaux is the bitterness and ribaldry
with which they scoff at female weaknesses.
The reader must not then imagine that he finds
portrayed in this collection of tales the Eastern
as opposed to the Western estimate of woman. *
What he does find is the medieval as opposed
to the modern estimate of her ; and he will find
the same, only painted in far stronger colours, if
he turns to the European popular story-books
of the period.

Being productions of a more outspoken age,
many of the following tales are, as was to be

---

* The modern Eastern, or at least Turkish, estimate of
woman may be found in the works of such writers as Kemāl,
Ekrem, and 'Abd-ul-Haqq Hāmid.

expected, of a character that is contrary to the taste of the present time. I have, however, omitted nothing in this book; but in the case of a few isolated passages and of three entire stories, the nature of which is such as to preclude the possibility of their publication in these days, I have been content to print the original transliterated into the Roman alphabet, but untranslated. The three stories in question are very similar in character in many of the Fabliaux, and I have little doubt that variants of them exist in one or more of the many collections of these tales. All such matters, it should be added, are as offensive to the modern Ottoman as to the modern English reader.

It only remains for me to say that I have made the Translation as literal as possible, adopting a simple style as being best suited to represent the quaint old-fashioned character of the original, which, notwithstanding what the writer says in the Dedication (the only high-flown piece in the whole book), is much less encumbered with literary conceits and verbal adornments than are most works due to the pens of Ottoman authors of the olden time.

April 1886. E. J. W. G.

Since writing the above, I have purchased from Mr. Quaritch two MSS. of the Forty Vezirs. The first of these, which was transcribed in A.H. 1010 (A.D. 1601), offers no new stories; but the second, which is undated, yields two. These have been translated and printed at the end of Appendix A, thus raising the total number of tales in this volume to one hundred and twelve. Unhappily, some leaves are lost from the beginning of both MSS., the first remaining page of the one commencing with the prefatory Story of Sultan Mahmūd; that of the other, with the Lady's Second Story. Of the hundred and twelve subordinate tales now collected, thirty-eight are common to all the five fairly complete texts I have seen (the Const. Text, the India Office MS., Behrnauer's translation of the Dresden MS., and the two Quaritch MSS.); two are peculiar to the Const. Text, four to the India Office MS., four to the Dresden MS., and two to the Quaritch MS. No. II.

TABLE OF CONTENTS.

(Figures within Brackets, thus [1], are introduced for the Purpose of numbering the several Stories for Reference.)

APPENDIX A—STORIES OCCURRING IN OTHER TEXTS
THAN THAT FROM WHICH THE TRANSLATION HAS
BEEN MADE.

THE

HISTORY OF THE FORTY VEZIRS.

In the Name of God, the Merciful, the Compassionate.

RAISES and lauds unbounded are due to that Creator (glorified be His glory! exalted be His power!) at the contemplation of whose greatness the eye of the understanding and the vision of the soul are mazed, and at the foot of the hill of the perfectness of whose sempiternity the farthest limit of the thoughts and the bourne of the perception of all creatures are dazed. And thanksgiving to that gracious One, to the compassing of the favour of whose graciousness the girdle of speech were strait : To the truth of the ray of whose beauty one may not win by that lantern, the lamp in the glass of the sight of the intellect ; and the voice of the herald of

B

whose grandeur may not be heard in the portico
of the ear, or yet on the tower of imagination :
The ocean of whose knowledge compasseth all
things known, of essential and of attributive, of
special and of general, seeing that—" With Him
are the keys of the unseen : none knoweth them
save He :"* And reverence is due to Him,
seeing that—" Then exalted be God, the King,
the Truth ; there is no god but He :"† And the
trust of all the faithful, and the confessors, and
the trusters, and the strivers is this hope, seeing
that—" Say, By the grace of God and by His
mercy :"‡ Save His pure self none is worthy
the attribute of Oneness, the praise of Unity,
seeing that—" And your God is One God :"§
And all perfectness of felicity's wonders is of
constancy in service at His threshold, seeing
that—" Then flee to God :"‖ And in the spirits
of all those passed away the light of His aid is
manifest, seeing that—" So take firm hold of
the rope of God altogether :"¶ And the praise
of all praisers is from the beginning of His work,
seeing that—" Verily, your Lord is God who
created the heavens and the earth,"** even to
the end of His words, seeing that—" Dwelling

---

* Koran, vi. 59.   † Ib. xxiii. 117.   ‡ Ib. x. 59.   § Ib. ii. 158.
‖ Ib. li. 50.   ¶ Ib. iii. 98.   ** Ib. vii. 52, and x. 3.

therein for aye, so long as dure the heavens
and the earth."* And be greetings limitless and
salutations boundless shed on yon pure tomb,
yon odorous sepulchre, to wit, that of Muhammed Mustafa (the peace of God on him,
and the blessing !), and be they shed upon his
Friends and Household !

To proceed : Now (through) the decree of
Divine Providence and the haps of empery
(there reigneth) the magnificent Sultan, the most
great Monarch, the Sovereign of the earth, the
Shadow of God over the believers, the Glorifier
of the world and the Faith, the Aidance of
Islam and the Muslims, the Proof, the Commander of the Faithful, the Sultan, the son of
the Sultan, MURĀD, the son of Muhammed the
son of Bāyezīd, the Khān—God aid his friends
and crush his foes ! God lengthen his life !

He's the Quarry of all justice, as the Mine of Grace him view :
The Shadow of the Lord, the Proof, Commander of the True.

For these ensigns of his glory are flashed to
all regions of the earth and all corners of the
world. Now, this is incumbent, that they of
religion and full assurance do by righteous
prayers and abounding lauds aid the majesty of
his empire, and that, according to the strength

---

* Koran, xi. 109, 110.

of their power and the measure of their ability,
they offer gifts at the threshold of glory. Those
gifts may be of the manner of the offerings of
the world, or of the matter of knowledge.
Now, it is not so worthy that majesty if those
gifts be of the gear of the world ; by two proofs :
the first is this, that a call hath been given to
his majesty from the manifestation of the case
and the divulgement of might and power, seeing
that—"What God hath given me is better
than what He hath given you."* The second
proof is this, that the world is little, seeing that
—"Say, The enjoyment of the world is little."†
Now, it is not according to reason to bring a
little thing to the King's majesty. So by these
conclusive proofs it is become known that the
gifts worthy that majesty were books on the
matter of wisdom. Now, by reason of this,
SHEYKH-ZĀDA hath written this book named
Hikāyetu-Erba'īna-Sabāhin wa Mesā, "THE
STORY OF THE FORTY MORNS AND EVES." In
the Arabian tongue it was a story bare of
elegance and of the ornaments of speech. Now,
we have bedecked it in every becoming place
with verses of the Koran, and Traditions,‡ and

---

* Koran, xxvii. 36.   † Ib. iv. 79.
‡ Hadīs-i Sherif, the traditional sayings of the Prophet
Muhammed.

with couplets and stanzas, with flowery **expressions** and heart-expanding graces, and have made it, bride-like, a fair, heart-resting sight for the eyes of the beholders of the outer and the inner, to the end that the King, bidding it be read, may hear on what wise were the stories of those by-gone monarchs, and know how that this tyrant Sphere hath crushed certain amongst them under foot.

To proceed : One day when that just king, Sultan Mahmūd the son of Sebuktekīn,* was conversing with his vezirs, some of those ministers, radiant of understanding, made mention of kings who had come into the world and departed, and died and passed away. And that Sultan, praiseworthy of disposition and auspicious of action, asked what were the names of those kings. And a vezir replied, " It is so long a time since those kings passed to the Palace of the Hereafter, that the name of not one in a thousand is known; it is only said, ' at such and such a time there was a king.'" Then said the Sultan, "Do ye contrive me a plan that my name shall be remembered in the

---

* Mahmūd the son of Sebuktekīn, the famous conqueror of India, ruled at Ghazni from A.H. 388 to 421 ; A.D. 998 to 1030.

palace of the earth, and my fame be celebrated till the Resurrection Day." The vezirs said, " Though you should set about the building of a great palace, in the course of ages it would fall in ruins, and your name should not dure ; neither would it be mentioned in other lands, and so your fame should not be celebrated." And they all said different things, but nothing was deemed suitable. Now Sultan Mahmūd had a favourite attendant named Ayāz who was exceeding resourceful, and at length he said, "Let a book be written in the name of my king, that it may remain until the Resurrection Day, and pass from land to land, and be read ; and by means of that book will the noble name of my king be remembered even till the end of time, and mentioned with blessings." The vezirs too deemed this suggestion befitting and this plan beseeming, and approved it. Sultan Mahmūd had there an all-accomplished, learned and intelligent master, by name Firdausī of Tūs. Him did the Sultan command, and he caused him to write in his name the book of the Shāh-Nāma, which consists of sixty thousand couplets ; and for every couplet he granted him a sequin. For that reason shall the name of Sultan Mahmūd dure till the Resurrection Day and be mentioned with blessings.

It is related that the wife of a great king
unjustly accused his son, by another mother, of
an act of treachery against his father ; and that
that king was wroth, and for forty mornings
caused his son to be led forth to be slain ; and
that that king had forty vezirs, all of whom
were peerless in the sea of understanding, and
in thoughtfulness and sagacity, and full of
plans and devices ; and that when the king
each morning caused his son to be led forth for
execution, these vezirs gave the king counsel,
and each morning a vezir, telling a story,
calmed the king's heart and turned away his
wrath, and saved the prince from his hand ;
and again, that each night that crafty lady, letting not the king rest, ever incited him to the
slaughter of the prince, and with enticing and beguiling words, repeated each night a story to the
king, and made his understanding forsake him ;
and that through the words of that crafty lady,
every morning for forty days he caused his son
to be led into his presence to be slain ; and that
the vezirs by each telling a story delivered him.
After forty days the innocence of the prince was
manifested and the falsehood and calumny of the
crafty lady disclosed ; and she received her due,

and the prince was greatly loved and esteemed before his father when the truth of his affair was known. The adventures of the king, and the lady and the prince, and his governor and the forty vezirs, and what befell between them, will be related ; and the stories told by the vezirs in the forty days, and by the lady in the forty nights will be set forth and narrated. " With God is grace : how excellent a Friend is He ! "

They tell in history books, that there was in Persia a great king, whose name was Khānqīn, and in the grasp of whose possession were the Seven Climes. As he was gracious and able and sagacious, kingliness and the bases of empire were present in him. God Most High had given him a fair son, by whose beauty the people of the world were bewildered. Whosoever looked upon his loveliness would say, " Is it magic, this ?"* and he who beheld his tall figure would exclaim, " This is no mortal ! "† Fair was his beauty and charming was his self, and desired of lovers. Moreover, his were accomplishments and perfections ; he had no rival in the reading of science, or in penmanship,

---

* Koran, lii. 15.   † Ib. xii. 31.

or in archery, or in horsemanship ; and his fair
character was talked of and celebrated among
high and low. The king, too, whenever he
saw him, experienced a hundred thousand
pleasures, and looked upon him as the source
of his life. The mother of this youth was of
the lovely ones of China.* One day she fell ill,
and at length, no remedy availing, she was
received into Mercy. Thereupon, after some
time had passed, his father married the daughter
of a great king and brought her to his palace.
After a while this lady fell in love with the
prince. For a long time she hid her love in
her heart, and, saying in herself, " He is my
step-son, what help for it ! " she disclosed it not.
But when, day after day, she looked upon his
beauty, she was no longer able to bear with
patience the fire of love, and, bringing into the
field the wallet of craft, she was busy night and
day with stratagems. Now the king had given
the prince to a governor to be taught the
sciences of astronomy and astrology, and the
boy was night and day occupied acquiring them.
One day the governor looked at the youth's
horoscope, and perceived there was a space of

---

* Not necessarily a Chinese woman, simply a beauty ; China
and Chinese Tartary being regarded as pre-eminent for the
beauty of their women.

forty days in most sinister aspect. Did he say
a word about this, he would be pointing out a
great calamity ; so he was exceeding grieved,
and his heart was contracted. But he said to
the prince, " I have this day looked at thy
horoscope and seen a most sinister aspect ; such
is it, my life,* that thou must obey the command
and decree of God Most High, and observe my
injunction, else thou shalt die." The prince
heard these words of his governor and his colour
changed, and he said to his teacher, " Order
what thou wilt : command is thine." Quoth the
teacher, " O son, the way of averting this
calamity is thus stated in the book : for the
space of forty days thou shalt not speak one
word though a naked sword be above thy
head." Then he bade the prince bear in mind
certain of the Holy Names and blessed litanies,
and sent him to his father. The governor
thereupon hid in a vault and concealed himself.†
When the prince came to his father, the latter
said to him, " My son, what hast thou read and
written this day ? " but the prince gave no
answer to his father. Again quoth the king,
" O my life, what does thy master ? " again he

---

* A term of endearment.
† Probably he was afraid lest the king should put him to death
for giving such bad news.

gave no answer. Again his father said, "O life of my life, what has befallen thee? Why dost thou not speak?" Again he gave no answer. Then said the king to his son's guardian, "The boy is sad to day, take him to his mother, may-be that his heart will expand." Then the guardian took the youth to the lady and said, "Lady, this youth is sad, he has not uttered one syllable to his father this day, therefore has he sent him to thee, that peradventure he may speak beside his mother." The lady was glad and said, "Clear the house, go, be off; that I may learn somewhat of the prince, and banish his sadness and grief." When she was alone with the youth the lady threw her arm round his neck, and said, "O my life, ah my lord, what has befallen thee that thy heart is thus sad, and that thou art disconsolate and mournful? Whatever thy father possesses is in my hand; if thou wilt make thy heart one with mine, and act according to my words, I will turn away thy sadness." To her too the prince gave no answer. Again said the lady, "Thou art a grown-up youth, I too am a young lady; thy father is a decrepit old man, with neither thought nor discernment, night and day he knows not one art; if thou wilt assure me, and swear to me, and accept me as thy legal

wife, I will make shift to kill thy father and
make thee king in his stead. First, I swear by
God, and for God, and in God, that I speak
these words from the bottom of my heart and
from my very soul, and that I will not falsify
these words; do thou likewise assure me, and
swear to me that I may act accordingly." The
prince answered not a word. Quoth the lady,
" O dearer than my life, should thou ask how I
will kill thy father; lo, in the treasury are many
kinds of poisons, of one of which if a person
eat, he turns ill and after three months dies.
The people will not know the cause of his
death, and will not suspect that he has eaten
poison. They will say he but took ill, and will
doubtless make thee king. Should thou say I
am thy step-mother and wonder how thou art
to marry me, the way is this : send me off to
my own country, and while yet on the road,
send someone after me who shall come in the
guise of a robber and pounce upon us by night
and seize me ; so it will be said that robbers
have seized me. Then buy me as a slave-girl
from that man, and make me thy wife ; so none
will know." But the prince answered her not at
all, and spake not. Then the lady grew
desperate at his not speaking, and her patience
was exhausted, and she said, "O my soul, O my

gliding angel, why wilt thou not speak to me ?"
And she put her arm round his neck and drew
him to her and made to kiss him. And the
prince was wroth, and he smote the lady's
mouth with the back of his hand, so that her
mouth filled with blood. When she saw this
conduct the fire of anger blazed up in the hearth
of her breast, and the sparks from the fumes of
her pride gained her heart, and she cried, " Out
on thee ! fool ! boy ! I sought to raise thee to
the throne and make thee king, and thou didst
strike me thus ; now will I speak to thy father
that he shall hew thee in pieces, small even as
thine ear." And she dishevelled her hair and
smeared the four sides of her robe with the
blood of her mouth and sat down, sad and
tearful, feeble and wailing. Then the youth
went to his private apartments. After a time
the king came to the harem, thinking to inquire
of the lady concerning the affair of the prince,
and he saw her seated besmeared with red
blood. And the king marvelled at this sight,
and said to the lady, " What is this matter ?
explain to me." She said, " O king, that
degenerate son of thine ! God forbid that he be
son of thine !" " What is the matter ?" said the
king. The lady replied, " I saw that degenerate
youth that he was sad, and I cleared the palace

that I might banish his sadness, and I said to him, ' My son, why art thou sad ? ' Then he stretched forth his hand and made to do me wrong, but I prevented him. Then he said to me, ' Why dost thou flee me ? if thou wilt be my mistress and make thy heart one with mine, and assure me thereof, it is my intention to kill my father and make thee my wife ; and the riches, and the country, and the throne, and the king-dom will be ours ? ' But I consented not, and he desired to kill me that I might not make known this matter to the king. And I cried out for the saving of my life, and he left me in this plight and went away. Now, O king, know of a surety that he purposes evil against thee, and see to the saving of thine own life, else crown and throne will go from thy hands ; so ere he kill thee do thou kill him that thou be secure from his wickedness." When the king heard these words from the lady he was wroth, and that night sleep came not to his eyes.

In the early morning he went forth and sat upon his throne, and caused the prince to be brought before him, that he might order the executioner to smite off his head. The courtiers who were beside him got the execu-tioner to delay, and at once sent word to the vezirs. As soon as they knew what was

happening, the whole Forty Vezirs came with all
speed to the presence of the king, and said, " O
king, how has the prince this day thus merited
the anger of the king ?" The king related to the
vezirs the events that had taken place, whereupon the Grand Vezir said, " Slay not thy son,
trusting on the woman's word ; do not a deed
beyond the ordinance of God and the law of the
Messenger :* and there is no permission in the
law for one to act on a woman's word. If there
were witnesses that the prince had done this
thing to the lady, then were command the
king's ; but spill not blood unjustly, that afterward thou suffer not regret and remorse. They
have said that whatsoever oppression there be
in a country it is incumbent on him who is
king to banish it ; where then were room for
kings to do deeds beyond the law and spill
blood unjustly ? If they be negligent in the
matter of banishing oppression, God Most High
will visit and afflict them with four sorts of
troubles : firstly, He will make their life short ;
secondly, He will let the enemy prevail against
them ; thirdly, He will give the enemy aid and
victory ; and fourthly, on the Resurrection Day
He will be wroth with them and consign them

---

* The Prophet Muhammed.

to the torment of Hell. He then is wise who will not for a five-day's life lose the Hereafter, and is not heedless. And, moreover, the Holy Messenger (peace on him!) when going to perform the ablution would first of all perform it with sand; the Companions asked, ' O Apostle of God, is it lawful to perform the sand-ablution when there is water?' The most noble Beloved of God replied, ' I fear lest death let me not reach the water.' Now, O king, be not presumptuous through worldly fortune and kingship, and consent not to a deed contrary to the law, and ruin not thy Hereafter, trusting in the woman's word. For by reason of the craft of woman has many a head been cut off; and the Blessed Messenger hath said, ' Whatsoever misfortunes befall my people will befall them through women.' Peradventure my king has not heard the story of the murdered Sheykh Shihāb-ud-Dīn; if it be thy high command I shall relate it." The king said, " Relate the story that I may hear it and learn its incidents." Quoth the vezir,

The First Vezir's Story.

" One day the doctors of the law were assembled in the council of the king of Egypt and were talking over the details of the Ascension.

They said, ' The **Most** Noble Apostle made the Ascension **and** God Most High showed him **the** Seven **Heavens, the** Eight Paradises, and **the** Seven **Hells, and** spake with him ninety **thou-**sand **words; and when** he **returned to** his place he found his bed **still warm, and** the water had not wholly run out **of an** ewer which **had been** upset beside **him, so** he straightway raised the ewer from the ground.'* The king **of Egypt** marvelled thereat and **said, '** These **words which** ye speak are remote from reason ; **the** depth **of** each of the **Seven** Heavens is **a** five-hundred years' **journey, and** the distance **between each is** a five-hundred years' journey, yet ye **say that he** traversed **the** Heavens and the Eight Paradises, and the **Seven Hells, and** conversed **to** the **ex-**tent **of ninety** thousand words **and came** back again and **found** his bed **warm and his ewer not** empty—that **is remote from reason.'** Although they insisted with him **that God Most High was** almighty, **it was in vain.** When **the** assembly broke up, news **of this reached** Sheykh Shihāb-

---

* Concerning **the** Mi'rāj, **or** Ascension, **of** Muhammed, **his** vision in which he **saw himself** transported to Heaven, **the com-**mentators tell many **wonderful** stories, of which the above **is an** example. All that the **Koran** says, **is** : " Celebrated be **the Glory** of Him who transported His servant by night **from the Sacred** Temple to the Remote Temple, whose precinct **We have blessed,** that We might show him of Our signs."—xvii. **1.**

ud-Dîn. So he arose and came to the palace
and shook hands with the king and sat down.
The king entreated the sheykh with great consideration and respect, and said, 'O sheykh, there
was no need for your coming here; if you had
but given us a hint we should have gone to visit
you: what need thus to weary your feet and
endure fatigue?' The sheykh replied, 'O king,
I have come this day to have somewhat of par-
ticular conversation with you.' Then quoth
the king, 'Welcome, and fair welcome!' Now
there were in the pavilion where the king was
sitting four windows which gave upon the desert.
The sheykh said, 'O king, let them shut the
windows for a little.' So the king ordered
them to be shut; and after they had conversed
for about an hour, the sheykh said, 'Order that
they open one of them.' When they had opened
one the king looked out and saw that the plain
was all full of armed soldiers, so that though the
stars in the sky might be reckoned, these could
not be numbered. They came on, their horses
pressing each against the other, and when the
king saw thus great an army on such wise, his
senses fled from him, and he cried out, 'What
manner of host is this? quick, go see!' The
sheykh said, 'My king, fear not, sit quiet in thy
place, it is nothing.' Then the king ordered them

to shut that window ; then they opened it again and the king looked and saw nothing. One of the windows likewise gave upon the city ; the sheykh told them to open it, and the king looked and saw that a fire was raging in the City of Cairo, and the flames were rising into the air. The king cried out, saying, 'What fire is this?' The sheykh replied, ' Have patience ; for this there is good reason.' Another window gave upon the river, it also they opened ; and the king saw that the River Nile had overflowed and was approaching, so that he feared exceedingly for the fury of the water. 'Help, O sheykh!' he cried, so the sheykh ordered them to shut that window. The other window looked fair upon the plain ; it also they opened, and the king saw that all that plain from end to end was become a garden, wherein were running streams, and fruits, and all manner of flowers, and parrots and turtle-doves and nightingales warbling—a place like Paradise. When the king saw this he said, ' O sheykh, let them not shut this window for a time, that we may enjoy it ;' and he looked on marvelling for about an hour. The sheykh let open again the shut windows, and nothing was visible. Then he bade bring a tub and fill it with water ; and the king told them to obey, so they brought it. The sheykh said, ' O king, hold about thee a

towel, and plunge once into this water, then come
out and sit down, and I will show thee a wonder.'
Then the king held about him a towel and went
into the tub and plunged in it, and when he
put out his head he saw himself on the skirt
of a trackless mountain by the sea-shore.   Then
was the king bewildered, and he cried, ' Dost
thou see ? the sheykh, he has by magic cast me
into the desert and seized my throne!'   Thus
thinking, he looked about and saw some persons
cutting wood on the mountain.   He went up to
them and saluted them, and they returned the
salute and asked, 'What man art thou ?'   The
king said, ' I am a merchant; the ship in which
I was sank in the sea, I laid hold of a plank and
was saved, and am come here.'   Then had they
compassion on him, and each of them gave him
some old garment, and they clothed him.   The
king said to them, ' Who are ye and whence are
ye ? '   They replied, ' Behind this mountain is a
city, we belong to it.'   Then the king went with
them to that city, and while he was wandering
through the bazaar he happened on the shop of
an aged farrier.   The farrier said to him, ' O
youth, whence art thou come ?'   And the king
again declared that he was a merchant whose ship
had sunk, and that he had managed to save himself ; and he asked for advice.   The old man said,

'As thou art a stranger, go sit at the door of the bath, and ask of every woman that comes out if she have a husband, and according to the custom of this city, whatsoever woman says to thee that she has no husband shall be thy wife.' So the poor king went and sat at the door of the bath and asked the ladies that came out; but they each answered, 'I have a husband,' and went away. Of a sudden a lady attended by several servants came out, and when he said to her, 'Hast thou a husband?' she replied, 'No,' and passed on. Afterward one of that lady's servants returned and took the king and brought him to her. She said, 'By the command of God I am become thy wife;' and the king was thankful for that event. He lived seven years with that lady and had two sons and a daughter. At length all her means were used up and they had nothing left to eat, and the lady said to him, 'O man, go earn something that we and our children may live.' Then the king was sad, and he went to the farrier and told him how things stood with him, and the farrier asked him if he knew any trade. The king replied that he knew none, so the farrier put a few pence into his hand and said, 'Go buy a rope and sit among the porters, and he whose load thou carriest will give thee two or three pence, and so thou shalt live.' The king

did as the farrier told him, and, having no other
resource, was for some days a porter and carried
loads. When he took up the loads the rope
would cut his shoulders, and he would think on
the estate he had enjoyed and weep. One day,
while strolling along, he came upon the sea-
shore. Now ablution had become necessary for
the king, so he went into the water and plunged
in it, and when he put his head out he beheld
himself in his own palace, and the sheykh was
sitting looking at him.* He said, 'O sheykh,
dost thou fear not God, and art thou not
ashamed before the Messenger?' The sheykh
replied, 'O king, wherefore art thou angry? thou
didst draw thy head for a moment under the water
and didst straightway put it out again; dost not
believe? see thy servants standing there, ask
them.' When he asked his servants they replied
as the sheykh had said. The king was amazed
and said, 'For seven years have I wandered
afar from my throne—what know ye?' And he
determined to slay the sheykh. The sheykh

---

* This trick of making one imagine that he has in a few
seconds experienced adventures that seem to have lasted over
a long period appears to have been a favourite one with the
dervishes. Several instances of it occur in the tales of 'Ali 'Aziz
that I have published under the title of "The Story of Jewād."
It may have been effected by means of some intoxicating preparation like hashish.

perceived this determination and said, 'O king,
what is there in this? lo, I too will go in.' So
he held the towel about him and plunged into
the water that was in the tub. The king signed
to the executioner to strike off the sheykh's head
without mercy as soon as he should put it out.
But when the sheykh put his head under the
water he found himself in the land of Syria; and
he wrote a letter to the king, saying, 'O king,
thou and I are slaves and creatures: thou drew-
est thy head under the water for a moment and
ere thou didst put it out again, the space of
seven years and all those troubles appeared to
thee. Thou wonderest that God Most High
should have shewn His Apostle the eighteen
thousand worlds, and that the Apostle on his
return should have found his bed warm, and that
the water should not have run out of the ewer;
and thou deniest the Ascension of that Apostle;
therefore have I done to thee this deed, that thou
doubt not nor question the might of God Most
High.' When the king read this letter his faith
was strengthened; but he forgot not the sufferings
he had endured through the sheykh, so he wrote
a letter to the governor of Syria asking him to
seize the sheykh and cut off his head and send
it to him. The letter reached the governor of
Syria, and as the sheykh lived in a cave without

the city, he sent men thither to seize and be-
head him. When they drew near the cave a
boundless host with weapons and horses appeared to them, so that they were unable to go
in to the sheykh. They informed the king of
this circumstance. So the king consulted with
his vezirs, and the vezirs said, 'The plan is this:
that we feign friendship with the sheykh, and
send him some boys and slave-girls, and with
them a crafty woman whom we shall instruct to
ask the sheykh, when she is alone with him,
what time he is impotent in prayer ; that time
she will find some means to kill him.' So the
king wrote a friendly letter to the sheykh and,
manifesting great affection, sent him with show
of much regard youths and girls like houris,*
and with them a crafty and wily woman. By the
divine decree the sheykh was off his guard, and
he passed some nights with the girls and was
pleased with them. Once when that crafty
sorceress was talking with the sheykh, she asked,
'Is there a time when thou art impotent in
these prayers ?' The sheykh replied, 'Speak not
such words ;' but woman is a devil, and she persisted, so the sheykh said, 'When in a state of

---

* This word is properly hūrī, and should be pronounced hooree,
not howri, the ou having its French sound, as our form *houri*
was introduced through that language.

ceremonial impurity I am impotent.' Straightway the woman sent word to the governor of
Syria, saying, 'On such and such a night the
sheykh will approach the girls, do thou send men
to seize him.' On that night the sheykh ap-
proached the girls, and when he left them he
went, according to his wont, to perform the ablution. But that night the crafty woman had
thrown the water that was in the jugs into the
desert, so that they were all empty, and when the
sheykh sought to wash he could find no water.
The woman said, 'I shall fetch water,' and went
out, when she told the men who were waiting,
and they entered straightway. When the sheykh
saw them he knew what had happened, and said,
'Resignation to destiny;' and taking in his
hands two candles that were burning in the can-
dlestick, he began to turn round. The men who
had come struck him with their swords and
martyred him."*

"Now, O king, know what sort of persons
have perished through the wiles of women.
Beware, slay not thy son in obedience to the
woman's word, or afterward thou shalt be sorry."
The king heard these words of the vezir, and
his advice seemed good to him, and he caused

---

* See Appendix B, Note 1.

the prince to be brought and said to him, " How
was thy affair with the lady ?"   But the prince
gave no answer, and sought for his governor,
but he was not to be found.   Quoth the vezir,
"O king, defer this matter till the morrow, peradventure the truth of it may be made manifest."
So the king sent the prince to the prison, and
went himself to the chase.

When it was evening he came to the palace
and entered the harem, and the lady came up to
him and asked, "How died thy son?"   The
king replied, "To-day have I deferred it and
sent him to the prison."   Quoth the lady, "O
king, do not thus defer, spare him not till the
morrow, for from crookedness straightness
comes not.   The sages have said that a man's
darling enemies are two—the one riches, the
other children.   O king, is not that degenerate
son of thine an enemy, who stretched forth his
hand to his step-mother and went about to slay
thee?   I tended him as a bird tends her young
ones, and now that he has become a man he
has dealt thus treacherously by thee and me.
Well have they said :—

> For many a day did I with care a puppy rear and tend,
> Which, when he grew a dog, did turn and fierce my feet did rend.

Now, O king, this youth is like a vicious dog,
he has bitten both thee and me ; judge then how

he will deal by others. The story of this youth
will be even as that of the king's son who was
unequalled in evil practices; mayhap my king
has not heard it." The king said, " Tell me
that story, let me hear it." Quoth the lady,

THE LADY'S FIRST STORY.

" Thus relate they: There was in the palace of
the world a great king, and he had one son, a
loveling of the earth. Him he had given to a
master, and he was busy acquiring knowledge
and good conduct. For the same purpose the
king had appointed the youth a governor perfect
in good conduct; and he had thus ordered the
master and the governor, ' If the boy do an un-
gracious act, beat him without mercy; if ye beat
him not, ye will regret it.' So the teacher used
to beat him for a slight fault, and the king would
send him to prison and let him remain for a day
and a night hungry and thirsty. When the
king was asked, ' Why dost thou thus?' he
would answer, ' He too will be king after me
and have to beat many men and put them in
prison; let him now taste what is each pain so
that when he rules he will know the plight of
the wretched and have compassion and mercy
toward the poor, and his reign will be on justice.
For that the lover who has not endured pain

knows not the value of delight, for that the
sufferer knows the sufferer's plight, let him now
endure pain, so that, having acquired instruc-
tion and humility and good conduct and knowledge, he may be profitable both to himself and
to us and be favoured by God with grace and
mercy and by the people with blessing.' Now
this king had feud with another great king who
likewise had a son who read with a teacher.
But that king ever warned his teacher and
governor thus, ' Be it not that anyone strike my
son or say a word to vex his heart, else will I
give him his reward.' And as he much im-
pressed this on them, no one dared say a word
to the boy. Although his vezirs used to say,
' Do not act thus with regard to the youth,' the
king paid no heed at all. Now the youth acquired as many evil habits as were in the world,
and when he grew older he began to seize the
nobles' sons and daughters, and whosoever said
a word to him he killed. The people were in
despair and they complained to the king, and
the king would scold him and say, ' Now leave
off this;' but it was no avail. At length one
night the youth struck his father with a dagger
where he lay and slew him ; and on the morrow
he ascended the throne and was king. And
through his cruelty he spilt much blood unjustly,

and day and night he left not to do evil. When
he was drunk there was no rescue from his hand
for the wives and sons of the nobles ; and he
would take a bow and arrows and pierce the
breasts of the nobles who sat and stood around
him, though they were guiltless, and make the
arrow stand out behind their backs. Then he
would say to those who sat by, ' Have not I
done well ?' He would seize him who said,
' Nay,' and strip him naked and bind his two
hands behind his back and lash him to a post,
then taking a long awl in his hand, he would
pierce the face and throat and breast and belly
of that noble, and with such tortures kill him.
And his custom was ever to kill men unjustly.
On market-days he would mount his horse and
go toward the market, and while the throng of
people were marketing he would shoot at them
with arrows from an open space, and ere they
could all flee away and disperse he would have
slain many men. The nobles and the poor were
in despair through him, and they would hurl
thousands of curses at his father, ' Why did he
not teach this youth good conduct when he was
little, and punish him by way of correction that
now .he too might know the plight of the
afflicted !' At length the nobles and the subjects and the poor consulted together, and they

secretly wrote this letter to the king who had
taught his son good conduct and knowledge :
' Protection and protection ! delay not, O king,
but send thy son with some troops against this
tyrant king. When he arrives we will turn
from this tyrant and go unto thy son and obey
him and assist him, and we will seize this tyrant
and make him over to thy son, and this country
shall be thy son's ; for we hear of the justice and
equity of thy son. O king, for the love of God
Most High, aid us.' When the letter arrived
and the king had read and understood it, he
straightway sent his son with some troops to
the country of that tyrant king. When the army
came, the people of the country turned away
from that tyrant and made over their lands to
the newly come king's son, and they seized the
tyrant and brought him before the prince. The
prince commanded them to bind his two hands
behind his back, and gave him to a man whose
father he had killed, saying, ' Even as he killed
thy father, so do thou kill him.' Then that
youth took an awl and stabbed the tyrant once
or twice so that he cried, ' For the love of God
grant me respite for a moment, I have somewhat to say to you.' So they granted him
respite, and he said, 'O God! O God ! what have I
done on earth ! had I known that the bitterness

of death was such, I had struck none even with a
rod. A thousand times cursed be my father that
he taught me not good conduct when little, and
punished me not, beating me and scolding me,
that I too might have known what was the
bitterness of death, then had not I hurt any, and
through my good conduct would he be alive and
I not a prey to this torment; nor should I have
killed those many Muslims with such torments.'
And when he made entreaty, ' Kill me not with
this torment,' the executioner came and smote
off his head from his body.   And the prince became king of that country by reason of good
conduct and through the blessings of his education by his father and mother and master; and
he acted with such justice and equity that they
called that kingdom the Kingdom of the Servant of the Protector.   And that unhappy one,
in that he learned not good conduct, first slew
his father and then perished himself."

" Now, O king, I have told this story for that
this youth too has adopted the way of that tyrant.
Dost not thou see that though thou speakest to
him, he respects not thy word and gives no
answer ?   In that he has not been beaten by his
master has he now learned profitless knowledge ;
lo, he has rebelled against thee and turned traitor
and gone about to slay thee, and stretched forth

his hand to me ; can there be a greater crime
than that ?   Lo, I have aided thee to thy life and
given thee word ; if thy life be needful for thee,
kill the youth and be free from anxiety, else
know of a surety that neither thyself nor thy
kingdom will remain, all will be destroyed."
When the king heard these enticing and beguiling words of the lady fear for his life took possession of him, and he said, " On the morrow will
I smite off his head."   And they went to bed.

When it was morning and the world was bright,
the king sat upon his throne and ordered the
executioner that he brought the youth, and then
he said, " Kill!" whereupon the Second Vezir
came forward and said, "O king, follow not,
without deliberation, the words of the evil. God
Most High knoweth that whoso stirreth up the
sea of trouble and setteth fire to the provender
and stores is unjust ; for they have said that it is
incumbent on kings that they act not on anyone's
word, neither fall before his spells, nor believe
calumny, so that they be not afterward regret-
ful nor suffer remorse, even as they say in this
couplet :

> A weakling, when he should decide, doth aye let pass his chance ;
> So that when gone, it turneth round against him from behind.

And as God Most High hath spoken in this verse,
'Say, Shall those who know be deemed equal

with those who know not ?'* Now, O king, look thou to these deeds; for in the latter times shall those who lie to one's face abound, even as saith the Apostle (peace on him!), 'Verily, before the Hour are mighty liars, be ye ware of them.' O king, it beseems thee to be not heedless, for many are the lies and tricks of women, so that if one of them but look at her great toe, she will hatch every day two-and-seventy different plots and tricks. And the stories of the craft and cunning of women are many, if the king command, I will display one mote from the sunbeam and one drop from the ocean." The king said, "Tell on, let us hear." The vezir said,

THE SECOND VEZIR'S STORY.

"There was in Hindustan a khoja † who had a beautiful wife. That woman had (God forefend the listeners!) a youthful lover. One day the khoja bought a parrot which knew well how to speak; and whenever it would speak, the khoja's heart reaped a hundred thousand joys and delights. One day the khoja went to a certain place and came not that night to his

---

* Koran, xxxix. 12.
† A khoja is a master of a household, also a teacher; in the former acceptation it is somewhat equivalent to the old English "goodman."

D

house. Forthwith the woman brought the
youth to the house, and that night passed they
in fun and frolic, and, joining soul to soul and
heart to heart, both reaped their desires. The
parrot watched this their secret from the cage,
and when it was morning the youth went
away and the khoja returned. As soon as it
saw the khoja, the parrot said, ' O khoja, this
night till morning the lady was with a youth,
eating, and drinking, and kissing, and clipping ;
lo, the youth is gone.' When the khoja heard
these words he said to his wife, ' Out on thee,
wife! who is that youth ?' The woman replied,
' What manner of speech is this ? dost thou
believe the word of a bird and act thereon ?'
And she fell to chattering and babbling, and
convinced the khoja, and gave the lie to the
parrot. One day the khoja again went to a
certain place, and the woman, according to her
wont, got the youth whom she told what the
parrot had said to the khoja. The youth said,
' Henceforward there can be no more frolic with
thee, this parrot is a hindrance to us, and will
make us disgraced before the world.' Quoth
the woman, ' My lord, be not dismayed, see
what a trick I will play the parrot.' And she
ordered the slave-girls and they brought a
sieve, an earthenware jar, some water, and a

piece of bullock hide. They put the hide over
the parrot's cage, and one of the girls struck on
it with a stick every now and again, while
another sprinkled water through the seive upon
the parrot, and a third put a looking-glass into the
jar which ever and anon she opened and closed
before the cage. So again the woman and the
youth made merry till the morning. When it
was morning the youth went away and the
khoja came; and as soon as the parrot saw
him, it said, ' Khoja, this night the lady and the
youth ate and drank and made merry till the
morning; but much did the rain rain and the
thunder roar and the lightning flash.' Then
quoth the lady, 'Dost thou see the parrot's lies?
did the rain rain, or the thunder roar, or the
lightning flash this night?' ' Nay,' said the
khoja. 'And thou believedst the lie spoken by
the bird,' quoth the woman. And the poor
khoja's trust was destroyed by this trick; and
as often as he went away the woman invited
that youth and made merry with him. And the
parrot ever said so, but the khoja would not
believe, and the woman would make mock of
the parrot's words, and split the khoja's head
by saying, 'And thou didst libel me on this
thing's word!'"

"Now, O king, I have told this story for

that thou mayst know that craft and trickery
such as this abound in women. Beware, slay
not thy son, trusting to the woman's word ; and
act not till thy son recover his speech and make
known his affair, and until it be evident where
is the truth, or it will hurt the present and the
Hereafter of the king. And the hurt of his
present will be this, the source of his life, his
only son, will be lost to him ; and the hurt of
his Hereafter will be this, that having spilt blood
unjustly, he will have done great sin, and will
inevitably enter Hell. O king, this were better,
that we have patience until the governor be
found ; belike he may know of the not speaking
of the prince, and of his every affair." The
king found the vezir's words good ; and sent
the prince to the prison, and went himself to
the chase.

When it was evening he returned from the
chase and went to the lady, who rose to greet
him, and they sat down. After the repast the
lady said, " Hast thou this day finished the
affair of that thy degenerate son ?" The king
replied, " To-day likewise they let me not alone,
so I have sent him back to the prison." Quoth
the lady, " O king, comply not with the words
of the vezirs, and be not negligent. ' Refuge
is in God Most High !' Now that youth has

made for the throne; **if it** pass into his hands,
he will sow the seed of tyranny and oppression."
Quoth the king, " To-day my vezir requested
wit, what could **I do ?"** The lady said, " God
forbid that he be **true son of** thine ; the story **of**
this youth resembles **that of a certain** king,
which mayhap **my king has** not heard." The
king said, " Tell on, let **us** hear." Quoth the
lady,

THE LADY'S SECOND STORY.

" Thus relate **they :** There was **a great king
who** had a sickly son, whom all the physicians
of that country had tried to cure, but in **vain.**
At length the physicians were reduced **to**
despair, when **from another country came a**
skilful leech, and the **king** summoned **him, and**
they took him to the **boy.** The physician felt
the boy's pulse **and** looked **at the colour of his**
face and said, ' **If it** please **God Most High, I**
will make this boy whole ; **but I would that**
you take me to his mother, **I have a** question
to ask of her, and **would** converse with her
privately ; **for** the affairs **of a** child should **be**
asked **of** his father **and** mother, but his **mother**
knows yet better than his father.' Then the
king commanded that they left the **physician**
alone with **his wife.** The physician said, ' O

ℵ

lady, I have a word to ask of thee, but speak
the truth if thou wish that the boy become
well, and if thou speak not the truth the blood
of the boy will be on thy head, for he will not
recover ; and this word shall remain between
thee and me.' And he protested with many
oaths and swore that it would be so, and said,
' O lady, my word to thee is this, and speak the
truth, whose is the boy ?' Said the lady, ' O
physician, what word is this thou speakest ?
who could enter the king's harem ?' Then
swore the physician by God and the Apostle,
saying, 'Speak the truth of it, be not guilty of
the boy's blood ; this word shall remain between
me and thee.' And the physician swore and
protested, and the lady refused, till the physician rose from his seat and was about to go,
when the lady caught hold of his skirt and said,
' Sit down ; thou hast sworn much to me ; what
use to hide from the people a thing known unto
God ? " And God Most High is the Hearer, the
Observant." O master, the truth of it is this, the
king has nor son nor daughter ; neither by me
nor by the other ladies has he any child at all
to take the throne after him. I saw that some
stranger would seize the throne after the king,
and I made merry with a youth, and this boy is
the issue.' Quoth the physician, ' What sort of

youth is that youth?' The lady said, 'He is of the Turkmans.' Then the physician went to the king and said, 'With the aid of God I will make thy son whole, for I have asked his mother, and know whence is his sickness. Now, O king, order that they cook some porridge* in the kitchen, and make ready a little curds and whey* and some brewis.'* So the king ordered and they prepared the whole of them. And the physician made the boy eat them before the king, and all the leeches and physicians that were present looked one at the other and said, 'We have laboured thus long a time with all manner of drugs, and have been unable to restore this boy to health, see this fool who would cure him with such odd stuffs.' When the boy had filled himself with these foods he came to himself a little. For three days the physician gave him these dishes, and he became all whole. And the king bestowed much wealth upon the physician."

"Now, O king, God forbid that this be true son of thine; if thou slay him not and he escape, he will bring about much evil; yea, for that he is evil he will slay thee." The king

---

* *Tarkhana, yoghurt, tutmaj,* favourite dishes of the wandering Turkman tribes; so, perhaps, their natural food. The translations are, of course, only approximate.

heard these beguiling words of the lady, and
his heart was troubled, and he said, " To-day
is past, to-morrow will I kill him." And they
went to bed and slept.

Early in the morning the king sat upon his
throne and caused the youth to be brought
before him, and ordered the executioner thus,
" Kill !" Whereupon the Third Vezir came forward and said, " O king, destroy not the prince
off-hand on the word of the woman ; for the
Holy Apostle hath said, ' Precipitation is from
the Devil and deliberation is from the Merciful.'
And wise is he who thinks a thousand times
over everything he does ; even as one, when a
thorn has run into his foot, takes his foot upon
his knee and moistens it many times with his
mouth, and picks out the thorn with the point
of a needle after many a difficulty and bearing
much pain, for till it be taken out he has no
rest.   And the prince is the darling of the
king's heart, and the light of his eyes, and the
source of his life ; and he is the support and
asylum of the people of the world ; and this is
incumbent upon us in this matter, that we endeavour to set it right.   For they have said
that if anyone see wrongness in any act of a
king and warn not the king, he must be reckoned of the crew of rebels and traitors.

O servant of the prince, to work! up then and strive thou **hard**!
That thou may be near unto him and in his favour **high**.
Thou know'st his nature, and thou shouldest counsel him **aright**,
Else, by the **Lord**! **a** traitor thou, and from the Truth dost fly.

And **wise is he who** looks **at the** beginning and end **of** an affair, like **as that** king **took** counsel with his sons **and his vezirs and the** elders of the country, **and was** prospered **alike** in **the** world and the Hereafter. And that story is a fair story; if the king grant **leave I will re-**late it." The king **said,** "Tell on." Quoth the vezir,

The Third Vezir's Story.

" There **was of** old time in the palace of **the** world **a great** king, such that the world was under his rule. He **had** lived **enjoying sove-**reignty for **a** hundred **and twenty years in the** palace of the world, **and was grown old and** knew that in the near future **he would be given to** drink of the potion **of** death. And the king had three moon-faced* **sons and likewise** three able **and** skilful vezirs. **One day** quoth the king **to his vezirs,** '**The end of** this my life draws nigh; the natural life **of man is a** hundred and **twenty years,** after that **not an old man** remains. **Now I have** reached **that state and**

---

* *i.e.*, beautiful.

the affair is thus, I wish to appoint one of my
sons to my place, and, leaning my back against
the wall of abdication, take rest.   Which of
my sons do ye deem worthy of the throne?'
The vezirs said, 'O king, long be thy life; a
person's good and bad are not known till he
have been proved; for two things are the touchstone of a man; the first is wine, the second,
office; in these two things is a person's manful-
ness apparent and manifest.   This were best,
for nine days let these thy three sons enjoy the
throne and sovereignty, and with this touchstone
let the king prove them; whatever be the character of each of them, it will appear; for the
rest, let the king order accordingly.'   When the
king heard these words from the vezirs they
seemed right good to his heart, and he commanded that each son should sit for three days
on the throne and exercise sovereignty, and declared that he would allow whatever they should
annul or appoint, and whatever they should grant
from the treasury, and whatever justice or oppression they might show, and that no one
should say aught.   Then the eldest son of the
king sat upon the throne and directed the
government, and he practised justice and equity
on such wise as cannot be described.   He loved
the doctors and turned from the foolish, and

gave the high offices to the learned, and withdrew from listening to things forbidden and
what was vain, and strove much in well-doing.
Then the king, to prove the judgment of his
son, sent him three persons from prison, one
was a murderer, and one a thief, and one an
adulterer; and with them he sent the complainants. When they came before the prince the
complainants stated their case and the witnesses
bore witness that these three persons were indeed guilty, and that these words were no
calumny against them, but true. When the
prince knew how the case was, he said, 'On a
man's coming into the world he is the blood of
his father's and mother's hearts; and, after bearing these many troubles and afflictions, a man in
forty years becomes mature; so it is not well to
slay him in a minute, as God Most High will
in the Hereafter surely punish him in Hell.' And
he made them vow that henceforward they would
do no such deeds, and set all three at liberty.
And for the whole three days he ruled with
justice. On the fourth day the turn came to
the middle son, and he likewise sat upon the
throne and directed the government. He
abased the learned and promoted the foolish;
and adopted as habit wine and music, and as profession avarice and meanness. Brief, he was the

opposite of his elder brother. According to the
custom, they sent to him too three criminals.
When the prince heard how the case was he said,
' Men like these are the thorns of the country ;'
and he ordered that the three of them perished.
When he too had ruled for three days, the turn
came to the youngest prince, and he likewise sat
upon the throne and directed the government.
He gave to the doctors the posts suitable to the
doctors, and to the learned the high offices, and to
the strong and impetuous young heroes, military
fiefs, and to the champions, feudal domains ; and
he registered their pay.   He honoured each of
them according to his position, and abased the un-
mannerly.   Brief, he put each one in his proper
place, like a string of pearls ; and he left not his
gate unlocked lest the foe should triumph over
him.   The king again sent three culprits from
the prison that he might try his judgment.
When they were present the servants informed
him, and he said, ' Bring them one by one.'
Then when the witnesses had borne witness that
the man had indeed committed murder, the
prince said, ' Murder is of two kinds, the one
intentional, the other accidental ; and the intentional is also of two kinds, the first when
a person strikes another with an iron instrument
and kills him, him it is needful to put to death

in retaliation ; and they have written in the Book
of Dues that if one person strike another with
a stick and kill him, or if he throw him into a
fire, then the fine for blood and the expiation
alike become necessary. And the other too is
accidental, when the expiation is incumbent, and
he is culpable, but the fine for blood does not become necessary. And that is accidental when a
person shoots an arrow at a deer, and it glances
and hits a man and kills him ; as God Most High
hath said, "Then whoso killeth a believer by mis-
chance, then (the expiation is) the freeing of a
believer from bondage .... but if he find
not (the means of doing so), then a fast for two
consecutive months."*' Then the prince asked
and learned that he had murdered intentionally ;
so they executed him. After that they brought
the thief ; and the prince said, ' If anyone, sane
and of age, steal ten minted dirhems of silver, his
hand must be cut off, as also if he steal one dīnār
of gold, even as saith the Apostle (peace on him!),
" No cutting save for a dīnār or ten dirhems."
When one thus commits theft his right hand
must be cut off at the wrist; if he commit theft
again, his left hand must be cut off; if he commit
it a third time, his right foot must be cut off; and

---

* Koran, iv. 94.

if he commit it yet again, he must be put in
prison till he repent.' Then the prince caused
the man to receive the due of his crime. After
that they brought him who had committed
adultery, his case also they exposed, and they
gave him the due of his sin conformably to the
law. The nine days were completed, and the
king assembled his vezirs and said, ' Lo, ye have
seen the rule of my three sons, which of them is
worthy the throne?' Quoth the first vezir, 'O
king, thy eldest son is worthy.' Quoth the
second vezir, 'Thy middle son is worthy.' Quoth
the third vezir, ' Thy youngest son is worthy.'
When the king heard these words of the vezirs
his doubts were not removed ; and he said, ' O
vezirs, the words of the three of ye are contrary
each to other.' And forthwith he commanded
the people of the country that on the morrow
they should all come out to the plain. The next
day the whole of the folk were assembled on the
plain ; then the king rose on his feet and said,
' O people, do not to-morrow on the Resurrection Day seize hold of my collar and say, " Thou
hast oppressed us," and so wrest from me my
meritorious acts and render me confounded and
ashamed. Now be ye kind and look not at my
kingship and know that before God Most High
there is none meaner or more abject than my-

self.' And he wept full bitterly. And the rich
and poor assembled there wept all of them together. Then turning again, the king said, 'O
friends, lo, my time is at hand ; do ye absolve me
for the Hereafter. I have three sons, whichever
of them ye wish, him will I seat upon the throne.
If he be just, ye will enjoy rest and bless me,
and I shall be at rest in the place where I lie ;
but if he be cruel, ye will not have rest neither
shall I have rest.' The people said, ' May the
king's life endure full many a year! may God
Most High be well pleased with our king! We
are well pleased with our king ; whatever we
may have against our king, let him be absolved.
We are pleased with whichever son he see
worthy the throne ; but since the king has given
the choice into our hands, let him seat his
youngest son upon the throne. He is wise as
well as learned and skilled in the affairs of the
world ; if the king see fit, the wise is worthy the
seat of honour, as this has come down in the
traditions, "A wise youth taketh precedence of a
foolish elder." For the rest, the king knows.'
Then the king went to the palace and ordered
that they adorned the throne, and the grandees
of the state came, and all were present. Then
he took his youngest son by the hand and made
to seat him on the throne, when his brothers

came forward and said, 'O father, all the folk say that he is accomplished and wise and that he knows well the law and the government; now we have some questions to ask of him, which if he answer, we also will contentedly resign to him the throne and stand in his presence with folded hands;* but if not, the crown and throne indeed become him not.' The king said to his youngest son, 'What sayest thou?' He replied, 'Whatsoever their questions be, let them ask them.' They said, 'What is meant by Sultan?' He answered, 'By Sultan is meant one who has certificate and warrant, that we obey the command and ordinance of God Most High : the Sultan is the shadow of God on the earth.' And they asked, 'To whom is it worthy to be king by birth?' He answered, 'First the king's lineage must be manifest, then his descent must be perfect, then he must observe the habits of the just monarchs.' They said, 'Who is just?' He answered, 'The just is he who transgresses not the law.' They said, 'Who is unjust?' He replied, 'He who rather than obey the law, brings in innovations of his own, so that it may be easy to amass wealth with oppression.' They said, 'What manner of persons should kings appoint vezirs?'

---

* As servants do.

He answered, 'They should appoint those persons in whom are two characteristics, the first of which is that they be endowed with prudence and resource, and the second that they be wise and accomplished ; for learning in a man is a second understanding.' They said, 'How many sorts of people are needful to kings?' He answered, 'Four kinds of people ; the first, skilful vezirs ; the second, valiant warriors ; the third, an accomplished scribe who is perfect in Arabic and Persian and the science of writing ; and the fourth, a clever physician who is most able in the science of philosophy.' They said, 'How many different things ought always to be in the thoughts of a king?' He answered, 'Four different things ; the first, to do justice to the people ; the second, to use aright the money that is in the treasury ; the third, to distribute offices properly ; and the fourth, to be not negligent concerning enemies.' They said, 'How many different traits should the king adopt as his wont?' He answered, 'Four ; the first is a smiling face ; the second, a sweet speech ; the third, generosity ; and the fourth, mercy to the poor.' They said, 'How many kinds of courtiers are needful to the king?' He answered, 'Four classes are requisite ; first, the wise ; second, the learned ; third, the valiant cham-

E

pions ; and fourth, musicians : from the wise
he will learn the law, from the learned he
will acquire the sciences, from the valiant
champions he will acquire chivalry, and by
the musicians will his heart be expanded'
They said, ' Of which class should the king consider himself one ?' He answered, ' Let him
consider himself of the great sheykhs who have
reached God, for it will cause him to be just.'
Then he turned to his brothers and said, ' O my
brothers, ye have put these many questions to
me and I have answered the whole of them
to the best of my power : I too have a question.'
So they said to him, ' Ask on.' Quoth he,
' What do the kings of the world resemble, and
what do their agents resemble, and what do the
people resemble, and what do the king's enemies
resemble, and what do the sheykhs resemble ?'
Then they both bent their heads and pondered.
After a time the prince again said, ' This is
no time for pondering ; lo, there the question ;
lo, there the throne.' Quoth they, ' We are un-
equal to this question.' Then the king took his
youngest son by the hand and seated him on
the throne and said, ' O son, may God ever aid
thee and may thy foes be overthrown !' Then
all the nobles of the State and the people came
and said, ' May the throne be blessed !' And

they made him king over them. Then the king
said, 'O son, do thou answer the question thou
puttest to thy brethren, that we may hear.'
Quoth the prince, 'O my father, this world resembles a pasture, and these people resemble
the sheep that wander in that pasture, and the
king resembles their shepherd, and the owner
of the sheep is God Most High, and the nobles
resemble that shepherd's dogs, and the enemy
resembles the wolf, and the sheykhs and the
·wise resemble the guardians appointed by God
Most High over the shepherd, who forbid the
shepherd by the order of God Most High
whenever he would do evil to the sheep. O
father, in very truth I am a feeble shepherd, I
see the sheep, and I perceive that even while
we say, " Let not them come and hurt the sheep,"
we become ourselves partners with the wolf.
Should the Owner of the sheep ask us about
His lambs, woe, woe to us!' And he wept full
bitterly. The princes acknowledged the sovereignty of their younger brother. Then the
king took up a handful of dust and put it on his
eye and said, 'O eye, how long a time is it I
have been king, and how great wealth have I
amassed and brought before thee by this much
oppression and justice, and thou wast never
satisfied! And with how many beauties have I

made merry and enjoyed the best of what they
had till thou hast lost all pleasure in taking it!
And how many delicacies have I eaten and how
many sherbets have I drunk, and thou art not
content! Why then didst thou not look to
these affairs and see not? True is it what they
say, " Nought fills the eye save a handful of
dust." Woe, woe, to us!' And he wept. And
all the nobles assembled there were moved to
pity and they wept together. Then the king
arose and went to his oratory and gave himself
up to devotion. After some time the king laid
his head upon the pillow of death and felt that
his life had touched its end, and he said, ' Do
now before my eyes that which ye should do
when I am dead, that I may see it.' Then they
laid the king upon his throne in the palace.
And they scattered sifted dust below the castle
and cut up strips of damask and strewed them
with dust. And all the slave-girls put on black
and dishevelled their hair and scattered dust
upon their heads and began to weep together,
crying, ' Alas! woe! alas!' so that hearts were
rent. Then came the vezirs who likewise fell
to weeping together and exclaiming, ' Shall a
king so just as this be found?' After that they
ordered that they brought a coffin with great
reverence; then the three princes, when they saw

the coffin, wept blood in place of tears and cried,
'This is the horse our father rideth now!' And
they adorned it with jewels and placed upon it
a jewel-set crown and held over it the royal
parasol. Then four great lords came and took
hold of the frame of the coffin and bare it away.
And before the coffin went the sheykhs singing
chants and hymns. And the devotees held
copies of the Sacred Volume before them;
and great nobles and nobles' sons marched in
front. Before them were a hundred sweet-
voiced dirge-singers who wept and cried, 'Ah!
woe! alas!' And from one side they scattered
gold and silver and jewels on the coffin; and
there were some ten thousand horsemen with
golden saddles and broken stirrups and snapped
bows. And behind these was an array of slave-
girls, all clad in black, whose wails and cries
rose to the heavens. When the king saw those
things he sighed and ordered that they took him
down from the throne; and he turned and said,
'While yet alive I have seen my death.' And
he took a handful of earth and threw it on his
head and said, 'Earth, though this long sovereignty has been mine, I have done no righteous
deed which will endure.' And again, 'O vezirs,
I would that ye endow for me.' Thereupon the
vezirs wrote what amounted to ten thousand

aspres a day ; and they founded free kitchens and
colleges, and they settled the revenues of certain
towns and villages on the free kitchens. When
the business of the endowments was finished, they
brought the sections of the Koran, and to each
section-reader they gave five sequins ; and to
each of the devotees and dervishes they gave
five hundred sequins.* Then they brought the
food, and all the plates were of gold or silver ;
and to all before whom they placed a dish they
said, ' Thine be food and plate.' When the
banquet too was finished they freed all the male
and female slaves ; and three days later the king
departed for the Abiding Home."†

" Now, O king, I have told this story for that
the king may, like that sovereign, enquire, and
act conformably to the words of the vezirs and
the people, and in compliance with the command of the law, that he be not a prey in the
world to remorse and in the Hereafter to torment." And he kissed the ground and made
intercession for the prince. When the king
heard of these wondrous events from the vezir,
he perceived how the world had no stability and

---

* In the time of Murād II. an aspre was worth about 2½d. stg.
Turkish sequins were not struck till the time of his successor,
Muhammed II., when they were equivalent to about 12s. 6d.
Foreign gold coins, especially Venetian, were used previously.

† See Appendix B, Note II.

he sighed and sent the youth to the prison and went himself to the chase.

When it was evening he returned and came to the palace, and went in to the lady who rose to greet him, and they sat down. After the repast the lady began to speak about the youth and asked concerning him. Quoth the king, "I have again sent him to the prison." The lady said, "This matter which has happened is no light matter, but thou art negligent and wouldst act upon everyone's word ; and they have said that the negligent person is not exempt from one of three conditions ; either he is a fool, or he is ignorant, or fortune has turned its face from him. O king, the negligent does no perfect deed ; be not negligent, for to be negligent in this affair is madness. O king, this thy story resembles that of another king, upon whom five times fell the enemy by reason of his negligence ; but mayhap my king has not heard that story." The king said, "Tell on, let us hear." Quoth the lady,

THE LADY'S THIRD STORY.

"There was of old time a king, and he had an enemy greater than himself. One day that hostile king assembled a mighty host and came against that weak king. The latter, having no

other resource, assembled all his army and went
forth to meet him. Although he much besought
that strong king and said, ' War is not a good
thing, come, consent not to this calamity, make
not thyself guilty of the blood of so many
Muslims;' and mentioned how the Holy Apostle
hath said, ' If two Muslims fight against each
other with swords or other implements of war,
and one kill the other, both the killer and the
killed shall enter Hell ;' and made many and
many an excuse, it was in vain. When the king
saw that all his entreaty was of no avail with the
enemy, he perceived that it was necessary to find
some plan to avert this evil. Now the king had
three skilful vezirs, these he summoned to give
counsel. He said, ' O my vezirs, what is your
advice in this matter ?' The chief vezir came
forward and said, ' My king, in the present circumstances the military might of our enemy is
great ; most assuredly are we unable to oppose
him. Now the best way were this, that we put
off the battle and return to our country ; he will
certainly come after us, but we will enter into a
strong castle and rest there till that time when
fortune will surely turn toward us likewise ;
thus are the affairs of the world, now gladness,
now woe.' He likewise asked the second vezir,
' What is thy advice, let us see ?' So he said,

'O my king, all that the first vezir has said is
wise ; but it is never allowable to show weakness before the enemy, for inasmuch as thou
displayest weakness will he become strong ; so
if now thou shun battle and flee, thou wilt be
giving him opportunity. Wise is he who, although the enemy appear overwhelming, fears
not death and gives the foe no answer but the
sword.' Then said the king to the third vezir,
'What is thine advice in this matter ?' The
vezir answered, 'O king, manliness is of ten
parts, nine of which are stratagem and one of
which is strength ; and by stratagem is the
affair of enemies ever finished, for they have
said that the affair which one stratagem finishes
a hundred thousand soldiers cannot finish. If
the king will be guided by this humble one,
to-night of a sudden we will attack the enemy
and fall upon his camp, and, if it please God
Most High, we will cut off the heads of many
of them.' The king approved this stratagem
of the vezir, so when it was midnight and the
enemy was negligent they fell upon his camp
from every side, and slaughtered the foes till
morning, and their king fled to his own country.
So was this weak king victorious, and he returned to his own land. But that fugitive king
went to his country and assembled an army,

and again marched against this king. Then
the weak king, having no other resource, went
forth to meet him, and they pitched opposite
each other. The weak king said to his vezirs,
'What is your advice this time, let us see?'
Then quoth the third vezir, 'O king, we shall
again finish our affair by stratagem.' Said the
king, 'What stratagem shall we use? they will
be very watchful this night.' The vezir replied,
'Stratagem is not one; let them keep watch
till morning, we shall this time employ another
stratagem.' Quoth the king, 'Speak on, let us
see.' The vezir said, 'We will hide in ambush
two thousand strong impetuous youths; and as
soon as it is morning we will go out against the
enemy and fight a little, then we will appear to
flee, and they shall follow after thinking to fall
upon us; and when the foremost of the host
reaches us we will turn and fight with them and
cut them down. Thereupon our soldiers who are
in ambush will rush into the field and take the
hostile army in the centre; and, if it please God
Most High, we will strike hard with our swords
and seize their leaders, and take their flags, and
tear in pieces their ensigns; and in this way
will we overcome the foe.' The king liked this
plan of the vezir, and by this stratagem they
sabred the foe and were again victorious. And

the king returned smiling to
other strong king in the great
cried out, 'What means this
king routs my army and puts
this wise! God Most High
whom He will!' Then he ass
of which he, himself, knew not t
went against that poor weak king. They gave
the king word, and he, having no other resource,
went forth again, and they pitched opposite each
other. Again the weak king questioned his
vezirs. Then the third vezir said, 'O my king,
our affair is finished by stratagem.' Quoth the
king, 'What stratagem shall we employ?' The
vezir said, 'O king, let us send an adroit headsman, who will go and by some stratagem kill
him; and when the head goes the foot is not
steady.' The king approved the vezir's words,
and sent a headsman with a dagger, who went
and somehow made shift to smite that strong
king that he well nigh slew him, and then took
flight. But while he was fleeing they caught
him and hewed him in pieces. When they
saw their king that he had reached the bounds
of death, they said, 'There is no fighting in
such plight;' and they fled, bearing their king.
They came to their country and appointed a
physician, and after some days the wound got

and er. And that king again assembled a host
th.nd came against the poor weak king. The
latter, having no other resource, went forth to
meet him and again sought counsel of his
vezirs. The third vezir said, 'O my king, our
affair is finished by stratagem.' The king
asked, 'What stratagem wilt thou employ this
time ?' The vezir said, 'This time let us send
an ambassador and offer some money and
some slave-girls and say, "We submit to thee."
And we will give poison to one of the slave-
girls we send, and tell her to give it to the king
to eat when she finds an opportunity ; and in
this way will we gain the victory over him.'
The king deemed the vezir's words good, and by
that stratagem they poisoned that king. And
this king mounted and attacked his army,
and, as when the head goes the foot is not
steady, it was beaten. They took their king,
and, after a thousand stratagems, conveyed him
to a castle and tended him, and at length he
recovered. Again he assembled an army, and
again they went against that weak king. So
the latter, having no other resource, again went
forth to meet him. He summoned his vezirs
and asked advice. Again the third vezir said,
'O king, our affair is finished by stratagem.'
Quoth the king, 'Give advice.' The vezir said,

' O king, this time he comes with great caution,
and has posted men on the roads and at the
stations who seize on every one who passes.
If the king deem good, we will write a letter
and address it to his vezirs and great nobles,
and it shall be on this wise :—" After greeting :
Be it not concealed that your letter has come
and all that you say is understood. Long life
and health to you ! We indeed hoped it from
you. Now let me see you. Display manliness
and valour. Seize him on the road and bring
him to me, and that country shall be yours ;
such and such a place to so and so, and such
and such a district to so and so." Then we
will seal .it, and split a staff and put it therein,
and give it to a man and send him to them.
They will find the staff and take it to the king,
who will undoubtedly read it, and look upon
those vezirs and nobles as traitors, and mur-
murings will arise among them and they will
split into parties. And by this stratagem we
will again find relief.' The king did so. And
in that way they brought the letter to that king,
and as soon as he had read it, fear for his life
fell upon him. Then he turned back and went
to his country and seized those vezirs and
nobles and slew them. At length all the nobles
turned from him and wrote a letter and sent it

to this king, and it was thus : ' For the love of
God come against this tyrant, and we will aid
thee.' When the king had read the letter he
assembled an army and went to that country,
and on the battle-day all the nobles came and
submitted to him, and they seized the other king
and surrendered him. So he took that country
through stratagem ; and because that strong king
was negligent he lost his country and his head,
for they slew him."

"Now, O king, I have told this story for that
my king may know and not be negligent, and
lose not life and kingdom through the stratagem
of that unworthy youth." When the king heard
this story from the lady he was wroth, and said,
" To-morrow will I slay him." And they went
to bed.

When it was morning and the sun showed
his face from behind the castle of Qāf,* and
illumined the world with light, the king came
and sat upon his throne, and commanded the
executioner that he brought the youth and he
gave the word, " Smite off his head." Then
the Fourth Vezir came forward and said, " O my
king, it is not seemly in kings to hasten in all

* Qāf is the name of a fabled mountain-chain, formerly supposed to encircle the world ; "the castle " is simply a metaphor
for the mountain-peaks.

things with precipitancy ; above all the spilling
of blood unjustly is deemed by the wise most
blameworthy and hateful. They have declared
that the trials of a king are four : one is haste ;
another, trusting to wrong ; another, considering
not the end of matters ; and another, negligence.
Haste is that which disappoints those who seek
good and profit for themselves ; wrong is that
which brings about wars and uses armies unjustly and does evil things ; considering not the
end of matters is that which employs hurry
instead of deliberation ; and negligence is that
which inclines to music, and lust, and taking
counsel of women. And they have said, ' Let
one take counsel of a woman and do the
opposite of what she says ;' even as spake the
Holy Apostle (peace on him !) 'Consult them and
do clear contrary.' * In compliance with this
Tradition the king must not obey the woman's
word ; and through the words of women have
many men suffered remorse and fallen under
the wrath of God. And the story of Balaam,
the son of Beor,† is a strange story ; if the king
grant leave, I will relate it." The king said,
" Tell on, let us hear." Quoth the vezir,

---

* This famous speech is usually attributed to 'Omar, the
second Khalif.
† Bal'ām-bin-Bā'ūr.

The Fourth Vezir's Story.

"One day Moses (peace on him!) went against a tribe, and they were of the people of 'Ad, and they called their chief Og the son of Anak.* One day Moses (peace on him!) by command of God summoned these to the Faith, and resolved to fight and war with them if they were not obedient. So Moses (peace on him!) assembled four hundred and four-score thousand men and proceeded against the 'Adīs. When they were come near the 'Adīs, he sent twelve men as ambassadors to that tribe. Now Og had gone out to look about and he saw the twelve men coming, so he put the whole of them into his sack and slung it over his shoulder and turned back and went away. He brought them to his tribe the 'Adīs and said, ' See the host of the Messenger Moses which is come seeking to make war with us;' and he held the mouth of the sack downward and the twelve men rolled out. And that tribe saw them that they were small of stature, for their own stature was twice that of these. And they all made mock of them and laughed at them; but they killed them not, but sent them back. They returned

* 'Uj-bin-'Unuq. He is said, in the Talmud, to have been a monstrous giant. The 'Adīs, we are told, were from 60 to 100 cubits high. Compare Numbers, XIII, 33.

and told these things to Saint Moses, and fear fell upon all the host. Then Saint Moses (peace on him!) took his rod in his hand and went against that tribe of 'Ad. Og the son of Anak saw that Moses (peace on him!) was himself coming, and straightway he went and pulled up a rock like a mountain and put it on his head, and went that he might cast it upon the host of Moses (peace on him!). But God Most High commanded an angel that he went in the likeness of a bird and smote that rock with his beak and clave it, and thereupon it passed like a circle of cursers down before the face of Og. And straightway Saint Moses came up, and his stature grew to forty cubits, and his rod to forty cubits, and he leaped up forty cubits, and smote Og on the heel with his rod; and God Most High slew Og. Then Saint Moses (peace on him!) returned to his people and gave them tidings of Og being slain; and they were all glad. Then Saint Moses passed thence and made for the country of Sheykh Balaam the son of Beor. When he was come nigh, they brought word to the sheykh that Saint Moses was coming against him with many warriors. Whereupon the sheykh's disciples said, 'O sheykh, if that host come into our land, it will lay waste all our land; thou must find some help for this.'

F

Then were they silent. The sheykh said, 'What should we do?' They answered, 'Curse him.' The sheykh said, 'He is a Messenger; I cannot curse him.' And howsoever much they urged the sheykh, it was in vain. Now the sheykh had a cunning brawling wife; her they besought, saying, 'Speak to the sheykh, and we will give thee much money.' The woman answered, 'I will manage it.' When the sheykh came to his house he desired to take counsel of his wife; she said, 'Curse him.' The sheykh replied, 'He is a Messenger; how can I curse him?' The woman persisted so that the sheykh was constrained to lift up his hands and curse him. His curse was heard; and Saint Moses, who was fourteen leagues distant, remained for forty years in the wilderness; even as God Most High saith in His Word, 'For forty years shall they wander about in the earth.'* Then Saint Moses knew that there was some reason for this, and he prayed and humbled himself before God Most High, and said, 'My God, send him who is the cause of our thus wandering, from the world to the Hereafter without the Faith.' His prayer was accepted at the Court of God, and that sheykh went from the world to the Here-

---

* Koran, v. 29.

after without the Faith by reason of a woman ;
even as God Most High hath said, 'And his likeness was as the likeness of a dog.'" *

"Now, O king, I have told this story for
that these many men have been cast forth from
the Court of God for following the words of
women. Then is it incumbent on the king that
he judge accordingly, so that he become not a prey
to remorse ; for too late repentance profits not.
Beware and beware, slay not the prince on the
woman's word." And he kissed the ground
and made intercession for the prince for that
day. When the king heard this story from the
vezir, he sent the prince to the prison and went
himself to the chase.

When it was evening the king came to the
palace, and the lady rose to greet him, and they
sat down. After the repast the lady again
began to speak about the youth, and the king
said, "This day too my vezirs would not let me
be, so I have sent him to the prison." Quoth
the lady, "I know all the plot of those
vezirs, day by day each of them plans some
trick or wile ; they purpose to discredit me with
thee, so they say that women are lacking in
understanding, and that by reason thereof they

---

* Koran, vii. 175. See Appendix B, Note III.

F 2

are plotters and liars. These words of theirs
are false, do not assail the truth; for these see
me, that my trust in my king is strong. Yet I
am aware of their case and their hurtful deeds;
and for that I would defend my king from their
craft and malice, are they enemies to me. An
thou desire, my king, I shall say no more; and
they may do whatsoever they will. But all
these are of single tongue and single aim, and I
fear they will bring some calamity upon thee
and some evil upon me; and afterward thou
shalt repent, but it will avail not. My king,
thou hast assembled some men of low birth and
made them vezirs and confided all thy affairs to
them, and thou thinkest them honest; Heaven
forefend they should be honest when some of them
are the sons of cooks, and some of bakers, and
some of butchers; it is even as when Khizr* (peace
on him!) showed another king the origin of his
vezirs, but mayhap my king has not heard that
story." The king said, " Tell on, let us hear."
Quoth the lady,

---

* A mysterious being, of the number of the Prophets, who
appears to and aids Muslims in distress; he is frequently mentioned in Muhammedan fiction, where he plays a part similar to
that of Elijah in the Talmud.

THE LADY'S FOURTH STORY.

" There was in the palace of the world a king who was very desirous of seeing Khizr (peace on him !) ; and he would ever say, ' If there be anyone who will show me Khizr, I will give him whatsoever he may wish.' Now there was at that time a man poor of estate; and from the greatness of his poverty he said in himself, ' Let me go and bespeak the king that if he provide for me during three years I will show him Khizr; by three years either I shall be dead or the king will be dead, or he will forgive me my fault, or I shall on somewise win to escape : and in this way shall I make merry for a time.' So he went to the king and spake those words to him. The king said, ' An thou show him not then, I will kill thee ;' and that poor man consented. Then the king let give him much wealth and money, and the poor man took that wealth and money and went to his house. Three years he spent in merriment and delight, and he rested at ease till the term was accomplished. At the end of the time he fled and hid himself in a trackless place, and he began to quake for fear. Of a sudden he saw a personage with white raiment and shining face who saluted him. The poor man returned the salutation, and the

radiant being asked, 'Why art thou thus sad?'
but he gave no answer. Again the radiant
being asked him and sware to him, saying, 'Do
indeed tell to me thy plight that I may find thee
some remedy.' So that hapless one narrated
his story from its beginning to its end; and the
radiant being said, 'Come, I will go with thee to
the king and I will answer for thee;' so they
arose. Now the king wanted that hapless one;
and, while they were going, some of the king's
officers who were seeking met them, and they
straightway seized the poor man and brought
him to the king. Quoth the king, 'Lo, the three
years are accomplished; come now show me
Khizr.' That poor man said, 'My king, grace
and bounty are the work of kings; forgive my
sin.' Quoth the king, 'I made a pact; till I have
killed thee I shall not have fulfilled it!' And
he looked to his chief vezir and said, 'How
should this be done?' Quoth the vezir, 'This
man should be hewn in many pieces, and these
hung up on butcher's hooks, that others may see
and lie not before the king.' Said that radiant
being, 'True spake the vezir; all things return
to their origin.' Then the king looked to the
second vezir and said, 'What sayest thou?'
He replied, 'This man should be boiled in a
cauldron.' Said that radiant being, 'True spake

the vezir; all things return to their origin.'
The king looked to the third vezir and said,
'What sayest thou?' The vezir replied, 'This
man should be hewn in small pieces and baked
in an oven.' Again said that elder, 'True spake
the vezir; all things return to their origin.'
Then quoth the king to the fourth vezir, 'Let us
see, what sayest thou?' The vezir replied, 'O
king, the wealth thou gavest this poor creature
was for the love of Khizr (peace on him!).
He, thinking to find him, accepted it; now that
he has not found him he seeks pardon; this were
befitting, that thou set free this poor creature for
the love of Khizr.' Said that elder, 'True spake
the vezir; all things return to their origin.'
Then the king said to the elder, 'O elder, all
my vezirs have said different things, contrary
the one to the other, and thou hast said concerning each of them, "True spake the vezir; all
things return to their origin." What is the
reason thereof?' That elder replied, 'O king,
thy first vezir is a butcher's son, therefore did
he draw to his origin; thy second vezir is a
cook's son, he likewise proposed a punishment
as became his origin; thy third vezir is a
baker's son, he likewise proposed a punishment
as became his origin; but thy fourth vezir is of
gentle birth, compassion therefore becomes his

origin ; so he had compassion on that hapless one and sought to do good and counseled liberation. O king, all things draw to their origin.'* And he gave the king much counsel and at last said, 'Lo, I am Khizr!' and vanished. Then the king went forth from his palace, but could see no sign or trace of that radiant elder ; and he said, ' I much longed to see Khizr (peace on him!) ; praise be to God, I have attained thereto, and he has told me the origin of my vezirs.' And he commanded that they gave that poor man much wealth."†

" Now, O king, I have told this story for that thou mayst know that thy vezirs are of low origin, and that fidelity will not proceed from them. In this matter too their words tally with their origin ; lose not the opportunity, for to spare an enemy is great folly." The king heard this story from the lady, and said, "To-morrow will I roll up the scroll of his life." And they went to bed.

When it was morning and the world, like to him who had won to Khizr, was illumined with light, the king sat upon his throne and commanded

---

* Compare Boethius thus translated by Chaucer : All thynges seken ayen to hir propre course, and all thynges rejoysen on hir retourninge agayne to hir nature.

† See Appendix B, Note IV.

the executioner that he brought the youth, and he gave the word, "Smite off his head." Thereupon the Fifth Vezir came forward and said, "O king of the world, slay not the prince thus hastily, and cast not to the winds the counsels of these many vezirs; for as they take pearls from the sea and string them, so do these string their words; they are speakers such that Mercury in the sky could not match their suggestions. O king, the reason of that which thy vezirs have said to thee is this, that the Apostle (peace on him!) hath said that whoso seeth his king do an act contrary to the law, and hindereth him not therefrom, hath departed from the Canon. Now, O king, deem not the words of thy vezirs mistaken; it is even as they have said, 'Let him who would see Khizr in the flesh, look upon a wise, accomplished and learned vezir.' And again, 'If one seek to do a righteous deed, let him arrange the affair of some poor creature with a king.' Mayhap the king has not heard the story of Khizr and a vezir." The king said, "Tell on, let us hear." Quoth the vezir,

The Fifth Vezir's Story.

"There was, of old time, a king who had an experienced vezir; and Khizr (peace on him!) would ever come to that vezir. One day the

vezir looked upon the affairs of the world, how
they abode not with anyone; and he withdrew from the vezirship, and chose the corner
of retirement, and gave himself up to worship.
A long time passed, and Khizr (peace on him!)
never once came to him. The vezir marvelled
and said, 'Why does not Khizr (peace on him!)
come to me? Now ought he to come every
day.' Then he said, 'There must indeed be
some reason for this.' Thereupon he saw that
Khizr had appeared, and he said, 'O Khizr,
while I was vezir thou didst ever come to me,
is it for that I have withdrawn from the world
that thou comest not now?' Khizr (peace on
him!) replied, 'O vezir, outwardly thou didst
perform the duties of vezir, inwardly I did;
therefore was there a bond between us;
now thou hast withdrawn therefrom, and that
bond is gone from between us, so I come not
to thee.' When the vezir heard these words
from Khizr, he went and asked back the vezirship, and he received it, and Khizr (peace on
him!) came to him as before and ceased not."

"O king, I have told this story for that the
king may hearken to the vezirs' words and
follow them, and pass his life in happiness.
Beware, O king, be not over hasty in this affair,
that afterward thou suffer not remorse." When

the king heard this story from the vezir, he
sent the prince to the prison and went himself
to the chase, and that day he took much game.

In the evening he came to the palace, and
the lady rose to greet him, and they sat down.
After the repast the lady asked about the
youth ; the king said, " This day again such an
one of my vezirs made intercession for him, and
I sent him to the prison." Quoth the lady, " O
my king, how good were it, could he be re-
formed by such conduct ; but this youth is
incapable of reform ; for he resembles that
snake which first stings his mother as she bears
him and kills her, and then stings his father
and kills him. God Most High will take vengeance on him ; and his eyes will be blinded as
though he had looked upon an emerald.* If a
drop of an April shower fall upon a snake it
becomes poison, but if it fall into an oyster it
becomes a pearl ; † and if the Koran, great of
glory, fall upon a believer's heart, it is faith and
knowledge. And it is notorious that whoever
nurses a snake falls at last a prey to its poison.
A certain man formed a friendship with a snake
and used every day to bring it a portion of

---

* The emerald was supposed to have the effect of blinding
snakes when they looked upon it.
† There is an Eastern myth to that effect.

food.   He went to the snake's hole and laid it
there, and the snake would put its head out
of its hole and eat that food, and when it was
satisfied it would frolic about, and that man
would play with it.   One day he came and saw
that the snake was out of its place and quite
stiff from cold ; 'O poor thing,' he said, and
took and put it in his bosom.   When the snake
got warm it at once raised its head and stang
that unhappy man, and killed him, and fled and
entered its hole.   And thus have they said,
that if one foster a swine, that brute will not
leave off till in the end it hurt him.   It is even
as the story of that sherbet-seller and the
Moor."   Said the king, " Tell on, let us hear."
Quoth the lady,

The Lady's Fifth Story.

 " There was of old time in a great city a
sherbet-seller, and he had a son, a loveling of
the age, who was so fair that he seemed a
second Joseph ;* and he used to sell sherbet
in the shop.   The folk would come to gaze
upon this youth's beauty, and they would give
a sequin for each cup of sherbet, and drain it ;
and whenever they drank a cup they would say

---

* Joseph is the type of youthful beauty.

it was the water of life. Now one day a
swarthy Moor came to that country; and as
soon as he saw the youth, the hapless Moor's
power of speech left him, and he could not stir
one step from where he stood, but leaned
against the opposite wall bewildered. After a
time he recovered his understanding, and, rising
and falling like one drunk, he came up as best
he could to the youth, and gave a sequin and
drank a cup of sherbet, and went away. For a
time he came every day and drank cups of sherbet
at a sequin each, and looked on the beauty of the
youth. One day the youth told this thing to
his father, and his father perceived that the
Moor was ravished with the boy, and said, 'O
my son, bring that Moor to the house to-
morrow, and let us see what manner of man he
is.' The next day when the Moor came to the
youth, he invited him to his house, and took
him and went to his father. After they had
eaten, the father of the boy asked of the Moor's
case and dwelling. The Moor saw what his
intention was, and answered, ' I have no dwelling, I am a stranger.' The boy's father said,
' Thou art a stranger; we will give thee a
dwelling, stay with us.' The Moor was glad
and counted it a boon to his soul; even as they
have said, ' The loved one's ward is Paradise.'

So they showed the Moor a dwelling. He abode for some days, and gradually his love for the boy increased ; and one day he showed him a precious stone, and said, ' An thou let me take one kiss of thee, I will give thee this stone.' With a thousand graces the boy consented, and the Moor gave him the stone and kissed him, and said, ' My life, my master, I love thee from heart and soul, flee me not; I know a talisman which will open before thee ; if thou wilt come with me I will open it, and give thee so much gold that thou shalt never again know poverty.' The youth told this thing to his father, and his father gave him leave ; so the Moor took him, and they went without the city ; and he brought him to a ruin. Now there was a well there, full to the mouth with water ; and the Moor wrote on a piece of paper and laid it on the well, and thereupon all the water vanished from the well. The Moor and the boy descended to the bottom of the well, and saw a locked door. The Moor wrote a charm and fastened it on the lock, and it opened forthwith. They went in and saw a negro holding in one hand a great stone to throw upon anyone who entered. The Moor repeated a charm and blew upon the negro, and the negro laid the stone that was in his

hand upon the ground, and let them pass.
They went on and saw a dome of crystal, and
at the door of the domed building were two
dragons, who stood facing one the other with
open mouths like caverns. When they came
near, these flew at them, but the Moor repeated
a charm and blew on them, and they vanished.
Then the door of the domed building opened
and they went in, and they saw that in one
corner thereof was gold, in another corner
silver, in another corner all manner of jewels,
and in another corner was raised a throne upon
black earth, and on that throne was a coffin,
and in that coffin lay a renowned man dead.
Upon his breast was a gold tablet, and on that
tablet was written : 'I was a king, and I ruled
the whole earth, and whithersoever I went in
this world I conquered. I had many many
champions and great wealth and treasure. Some
little of the wealth I owned I gathered here.
Me too Death spared not ; but made me even
as though I had not come into the world. Now,
O thou who seest me in this plight, take warning by me, and remember my soul in prayer,
and be not presumptuous through the wealth of
this world for a few days' life.' And that was all.
Then the Moor and the youth took as much
as they desired of the gold and silver and pre-

cious stones and black earth, which was the Philosopher's Stone, and went out. The Moor repeated a charm and blew upon the well, and it was again all full of water ; and he went back with the boy to their house, and they gave themselves up to mirth and merriment. Day and night they ceased not therefrom an instant. One day the boy asked the Moor to teach him the charms he had repeated in the talisman. The Moor consented, and instructed him for many days and taught him. One day, of a sudden, the boy said to his father, ' O father, I have learned the whole of the charms for the talisman, so we have no longer any need of the Moor ; let us poison him.' But his father consented not, and said, ' Let us turn him away ; let him go elsewhither.' Quoth the youth, ' The turning away of him would not do ; he is a great master, he might do us an injury, so let us poison him ere he play us some trick ; and I will take as much gold and silver as is needful from that buried treasure.' The Moor heard him and knew that fairness purposed foulness, and he straightway disappeared from there."*

"Now, O king, I have told this story for that the king may know that no good has ever hap-

---

* See Appendix B, Note V.

pened **to anyone** from youths. Yea, O king,
be **not** negligent, kill the youth, else **the affair**
will **end in** evil." **When** the king heard **this**
story from the lady he was wroth and said,
" On the morrow **will I slay him."** And they
went to bed.

When it was morning the king sat **upon his**
throne and caused the youth to **be** brought, and
commanded the executioner, " Smite off his
head." The Sixth Vezir came forward and said,
" **O** king of the world, beware, act **not on any-**
one's word **till** the crime be proved against the
prince; for **the** Resurrection is at hand, **and**
lying and cunning **and** craft abound. The wise
man is he **who** turns **off** sin and **evil** that he
may not afterward **begin to** bite upon the
finger with regret and remorse and be repentant,
and who takes **the** woful by the hand and gives
happiness to the unhappy, and **who** repulses
not him who comes to his **door,** but sees his
needs and provides for him, and who never lets
himself be deceived by a woman's word ; for
these laugh in one's face. Mayhap my king
has not heard the story of the tailor youth and
the woman." **The** king said, " **Tell** on, let us
hear." Quoth **the vezir,**

G

The Sixth Vezir's Story.

" Thus relate they : In the time of Saint Jesus (peace on him !) there was a tailor youth who had a fair wife, and they greatly loved one another.   One day they made a pact that if the woman died first, her husband should take no other wife, but throw his arms round her tombstone, and weep till morning ; and if the youth died first, the woman should do likewise.   By the decree of God the woman died.   After the tailor had wept and lamented he buried her, and fulfilled his pact, and threw his arms round his wife's tombstone and wept.   And he constantly kept watch over the grave.   One day Jesus (peace on him !) when passing by that place, saw a youth weeping and embracing a tombstone, and he went up to him and asked why he wept.   The youth related all.   Then Jesus (peace on him !) prayed, and the woman became alive, and came forth from the grave in her shroud.   And Jesus (peace on him !) proceeded on his way.   The youth said, ' One cannot go thus in a shroud ; wait thou here a moment till I go and fetch clothes from the house ; then thou shalt put on these clothes, and we will go together.'   And he went quickly to the house, leaving the woman there.   Suddenly

the son of the king of that country passed that
spot, and saw a fair woman sitting wrapped in
a shroud.   As soon as the prince saw that
woman he fell in love with her from heart and
soul, and he said to her, 'Who art thou?' She
answered, 'I am a stranger; a robber has
stripped me.'   Thereupon the prince ordered
his servants to take the woman to the palace,
and clothe her in clean garments.   When the
youth returned with the clothes he found not
the woman there, and he cried and asked of the
passers-by.   No one had seen her.   The poor
man, asking and asking, met the prince's servants.   These asked the tailor why he wept.
He replied, 'For a time my wife was dead;
but now, praise be to God, she is become alive
through the prayer of the Messenger Jesus; I
went to fetch her clothes, but she has disappeared: therefore do I weep.'   They answered,
'The prince sent that lady to the palace this
day.'   Thereupon the tailor went before the
prince and complained, saying, 'The woman
thou hast taken is my wife.'   The prince asked
the lady, she denied and said, 'This is the
robber who stripped me of my clothes and
made off; praise be to God, if thou kill him
now, thou shalt gain great reward.'   The prince
commanded that they bound both the tailor's

hands behind his back. Although the poor
tailor cried aloud, it was no avail; they put a
rope round his neck and led him to the gallows.
Then they perceived Saint Jesus on the road,
and they waited. When he came near he asked
of their case, and they told him. Then he bade
them stop and went himself to the prince; they
called the woman, and he said, ' This woman is
the wife of yonder youth; I prayed and she
became alive.' When the woman saw the
Messenger she was unable to deny, but spake
the truth. Jesus (peace on him!) prayed again,
and that woman died; and the youth was
rescued from the abyss whereinto he had fallen,
and he repented of his having wept so long a
time."

" Now, O king, I have told this story for
that thou mayst know that the inclinations of
women are ever to works of evil, craft, and
wickedness." And he kissed the ground and
made intercession for the prince's life. When
the king heard this story from the vezir he sent
the prince to the prison, and went himself to
the chase.

In the evening he returned from the chase
and came to the palace, and the lady rose to
greet him, and they sat down. After the repast
the lady fell to speaking about the youth. The

king said, " To-day such an one of my vezirs
made intercession for him, so I have again sent
him to the prison." Quoth the lady, "O king,
thou dost not believe my words ; but at length,
in the near future, some hurt will befall thee
from the youth ; for this night I saw a vision,
which it is, as it were, a duty on me to tell my
king, and incumbent on thee to hear." Said
the king, " Tell on, let us hear." The lady
said, " This night thou wast holding in thy hand
a golden ball, and that ball was adorned and
set round with rubies and jewels, and its bril-
liancy lit up the world ; and thou wast playing,
throwing up the ball and catching it in thy
hand. And this youth was sitting by thy side
watching, and ever and anon he asked for the
ball, but thou gavest him it not. Of a sudden,
while thou wast heedless, he snatched the ball,
and for that thou hadst not given it him when
he had asked was he angry, and he struck the
ball upon a stone, so that it was shattered in
pieces. And I was grieved, and I went and
picked up the fragments of the ball, and gave
them into thy hand, and thou didst look upon
those fragments and didst marvel, and with that
I awoke." Quoth the king, " What may the
interpretation of this vision be ? " The lady
said, " I interpreted this dream : that ball is thy

kingdom ; and this youth's snatching it from thy
hand is this, that this youth came to me and
said, ' I wish to kill my father and sit upon the
throne, and I desire to make thee my wife ;
and all the men of the kingdom have turned to
me, and now the kingdom is wholly mine, do
thou likewise submit to me ?' Had I submitted
to him, ere now he had killed thee and accomplished his affair. Ah! the fortune and auspiciousness of my king averted it. And his
striking the ball upon the stone is this, that if
he had become king after thee, he would have
utterly ruined the kingdom. And my going and
picking up the fragments and giving them to
the king is this, that for that I obeyed not the
youth, but came and told the king, he seized
him, and the kingdom remained in his hand.
But had not I done so, know of a surety that
ere now the kingdom would have passed from
thy hand ; yea, thy life, too, would have gone.
That is the interpretation of the dream. O
king, the story of this degenerate youth resembles that of a certain king's son; mayhap
my king has not heard it." The king said, " Tell
on, let us hear." Quoth the lady,

THE LADY'S SIXTH STORY.

"In the palace of the world there was a king
in whose country was a robber, such that none
could escape from his hands. And in that
king's country was a great khoja. That khoja
and his wife were travelling with some money,
when of a sudden, while they were on the road,
they met that robber. He forthwith stripped
them and made them naked and took them
captives. He put their clothes in the cave
which he had chosen for his dwelling, and
bound both the khoja's hands behind his back
and laid him in a corner; and then he gave
himself up to mirth and merriment with the
woman. A time passed thus, and the woman
conceived by the robber. After seven or eight
months the robber released the khoja and his
wife. So these went forth from the cave, and
saying, 'There is nor strength nor power save in
God, the High, the Mighty,' they set their faces
in a certain direction, and fared on till one day
they entered a city. And they took a dwelling
in that city and settled there. When the
woman's time was come she gave birth to a
boy; but as they knew that the boy was the
robber's, they would not accept him, and they
laid him at the door of the mosque. The king

of that country happened to pass by and asked
concerning him, and the people who were
present answered that his parents had no means
of bringing him up and so had left him there.
Now the king had no son, and he took pity on
this child and adopted him and made him his
son, and said, ' If God give him life and he die
not, he shall sit on the throne after me and
be king.' So they took the boy and brought
him to the palace, and appointed him a nurse,
and made him clothes of all manner of stuffs.
Day by day he grew, and when he had
reached his seventh year he was a moon-
faced boy, such that he who looked upon
his countenance desired to look thereon again.
And the king appointed a teacher and a
governor for the boy, and he learned science
and good-conduct. When he had reached his
twelfth year he had acquired sciences and
accomplishments. After that, they instructed
him in horsemanship; that too he acquired in a
few days. And every day he would go into
the square and take a ball and play ; and all the
world marvelled at his beauty and dexterity,
and the king felt delight as often as he looked
upon him. Now the king had also a daughter
peerless in beauty. In the course of a few
years this girl grew up and reached the age of

puberty, and the boy fell in love **with her.** He
would brood over this, saying, ' Alas ! would she
were **not my** sister, **that** I might marry her.'
Now the boy was a valiant youth, such that the
king's emirs and vezirs applauded **his valour ;**
and he overcame the king's enemies **who were**
round about, and made them subject to **his**
father ; and no one could **stand** before **his**
sword. The king **had** betrothed his daughter
to another king's son, and when the time was
come they wished to take **the girl from the king.**
And the king commanded that they should make
ready ; and thereupon the youth, to make clear
what was in his heart, asked a legist this question, ' If a person have a garden and **the fruit of**
that garden ripen, should that person eat it or
another ?' **The** legist replied, ' **It were better**
that person should eat it than another.' **Now**
the prince had a learned companion, **and** that
companion knew the prince's desire ; **for** science
is of three kinds : one the science of the Faith,
another the science of physiognomy, and another
the science of the body ; but unless there be the
science of physiognomy, other science avails not.
Straightway that companion said, ' O prince, if
there be in that garden you ask **of,** a fruit forbidden by God Most High, it were better
that the owner eat it not ; but if **God Most**

High have not forbidden it, then is it lawful for that person to eat it.' Quoth the prince, 'Thou knowest not as much as a legist; yon man is a legist; I look to his decision.' And he arose and went to his sister's palace, and that hour he took his sister and went forth the city, and made for another city. Then the slave-girls with great crying informed the king, and thereupon the king's senses forsook him, and he commanded, 'Let the soldiers forthwith mount their horses and pursue the youth and seize him.' Straightway the soldiers mounted and went after the youth; and the king said, 'From the low born fidelity comes not;' and he repented him of his having taken him to son. The king and the soldiers appeared behind the youth, and the latter sprang into a hiding-place. And while the king and the soldiers were passing he slew the king from that hiding-place; and when the soldiers saw that the king was slain they each one fled in a different direction, and were scattered in confusion. And the youth took the girl and went to a city and took a house therein, and made her his wife; and he adopted the whole of what had been his father's business, and turned robber."

"Now, O king, I have told this story, for that thou mayst know that the desire of this degenerate youth is to kill his father as that low born one slew his, and even as that youth took his sister does this one wish to take his mother; the rest the king knows." When the king heard this strange thing from the lady, he said, "On the morrow will I slay him." And they went to bed.

When it was morning the king went and sat upon his throne, and he caused the youth to be brought and commanded the executioner, "Smite off his head." Whereupon the Seventh Vezir came forward and said, "O king of the world, first look to the end of every business thou undertakest and then act accordingly; for on the day of battle it is needful first to think of the way of retreat and then to set to, so that when it is 'or fate or state,' one may save his life. They have said, 'On the day of strife be not far from the nobles: in the chase and the palace go not near them;' and 'He is profitable in the councils of a king, who in the day of security looks to the matters of war and the provision of weapons, and stints not money to the troops that these on the day of battle may be lavish with their lives in the king's cause.' It is incumbent on the king that he kill those who flee when they see the enemy (and after that the foes); for they resemble those who give up a stronghold to the adversary. And they have said that a good scribe and a man who knows the science of the sword are very needful for a king ; for with the pen is wealth collected, and with the sword are countries taken. Mayhap the king has not heard the story of a certain king and a vezir." The king said, " Tell on, let us hear." Quoth the vezir,

The Seventh Vezir's Story.

" There was in the palace of the world a king and he had two vezirs, one of whom was wise and learned and one of whom was foolish and ignorant. On the king's taking counsel of them concerning the management of the affairs of the state, the ignorant vezir said, ' O king, expend not money, give not money to the soldiers and warriors, or if thou give, give little ; and let him who will stay, stay ; and let him who will not stay, go. When thou hast money on the battle-day, many will be soldiers to thee : where the honey is, there surely come the flies.' His words seemed good to the king, who one day said to the learned vezir, ' Get me a few men who will be content with little pay.' On the vezir's replying, ' Men without pay are not to be had,' the king said, ' I shall have money when anything befalls, and shall find many men.' Quoth the vezir, 'So be it, I shall find men for the king who will take no pay and stir not day or night from his gate.' The king was glad and said, 'Get them, let us see.' The vezir went and found a painter and brought him, and he painted a large room in the palace so that the four walls of that room were covered with pictured figures of men, and he decked all the figures with arms and implements of war, he depicted a mounted and armed host standing rank on rank. When it was completed the vezir called the king, and the king arose and went with him to that wall of pictures, and he showed the king the whole of them. The king looked and said, 'What are these pictures? why hast thou ranged these here rank on rank?' The vezir replied, 'O king, thou desiredst of me men without pay; lo, these youths want no pay; so they will serve the king.' The king said, 'There is no life in these; how can they serve?' The vezir answered, 'O king, if lifeless pictures will not serve, no more will payless soldiers serve. Fief and pay are as the life of the soldier; when thou givest not a man his fief or pay, it is as though thou tookest away his life; judge if a lifeless man could serve.' Again, 'O king, if a paid army be not needful for thee, these will suffice; but living men require to eat and drink.

If they get no pay they will not sacrifice their
lives in the cause of the king or face the enemy ;
but they will hate the king and turn from him,
and evil will befall the king ; but if the king be
bountiful they will obey.   Thus a noble had a
young steward who used to serve him.   One
day the noble asked the youth his name.   He
replied, "God on thee, my name is Wittol."
Said the noble, "Can anyone be so called ?"
The youth answered, "Anyhow it is my nick-
name, never mind."   So they used to call that
youth Wittol so long as he was at that noble's
gate.   One day he went from that noble's gate
to another's.   One day that noble in whose service he had been happened to meet him, when
he cried out, "Ho Wittol, how art thou ?"   The
youth replied, "O noble, say not so again, or thou
shalt see." The noble said, "My life, thou didst
tell me Wittol was thy name ; why art thou now
angered ?"   The youth answered, "Then did I
serve thee, and thou bestowedest on me worlds
of bounties, so though thou calledst me Wittol,
it offended me not ; but now I never get a
favour from this man that he should call me so."
Quoth the noble, "He who called thee so just
now was I, not he ; yet thou wast angered with
me."   The youth replied, "God forbid I should
be angered with thee ; but if to-morrow the

other were to hear that word from thee, he too
would wish to use it ; now was I angered lest
he should call me so."' Then that vezir laid a
dish of honey before the king ; as it was night
no flies came to it. And the vezir said, ' They
say that where there is honey, thither will the flies
surely flock ; lo, here is honey, where are the
flies ?' Quoth the king, ' It is night, therefore
they come not.' The vezir said, ' My king, it
is necessary to give soldiers money at the proper
time ; for bringing out money on the battle-day
is like bringing out honey at night.' When the
king heard these words from the vezir he was
ashamed ; but he greatly applauded the vezir,
and thenceforth did whatsoever he advised."

" Now, O king, I have told this story for that
thou mayst know that attendants and servants
are needful for kings, and that masters of device
and resource are requisite. Kings should take
counsel of their vezirs in such matters that no
defect may mar their fortune in the world or
the Hereafter. Now the prince is thy support
and asylum, and all the folk, high and low, ask
why he is fettered with the bonds of woe and a
prisoner of the dungeon. And slaying the
prince were like slaying the vezirs and all the
world. Who would sit on the throne after thee
that should know our circumstances ? All the

grandees of the empire and lords of the state and noble seyyids would be cast down, and scattered to the winds and ruined. This woman is a woman lacking in religion and understanding; to give ear to and thus countenance those who are so lacking is not worthy our king." And he kissed the ground and begged for the prince. So the king sent him to the prison.

Having returned from the chase, the king went to the palace, and the lady rose to greet him, and they passed on and sat down. After the repast the lady again asked for news of the youth. The king answered, "To-day too I have sent him to the prison." The lady said, " Thou art a wise and just king; we will talk together this night and see whether or no by principle, by the Law, and by custom, thou dost sin in thus vexing my heart. O king, there are many rights between husband and wife. First, the husband's right over the wife is this, that if he have a hurt in the bottom of his tooth, she must lick that hurt and cleanse his tooth ;* another is, if his heart desire solacement of love, she must, even though kneading dough with tucked-up sleeves, submit to him, ere she wash her hands. But the wife's right over the hus-

---

* *I.e.* tend him in every illness, whatever it may be, to the best of her power.

band is; first, that he leave her not naked or
hungry or bid her work out of doors, and that
he vex not her heart and she innocent, and that
he deny her not money. For women's words
and skirts are short, and they are slaves and
helpless before men, therefore should the latter
cherish them and heed not though they be sometimes froward, but caress them. And they have
said that it is better to give a woman a handful
of words than a skirtful of money. Mayhap
the king has not heard the story of the sparrow
and his mate." The king said, "Relate it, let
us hear." Quoth the lady,

THE LADY'S SEVENTH STORY.

"There was in the blessed service of Saint
Solomon (peace on him!) a little sparrow whose
many tricks and gambols were ever pleasing to
Saint Solomon. One day Saint Solomon saw
not the sparrow by him, and he commanded the
simurgh* bird to go fetch the sparrow wherever
he might find him. For a long time the sparrow
had not gone to his mate, and his mate had upbraided him, saying, 'For this long time thou

---

* A fabulous bird of great size. Solomon, it should be said,
according to the Talmudic and Koranic legends, was acquainted
with the language of beasts and birds, with whom he used often
to converse.

H

hast left me and been with Solomon; dost thou
love him more than me, or dost thou fear him?
tell me.' The sparrow answered, 'By God, I
would not give thee for the world: I am come
but once to earth and shall not come again; I go
to Solomon for diversion, I have no dread of
him.' While he was talking with many such
vaunts and boasts, the sīmurgh arrived in haste
and heard the sparrow bragging and said
harshly, ' Up, let us off; Saint Solomon wants
thee.' Then the sparrow, being beside his mate,
plucked up courage and replied, ' Off, begone, I
will not go.' The sīmurgh said, ' I will indeed
take thee.' The sparrow answered, 'Off with
thee, get thee hence, or I will seize thee and rend
thee in twain.' Quoth the sīmurgh, ' Until I
take thee with me I will not budge from here.'
Yet the sparrow heeded not, and the sīmurgh
waited awhile, but the sparrow would not go.
Again said the sīmurgh to the sparrow, ' O my
life, give me an answer.' Quoth the sparrow, ' I
tell thee begone from here; if thou speak again,
my heart will bid me do somewhat else; but no,
I will not slay thee. Off, begone, or I will do thee
some hurt, and then go to Solomon's palace and
smite it with my foot, and overturn it from its
foundations and pull it down about his head;
now then, away fool, off, begone the road thou

camest. Thou chatterest here and sayest not,
" This is the sparrow's harem ; he is ill."' And
he gave the sīmurgh a kick such that the latter
knew not where it touched him, but he flew
thence and reported the sparrow's words to Saint
Solomon. Solomon said, 'When the sparrow
spake these words where was he ?' 'His mate
was there,' answered the sīmurgh. Then quoth
Solomon (peace on him!), ' There is no harm in
one thus boasting and bragging in his own
house before his wife. Though every stone of this
my palace was raised by the toil of these many
demons, still wonder not at his saying when
beside his wife that he could shatter it with
one foot.' And this was pleasing to Solomon
(peace on him!), and when the sparrow came he
made him of his boon-companions."*

" O king, I have told this story for that thou
mayst know that one should thus love his wife
and vex not her little heart, so that his wife may
have nought against him. And God Most High
has given thee understanding; weigh my words
in the balance of understanding, and try them on
the touchstone of the heart ; if they stand not the
test, I shall speak no more. I tell thee that this
youth has stretched forth his hand to me and

---

* See Appendix B, Note VI.

has been treacherous, and has moreover purposed against thy life ; can there be greater
crimes than these ? O king, beware, be not negligent in this matter; for there is fear and danger
for thy life and kingdom." When the king heard
these beguiling words of the lady he said, " On
the morrow will I make an end of his affair."
And they went to bed.

When it was morning the king sat upon his
throne and commanded the executioner that he
brought the youth, and he said, " Smite off his
head." Whereupon the Eighth Vezir came forward and said, " O king of the world, slay not
the prince on the woman's word.   One should
be forgiving; above all, as no man is exempt
from sin ; for they have said that humanity is
composed of forgetfulness. A man falls sometimes through the intrigues of an enemy and
sometimes through the maleficence of the cruel
Sphere ; or else he attains prosperity and falls
into adversity. Mayhap the king has not heard
the story of a certain vezir." The king said,
" Tell on, let us hear." Quoth the vezir,

THE EIGHTH VEZIR'S STORY.

" Of old time there was a king, and he had an
experienced and learned vezir. One day the
latter went to the bath, and while he was sitting

beside the basin, his ring fell from his finger into
the water; and it sank not in the water, but
floated on the surface. Whenever the vezir saw
this he sent men to his house and treasury, saying, 'Go quickly, and hide in a certain place
whatsoever I have in the treasury of gold and
silver or rubies and jewels; for now is the king
about to seize me.' Then they went and acted
according to his order. And as the vezir was
coming out from the bath, men from the king
arrived and seized him; and they put him in
prison and took possession of whatever he had
in his house and treasury. One day, after the
vezir had been imprisoned for a certain time, his
heart longed for a conserve of pomegranate pips,
and he ordered the gaoler, saying, 'Make me
ready a conserve and bring it, for my heart doth
greatly desire it.' Now the king had forbidden
that dish, and the gaoler was afraid and made it
not. And the vezir's desire increased and he
begged it of all who came to him, but no one
made it and brought it through fear of the king.
Brief, the vezir lay for a year in prison and
longed for that dish, but no one found means
to bring him it. One day the gaoler made
shift to cook that dish and bring it to the vezir.
As soon as the vezir saw it he was glad; and
they put it before him, but ere he had stretched

out his hand to it, two mice, that were struggling
with each other above, fell into the dish, and the
food became unclean. Thereupon the vezir said,
'It is good;' and he arose and commanded his
servants, saying, 'Go, furnish the mansion, put
that wealth you hid back into its proper place;
my king is about to take me from prison and
make me vezir.' Then his retainers went and
did as he had commanded. Hereupon came a
man from the king who took the vezir from the
prison and brought him before the king. Then
said the king to comfort the vezir's heart, 'I put
thee in prison seemingly to afflict thee; but
really that thou mightest know, from experienc-
ing imprisonment, speedily to intercede for the
men whom I cast into gaol.' Quoth the vezir,
'Nearness to a sultan is a burning fire: whatsoever conduct be observed toward me by the king
is pleasant teaching.' The king was pleased and
commanded that they brought a robe of honour,
and he put it on him and made him again vezir.
Then when the vezir was come to his mansion
his retainers and others asked him, saying,
'Whence knewest thou of the king's being about
to imprison thee and seize thy wealth, and
whence knewest thou of his being about to take
thee out and make thee vezir?' The vezir replied, 'While in the bath my ring fell into the

water and sank not, so I knew that my fortune
had reached its perfection, and that what follows
every perfection is declension, therefore did I so
command; and for a whole year, while I was in
prison, I longed for a dish of pomegranate pips,
at length I got it, and mice polluted it so that I
could not eat it, so I knew that my misfortune
was complete and that my former estate was
returned. And I was glad.'"

"Now, O king, I have told this story for that
the king may likewise know that every perfection has its declension. Until now the prince
and the vezirs were safe and esteemed before
the king. Now he knows not in what malefic
sign our stars may be imprisoned. A woman
has rendered us despicable before the king and
has bound him about with craft and wiles, so
that these many learned and sagacious vezirs are
impotent against her incitements; even as it
is clear that when a fool throws a stone down
a well a wise man is powerless to get it up again.
O king, haste not in this affair; too late repentance
profits not; for the prince is like a young bird
that can neither fly nor flee, grant him a few
days' respite, haply this difficulty may be solved;
and there is a reason for his not speaking. He
is ever as a prisoner in thy hand; afterward, if
thou will, kill him; if thou will, free him." And

he kissed the ground and begged for the prince.
When the king heard this story from the vezir
the fire that was in his heart was increased tenfold and the tears poured from his eyes; and
he sent the prince to the prison and mounted
for the chase with his own cares.

When the king returned he entered the
palace, and the lady rose to greet him, and
they sat down. After the repast the lady
asked for news of the youth. The king said,
" To-day too such an one of my vezirs made intercession for him, and I sent him to the prison."
Quoth the lady, " O king, I have given thee
this much counsel, and it has produced no effect
upon thee. It is as though a physician treated
a sick man, and the treatment was without
result, and that physician was powerless and
attempted no other treatment, but left off; for if
he treated that sick man again, he would kill
him. Now, I too am powerless to speak to
thee. I should say, ' I will speak no more nor
waste my breath in vain;' still my heart pities
thee, for the king's realm and life will be
destroyed. My head, too, will fall; for that I am
in the same peril with the king do I speak. It
is even as once when they cut off a person's
hand and he uttered no sound; afterward he
saw someone whose hand had been cut off, and

he wailed aloud and wept. Those who were present wondered and asked, saying, 'O man, when thy hand was cut off thou didst not weep; why weepest thou now?' That person answered, 'By God, then, when they cut off my hand, I saw that there was not among you one who had met the like, and I said in myself that if I wept each of you would speak ill of me, for ye knew not the pain of it; now that I have found a companion in my plight do I weep, for he knows the anguish I have suffered.' Now, O king, thy head and my head are like to fall; if the king know not my plight, who should know it? Mayhap my king has not heard the story of the three princes and the cadi." The king said, "Tell on, let us hear." Quoth the lady,

The Lady's Eighth Story.

" In the palace of the world there was a king and he had three sons. One day this king laid his head on the pillow of death and called those sons to his side, and spake privately with them. He said, ' In such and such a corner of the palace I have hidden a vase full of pearls and jewels and diverse gems; when I am dead do ye wash me well and bury me, then go and take that vase from its place and divide its contents.' The king lay for three days, and

on the fourth day he drained the wine of death
and set forth for the Abiding Home. When
the princes had buried their father according to
his injunctions, they came together and went
and beheld that in the place of those jewels the
winds blew. Now the princes began to dispute,
and they said, 'Our father told this to us three
in private, this trick has been played by one of
us.' And the three of them went to the cadi,
and told their complaint. The cadi listened
and then said to them, ' Come, I will tell you a
story, and after that I will settle your dispute.
Once, in a certain city, a youth and a girl loved
each other, and that girl was betrothed to
another youth. When the lover was alone
with that girl he said, " O my life, now thou
comest to me and I am happy with thee; to-
morrow when thou art the bride of thy betrothed, how will be my plight ?" The girl
said, "My master, do not grieve; that night when
I am bride, until I have come to thee and seen
thee, I will not give the bridegroom his desire."
And they made a pact to that end. Brief,
when the bridal night arrived, the girl and the
youth went apart; and when all the people
were dispersed and the place was clear of
others, the girl told the bridegroom of the pact
between her and the stricken lover, and be-

sought leave to fulfil it. Whenever the bridegroom heard these words from the bride he
said, " Go, fulfil thy plight and come again in
safety." So the bride went forth, but while on
the road she met a robber. The robber looked
at her attentively, and saw that she was a
beautiful girl like the moon of fourteen nights ;
never in his life had he seen such a girl, and
upon her was endless gold, and she was
covered with diverse jewels such as cannot be
described. Thereupon the bridle of choice
slipped from the robber's hands ; and as the
hungry wolf springs upon the sheep, so did the
robber spring upon that girl. Straightway the
girl began to sigh, and the robber felt pity and
questioned her. So the bride related to the
robber her story from its beginning to its end,
whereupon the robber exclaimed, " That is no
common generosity ! nor shall I do any hurt or
evil thing to her." Then said he to the girl,
" Come, I will take thee to thy lover." And
he took her and led to her lover's door and
said, " Now go in and be with thy lover."
Then the girl knocked at the door, and that
youth, who lay sighing, heard the knocking and
went with haste and said, " Who is that ?"
The girl answered, " Open the door ; lo, I have
kept my plight, nor have I broken it, I am

come to thee." The youth opened the door
and came to the girl and said, "O my life, my
mistress, welcome, and fair welcome! how hast
thou done it?" She replied, "The folk assembled and gave me to the bridegroom, then all
dispersed and each went his way. And I explained my case to the bridegroom and he gave
me leave. While on the road I met a robber,
and that robber wished to stretch forth his
hand to me, but I wept and told him of my
plight with thee, and he had pity and brought
me to the door and left me, and has gone
away." When the youth heard these things
from the girl he said, "Since the bridegroom is
thus generous, and has given thee leave to
fulfil thy plight with me, and sent thee to me,
there were no generosity in me did I stretch
forth my hand to thee and deal treacherously;
from this day be thou my sister; go, return to thy
husband." And he sent her off. When the
girl went out she saw that robber standing by
the door; and he walked in front of her, and
conducted her to the bridegroom's door. And
the girl went in, and the robber departed to his
own affairs. While the bridegroom was marvelling the bride entered, and the bridegroom
leaped up and took the bride's hands in his,
and they sat upon the bed. And the bride-

groom turned and asked her news of the bride; and she told all her adventures from their beginning to their end. And the bridegroom was pleased,* and they both attained their desire. God grant to all of us our desire. Amen.' Then quoth the cadi, 'O my sons, which of those showed manliness and generosity in this matter?' The eldest youth said, 'The bridegroom, who, while she was his lawful bride, and when he had spent thus much upon her, and was about to gain his desire, gave the girl leave. What excellent generosity did he display!' The middle youth said, 'The generosity was that lover's, who, while there was so much love between them, had patience when they were alone in the night and she so fair of form and in such splendid dress, and sent her back. What excellent generosity: can there be greater than this!' Then asked he of the youngest boy, 'O you, what say you?' Quoth he, 'O ye, what say ye? when one hunting in the night met thus fair a beauty, a torment of the world, a fresh rose; above all, laden with these many jewels, and yet coveted her not but took her to her place. What excellent patience, what excellent generosity!' When the cadi heard

---

* Or, as the text has it, Guwegi baqdi qizin bākiriyeti bozilmamish.

these words of the youngest boy he said, ' O
prince, the jewels are with thee ; for the lover
praised the lover; and the trustful, the trustful ;
and the robber, the robber.'   The prince was
unable to deny it, and he took the jewels from
his breast and laid them before the cadi."*

" Now, O king, I have told this story for
that thou mayst know that in that I am true I
would aid my king ; and that the vezirs, in that
they are traitors, would aid the traitor prince.
And they are forty men, each one of them a
wonder of the world, while as for me, I am but
one and a woman, lacking in understanding : the
rest the king knows."   When the king heard
these enticing and beguiling words of the lady
he said, " Grieve not, to-morrow will I kill
him."   And they went to bed.

When it was morning the king sat upon his
throne and thus commanded the executioner,
" Smite off the head of that traitor youth."
Whereupon the Ninth Vezir came forward and
said, " O king of the world, beware, slay not thy
son on the woman's word, and be not heedless
of the import of this verse which God Most
High hath spoken in His Word : ' And the
stiflers of wrath, and the pardoners of men ;

---

* See Appendix B, Note VII.

and God loveth the beneficent :'* that is they
are **His peculiar** servants.   And the **Holy**
Apostle **(peace on him!)** hath said, 'Whoso
bridleth his anger, he having power to avenge,
—God will call him on the Resurrection-Day
over the heads **of the creatures** that He may
give him to choose from **the** houris which he
pleaseth :' that is he shall surely **enter** Paradise.
Let one pardon him who has wronged him and
forgive his servants their misdeeds, **that God
Most High may pardon him** and be beneficent
to him ; **even as** saith the Apostle (peace **on**
him!) '**The** proclaimer shall proclaim on **the**
Resurrection-Day : — **Where** are they whose
reward is (incumbent) **upon God : none** shall
rise save him who hath forgiven.'   Mayhap the
king has not heard **the story of** Hārūn-er-
Reshīd † and the slave-girl."   **The** king **said,**
" Tell on, let us **hear."**   Quoth the vezir,

The Ninth Vezir's Story.

" Once the **Khalif** Hārūn-er-Reshīd sat **upon**
his throne of estate ; and the people of the city
of Baghdad were late in coming to salute **him.**
Therefore **was the Khalif** exceeding **wroth,**

---

* Koran, iii. 128.
† The celebrated Khalif of Baghdad, and hero of **so many of**
the stories in the Thousand and One Nights.

and he thus commanded the chamberlains, 'Whoso comes now do ye turn off and cast into prison.' And they seized and cast into prison all of the grandees of the city who came. For three days the Khalif went not out, neither spake with anyone; but sat full of fury: who could have dared to address a word to him? While in this state he desired to eat, and he ordered one of the slave-girls to bring food. She brought it before him, but while laying down the dish, she was careless and spilt some part of it over the Khalif. Forthwith the Khalif rose in wrath and was about to hew the girl in pieces, when she said, 'O Khalif, God Most High saith in His Glorious Word, "And the stiflers of wrath." '* Straightway the Khalif's wrath was calmed. Again saith the slave-girl, "'And the pardoners of men."'* Quoth the Khalif, 'I have forgiven the crimes of all the criminals who may be in prison.' Again said the slave-girl, ' " And God loveth the beneficent."' * Quoth the Khalif, 'God be witness that I have with my own wealth freed thee and as many unfreed male and female slaves as I have, and that this day I have for the love of God given the half of all

---

* Koran, iii. 128.

my wealth to the poor in alms.' After that
he let bring into his presence all the prisoners
who were in the gaol and begged absolution
of them ; and as he had attained to the import
of that noble verse, he put on each of them a
robe of honour, and devoted himself to justice
and equity. And now whoso mentions him
doth add, ' The mercy of God on him !' "*

"O king, I have told this story for that I
have seen this day that thy wrath was great.
I would that thou pardon the prince and grant
him his life and so do a meritorious deed ; and
in this matter, beyond doubt and beyond uncertainty, thou shalt become deserving of the
mercy and Paradise of God Most High." And
he kissed the ground and begged for the
prince. When the king heard this story from
the vezir he sent the youth to the prison and
mounted for the chase.

That day he found no game and returned
in wrath to the palace. Again the lady rose
to greet him and they sat down. After the
repast the lady began to speak of the youth.
The king said, " Look, my mistress, now all
is over, and my prince is still upon thy

---

* D'Herbelot relates the same story in his Bibliothèque
Orientale, but substitutes Hasan son of 'Ali, the Prophet's son-
in-law, for Hārūn-er-Reshīd.

I

tongue ; to-day too one of my vezirs begged for
him and I sent him to the prison." The lady
saw that the king was vexed and said, " My
king, be kind, be not vexed with me ; for I
know that soon no good will befall thee from
that youth, for he is very covetous of wealth
and kingship, and the covetous is ever balked.
I saw him without understanding and without
discretion ; he knows neither his words nor
himself; he is even as the sons of that king
who took the metaphorical words of their father
as literal, and at length lost what wealth was in
their hands. Mayhap my king has not heard
that story." The king said, " Tell on, let us
hear." Quoth the lady,

The Lady's Ninth Story.

" There was in the palace of the world a
great king, and he had three sons. One day
that king laid his head upon the pillow of
death and called his sons before him and said,
' O my sons, my life has reached its end; I have
counsel to give you, which when I am dead do
ye observe.' His sons replied, ' On our heads
be it ; speak, father.' To his eldest son he
said, ' Build thou a house in every city.' And
to his middle son, ' Marry thou a virgin every
night.' And to his youngest son, ' Whenever

thou eatest, eat honey and butter.' The king lived not long after giving these injunctions, but died. The eldest son fell to building a house in every city; the middle son married a virgin every night, and on the morrow gave her her dower and sent her to her father's house ; and the youngest son, whenever he ate, mixed honey and butter and ate it. A long time passed on this wise; we may say that though the middle and the youngest sons spent money, they at least had pleasure for it; but that bewildered and senseless eldest son spent this much money, and if the buildings he raised were fit for habitation, still they pointed to folly. One day a wise man asked them, 'Why do ye thus ?' The princes answered, 'By God, our father thus enjoined us.' The wise man said, 'Your father's injunctions were not thus, but ye have not understood his riddles. And there is a tale suitable to this your plight, I will tell it you; afterward I will teach you your father's riddles.' The princes said, 'Pray do so.' Quoth the wise man, 'Once there was a king who always exacted tribute from the infidels. One day those infidels assembled their monks and said, "Let us find some trick which the king will be unable to understand, that thereby we may escape from

this tribute : now do ye each think of some
plan." Thereupon they dispersed and went
away. After a time a monk came to the
infidel who was their chief and said, " I shall
go to them and put to them a question, and
if they can answer it we will give them
tribute." So the unbelieving king gave that
monk a little money and sent him. One day
he entered the realms of Islam, and the event
was reported to the king, who said, " Our
learned men of the Faith will surely answer
an infidel without the Faith ; let him come."
They brought him into the presence of the
king ; and the king straightway assembled
his doctors and pious men and grandees.
Then the king said, " O monk, now what is
thy question ; speak, let us see ? " The monk
first opened the five fingers of his hand and
held the palm opposite the folk, then he let
the five fingers droop downward, and said,
" What means that ? know ye ? " And all the
doctors were silent and began to ponder, and
they reflected, saying, " What riddles can these
riddles be ? There is no such thing in the
Commentaries or the Traditions." Now there
was there a learned wanderer, and forthwith
he came forward and asked leave of the king
that he might answer. The king gladly gave

leave ; then that wanderer came forward and
said to the monk, " What is thy question ?
what need for the doctors ? poor I can
answer." Then the monk came forward and
opened his hand and held it so before the
dervish ; straightway the dervish closed his fist
and held it opposite the monk. Then the monk
let his five fingers droop downward ; the dervish
opened his fist and held his five fingers upward.
When the monk saw these signs of the dervish,
he said, " That is the answer," and gave up
the money he had brought. But the king
knew not what these riddles meant, and he
took the dervish apart and asked him. The
dervish replied, " When he opened his fingers
and held his hand so to me, it meant, 'now I
strike thee so on the face ;' so I showed him
my fist, which meant, ' I strike thy throat with
my fist ;' he turned and let his fingers droop
downward, which meant, ' thou dost so, then I
strike lower and seize thy throat with my
hand ;' and my raising my fingers upward meant,
' if thou seekest to seize my throat, I too shall
grasp thy throat from underneath ;' so we
fought with one another by signs." Then the
king called the monk and said, " Thou madest
signs with the dervish, but what meant those
signs ?" The monk replied, " I held my five

fingers opposite him, that meant, 'the five times
ye do worship, is it right ?' The dervish presented his fist, which meant, 'it is right.' Then
I held my fingers downward, which meant,
'why does the rain come down from heaven ?'
The dervish held his fingers upward, which
meant, 'the rain falls down from heaven that
the grass may spring up from the earth.' Now
such are the answers to those questions in our
books." Then he returned to his country.
And the king knew that the dervish had
not understood the monk's riddles ; but the
king was well pleased for that he had done
what was suitable ; and he bestowed on the
dervish a portion of the money which the
monk had left. O princes, ye have not understood your father's riddles and ye have wasted
your wealth in vain.' The princes said, 'What
meant our father's riddles ?' He replied,
'Firstly, when he said, " Build thou a house
in every city," he meant, " gain thou a friend in
every city, so that when thou goest to a city the
house of the friend thou hast gained may be
thine." Secondly, when he said, " Embrace
thou a virgin whenever thou embracest," he
meant, " be moderate in thy pleasures that thou
mayst enjoy them the more." Thirdly, when
he said, " Whenever thou eatest, eat honey and

butter," he meant, "never when thou eatest, eat to repletion; but eat so that if it be but dry bread thou eatest, it will be to thee as honey and butter."' When the princes heard the words of the wise dervish they knew that their father's signs to them were so, and not that which they had done; and they left off doing those things."

"Now, O king, I have told this story for that with youths is no discretion, but in them ignorance and heedlessness abound. Though thou through understanding have compassion on him, yet will he have none on thee; it will be even as when one day Saint Bāyezīd of Bestām* saw a mangy dog, and through pity took it and laid it in a place and tended it many days till it became well, whereon it bit his foot. Bāyezīd said, 'O dog, this is the return for the kindness I did thee—that thou bitest me.' God Most High gave speech to that dog, and it said, 'O Bāyezīd, is not the proverb well known, "A man acts as a man; a dog, as a dog"?' Methinks, O king, that in that youth must be an evil vein: for if kindness be to kindness, never so long as he lived could

---

* Bāyezīd of Bestām was a famous saint who, according to Ibn-Khallikān, died in 261 or 264 (A.D. 875 or 878).

that unworthy one have cast on me an envious
glance ; above all, never could he have sought
to slay my king, his father, the source of his
being.   I, where am I ?   Take warning."
And she incited the king with very many evil
words, so that he was afraid and said, " Grieve
not, to-morrow will I slay him."   And they
went to bed, and that night was grievous to the
king.

Scarce was it morning and had the sun
shown forth the riddle of the whiteness of
dawn, like as that dervish showed to the king's
sons the riddles of their father, and illumined
the world with light, ere the king sat upon
his throne and caused the youth to be brought
and ordered the executioner, " Smite off his
head."   Then the Tenth Vezir came forward
and said, " O king of the world, every king
desires that whithersoever he go he may
triumph and conquer ; and that the earth be
subject to his hand ; and that whoso comes to
his gate hoping, may find that which he seeks ;
and that the heart of none be vexed.   When
in the country of a king despairing hearts are
many, that host of despairing hearts gathers
together and utterly destroys another gay host.
Thus it becomes the greatness and glory of
kings, that when they see a beast under a

heavy load they have compassion on that beast;
even as it was when an ass came, dragging itself
along, to the chain of the justice of Nūshīrvān
the Just.* Straightway the king caused it to
be brought into his presence, and he saw it to
be a lean and worn black ass, whose back
was broken with bearing loads. When the
king saw that animal in such plight his heart
bled, and he laid his hand on the beast's face
and wept full bitterly and said, ' See ye how
this poor creature has been oppressed in my
kingdom ?' And he called for a physician
and said to him, ' Go, tend the wounds of this
beast, and give it abundance to eat, and wrap
round it a good horse-cloth that it be at ease.'
Now, it is incumbent on kings that they
have compassion on the unhappy and the weak,
and pity them, and believe not plotters and
liars, nor trust their evil wicked words; and
such folk are very many. Mayhap my king
has not heard the story of the king's son of
Egypt and the crafty woman." The king
said, " Relate it, let us hear." Quoth the
vezir,

---

* One of the most famous kings of pre-Islamitic Persia, he
reigned from A.D. 531 to 579.

The Tenth Vezir's Story.

" In the city of Cairo there was a king and he had two sons. One day he reflected on the doings of the cruel Sphere and saw how the world was without constancy and remained not to king nor yet to beggar, but trod all under foot. At length he bethought him how it would not endure for himself either ; and he took his younger son and made him apprentice to a master tailor, and said, 'After all, a trade is needful for a man ; and they have said that the least knowledge of a trade is better than a hundred thousand sequins.' So in a short while the prince became a tailor such that there was not in the city of Cairo one who could ply his scissors and needle. One day the king passed to the Abiding Home, and his elder son became king. His brother the tailor, fearing for his head, fled and went to the Ka'ba.* While making the circumambulation,† his foot struck against something hard, he looked and saw a girdle and took it up and bound it round his loins, and continued the circumambulation. After a while he saw a khoja who had a stone in either hand and who was beating his breast

---

* The Cubical (House), *i.e.*, the Sacred Temple at Mekka.
† One of the ceremonies performed by the pilgrims at Mekka.

with these stones and crying, 'Ah woe! alas! I
had hidden in that girdle all the wealth I have
gained from my youth; whatever Muslim has
found it, let him give it me for the love of God
and the honour of the Ka'ba, and the half of it
shall be lawful for him as his mother's milk.'
When the prince saw and heard him he knew
that that girdle was his, and he said in his heart,
'What has this much wealth and the kingdom
of my father done for me? and what should
this do for me? I shall not let this poor man
weep; I shall give it him.' And he went round
and came before the khoja and said, 'O khoja, I
have found that girdle of thine; lo, it is round
my loins.' The khoja clung fast to the prince,
and the prince said, 'What reward wilt thou give
me? lo, the girdle is round my loins.' Then the
khoja took the prince and brought him to his
own tent; and the prince loosed the girdle from
his loins and laid it before the khoja, and the
khoja took it and clasped it to his heart. Then
he brake the seal and poured out what was in it;
and the prince saw it to be full of precious stones.
The khoja divided these stones into three heaps
and said, 'O youth, wilt thou take one heap
with my good-will, or two without it?' The
prince replied, 'Give me one heap with thy
good-will.' Then the khoja divided one of

those heaps into two and said, 'Which of them wilt thou take with my good-will?' Again the prince made choice of a heap. At length the khoja said, 'Youth, wouldest thou have these remaining jewels, or wouldest thou that we go and that I pray for thee under the Golden Spout?'* The prince answered, 'Wealth perishes, but prayers endure; do thou bless me, I have relinquished all these riches.' And they went, and he held up his hands and said to the prince, 'Say thou, "Amen."' So the youth raised up his hands and the khoja began to pray. He repeated many prayers in himself, and the prince said, 'Amen.' The khoja drew his hands down his face and said, 'O youth, I have prayed much for thee; now go, and may thy end be good.' The prince went away; but after a little he thought in himself, 'If I go now to Cairo my brother will kill me, let me go along with this khoja to Baghdad.' So he went back to the khoja and said, 'O khoja, I would go with thee to Baghdad; take me that I may serve thee on the road.' So the khoja took him; and the prince was in the khoja's service, and they entered Baghdad and lighted at the khoja's dwelling.

---

* For a description of it see Capt. Burton's Pilgrimage, vol. III, p. 164.

For some days the prince abode there, then he said to the khoja, 'I may not stay here thus idling; I have a trade, I am a master tailor, if thou hast any tailor friend, pray take me to him that he may give me some work to do.' Now the khoja had a tailor friend, and he straightway took the prince and brought him to the shop of that tailor and commended him to him, and the tailor consented. Then the prince sat down and his master cut out cloth for a robe and gave it him; now the prince had checkmated the Cairo tailors, where then were those of Baghdad? The prince sewed that robe and returned it, and the master took it and looked at it and saw that it was a beautiful robe, made so that in all his life he had not seen the like of it, and he said, 'A thousand times well-done, youth.' This news spread among the masters, and they all came to that shop and saw it and admired; and this prince became very famous in that country. The work in that master's shop was now increased tenfold, and customers in like measure. One day that khoja had a quarrel with his wife, and in the greatness of his heat the words of the triple divorce passed his lips. Then he repented and would have got back his wife, and his wife also was willing. They sought a legal decision, but the mufti said, ' It may not be without an intermediary.' * The khoja bethought him whom he could get for intermediary when the prince came into his mind, and he said in himself, ' That stranger youth is he ; I shall make him intermediary.' So he married the woman to the prince. When it was evening he took him and put him into a dark house with the lady ; but the lady made shift to light a candle, and as soon as she saw the prince she fell in love with him with all her heart. And the prince, as soon as he saw her, fell in love with her with all his heart. Then these two moons came together, and, after making merry, the lady showed the prince sumptuous stuffs, and countless gold, and precious stones, such as the tale and number of them cannot be written, and she said, ' O my life, all this wealth is mine, it is my inheritance from my mother and my father, and all the wealth too that that khoja has is mine ; if thou will not dismiss me to-morrow, but accept me as thy legal wife, all this wealth is thine.' The prince consented to this proposal, and the woman said, ' O youth, when the khoja comes to-morrow he will say, " Come, let us go to the cadi ;" say thou, " Why should we go to the

---

* Such as is required by the Muhammedan law in case of a triple divorce.

cadi ?" If he say, "Divorce the woman," do thou reply, " By God, it were shame in us to take a wife and then divorce her." And he will be unable to find any answer thereto.' The prince was glad and accepted the lady's advice. When it was morning the khoja came and knocked at the door, and the prince went forth and kissed the khoja's hand. The khoja said, ' Come, let us go to the cadi ; ' the prince answered, ' Why should we go to the cadi ?' Quoth the khoja, 'Divorce the woman.' The prince replied, ' By God, it were mighty shame in us to divorce the woman ; I will not divorce her.' The khoja exclaimed, 'Ah youth, what word is that? I trusted thee, thinking thee an upright youth, why speakest thou thus ?' The prince answered, ' Is not this which I have said the commandment of God and the word of the Apostle ?' The khoja looked and saw that there was no help ; he wished to go to the cadi, but the folk said to him, ' Khoja, now that woman is his, she is pleased with him and he is pleased with her, they cannot be divorced by force.' The khoja was filled with grief and said, ' He shall not be questioned concerning what He doth ; '* and he ceased from trying.

---

* Koran, xxi. 23.

He fell ill from his rage and became bedridden ; then he called the prince and said to him, ' Hast thou any knowledge of what I prayed for thee under the Golden Spout ? ' The prince replied, 'I know nought of it.' The khoja said, 'Although I would have prayed otherwise, this came upon my tongue : " My God, apportion to this youth my wealth, my sustenance, and my wife." O youth, would I had not taken from thee yon girdle ! O youth, my wife was my existence, now that too is become thine. Now let these sitting here be witnesses that when I am dead all that I possess belongs to thee." Three days afterward he died ; he perished through grief for that scheming woman ; and the prince became possessor of his wealth." *

"O king, I have told this story for that thou mayst know that fidelity comes not from women, and that their love is not to be trusted. When they cannot help it, they are obedient to their husbands, and, fearing the rod of the law, they wrap their feet in their skirts and sit quiet, otherwise they would ruin the world with craft and trickery. Now, O king, act not on the woman's word." From seven places he performed the salutation due to kings, and begged

---

* See Appendix B, Note VIII.

for the prince's life. The king heard this story
from the vezir, and that day, too, he sent his
son to the prison, and went himself to the chase.

When it was evening, the king returned from
the chase and came to the palace, and the lady
rose to greet him, and they sat down. After
the repast, the lady brought about an opportunity, and began upon the youth. The king
said, " To-day such an one of my vezirs made
intercession for him, and I have sent him to the
prison." Quoth the lady, " These vezirs are
all of them traitors to thee, and they are schemers
and plotters. Each of them says words concerning me which if he heard, no true man would
bear ; a man's wife is equal with his life. All
the people marvel at thee, and say thou hast no
sense of honour. But these vezirs have be-
witched thee. Thy lies, too, are many ; every
night thou sayest, ' I will kill this youth ;' then
thou killest him not, and falsifiest thy words.
O king, through truth is one acceptable both to
God and man. O king, no good will come from
a youth like this ; it were better such a son did
not remain after thee than that he did remain.
Mayhap my king has not heard the story of a
certain merchant." The king said, " Tell on ;
let us hear." Quoth the lady,

The Lady's Tenth Story.

" There was of old time a great merchant, and he had two sons. One day the merchant laid his head on the pillow of death, and he called his sons before him, and brought together some wise persons, and said, 'Muslims, if it please God Most High, these boys will live for many years; reckon at the rate of a hundred years from to-day, and allow to each of them a daily grant of a thousand aspres, and whatever the sum may amount to, that sum will I give them, that after me they may stand in need of no one till they die, but pass their lives in ease in this transient world.' Then they reckoned up, and he gave them much money; and a few days afterward he passed to the Abiding Home. The sons buried their father, and then began to waste that money. Their father's friends gave them much advice, but they would not accept it. One of them would enter the shop of a confectioner and buy up all the sweetmeats that were therein, and load porters with them, and take them to the square of the city, and cry out, ' This is spoil!' and the folk would scramble for them, and he would laugh. And his business was ever thus. The other youth would buy wine and meat, and enter a ship with some flattering

buffoons, and eat and drink and make merry;
and when he was drunk he would mix up gold
and silver coins before him, and throw them by
handfuls into the sea, and their flashing into the
water pleased him, and he would laugh. And
his business likewise was ever thus. By reason
of these follies, the wealth of both of them came
to an end in little time, in such wise that they
were penniless, so that they sat by the way and
begged. At length the merchants, their father's
friends, came together, and went to the king
and said, 'The sons of such and such a merchant are fallen a prey to a plight like this; if
they be not disgraced now, to-morrow will our
sons also act like them. Do thou now put them
to death, for the love of God, that they may be
an example, and that others may not act as they.'
Then the king commanded that they brought
them both into his presence, and the king said
to them, 'O unhappy ones, what plight is this
plight in which ye are? Where is the headsman?' And he ordered them to be killed.
They said, 'O king, be not wroth at our having
fallen into this plight, and kill us not; our father
is the cause of our being thus, for he commended us not to God Most High, but commended us to money; and the end of the child
who is commended to money is thus.' Their

words seemed good to the king, and he said, 'By God, had ye not answered thus, I had cleft ye in twain.' And then he bestowed on each of them a village."

"Now, O king, I have related this story for that among youths there is nor shame nor honour, neither is there zeal for friend or foe. Beware and beware, be not negligent, ere the youth kill thee do thou kill him; else thou shalt perish." When the king heard this story from the lady he said, "On the morrow will I kill him." And they went to bed.

When it was morning, and the darkness of night, like the wealth of that merchant, was scattered, the king sat upon his throne and commanded the executioner, saying, "Smite off the youth's head." Then the Eleventh Vezir came forward and said, "O king of the world, hurry not in this affair, and whatsoever thou doest, do according to the command of God and the word of the Apostle; and the Holy Apostle hath said that when the Resurrection is near, knowledge will vanish and ignorance will increase and the spilling of blood will be oft. O king, leave not the Law, and spill not blood unjustly on thine own account, and pity the innocent; for they have said that whoso taketh a fallen one by the hand to raise him shall be happy; but whoso, having the power, raiseth him not shall himself burn in the fire of regret. Mayhap the king has not heard the story of a certain king and a vezir's son." The king said, "Tell on, let us hear." Quoth the vezir,

THE ELEVENTH VEZIR'S STORY.

"Of old time there was a king, and that king had a sage vezir. God Most High had given that vezir a son; and the people of the world were bewildered at the beauty of that boy. And the king loved him so that he could not endure to be a moment without seeing him, and he never parted from him. So his parents yearned for the boy, but what avail? they had needs have patience through fear of the king. One day, the king while drunk entered the palace and saw this boy playing with another page, and thereupon was he wroth and he commanded the executioner, 'Smite off the head of this degenerate boy.' And they dragged the boy out. Thereupon word was sent to the vezir, and he came straightway, and crying, 'My life! my son!' went up to the headsman and said, 'O headsman, now is the king drunk and senseless and he knows not the words he says; if thou kill the boy to-night, to-morrow the king will not spare thee;

but will kill thee likewise.' The headsman
said, 'How should we do? he said to me,
"Quick, smite off his head and bring it."'
The vezir answered, 'Go to the prison and
smite off the head of some man meriting death,
and bring it; at this time the king has not his
senses and will believe it.' And he gave the
headsman much gold. The headsman took the
sequins and was glad, and went forthwith to
the prison and smote off the head of a robber
and brought it to the king. The king was
pleased and gave the headsman a robe of
honour. And the vezir took the boy and
brought him to his own house and hid him
there. When it was morning and the king's
senses returned, he asked for the boy, and they
said, 'This night thou didst command the
executioner that he smote off the boy's head.'
As soon as the king heard this he fell senseless
and his understanding forsook him. After a
while his understanding returned and he sat
beating his knees and he fell a-weeping. Then
the vezir, feigning not to know, came before the
king and said, 'O king, what plight is this?'
Quoth the king, 'O vezir, where is that source
of my life? where is that spring of my soul?'
The vezir said, 'O king, whom meanest thou?'
The king replied, 'Thy son, who was the joy

of my heart.' And he cried and wept beyond
control, and the vezir rent his collar and wailed
and lamented. For two months the one
business of the king was sighing and crying;
during the nights he would not sleep till dawn
for weeping, and he would say, ' My God, shall
I never behold his face? mayhap I shall behold
it at the Resurrection. To me henceforth life
is not beseeming.' Mad words like these
would he utter. And he ceased from eating
and drinking, and retired from the throne and
sought a private house and wept ever, and it
wanted little but he died. When the vezir
saw this, he one day decked out the boy like a
flower and took him and went to the private
place where the king dwelt. He left the boy
at the door and went in himself and saw that
the king had bowed his head in adoration and
was praying to God and weeping and thus
saying, ' My God, henceforth is life unlawful
for me, do Thou in Thy mercy take my soul;'
and he was lamenting, recalling the darling
fashions of the boy. The vezir heard this wail
of the king and said, ' O king, how thou
weepest! thou hast forsaken manhood and art
become a by-word in the world.' The king
replied, ' Henceforth advice profits me not; lo,
begone.' Quoth the vezir, ' O king, if God

Most High took pity on thee and brought the
boy to life, wouldst thou forgive his fault? and
what wouldst thou give to him who brought
thee news thereof?' The king said, ' O would
that it could be so! all the wealth that I have
in my treasury would I give to him who brought
me news thereof, and my kingdom would I
give to the boy; and I should be content to
look from time to time on the boy's face.'
Then the vezir beckoned to the boy and he came
in, and went and kissed the king's hand. As
soon as the king saw the boy his senses
forsook him, and the vezir sprinkled rose-water
on the king's face and withdrew. When the
king's senses returned he saw the boy beside
him and he thought that his soul had gone and
returned. When it was morning the vezir came
before the king, and the king said, ' As thou
hast brought the boy to me whole, go, all
that is in my treasury is thine.' The vezir
answered, ' O king of the world, rather is the
wealth which is in my treasury thine; we are
both of us the meanest of the king's slaves.
May God (glorified and exalted be He!) grant
fortune to our king and long life! We too
shall live in thy felicity.' The king was
glad at the words of the vezir, and bestowed
many towns and villages on the son of the

vezir, and offered up many sacrifices, and gave away much alms."

"O king, I have told this story for that the king may take profit and not do a deed without reflection, that he be not afterward repentant, like that king, and suffer not bitter regret and remorse. That king suffered so great regret and remorse for a vezir's son, yet this one is the darling of thine own heart. The rest the king knows. Beware, O king, slay not the prince on the woman's word." And he kissed the ground and made intercession for the prince for that day. So the king sent the youth to the prison and went himself to the chase.

When it was evening the king returned from the chase and came to the palace, and the lady rose to greet him, and they sat down. After the repast the lady commenced to speak about the youth. The king said, " To-day too such an one of my vezirs made intercession for him and I sent him to the prison." The lady said, "O king, three things are the signs of folly ; the first is to put off to-day's business till to-morrow, the second is to speak words foolishly, and the third is to act upon senseless words. O king, whatsoever thy vezirs say, that thou believest straightway and actest upon.

Satan is of a surety entered into these thy
vezirs and into thy boy; in whose heart soever he
plants the love of office or of wealth, him in the
end does he leave without the Faith.   Mayhap
the king has not heard the story of the devotee
Barsīsā."   The king said, "Tell on, let us
hear."   Quoth the lady,

The Lady's Eleventh Story.

"Of old time there was a devotee called
Barsīsā who had worshipped in his cell for a
hundred years, standing up in prayer during the
night and fasting during the day, and not an
hour did he cease from devotion.   The people
of the age believed in him, so that for one word
of his they would give their lives, and some of
them were his disciples and some were his
friends.   Whatever sick person he breathed on
and prayed over was restored to health.   He
was one whose prayers were answered, and his
miracles were evident.   A daughter of the king
of that Clime was sick and the physicians were
powerless to cure her.   At length the king said,
'Go, take her to Barsīsā, the devotee, that he
may pray over her, haply she may be cured.'
So the eunuchs took the girl and brought her to
Barsīsā.   Barsīsā saw the girl that she was a
lady of wondrous beauty, and his heart inclined

unto her. That same hour Satan tempted him, and the flesh overcame him. Satan said, 'O sheykh, when shall an opportunity such as this, and a beauty such as this be in thy power again?' The sheykh said in his heart, 'How shall I make shift to accomplish my desire?' Quoth Satan, 'Thou must say to the eunuchs who came with the girl, "Let the girl remain here this night; do ye go; and when it is near morning I shall pray over her that she may find health, then come ye and take her and go your ways." They will not question thy words, but leave the girl and go; and from night till morn thou canst make merry with her. When it is near morning, pray over her that she may find health; and they will come and take the girl; and the girl will go, and she will not say, "The sheykh did so by me;" and even if she do, none will believe her. And the pleasure thou hast had will be thine.' So the sheykh, reflecting not on the end thereof, how that his face would be black in the world and the Hereafter, said to the eunuchs, 'Leave the girl here this night, and go your ways.' The eunuchs told the king, and the king said, 'What evil would come from the sheykh? let her stay.' As soon as it was night, Satan came and said, 'O sheykh, how sittest thou still? into whose hand comes

a beauty like this? up, make merry with her.'
The poor sheykh's veins began to throb and he
could not drive from his heart the whisperings
of Satan, and the cruel flesh overcame him.   So
he arose and took to him the girl, and kissed
her and embraced her.* No sooner was the
passion of the sheykh fulfilled than he repented
him of what he had done.   Thereupon Satan
appeared before him and said, 'O sheykh, when
the king sees his daughter in this plight his
killing thee is certain.'   Said the sheykh, 'What
can I do?'   Satan answered, 'Kill the girl, and
bury her in a secret place; and if they come in
the morning and ask for the girl, say thou, "I
prayed over her, and she became well and is
gone."   And they will believe thy words and go
and search in vain, and, finding her not, will
leave off; and thou shalt escape.'   The sheykh
gave way to the tempting of Satan, and slew
the girl and buried her in a corner of his cell.
When it was morning the eunuchs came from the
king and asked for the girl.   The sheykh said,
'Early in the morning I prayed over her and
she found health, and went out and is not returned.'   The eunuchs searched every corner of
the city, but found her not.   Then Satan, taking

---

* 'Aqibet qizin muhr-i bekāretin bozdi, adds the original.

the form of an old man, came and said to the
eunuchs, 'What seek ye?' The eunuchs replied, 'We want the girl.' Satan related to
them all the evils, one by one, which the sheykh
had done to the girl and said, 'If ye believe
not, go, see, she is buried in such and such a
corner of the cell.' They went quickly and dug
up that place as Satan had told them, and took
out the girl. And they seized the sheykh and
took him with the girl before the king. When
the king saw his daughter in this plight he
sighed and wept. And he brought together
the doctors and sheykhs of that Clime and told
them the foul deeds of the sheykh, and they all
marvelled and gave leave for his execution.
The king said, 'Hang ye him.' When they
raised the sheykh on the gallows, Satan came
before him and said, 'O sheykh, if I save thee
from this evil, wilt thou call me God and adore
me?' The sheykh said, 'I will.' Then quoth
Satan, 'Adore me now with thine eyes and eye-
brows.' And the sheykh adored Satan with the
corner of his eye; but it availed not, and they
hanged him. And Satan said, 'There is one who
has turned thee from the Path and in the end
has made thy life to go; and thou hast abandoned
the Faith, and art not delivered.' And he spat
in his face and vanished. Now, such a sheykh,

whose prayers had been answered, was in the end,
by Satan the accursed, turned from the Path and
left in this wise."

"O king, I have told this story that thou
mayst know that, Satan seeing how he led astray
a devotee like that, is surely able to deceive
thy son and thy vezirs. And they have said
that Satan has three different snares, each
subtler than the other : when a believer seeks
to found charitable buildings, he comes and says,
'Why dost thou waste thy substance ? when old
age comes upon thee, how will be thy case ?'
or, 'After thee thy sons will be orphans, will·
not they need the means of livelihood ?' If the
believer pass that snare, then Satan comes and
says, 'If thou wilt build such things, build but
little ;' or, 'If thou wilt make free-kitchen or
bridge, make a little one and endow it scantly.'
If he pass that too and turn away, Satan says,
'If thou wilt build such, speak to the folk that
they may know that it is thou who hast done
it.' So that it may be hypocrisy, and the good
may be rendered of none effect. Now, O king,
the works of these are ever evil ; Satan has
turned these altogether to himself. Beware,
have great heed of them ; for they have aimed
at thy life and wealth." When the king heard
these beguiling words of the lady he said, "On

the morrow will I slay him." And they went to bed.

When it was morning the king came and sat upon his throne and caused them to bring the prince and ordered the executioner, "Smite off his head." Whereupon the Twelfth Vezir came forward and said, "O king, the counsel of the Kings of the East is, 'Tell not secrets to women and confide not thy business to them.' And beware of avarice, for the avaricious shall not enter Paradise. The Holy Apostle hath said, ' The avaricious man shall not enter Paradise, even though he be a devotee.' Love not the avaricious. And women are lacking in honesty; it is not worthy of kings to give their free-will into a woman's hands and reject the counsel of these many vezirs. O king, the hostility of the learned and wise is better than the friendship of foolish persons. The time may be when much evil may arise from the true words of the foolish, and much good may arise from the untrue words of the wise. The learned have said that that falsehood which betters one's affair is before that truth which ruins his affair. And the Holy Apostle hath said, ' That person who says what is untrue and so makes peace between two persons, does better than if he spake the truth.'

There is a story suitable to this." The king said, " Relate, let us hear." Quoth the vezir,

The Twelfth Vezir's Story.

"Sultan Mahmūd* had a favourite vezir called Ayāz. One day a dervish came to Ayāz and said, ' For the love of God get somewhat for me from the king.' Ayāz answered, ' To-morrow the king will go to the chase, do thou come before the king and pray and say, " O king, I know the language of birds." If the king ask me, I shall answer and get somewhat for thee from the king.' So on the morrow the dervish did so. Ayāz was by the king's side and he said, ' O king, give me this dervish that I may learn the language of birds.' The king answered, ' Take him, let him bide with thee.' Ayāz said, ' O king, give this dervish some little thing that may be an allowance to him till thy slave learn the language of birds.' So the king gave the dervish a daily allowance of a gold sequin. For a time the dervish abode with Ayāz ; and after that, Ayāz went before the king and said, ' O king, I have learned the language of birds from the dervish.' And he caused them to give the dervish much wealth ;

---

* Sultan Mahmūd of Ghazni.

and the dervish went away. One day Sultan Mahmūd went to the chase with Ayāz. While on the road the king saw that there were two trees growing, one on either side of the way, and upon each an owl was perched, and these were screaming across to each other. The king said, 'O Ayāz, thou sayest that thou knowest the language of birds; what are these birds saying? Listen and tell me.' Ayāz listened for a little while and then said, 'O king, this bird has a son and this other has a daughter, and this one wants the other's daughter for his son, and the other wants five hundred ruined villages and towns as dower for his daughter, and this one answers, "What is five hundred villages! since Sultan Mahmūd is king over this Clime, if thou wish a thousand I shall give thee them."' Sultan Mahmūd heard this answer from Ayāz and said, 'Am I such a tyrant that in my time towns and villages are ruined?' And he straightway ordered that they restored all the ruined towns and villages in his country. So by reason of that untruth he set about acting with justice; and now, whenever his name is recalled, they say, 'The mercy of God on him!'"

"O king, I have related this story for that the king may know that because Sultan Mahmūd believed his vezir's words and acted accordingly,

L

beside gaining great reward in Heaven, he will
be remembered till the Resurrection.   So what
beseems the king is this, that in every instance
he act according to his vezir's words.   If any
hurt befall the king, be the condition that he
smite off the heads of the whole of us forty
vezirs."   And all the vezirs said, " We agree to
this."   And they kissed the ground and made
intercession for the prince.   When the king
heard this story from the vezir he sent the
prince to the prison and himself mounted for
the chase.

When it was evening the king returned to
the palace from the chase, and the lady rose to
greet him, and they sat down.   After the repast,
the lady began to speak about the youth.   The
king said, " This day too, such an one of my
vezirs made intercession for him and I sent
him to the prison."   The lady said, " Dost thou
see how thou believest me not ?   Lo, now all
of them are allied, they wish to release this
youth from thy hand and set him free, that
afterward when they find an opportunity they
may finish their affair.   O king, this night I had
a dream ; without doubt or uncertainty God
Most High hath made manifest to me the
treachery of these, it is even as the Holy Apostle
hath said, ' The dream is the inspiration of the

believer.' O king, this night I saw in my dream
that thou wast seated on thy throne, when a
poisonous dragon appeared before thee; I
counted and it had forty heads, each of which
was poison-smeared, and behind it crept an
untold innumerable host of snakes. And they
came on till that dragon took the king and
his throne in its mouth, but it could not swallow
them and so put them out again. Three times it
tried thus, and at length, unable to avail, it
gathered into one place all the venom that was in
its forty heads, when, while it was making to
shower that over the king, I cried out from
opposite, ' O king, the dragon is about to shower
venom over thee.' And I cried so that I awoke
through fear." Then was the king afraid, and
he said, " What may the interpretation of this
dream be ? " The lady answered, " O king, the
interpretation of this dream is clear; that dragon
is this youth, and those forty heads are thy
vezirs, each one of whom is full of poison, and
that host of snakes is the rabble who follow
them ; that dragon which three times sought to
swallow thee is again this youth who purposed
evil against thee, and his succeeding not is his
being feeble, and his making to shower over
thee the poison that was in those his forty heads
is the forty vezirs' being one, and his wishing

to slay thee by their aid ; and my crying out is my saying every day, ' O king, have great care.' That is the interpretation of this my vision.   O king, be thou ware of these, take my counsel ; every day thou sayest, ' I will kill him ;' yet thou killest him not.   My story with thee resembles the story of a certain king and a weaver."   The king said, " Relate it, let us hear."   Quoth the lady,

The Lady's Twelfth Story.

" Of old time there was a great king.   One day a man came before him and said, ' My king, I shall weave a turban such that one born in wedlock will see it, while the bastard will see it not.'   The king marvelled and ordered that that weaver should weave that turban ; and the weaver received an allowance from the king and tarried a long while.   One day he folded up this side and that side of a paper and brought it and laid it before the king and said, ' O king, I have woven that turban.'   So the king opened the paper and saw that there was nothing ; and all the vezirs and nobles who stood there looked on the paper and saw nothing.   Then the king said in his heart, ' Dost thou see ?   I am then a bastard ;' and he was sad.   And he thought, ' Now, the remedy is this, that I say it is a goodly

turban and admire it, else will I be put to shame
before the folk.' And he said 'Blessed be God!
O master, it is a goodly turban, I like it much.'
Then that weaver youth said, 'O king, let them
bring a cap that I may wind the turban for the
king.' They brought a cap, and the weaver
youth laid that paper before him and moved his
hands as though he wound the turban, and he
put it on the king's head. All the nobles who
were standing there said, 'Blessed be it! O
king, how fair, how beautiful a turban!' and they
applauded it much. Then the king rose and
went with two vezirs into a private room and
said, 'O vezirs, I am then a bastard ; I see not
the turban.' Quoth the vezirs, 'O king, we too
see it not.' At length they knew of a surety that
the turban had no existence, and that that weaver
had thus played a trick for the sake of money."

" O king, thou too sayest, 'On the morrow
will I kill him ; I will do this and I will do
that;' and yet there is nothing. O king, I had
that dream this night, there is no doubt that
it is as I have interpreted. O king, if the
king's life and throne go, who knows what they
will do to hapless me ?" And she began to
weep. When the king saw the lady thus
weeping his heart was pained and he said, " On
the morrow I will indeed refuse the words of

whichsoever of my vezirs makes intercession for him, and I will indeed kill the youth; for, according to the dream thou hast had, this is no light affair." And they went to bed.

When it was morning the king came and sat upon his throne, and he caused the youth to be brought and commanded the executioner, " Smite off his head." Whereupon the Thirteenth Vezir came forward and sought to make intercession, but the king was wroth and said, " Be silent, speak not." Thereupon the vezir drew a paper from his breast and said, " For God's sake read this paper, then thou wilt know." Then the king looked at the paper and saw that there was written thereon, ' O king, yesterday I looked at the astrolabe; for forty days is the prince's ruling star in very evil aspect, such that the prince may even lose his head.' Then all the forty vezirs came forward at once and said, " O king, for the love of God and the honour of Muhammed Mustafa, for the forty days have patience and slay not the prince; thereafter it is certain that this affair will be made clear, and when its origin is known must each one receive his due." Then said the vezir, " There is a story suitable to this; if the king grant leave I will tell it." The king said, " Tell on, let us hear." Quoth the vezir,

THE THIRTEENTH VEZIR'S STORY.

"There was in the palace of the world a great king and he ruled over the Seven Climes. But he had neither son nor daughter, and he was ever offering sacrifices in the way of God. One day God Most High accepted his sacrifice and bestowed on him from His bounty a fair son who was in his time a second Joseph. So the king was glad, and that day he held a high feast, and at that feast he gave robes of honour and money to many men. After that he assembled the astrologers and made them cast the prince's horoscope; and the astrologers looked the one at the other and were bewildered and confounded. Then the king said, 'What see ye that ye stand looking the one at the other?' The astrologers replied, 'O king of the world, we have cast the prince's horoscope; and in the astrolabe and the Jāmesb-Nāma they thus rule, that from his thirtieth year to his sixtieth the prince's ruling star is afflicted so that he shall wander in strange lands, with tribulation and pain for his companions: "None . . . . knoweth the unseen save God."'* After the king had heard these things from the astrologers, at times his heart would be sad and

---

* Koran, xxvii. 66

at times he would plunge into the ocean of
deliberation. Saying, 'God knows the end of
the boy,' he began to train up the prince.
When the latter entered his seventh year he
appointed him a teacher, and he passed some
years in acquiring reading and writing. When
he was become a young man his father got for
him a king's daughter; and after a time the
prince had two sons. These children, too, in a
little time acquired knowledge; and from time
to time they would go out a-pleasuring with
their father. One day the prince's heart desired a sea-voyage, and he commanded that
they prepared a ship, and with his children and
forty slaves and attendants he entered the ship.
For many days they sailed the sea full pleasantly. But there was there a Frankish corsair
filled with infidels, and they encountered
the prince's ship and straightway flung their
grappling-irons, and took captive the prince
and his two sons and forty servants, and went
off. They took the prince and the forty men
and sold them to the cannibal negroes; but the
two boys they sold not, but kept by them.
The negroes fed up the prince and the men
with delicate and delicious foods, and every day
they took one of them to their king's kitchen
and cut his throat, and cooked him at the fire

and ate him. When they had eaten the forty men,
the prince's turn came, him too they took and
brought to the kitchen that they might cut his
throat. The prince perceived that plight, and
he entreated God in his heart to give him
strength, and he burst the fetters that were
round his wrists and, striking about with the
chains that were in his hands, he slipped through
them and rushed out. While he was running
on, a vast forest appeared before him, he entered
it, and although the negroes searched for him they
could not find him. Then he came out thence
and fared on many stages till one day he came
to a great city. The people crying, ' He is an
enemy,' rushed upon him. And the prince
exclaimed, ' O Lord! what tribulation is this!'
and fought with them. Word was brought to
their king, and he came and saw that the prince
was fighting like a dragon. When the king
saw the prince's valour he admired it, and said
to his soldiers who were there, ' Let no one
attack the stranger.' Then the soldiers dispersed, and the king took the prince and went
to the palace. He prepared a suit of clothes,
and sent him to the bath, and caused his head
to be shaven and made him put on those clothes,
and brought him back to the palace. The king
said, ' Come, remain by me, I have a daughter,

I will give her thee.' The prince consented ;
so they gave him the king's daughter ; and he
remained there two years and his lot was right
pleasant.   One day the prince's wife died ; now
this was their custom, they had a great deep
pit, and if a man died they put his wife with
him alive into that pit, and if a woman died
they did the same with her husband ; and they
let down along with them a loaf of bread and a
pitcher of water, and covered over the pit with
a great stone.   So they brought the prince and
his wife with a loaf of bread and a pitcher of
water to that pit, and, saying, ' It is our custom,'
lowered both of them into the pit and placed
that great stone over them.   When the prince
saw himself in such case he was bewildered and
said, ' My God! what plight is this!' and he
prayed to God.   And he searched the inside of
the pit carefully and saw a fair girl seated there,
and he asked her, ' What manner of girl art
thou ?'   She replied, ' I am a young bride ; they
have put me into this pit with my husband.'
And the prince examined the pit, and saw
it to be all full of the bodies of men, some
of which were decayed and some of which
were writhing in the agonies of death ; and
dread overcame the prince.   Of a sudden,
while he was seated, a rustling sound came from

one part of the pit ; the prince knew that it was some beast, and he arose and went with the girl straight to that place, and he found the passage through which that beast had come in. They went for a time through that passage, and at length came out on the skirt of a mountain on the bank of a great river. And they were glad thereat, and thanked God much. And there they found a boat, and they gathered fruit from that mountain and filled the boat, and they both entered the boat and went along with the current of the river. That river grew wider day by day ; but it passed underneath a great mountain. When they came near to the tunnel under that mountain they could not govern the boat, and the water took the boat and bore it under the mountain. When the prince saw this he exclaimed, ' My God ! O Lord ! what tribulation is this too ! how shall we escape from this !' Helpless they sat in the boat ; now the water dashed the boat against the rocks, now it made it fly down precipices, and now the mountain became low and pushed the boat under the water ; and they, never ceasing, emptied the water out of the boat. They knew not at all whither the boat was going, neither did they know whether it was night or day. For a long time they were a prey to that an-

guish ; and scarce a spark of life remained in
their bodies when, at length, after a hundred
thousand perils, their boat came out from under
the mountain on to the surface of the earth.
They were glad, and they drew their boat to
the shore and got out of it, and took fruits from
the trees that were there, and ate them.   While
standing there they saw a great white vaulted
building, the dome whereof was of crystal. The
prince and the girl went up to it, and they saw
that it was a great castle, and that the domed
building was within the castle, and on the door
of the castle was written, 'O thou who wouldst
open this door, O thou who desirest to overcome this talisman, bring a five-footed animal
and kill it before here, that the bolts of this
talisman may be opened thereby.'   The prince
marvelled and said, ' Is there in the world a five-
footed animal ?' and he wondered.   And they
sat by the gate of the castle and lice tormented
them, and they began to louse themselves. The
prince killed a louse, and straightway the bolts
of the castle fell, and they knew that the said
five-footed animal was the louse.   Then they
both entered by a door, and they saw a garden,
such that of every tree which is in the world
there was therein ; and ripe fruits were hanging
there and running streams were flowing.   And

the prince felt a longing for those fruits and he
went to pluck one of them that he might eat it,
when he saw that those trees were of gold and
their fruits of silver and jewels, and that precious
stones were lying at the foot of the trees, scattered like pebbles in a brook. They passed
through and came to that dome, it was fashioned
of crystal, they entered by a silver door and saw
that within that dome was another dome all of
pure gold. It too they entered and saw yet another dome, all the walls and the top of which
were of ruby, built after the fashion of Paradise.
They entered it and saw a throne upon which
was a coffin made of jewels, and at the head of
the coffin was a tablet whereon was written:
'O son of Adam, who comest hither and seest
me, know thou that I was a king, and that all the
world was in my hands, and my wealth was beyond bounds or computation. Men and demons
and fairies and jinn were my warriors; and I
lived in the world for a thousand years, and I
never said, "I shall die;" and I made not any
preparation against death. One day, of a sudden,
I fell sick, and I knew of a surety that I was
about to die, and I commanded that this dome
was built in three days, and I made it a sepulchre
for myself. And by my head are two fountains;
drink, and pray for me.' And the prince saw

those two fountains and drank ; and from one of them flowed sugared sherbet and from the other milk. And they drank of both of them and remained a long while by that grave, and they nourished themselves on the milk and drank of the sherbet. At length they found some vases, and they took of the milk and the sherbet and the jewels and the gold, and filled their boat with them, and again set forth on their voyage. After they had gone for a time the wind drove their boat upon an island, and they went forth from the boat to look for fruit on the mountain that they might eat. Of a sudden a body of men came and seized them ; and the prince saw these that they had no heads, their mouths were in their breasts and their eyes in their shoulders, and their speech, when they spake together, was as the chirping of birds. And they took the two and brought them to their king ; and they remained there prisoners a long time. At length one day they found an opportunity and escaped, and again they entered their boat and sailed for a long time upon the sea. Brief, the prince wandered for thirty years upon the seas, sometimes happening among nine-headed men, and sometimes among bird-headed, and sometimes falling among elephant-headed folk, and sometimes among ox-headed, and then escaping ;

and each of them inflicted different torments on
the prince. Still God Most High opened a way
and he escaped. And he saw these strange and
wondrous creatures, and he marvelled. At length,
through the grace of God (glorified and exalted
be He!), the wind drove the prince's ship before
a city, and he saw that the inhabitants of that
country were all men, and he came out. When
these saw the prince they cried, ' He is a spy,'
and seized him and bound his arms behind his
back, and tied a rope round his neck, and took
him alongside a horse, and said, ' Our lord has
put down: when ships come from the sea and
touch at our country, seize their spies and take
them to our king.' And the prince exclaimed,
' What tribulation is this too! how to go alongside a horse!' And while he was praying in
his heart they reached the city. And they took
the prince in this plight to their king. When the
king saw the prince he asked, ' What manner of
man art thou?' The prince said, ' Many mar-
vellous things have befallen me;' and he related his adventures from their beginning to their
end. When the king heard his story he loosed
the prince's bands and took him to his side and
clad him in sumptuous robes of honour. The
prince asked for the jewels that were in his ship.
The king bade bring them and said, ' O prince, I

know thy kingdom, and I heard that the Franks
had taken thee ; and I know thy father too.
Come, go not away, stay ; I have a daughter, I
will give her thee, and we shall live pleasantly
together.' The prince replied, 'O king, when I
was born of my mother, my father caused my
horoscope to be cast, and the astrologers thus
ruled, that my life was afflicted for thirty years ;
mayhap if I took the king's daughter, some evil
might befall the king's daughter by reason of my
affliction ; I may not consent.' Then the king
brought the astrologers and made them cast the
prince's horoscope. The astrologers gave good
news, saying, 'Glad tidings be to thee, those
thirty afflicted years are passed, now his ruling
star has entered the sign of good fortune.' The
prince was exceeding glad and joyful. Thereupon the king commanded that they made ready
a festival, and he gave his daughter to the prince,
and he greatly honoured and reverenced him.
After some time the king died, and the prince
became king in his stead. One day when he was
seated on his throne they said, 'O king, a Frank
has come with much merchandise ; if the king
grant leave, he will bring his merchandise.' The
king replied, 'There is leave, let him bring it.'
And the Frank brought his merchandise before
the king. The king saw his two sons at the

Frank's side, then the blood of love boiled, and
the affection of paternity yearned for them ; and
he asked that Frank, 'Are these youths thine ?'
The Frank answered, ' They are my slaves.'
The king said, 'I will buy them.' And he took
the youths to a place apart and said, ' Where did
this Frank get you ?' Then they related their
adventures from their beginning to their end ;
and the king knew of a certainty that they were
his own sons, and he pressed them to his heart
and kissed each of them on the eyes, and said,
' I am your father.' Then the king arose ; and
they killed the Frank with a thousand torments." *

"O king, I have told this story for that the
king may know that haps such as this often
befall princes. Their happy fortune passes
into the sign of inauspiciousness, and they become a prey to a thousand tribulations and dis-
tresses, so that even gold turns into black earth
in their hands, and all their friends become
enemies to them. Afterward the malefic aspect
gives place to prosperity and auspiciousness,
then everyone is their friend. O king, this
youth's ruling star is likewise afflicted for a few
days. Beware, O king, until the days of the

* See Appendix B, Note IX.

malefic aspect be fulfilled, slay not the youth,
else afterward thou wilt be repentant, and too
late repentance profits not.   The rest the king
knows."   When the king heard this story from
the vezir he asked for the youth's governor, but
he could not be found.   So again he sent the
youth to the prison and went himself to the
chase.

When it was evening the king returned from
the chase and came to the palace, and the lady
rose to greet him, and they sat down.   After
the repast the lady again began to speak about
the youth.   The king said, " To-day also such
an one of my vezirs made intercession for him
and I sent him to the prison."   And he related
to the lady that story which the vezir had told.
Then said the lady, "O king, the reason of
these vezirs stirring up trouble is that they wish
to sow enmity between thee and me.   Beware,
O king, go not by the words of these, but follow
well my words, that thy present state and thy
Hereafter may be happy.   When God Most
High decrees good between husband and wife
He gives mildness and accord.   And, moreover,
O king, be it good news to thee, a week ago
did I conceive by thee ; till now I have not told
thee, but now I have told thee and do thou
believe it true."   And the king believed it.

Then she continued, "O king, lo, these vezirs say that this youth's star has fallen into a malefic aspect. His star became afflicted what time he made for thy life and thy kingdom and for me. God Most High aided us and afflicted his star and brought down his head." And the lady was glad and said, "Thy true son is he that is in my womb; that youth is without doubt base-born. Mayhap the king has not heard the story of him who had no sons." The king said, "Tell on, let us hear." Quoth the lady,

The Lady's Thirteenth Story.

"There was in the palace of the world a great king, and he had neither son nor daughter. And there was in his country a sheykh whose prayers were answered. One day the king, while conversing with the sheykh, said, 'O sheykh, God Most High has given me no son; do thou strive in prayer that God Most High give me a son.' The sheykh replied, 'Send an offering to the convent that the dervishes may eat, and we shall pray for thee; God Most High is a gracious King, He will give thee a son.' Now the king had a golden-ankleted fat ram that was valiant in fight; and he sent that ram to the sheykh's convent with some loads of

M 2

rice and honey and oil. That night the dervishes ate and were pleased ; and the sheykh
sent of that meat in an earthen bowl to the
king, saying, ' Let him desire a son and eat of
the dervishes' portion.' Then the dervishes
danced, after which they prayed and besought
of God a son for the king. By the divine decree the king's wife conceived that night, and in a
short time she brought forth a moon-faced boy.
The king was delighted, and called the people
of the country to the feast; and he took the prince
and laid him on the sheykh's skirt, and he bestowed many gifts on the sheykh's convent.
One day, some time after that, when the king
was conversing with the sheykh, he said, ' O
sheykh, what if thou were to pray and beseech
of God another son for me ?' The sheykh
replied, ' The favours of God are many; to pray
is ours, to give is His ; send then an offering
to the dervishes.' Now the king had a favourite plump horse, that sent he forthwith to the
convent. The devotees cut its throat and
roasted it, and again sent an earthen bowl of it
to the king. They ate the rest themselves, and
prayed and besought of God a son for the king.
By the divine decree the lady again conceived,
and in a short time she brought forth a moon-
faced boy. And the king was delighted and

sent many gifts to the dervishes. Some time
afterward the king requested the sheykh to
beg of God yet another son. The sheykh
said, ' To pray is ours, to give is God's ; send
again an offering to the devotees.' Now the
king had a good mule, that sent he to the convent. The devotees sold that mule and took
its price and therewith prepared a confection.
And they sent a bowl of that too to the king.
After the dance they prayed and besought of
God a son for the king. Again the king's wife
conceived and gave birth to a moon-faced boy.
And the king was glad and sent many gifts to
the dervishes. When the king's sons grew up,
the eldest turned out very valiant ; the second
proved swift of foot and accomplished and possessed of understanding and sagacity ; but the
youngest was ill-omened and ill-natured, and
oppressed men, and wounded and wasted the
hearts of many poor creatures with the sword
of his tongue. And the king was sore grieved
because of him. One day while conversing with
the sheykh he complained of his youngest son
and said, ' O sheykh, would that we had not
besought of God that youngest boy.' The
sheykh replied, ' O king, why art thou grieved ?
thou art thyself the cause of that youth being
thus.' The king asked, ' How am I the cause ?'

The sheykh answered, 'First thou gavest in
the cause of God a ram among beasts, and God
Most High hath given thee a ram among men*;
then thou gavest in the cause of God a courser
of the plain of earth among beasts, and God
Most High hath given thee a courser of the
plain of glory and fortune and understanding
and accomplishments among men; and after
that thou gavest in the cause of God an ill-
omened and base-born brute among beasts,
and God hath given thee such an one among
men. O king, he who sows barley reaps not
wheat.' In the end the king got no rest until he
had killed the youth."

"Now, O king, I have told this story for that
the king may know that from this ill-omened,
base-born one no good will come. They have
said that the base-born are of two classes;
the one the fruit of adultery, the other the fruit
of an unlawful morsel. This thy son is without doubt of one of these two sets; lo, thy true-
born offspring is about to come into existence."
When the king heard these beguiling words of
the lady he said, "On the morrow will I kill
the youth, be not sad." And they went to bed.

When it was morning the king came and sat

---

* The ram is a type of courage.

upon his **throne and** ordered the executioner that **he** brought **the** youth, and he said, " Smite off his head." **The** Fourteenth Vezir came forward and said, **" O king of the** world, it **is** not seemly **to kill the prince in** compliance with the woman's word, for **the** angels **that are in** Heaven **are** not safe against **woman's** wiles ; such is the story of Hārūt and **Mārūt ;** mayhap my king **has** not heard it." The king said, " Tell **on, let us hear."** Quoth **the vezir,**

The Fourteenth Vezir's Story.

" They **have related** that what time God Most High said to **the** angels, **' I will** place a vicegerent upon earth,' the angels **said, ' Thou** wilt make a vicegerent, and **they will do evil on** the earth and shed **blood ; we** celebrate **Thy** praise.' **The** glorious answer **proceeded from** God Most High, **' Ye know not what I know.'** Then God Most High brought Adam **from the** world of non-existence into the world **of** being ; and **Adam's** children multiplied and **did** evil and **shed blood.** And the angels said, **' O** our Lord, **Thou hast created** Adam ; and his children commit **adultery and do evil** and shed blood.' God **Most** High replied, **' O my** angels, had I given **to you the passions I have** given to them, ye too **would have done all** manner evil and wrought works of wickedness.' They said, 'We celebrate the praise of God; far be it that we should do evil like the sons of Adam.' Then said God Most High, 'Which among you is the most devout and austere, that I may give him passions such as I have given the sons of Adam and send him down to earth, that ye may see what he will do and what he will not do?' Then the angels chose Hārūt and Mārūt; and God Most High gave them passions like the passions of men and sent them down to earth. When these came down from Heaven to earth they went to a house and became guests. In that house there was a woman, a loveling of the age; and they both of them were ravished with that woman as soon as ever they saw her. The woman also inclined to them and showed love toward them, so that they stayed with the woman that night and sought to make merry with her. The woman said, 'If ye wish, I am content; bring wine that we may sit and drink and make merry together.' They asked, 'What is wine?' The woman rose from her place and went and brought wine to them, and they sat and drank. And when they were drunk their passions overcame them and they sought to stretch forth the hand to the woman. She said, 'I have a husband ; if he come and see you here, he will leave whole nor you nor me.' They asked, ' What is a husband ? what do they call a husband ?' The woman replied, ' He is coming now, as soon as he comes do ye smite him and kill him that I may be subject to you.' They both agreed thereto ; and when that woman's husband came to the house they smote him and slew him. God Most High said to the angels, ' Have ye seen your devout ones, how they have committed adultery and shed blood and drunk wine and done evil ?' The angels were ashamed and bowed their heads and said, ' Our Lord, Thou knowest, and we know not as Thou knowest.' And God Most High turned that woman's form into a star and placed it in the sky; and what they now call the star Venus is that woman. Then God Most High offered Hārūt and Mārūt the choice between the torment of the world and the torment of the Here-after. They said, ' O God, not the torment of the Hereafter, torment us in the world ; for the world is transient and its torment ends, but the torment of the Hereafter is enduring and ends not.' Then God Most High commanded so that, after they had performed the evening wor-ship, they hanged those two angels in the well at Babylon with their heads downward ; and they must suffer that torment till the Resurrection Day by reason of a woman."

" Now, O king, I have told this story for that the king may know that the angels are not safe from the craft and trickery of women ; where then were the prince ? Then is it incumbent on the king that he beware of following the woman's word and that he grant the prince his this day's life." The king heard this story from the vezir and he sent the youth to the prison and went himself to the chase.

When it was evening the king came to the palace, and the lady rose to greet him, and they passed on and sat down. After the repast the lady commenced to speak about the youth. The king said, " To-day too such an one of my vezirs made intercession for him and I sent him to the prison." The lady said, " O king, to-day I caused the astrologers to be brought and made them cast the horoscope of that which is in my womb, to see whether it be male or female ; and they answered, ' It is male, and will be exceeding fortunate, just and glorious.' Now, O king, this is thy fortunate son ; leave that unworthy one, there will no good come to thee from him. Beware, O king, be not negligent in this affair, that thy story resemble not the story of those opium-eaters." The king

said, "Tell that story, let us hear it." Quoth
the lady,

The Lady's Fourteenth Story.

"Certain opium-eaters, while walking abroad,
found a sequin ; they said, 'Let us go to a cook
and buy food and eat.' So they went and
entered a cook-shop and said, 'Master, give
us a sequin's worth of food.' The cook prepared all manner of foods and loaded a porter
with them ; and the opium-eaters took him
without the city where there was a tomb,*
whereinto they entered and sat down, and the
porter laid down the food and went away. The
opium-eaters fell to eating of the food, when, of
a sudden, one of them said, 'The gate is open,
stay, do one of you shut the gate, else other
opium-eaters will come and trouble us ; even
though they be friends they will do the deeds
of foes.' One of them replied, 'Go thou and
shut the gate,' and they fell a-quarrelling. At
length one said, 'Come, let us agree that whosoever of us first speak or laugh shall rise and
make fast the gate.' They all agreed to this
proposal, and left the food and sat quite still.

---

* A tomb enclosed by four walls.

Suddenly a bitch and fifteen dogs came in ; not
one of the opium-eaters stirred or spake, for if
one spake he must needs rise and shut the
gate ; so they spake not. The dogs made an
end of the food and ate it all up. Just then
another dog leaped in from without, but no
food remained. Now one of the opium-eaters
had partaken of everything, and some of the
food remained about his mouth and on his
beard. That new-come dog licked up the
morsels of food that were on the opium-eater's
breast, and while he was licking up those about
his mouth he took his lip for a piece of meat
and bit it. The opium-eater stirred not, for he
said in himself, 'They will bid me shut the gate ;'
but to ease his soul he muttered, ' Ough !' inwardly cursing the dog. When the other opium-
eaters heard him make that noise they said,
' Rise, fasten the gate.' He replied, ' 'After loss,
attention ;' now that the food is gone and my
lip is wounded, what profit in shutting the
gate ? Through negligence and folly ye have
let this great good slip from your hands.' And
crying, ' Woe ! alas !' they went each in a different direction."

" O king, I have told this story for that the
king may not be repentant at the last moment."
When the king heard this story from the lady

he said, "To-morrow will I kill him." And
they went to bed.

When it was morning the king went forth
and sat upon his throne, and he caused the
youth to be brought and commanded the executioner, " Kill." When the Fifteenth Vezir
came forward and said,

The Fifteenth Vezir's Story.

" There was in the palace of the world a
famous king and God Most High had given
him a son. After some time the son became
afflicted with a heartburn, and he would ever
complain of his heart. The king brought
together all the physicians that were to be got,
and they treated the boy's ailment; but it was
in vain, the physicians were powerless. As
often as the boy said, 'Father, my heart,' the
king would say, 'Son, my heart aches more
than thy heart;' and the king was afflicted at
his pain. At length the boy died. After the
dismay, the king came up by the boy and said,
'Cut him open that I may see what pain was in
his heart.' When they had cut open the boy
the king saw that a bone had grown on the top
of his heart. The king ordered that they took
out that bone and then buried the boy; and the
king caused that bone to be made into the

handle of a knife.   One day they placed a
water-melon before the king; the king cut the
melon with that knife and ate some of it, and he
stuck the knife into the remains of the melon
and left it.   Then the king caused the chess
things to be brought and he began to play;
afterward he went to take up the knife when he
saw that the part of the handle which had pene-
trated into the melon was melted and had
vanished.   As soon as the king saw this he
exclaimed, ' Dost thou see ? the cure for my
son's sickness was water-melon ; and I knew it
not.'   And his heart was grieved thereat, and
he began to weep, and said, ' Son, it has gone
from thy heart and come into my heart; would
that thou hadst not come to earth !'   And at
length that king died of anguish of soul."

" Now, O king, I have told this story for that
thou mayst beware and slay not thy child on
the woman's word, lest thou too die of anguish
of soul."   And he kissed the ground and made
intercession for the prince.   When the king
heard this story from the vezir he sent the
youth to the prison and went himself to the
chase.

When it was evening the king returned from
the chase and came to the palace, and the lady
rose to greet him, and they passed on and sat

down. After the repast the lady began to speak
about the youth. The king said, "This day
also such an one of my vezirs made intercession
for him and I sent him to the prison." The lady
said, "O king, this youth is a dragon, until he
be killed thou shalt not be safe from his malice ;
it is even as it was with a certain king who
until he had killed his son could not escape from
his pain ; mayhap the king has not heard that
story." Then the king said, "Tell on, let us
hear." Quoth the lady,

THE LADY'S FIFTEENTH STORY.

"They have related that a great king was
wroth with Luqmān,* and commanded that they
lowered him into a pit and closed up the
mouth of the pit with a great stone. By
Luqmān the sage was a pill, of the bigness
of a walnut, which he had made by his science.
He ever smelled it, and his hunger was satisfied
and his thirst was quenched ; and for a long
time he remained in that pit. The king who
imprisoned him died, and his son became king
in his stead. And sickness seized upon this
king ; and the physicians treated him, but he
grew no better, and his trouble increased upon

---

* A legendary sage. He here pretends to kill the boy, that
the king may recover through joy on finding his son alive.

him. They were helpless and said, 'O king, had Luqmān been alive he could have cured thy pain.' Then said the king, 'What manner of man was Luqmān?' They replied, 'Thy father was wroth with him and put him into the pit; by now his bones are rotten. But Luqmān was a man such that God Most High hath mentioned him in the noble Koran; such a sage has never come to earth.' The king said, 'If it be so, open the pit, belike he has in some way saved himself.' They went and opened that pit and went down and saw him sitting there, and they came and told the king. The king said, 'Quick, go bring him.' They went to pull him out of the pit, when Luqmān said, 'If the king wish me, wrap me in cotton and draw me out; and bring to me a virgin every night.' They did so, and after forty days he arose and came before the king, and he saw the king lying without strength. After praising and lauding him, he asked of the king's trouble and felt his pulse, and said, 'O king, thou hast a hard sickness.' Then he asked, "Has the king a son?' They replied, 'He has.' Luqmān said, 'O king, until the throat of thy son be cut and his blood rubbed on thy body, this thy pain will not leave thee.' The king answered, 'O Luqmān, thou art thyself a

great man ; I will consent to my own death,
but I will not consent to my son's.' Quoth
Luqmān, 'O king, I have told thee the cure ;
the rest thou knowest.' And he arose and
went away. After some days the king's trouble
increased, and he called Luqmān to his side
and said, ' O Luqmān, is there no other remedy?'
Luqmān answered, 'O king, there is no cure
save the cutting of thy son's throat.' The
king's soul came up to his throat through that
trouble. Quoth Luqmān, ' O king, when thou
art well, sons will not be lacking thee.' Then
said the king, ' Now get the boy and cut his
throat in a distant place that mine eyes see it
not.' Luqmān said, ' There is no good if it be
done in another place, it is needful that it be
done before thine eyes.' Then they gave the
boy into Luqmān's hands. And Luqmān bound
the boy's hands and feet, and cunningly tied a
bladder filled with blood round the boy's throat,
and laid him down before the king. Then he
took a diamond knife in his hand and said, ' O
king, now look, see how I cut the prince's
throat.' When the king's two eyes were fixed
on the boy, he struck against the boy's throat
with the knife and the blood gushed out. When
the king saw the blood on the boy's throat he
sighed ; and when Luqmān saw him he thanked

N

God. And straightway he raised the boy from
the ground and kissed his two eyes ; and
Luqmān said, 'O king, I could find no other
way to turn off thy sickness than this trick.'
Then the king greatly applauded Luqmān and
bestowed upon him much wealth."

" Now, O king, I have told this story for that
until the king have killed his son, he too will have
no security from trouble." When the king heard this
story from the lady he was wroth and said, " To-
morrow will I kill him." And they went to bed.

When it was morning the king went and sat
upon his throne and he caused the youth to be
brought and ordered the executioner, " Smite off
his head." The Sixteenth Vezir came forward
and said, " O king of the world, it is not
beseeming thy glory that thou castest to the
waters the words of the vezirs ; for men are
either good or bad concerning the king, whatsoever they say, the king is informed thereof,
and the king is given word of evil or hurt about
to be, and all that goes on without is known to
the king, that he may make preparation accordingly. It is even as in the Tradition, 'Speak
to men according to their understanding.' Mayhap my king has not heard the story of the
dervish and the king." The king said, " Tell
on, let us hear." Quoth the vezir,

The Sixteenth Vezir's Story.

"There was in a palace of the world a king and his name was Aydin (light). One day a dervish came before him and spake pleasantly with fair discretion; and whatsoever they asked, he answered the whole of it, and his every word seemed good to the king. The king said, 'O dervish, go not away, let us spend this evening together.' The dervish blessed him and said, 'On head and eye.' Now it was then very cold. So the king took the dervish, and they went to the palace and sat down. The king ordered that they laid wood upon the fire-place and set light to it, whereupon the dervish repeated these verses—

'Take in winter fire from garden-land ;
Take the goblet from the drunken band ;
Should there no loveling for cup-bearer be,
Take from orange-breasted damsel's hand.'

As these verses seemed right good to the king, he wrote them in his album ; and he said to the dervish, 'Tell some merry story.' Quoth the dervish, 'O king, once there was a king, and by him there was a devotee. One day they said to the king, "Yon devotee is a Ráfizí.*" The king, to try him, one day asked that devotee, "O

---

* An adherent of the Shi'a sect, which acknowledges 'Alí, but rejects Abu-Bekr, 'Othmán and 'Omar as lawful Khalifs.

devotee, lovest thou Saint Abu Bekr the True ? " The devotee replied, " Nay." He said, "Lovest thou Saint 'Omar?" He answered, " Nay." " Then lovest thou Saint 'Othmān ? " He answered, " Nay, nay." " Then lovest thou Saint 'Alī the Approved ? " He answered " Nay." Thereupon the king's difficulties from being one became two, and he thought and said in himself, " If this devotee were a Rāfizī, he would love Saint 'Alī, though he loved not the other Noble Companions our Lords ; if he were a Sunnī, he would love all of the Four Chosen Friends our Lords." And he turned and said to the devotee, " Thou lovest none of the Glorious Companions, whom then lovest thou ? " The devotee replied, " There is at the gate of the bazaar a loveling of the age ; lo, that is whom I love." The king was pleased with this jest of the devotee and gave him many gifts.' And that dervish told stories such as this to the king, and he amused the king with many jests. That night they ate and drank, and when their converse was finished, drowsiness came upon the king, and he would have lain down, but the devotee was at ease and would not rise and go. The slaves thought to say to the devotee, ' Arise and go,' but they feared the king and were silent. The king too wished that the devotee might perceive by his discretion that he should arise ; but where was that discretion ? The king looked, but it was not. Then he called to his servants, ' Strike the fagot that the glow (ishiq) may go out.' The servants understood not and remained still. Thereupon the devotee said, ' Why wait ye ? Strike the log that the light (aydin) may spring up.' Now the king's name was Aydin (light) and the devotee's name was Ishiq (glow).* The king said, ' I sent thee off with a fagot, that is struck thee with a fagot, but thou didst strike me with a log.' The devotee said, ' My king, thou didst not strike me with a fagot, neither did I strike my king with a log ; so do thou rest on the one side of the hearth and I shall rest on the other.' And the king was pleased with these words of the devotee ; and they lay down and rested."

" Now, O king, I have told this story for that thou mayst know that a certain freedom is usual with the accomplished. Now there are no learned men equal to these forty vezirs of my king, each one of whom utters these many good sayings and fair words ; and indeed the good or bad of these has many a time been tried. And

---

* So the point of this story turns upon an untranslatable pun.

what is incumbent upon my king is this, that he
listen not to the words of these inattentively
nor cast them to the winds." The king said,
" This demand leaves me in bewilderment.
Our Lord the Apostle of God hath said concerning women, that they are enemies to you,
but that one of them is needful to each of you.
And God Most High hath said in His Glorious
Word, ' Your wealth and your children are but
a trial.'* Now I ask these affairs of this youth
and he answers not at all ; and so long as he will
not speak, will my difficulty remain unsolved.
Thus it seems to me that this youth has done
this wantonness, and therefore cannot speak."
When the vezir saw this much consideration on
the part of the king he said, " My king, in
every thing the mysterious workings of God
Most High are many ; let not my king regard
the not speaking of the youth. One day will
he speak indeed ; yea, there is also in that noble
verse concerning children, ' And God : with
Him is great reward.' "* And he kissed the
ground and made intercession for the prince.
And the king sent the youth to the prison and
went himself to the chase. That day, when they
were hunting, a deer rose, and the hounds pur-

---

* Koran, viii. 128, and lxiv. 15.

sued it, and all the attendants pushed their
horses after that deer, and the king too pushed
on.   Each one went in a different direction, and
the king was left alone.   When it was evening
there was with him no attendant nor anyone ;
the king looked and there was none, and he
said, " There is in this some divine working."
And straightway he disguised himself and
pushed on and came to a village and was guest
in a shepherd's house.

On the morrow he rose betimes, and while he
was watching the sheep and lambs, he looked and
saw a lamb that had lost its mother.   Seeking
about, it went up to a sheep, and that sheep
butted at the lamb, and the lamb fell.   It rose
again and went to another sheep ; and that
sheep likewise butted at the lamb.   The king
asked this from the shepherd, " Why do these
sheep butt at that lamb ?"   The shepherd said,
" To-day this lamb's mother died ; these, being not
its mother, receive it not."   Then the king sighed
in his soul and said in his heart, "May God Most
High leave not a servant of His an orphan."

Let us to our story : The attendants returned to the city, and each one turned his
horse's head straight to the palace. They
arrived at the castle, and one of them called out
and learned the circumstance (of the king's

absence) from the watchmen ; so they went to
look for news of the king.   On the other hand
the watchmen informed the grand vezir of the
matter ; and straightway the grand vezir commanded that all of those watchmen were secured
in prison,* and he himself walked about the city
till morning.   He sent a vezir to the king's
attendants, saying, " Go tell the attendants that
they publish not this affair, and do thou go with
the whole of them to seek the king."   On her
part, the lady looked and the time passed and
the king came not, and she caused the grand
vezir to be questioned ; the vezir sent word to
her, " This night there is a great council ; our
king will not go in."   The vezir questioned the
king's attendants ; and while they were going
to the place where they had left the king, the
king himself set out from the village where he
was and came to the place where the attendants
had dispersed.   The attendants saw the king,
and brought word to the vezir ; so the vezir
pushed on his horse and came up to the king.
The king said in his heart, " These will have
enthroned the prince and sent this vezir to me ;
now is he coming to give me the sherbet ; O
how the lady's words were true !"   The vezir

---

* To prevent their spreading the report of the king's dis-
appearance.

saw from the king's countenance that he was
thinking thus, and he came up quickly to him,
and kissed the ground before the king, and said,
"My king, what plight is this plight? Is it
beseeming to remain without at such a time?
Above all, as the prince has been these many
days imprisoned, everyone says that the king's
senses have well nigh left him." Thereupon
the king said, "Have ye taken the prince from
prison?" The vezir replied, "Nay, my king;
the grand vezir secured in prison the watchmen
who had learned of my king's remaining out in
the evening from the attendants who came to
the gate; and he sent me and the attendants to
seek my king." The king's mind was somewhat comforted, but his heart would not believe.
Then the vezir perceived that the king's heart
was not at ease and he said to the king, "My
king, thy grand vezir sent me hither in the
evening; to learn the events of to-day are my
eyes now on the road." And he kissed the ground
and was silent. The king said, "If we went
on now it were too quick; but let an attendant
go and inform the vezir of the affair." They
sent on an attendant; and that day, when it was
evening, the king came to the palace and found
everything in its proper place, and his heart
was again at rest concerning his vezir.

After the repast he entered the harem. The
lady had rubbed a dye upon her eyes and made
them red, and she rose to greet the king as if
weeping ; and the king passed on and sat in
his place. When coffee and sherbets had
been drunk she asked of the haps of the
night, and the king related the events to her.
She said, " O king, the thing thou hast done
might be in two ways ; the one, of purpose, to
distinguish between friend and foe ; the other,
by chance. In this instance thou hast passed
the evening outside by chance, and thy heart is
at ease for that thy vezirs have done no un-
seemly deed. But, my king, beware, trust not
these vezirs ; for they would make the youth
king. Praise be to God ! thou art well, but
they still watch their opportunity ; and this
youth has no dread of thee, thou hast brought
him up full insolent ; that is not good. And
they have said that if a person treat thee as a
brother, do thou treat him as a master and
deem him great. Kings are like fire ; if thou
be a lion, thou must be on thy guard against
the fire, even as lions are on their guard against
fire. There is a fable suitable to this : The
lynxes go along with the lion, but they go not
close to him. One day they asked one of them,
' Thou goest along with the lion ; why goest

thou not near to him?' He replied, 'Firstly, the lion hunts beasts and I eat his leavings; secondly, when an enemy comes against me I go to him and take refuge; as these two things are good for me I go along with him. And the reason of my going not near is this, that his glory is that of a render, one day it might be that he should rend me like the leopard; therefore go I not near him.' Wise is he who acts before kings like the lynx; for nearness to the sultan is a burning fire. Even as the lynx is content with and eats the lion's leavings, must the wise man be content with the king's leavings; else, if he stretch forth his hand to the morsel that is in the king's mouth—the plight of him who stretches forth his hand is notorious. If an enemy appear, it is needful to take refuge with the king; so one must ever be between dread and entreaty, and must measure his words. A word is like an arrow that has left the bow, when once it leaves the mouth it returns not again. Mayhap my king has not heard the story of Sultan Mahmúd* and Hasan of Maymand.†" The king said, "Tell on, let us hear." Quoth the lady,

---

* Sultan Mahmúd, the son of Sebuktekin, of Ghazní.

† Hasan of Maymand was a minister, not of Sultan Mahmúd, but of that monarch's father. Hasan's son, Ahmed, was Mahmúd's vezir.

The Lady's Sixteenth Story.

" A word was the cause of Sultan Mahmūd dismissing his vezir Hasan of Maymand, and confiscating all his property and banishing him. So what could Hasan of Maymand do but yield consent to misfortune and bear calamity with patience ? One day, during his exile, while he was passing along a street, a group of children were playing, one was prince and one was vezir. The prince got angry and wished to banish the vezir and confiscate his property. The child who was vezir said, ' Art thou just or art thou a tyrant ?' The prince answered, ' I am just.' Then said the vezir, ' Thou art just ; well, when I came to thee I was young, and I have spent my life in thy service and gained my property ; now thou confiscatest my property and takest away my office, I now ask back from thee my life that I have spent in thy service ; if thou be just, it is right that thou give me my life.' The prince was silent and made that child vezir again. Hasan of Maymand liked the child's words, and straightway he went and composed a petition and sent it to Sultan Mahmūd. When the petition arrived they took it and gave it to the king. The king read it, and when he perceived its import, he straightway ordained that he was pardoned and reinstated in his office. So he was dismissed by one word and reinstated by one word."

" O king, I deemed this story suitable in that a master of speech comes not readily to hand ; and a master of speech is one who knows the speech that ought to be spoken. For speech is of two kinds; one kind is truth, another kind is folly. A wise man distinguishes between the speech of a sage and the speech of a fool. A sage speaks with understanding, but a fool speaks with trickery. The man who distinguishes not between these is like a beast, for a beast knows only when it is hungry and when it is full. Now this thy degenerate son has made for thy life and thy throne; this is beseeming, that thou give him neither grace nor time. Thou must kill him to-morrow, else he will slay thee." When the king heard this story from the lady he said, " To-morrow will I finish his affair." And they rose and went to bed.

When it was morning and the sun shed light (aydin) and, like the words of the king and the dervish, the glow (ishiq) appeared, and the world was illuminated with radiance, the happy-fortuned king passed and sat upon his throne, and he caused the executioner to bring the youth and commanded, " Smite off his head."

The Seventeenth Vezir came forward and said, " O king of the world, haste not in slaying the prince ; both sides of the question are not yet known, kill him not until the accused and the accuser come together. At present he is innocent and much cruelty has been done him ; and this calamity has befallen those who are in thy service. If thou forgive, all the troubles brought upon him will be forgotten : and the Holy Apostle hath said, 'Verily, God will not require of my people that whereto their passions have urged them, if they have not spoken it or done it.' If thou slay the prince, on the Resurrection Day God Most High will ask of thee if thou killedst thy son in accordance with the Law ; how wilt thou answer Him, if the sin be the woman's ? For they have said that the lust of man is as one and that of woman as nine ; for Gabriel (peace on him !) brought to our father Saint Adam (peace on him !) ten apples and said, ' Adam, these apples are lust ; beware, let not Eve eat them, eat the whole of them thyself.' Adam (peace on him !) ate one of them, then as some wondrous sight appeared in the alleys of Paradise, he gave the nine of them in charge to Eve and warned her, saying, ' Take heed, eat them not,' and went off. When Eve was alone, Satan came and tempted her, and

Eve ate those nine apples. Therefore is the lust of man one and the lust of woman nine. There is a story on the greatness of woman's lust, if the king grant leave I will relate it." The king said, "Relate it, let us hear." Quoth the vezir,

The Seventeenth Vezir's Story.

"One year there was a famine in Mekka the Revered. And there was there a woman, and she had much wheat which she sold. A youth came and asked wheat from her. The woman admired that youth and was ravished with him, and she said to him, 'The wheat is finished.' What could the youth do? His strength and power were gone through hunger, and he began to beseech the woman. Then the woman with a thousand airs and graces said to the youth, 'I will present thee with a load of the wheat I am about to eat myself, if thou wilt come and make merry with me.' The youth said, 'We take refuge in God. God forbid that I should commit that sin in this most holy spot, or in any other place.' The woman answered, 'Come, make merry with me, else shall I now call out, "This youth has come and broken into my house and seeks to do me wrong," and so put thee to shame before the world.' The youth was

bewildered and said in himself, 'See what an
evil has befallen me! if I do this, to-morrow on
the Day of Retribution how shall I answer God
Most High?   And if I do it not, she will put
me to shame before the world.'   He pondered
a while and then determined to go into a
chamber of that house and there geld himself;
and he went into that house with that purpose.
He looked and saw that the wall of that
chamber was cracked and that there was a
way of escape.   So the youth went out that
way, and he saw ten camels standing, all laden
with loads of wheat, and they had no master.
The youth knew them to be the gift of God
Most High, and he took them and led them
to his house.   And the woman was longing for
the youth, so she went into the chamber but
could find neither şign nor trace of him; and
night and day was she oppressed with sorrow.
If anyone fear God Most High, God Most
High will not leave him in straits, but will give
him untold good."

   " Now, O king, I have told this story for that
thou mayst know that overpowering passion
such as that abounds in women.   Refuge in
God! may the wiles of woman hurt not the
prince too.   Now, in this affair it is incumbent
on the king that he hurry not, but enquire dili-

gently." And he made intercession with the king for the prince for that day. When the king heard this story from the vezir he sent the youth to the prison and mounted for the chase. The grand vezir sought to prevent him, but he was unable. And that day he found his way with difficulty in the evening.

He came to the palace, and the lady rose to greet him, and they sat down. After the repast the lady began to talk ; now day and night the lady's thoughts were taken up with the youth, so she asked about him. The king answered, " To-day also such an one of my vezirs made intercession for him and I sent him to the prison." The lady said, " O king, Hippocrates the sage hath said, ' Be eager in the search for thy faults because of thine enemy.' And Plato the sage hath said, ' Let whoso desireth that his friends be glad and his foes confounded endeavour to abandon his faults.' Thus a man went to a friend of his and said, ' Such and such a man speaks ill of me.' The friend replied, ' Go thou and shame that man by good deeds.' He said, ' He spake ill of thee likewise.' The other answered, ' Let be, vex me not; he doth blot out my sin,' and he left him. Now, thus do the vezirs bring forward my sins before the king ; but, praise be to God ! I am free from all sin. Then, if thy life be needful for thee, leave not the youth alive, for he is a sharper. His story resembles the story of a certain sharper; mayhap my king has not heard it." The king said, "Relate it, let us hear." Quoth the lady,

The Lady's Seventeenth Story.

"Of old time there were in the city of Baghdad forty sharpers, and one among them a youth. One night, when these were talking together, their chief pulled out a sequin and laid it on the ground in the middle of them and said, 'Which of you can go and buy a sequin's worth of sweetmeats and bring back both sweetmeats and sequin?' None answered. Then the youth rose and took the sequin and went with some young men to a confectioner's shop, bought the sweetmats, gave the sequin, and sent the sweetmeats away with those young men. The youth stole the sequin from the place where the confectioner had put it, and went out into the street. The confectioner saw that the sequin was gone and knew that the youth had stolen it, so he took two jugs in his hand and went and arrived before the youth at the door of the house where his fellows dwelt. He stood there, and the youth came across;

then the confectioner said, 'Youth, hast thou stolen the sequin?' The youth, thinking him to be of his fellows, replied, 'I have stolen it.' The other said, 'Come, give it me and do thou fill these jugs.' The youth gave him the sequin, took the jugs, and went to the river; and the confectioner took the sequin and made for his own house. When the youth had filled the jugs he returned, and the sharpers, as soon as they saw him, said, 'Where is the sequin?' The youth perceived that it was the confectioner who had been at the door, and he straightway ran off, and ere the confectioner had reached his house he arrived there, and disguising himself as a woman, stood behind the door. When the confectioner came, the youth said, 'Why standest thou there? the ass has broken loose and gone out into the street; go, catch it and bring it.' The confectioner thought the speaker was his wife and saying, 'Take this sequin,' gave it him. The youth took the sequin and went off. The confectioner went and saw no ass and he returned and said to his wife, 'I have not found it.' His wife asked, 'What hast thou not found?' The confectioner answered, 'The ass.' His wife said, 'Fellow, art thou mad? who asked thee about the ass? or dost thou make mock of me?' The confectioner

replied, 'My life, why should I make mock of
thee? it seems to me it is thou who art mad.'
His wife said, 'How am I mad?' The confectioner said, 'Give me that sequin I gave
thee.' His wife answered, 'I have no knowledge of the sequin.' Then the confectioner
perceived that it was the work of the sharper,
so he took a pitcher in his hand, and ran and
came to the sharper's door. The youth had not
yet returned. He saw the youth coming and he
went forward and said to him, 'Well, youth,
hast thou contrived to get the sequin this time?'
The youth said, 'I have got it.' Then the confectioner said, 'Come, let me see it.' The
youth gave it him, and the confectioner said,
'Take this pitcher and get a little water in it
and bring it.' The youth took the pitcher, got
water in it, and returned. He saw that there
was no one, and perceived that it had been the
confectioner again. He went quickly and
entered the confectioner's house, and saw that
the confectioner and his wife were lying
sleeping. He stripped himself and slipped in
between them, and, after waiting a little, said to
the confectioner, 'Come, husband, where didst
thou put the sequin? I shall hide it that the
sharper will not get it if he come again.' The
confectioner said, 'It is under the pillow.'

Thereupon the youth took it from under the pillow, and, before the sharpers had lain down, he returned and placed the sequin on the ground in the middle of them, and related to them the events that had happened. They all applauded him and said, ‘ Bravo, such sharping is in none of us.’ ”

“ Now, O king, I have told this story for that the king may know that cunning like to this abounds in youths. Beware, be not deceived by the youth’s gentleness, or afterward thou shalt be repentant, and too late repentance profits not.” When the king heard these enticing and beguiling words of the lady he said, “ On the morrow will I kill him, be not sad.” And they went to bed.

When it was morning and the sun had appeared, like as the ten camels laden with wheat appeared to that youth in Mekka for his fearing God Most High, and the world was illumined with radiance, the king came and sat upon his throne, and he caused the youth to be brought and commanded the executioner, “ Smite off his head.” The Eighteenth Vezir came forward and said, “ O king of the world, two things are indeed incumbent upon kings; the first is to have pity on the folk, and the second is to have mercy in the time of wrath.

Long will be the life of the king who is thus,
and God Most High will protect him from all
calamities.   It is even as said Our Lord the
Holy Apostle of God, 'Be merciful to those
upon the earth that the Dwellers in Heaven
may have mercy upon you.'   And the friends
of a king who is generous are many, and he
triumphs over his enemies, and is of the host
of the Prophets and the Saints.   And there is
a story of Sultan Mahmūd suitable to this ; if
the king grant leave, I will relate it."   The
king said, "Relate, let us hear."   Quoth the
vezir,

The Eighteenth Vezir's Story.

"One day while Sultan Mahmūd the son of
Sebuktekīn was hunting, he got separated from
his soldiers, and he saw some one going along
in a trackless place.   He pushed on and came
up to that man and saluted him and said, 'O
man, whence art thou and what is thy origin ?'
The man replied, 'From the kingdom ; and my
origin my mother knows.'   Then the Sultan
saw that he was wrapped up in black clothes and
mounted on a black ass ; and the king asked,
'Whither goest thou now ?'   That man replied,
'I go to Sultan Mahmūd.'   The king said,
'What is thy desire of the Sultan ?'   The man

answered, 'I want ten thousand aspres of him ; I have a debt, perchance he may give it me and I shall be freed from my debt.' The Sultan said, 'If he give it not, how wilt thou act ?' The man replied, 'If he will not give ten thousand, let him give one thousand.' Again the Sultan said, 'If he will not give even one thousand, what wilt thou do ?' The man replied, 'If he will not give a thousand aspres, let him give a hundred aspres.' The Sultan said, 'If he will not give even that, what wilt thou do ?' Then the fellow replied, 'If he will not give even a hundred aspres, I shall say, *Bu qara eshegimin durt ayaghi 'avretinin ferjine !** and shall turn and go.' The king wondered at this man's self and words. After a little he met his soldiers and went to his palace and sat upon his throne and thus commanded the grand chamberlain, 'A man clad in black and mounted on a black ass will come, give him leave to enter.' The next day, early in the morning, that man came, and the grand chamberlain took him and brought him into the king's presence. When he saw the king he knew that it was he whom he had seen yesterday, and straightway he prayed for the king and asked ten thousand

---

* I have thought it best to leave the uncivil remark of the owner of the black ass in the inimitable simplicity of the original.

aspres. The king said, 'May God give it thee.' The man said, 'Give one thousand aspres.' Again the king answered, 'May God give it thee.' The man said, 'Let it be a hundred aspres.' Again the king answered, 'May God give it thee.' Then the man said, ' Be thou well ; the black ass is tied at the door.' Thereupon a courtier* said, ' The king has bestowed nothing on thee ; let the black ass be.' The man said, ' If he has not, then it means, *eshegimin durt ayaghi 'avretinin ferjine !* And I shall be off.' But his boldness pleased the king who said, ' This poor man's desire is but to be delivered from distress and find rest, as he got no boon from us he mounts his ass and goes.' And this remained as a proverb, ' The black ass is tied at the door.' However, he bestowed on him somewhat."

"And this story resembles it : A certain khoja was going from Hindustan to Baghdad, and while on the road he thus thought, ' When I enter the city of Baghdad what goods should I buy ?' Anyhow he entered Baghdad, and there was there a naked abdal† who had

---

* In Belletéte this courtier is said to be Firdausí of Tús, and he is made to tell Mahmúd the following story of the khoja and the abdal, for which the Sultan rewards him with a purse of gold.

† A kind of religious mendicant.

plucked out his beard and put it in a piece of paper. He came up to the khoja and said, ' I have heard, O khoja, that thou hast come to buy goods ; I have something, buy it.' And he gave the paper into the khoja's hand. The khoja took it and opened it and saw in it the hairs of the beard, and he said, 'What shall I do with this ?' The abdal said, ' Take it, and give the money.' The khoja answered, ' I shall not give money for this.' The abdal said, 'Why wilt thou not give money ? that is indeed a beard ; is it not worth a hundred aspres ?' The khoja replied, ' It is not.' The abdal said, ' Let it be ten aspres ; is it not worth that ?' The khoja answered, ' It is not.' The abdal said, ' Let it be, five aspres ; is it not worth that ?' The khoja said, ' It is not.' Then said the abdal, 'A beard is not worth five aspres ; why then dost thou carry one ? shave it off and let it go.' The khoja was pleased with this jest of the abdal and gave him a hundred aspres."

" Now, O king, I have told these stories for that the king may know that it is needful for kings to raise the fallen and bestow favours on the poor." And he kissed the ground and made intercession for the prince. When the king heard these stories from the vezir he sent the prince to the prison and went himself to the chase.

When it was evening the king returned from the chase and came to the palace, and the lady rose to greet him, and they sat down. After the repast the lady asked for news about the youth. The king said, " To-day likewise such an one of my vezirs made intercession for him and I sent him to the prison." The lady said, " O king, think not thou this youth would maintain thy place after thee and observe the ordinances of kings. To exercise sovereignty is a hard work. I know that he is no true man ; he watches his opportunity, and one day he will slay thee and shed blood, and then they will kill him too. Moreover, family and descent are needful for one; he who is not of family cannot exercise sovereignty. And one's nature must be good. There are men of family and descent who are yet themselves of evil nature; for there is not honey in every bee nor a pearl in every oyster. Then this youth's nature is evil ; he has not the qualities of a king ; his work would ever be wickedness and he would do wrong to those who do good. It is like the story of a certain merchant's son ; mayhap my king has not heard it." The king said, " Tell on, let us hear." Quoth the lady,

THE LADY'S EIGHTEENTH STORY.

" There was of old time a cobbler in the city of Orfa. One day he saw a dervish passing, the seams of whose shoes had given way. The cobbler said, ' Dervish, come, sit down till I sew up the seams of thy shoes and patch the holes.' The dervish answered, ' If thou hast a remedy, apply it to the hole in my heart.' The cobbler gave him his right hand and he came and sat down ; and the cobbler gave him food to eat and sewed up the holes in his shoes and said, 'O dervish, I too wish to journey ; what counsel dost thou give me ?' The dervish answered, 'I have three counsels ; see thou keep them : my first is this, set not out on the journey till thou have found a good fellow-traveller ; for the Apostle of God hath said, " The companion, then the road." My second is this, light not in a waterless place. My third is this, enter great cities when the sun is rising.' Then he went his way. After some days the cobbler found some suitable fellow-travellers and set out. While they were on the road, one day in the afternoon a city appeared before them. The cobbler youth asked, ' What city is this city ?' The companions answered, ' It is the city of Aleppo.' The youth said,

'To-day it is near evening; I shall not enter
the city to-day.' Howsoever the companions
urged him, it was no use; so at length they left
him and went on. The youth went and lighted
on the bank of a stream and remained there
that night. Now there were tombs near the
youth; and when it was midnight he saw two
men coming from the city carrying something
which they laid in the graveyard, and then they
went away. Then the youth went up to that
grave, and, striking a light with a flint and
steel, lit a candle; he saw that they had laid
there a new coffin, and that from the four sides
of that coffin streams of blood were running.
The cobbler youth opened the lid of the coffin
and looked to see what he might see; there
was a body bathed in blood, the garments were
of massive gold embroidery and on the finger
was a ring in which a stone glittered. The
youth coveted the ring and took hold of it that he
might pull it off, whereupon the body raised its
head and said, 'O youth, fearest thou not God
that thou wouldst take my ring?' Then the
youth saw that it was a girl like the moon of
fourteen nights, a torment of the age, like a
lovely rose; and he said, 'What is this plight?'
The girl said, 'Now is not the time for questions; if thou be able, relieve me; and after-

ward I will help thine affairs.' Straightway the
youth pulled off his outer robe and tore it in
pieces and bound up the girl's wounds and laid
her in a place. When it was morning he took
her on his back and brought her into the city
and placed her in a cell in a certain place; and to
all who asked of her he said, 'She is my sister;
passion came upon me and I brought this plight
upon this poor creature, and she innocent.'
The youth tended the girl's wounds and in the
course of a month or two she became well.
One day she went to the bath, and when she
returned she asked the youth for inkhorn, reed,
and paper. The youth brought them and
placed them before her. The girl wrote a
letter and gave it into the youth's hands;
and therein was written thus: 'Thou who art
Khoja Dibāb, the superintendent of the bazaar,
give the bearer of this letter a hundred sequins
and send him to me; and disclose nothing to
my father of my health or my death; if thou
do, thou shalt reflect well upon the issue.' She
sealed it and said, 'Go, give this letter to a khoja
who sits in such and such a place in the bazaar,
and take whatever he gives thee and bring it.'
The youth took that letter and went to the bazaar
and asked, and they showed him to him, and
he gave the letter into his hand. When the

khoja opened the letter and read it, he kissed
it and raised it to his head, and straightway
drew forth a purse of gold and gave it to the
youth.   The youth brought it and laid it before
the girl.   The girl said, ' Go, take a house, and
buy with what is over clothes for thee and me.'
The youth went and took a house and bought
sumptuous clothes and brought them to the
girl.   And they arose and went to that house
which they had taken.   Again she wrote a
letter which she gave to the youth who took it
to the khoja, who this time gave him two
purses which he took to the girl.   She said to
him, ' Go, my youth, and buy some provisions
and furniture for the house.'   And the youth
went and bought them.   Then the girl got
another purse of sequins, and she said to the
youth, ' Go, buy thyself horses and arms and
male slaves and female slaves.'   And the youth
went and bought them, and he brought them
and gave them to the girl, and he said, ' Now
tell me what are these matters.'   The girl
answered, ' Now is not the time, by and bye.'
Gradually the girl built palaces there and increased the number of her male slaves and
female slaves, and whenever she gave the youth
a letter he went and got two or three purses of
gold from that khoja.   One day the girl gave

the youth a purse of gold and said, 'In the bazaar is a youth they call Ghazanfer Agha; now go and find him, and ask of him some precious stuff, and he will show it thee, and whatever price he ask for it, give him the double thereof, and take and bring it.' So the youth went and found him, and sat a while and talked with him ; and whatever the price of it was he gave the double, and took it ; and Ghazanfer Agha marvelled at this. The youth returned and gave it to the girl, and again he asked of these matters, but the girl said that this too was not the time. And she took out a purse of jewels and gave it to the youth and said, 'Take these jewels and go to Ghazanfer Agha and ask him to put a value on them, and take them out and lay them before him, and see what he will say to thee ; and when putting the jewels back into the purse present him with three of them.' So she sent him off. The youth said, ' I shall go ; but when I come back tell me the things that have befallen thee.' He went and did as the girl had said. When Ghazanfer Agha saw these gifts he said to the youth, ' O youth, thou hast made us ashamed ; pray be troubled to come once to our house and honour us that we may show our affection.' The youth replied, ' What though it be so ; to-morrow I shall go.

And he bade him farewell and he came and
told the girl, and the girl said, 'Go to-morrow;
but when thou enterest his house look not to
this side nor that side, but look straight before
thee.' And thus did she warn him. When it
was morning the youth arose; and Ghazanfer
Agha looked and saw the youth coming and he
said, 'Welcome!' and took him and led him to
his house. And the youth looked at nothing,
but passed on and sat down; and Ghazanfer
Agha treated and entertained that youth with
all manner of delicious foods, and then sent him
away. And the youth came and told the girl,
and she said, 'Go again to-morrow and talk
with him, and when thou risest, do thou too invite
him; and be not jealous.' And the youth reflected and said in his heart, 'This Ghazanfer
Agha must be the friend of this girl; anyhow
we shall see; whatever God does He does well.'
In the morning he went and invited him, and
then came to the girl and gave her word and
said, 'Tell me and let me hear of the matters of
that night.' The girl answered, 'Now is not
the time; go and get these things which are
needful.' The youth went and got them and
brought them and gave her them and said, 'Lo,
I have brought them; tell me.' The girl said,
'Now is the guest coming, it cannot be; by and

bye I will tell thee.' When Ghazanfer Agha
came the youth gave the girl word and she said,
' Go and meet him, and lead him and bring him
here.' The youth said in his heart, ' This is
not without reason ; but wait, we shall see.'
And he led him respectfully, and he entered and
sat down with the girl. After that, came foods
and they ate and drank and made merry till the
evening. Then the girl sent word and the
youth came in, and she said, ' Take care, be it
not that thou lettest Ghazanfer Agha leave this
evening.' And the youth said, ' What is this of
thee that thou dost not dismiss him ?' The girl
answered, ' I will tell thee afterward.' The
youth said in his heart, ' I shall slay the two of
you this night.' And he went out. When it
was night Ghazanfer Agha asked leave to go
away, but the youth would not let him, and
Ghazanfer Agha saw that it was not to be, so
he remained ; and they brought out a clean
coverlet and mattress and made a bed for him.
And Ghazanfer Agha lay down, and the youth
lay down with the girl, but he slept not that he
might watch the girl. When it was midnight
the girl arose and the youth saw her, but he
made no sound, and the girl went up close to
Ghazanfer Agha. The youth, unable to endure it any longer, rose from his place and

P

said fiercely to the girl, 'What seekest thou
there?' The girl saw that the youth spake
angrily and she took him by the hand and drew
him to a place apart and said, 'I am about to
slay this Ghazanfer Agha.' The youth said,
'What is the reason of it?' The girl replied,
'The reason of it is this: I am the daughter of
the king of this land, and this youth was a
butcher's apprentice. One day, when going to
the bath, I met this youth selling meat upon
the road; as soon as I saw him I fell in love
with him, and the bird, my heart, was taken, so
that I was without rest and could not remain
quiet. I saw there was no help for it, so I got
him by force of money, and sometimes I went
to his house, and sometimes I had him brought
in disguise to my palace. One night I went in
disguise to his house, and I saw him sitting conversing with a gipsy harlot, and I got angry
and I cursed the two of them. This youth was
wont to use the dagger, and he gave me many
wounds, and thought me dead and put me in a
coffin and sent me with two men who laid me
in that tomb thou sawest. Praise be to God!
my time was not yet; thou didst come to me
like Khizr: now, do thou kill him.' The youth
said, 'I shall kill him. Wilt thou marry me
according to the Ordinance of God?' She

answered, ' I will not marry thee ; but the vezir
has a daughter fairer than I, her will I get for
thee.' Then the youth smote him and killed
him. The girl said, ' In the morning go to my
father and give him good news; and go to-night
and bring here all the possessions of this youth.'
The youth said, ' To-morrow thy father will
bring them.' When it was morning the youth
went and gave the good news to the king. And
the king sent slave-girls who brought the girl
to the palace. And her mother was glad when
she saw her safe and sound.* And they con-
fiscated the property of Ghazanfer Agha and
bestowed it on that youth. But what would
the youth do with the wealth ? his desire was
the girl. The king's vezirs said, ' My king, it
were right if thou give the girl to the youth.'
The king answered, ' It is my desire too ; for
when my daughter disappeared and we sought
but could not find her, I made a promise, saying,
that to him who brought good news of my
daughter I should give her; but the girl does
not wish it.' The vezirs said, ' My king, our
daughters are thine ; make this youth thy client;
whichever girl thou pleasest, give her to him.'

---

* The original is somewhat more explicit here : *Validesi
qizin muhrini teftish* **eyledi**, **chun** *muhrini muhrlu buldi, qizin
iki guzinden updi.*

The king said, ' I shall make a proposal ;' and
he went and spake with her mother. And the
girl's mother went to her and with difficulty
persuaded her ; and then sent word to the king.
That hour they performed the marriage cere-
mony, and the king made the youth a vezir ;
and they lived for a long time in joyance and
delight."

" O king, I have told this story for that thou
mayst know that thy son will not accept counsel,
but purposes for thy life. Because that cobbler
youth accepted the words of the saints he
attained to fortune ; and that butcher's apprentice, for that he was a fool, wounded his bene-
factress, the king's daughter; and if the girl had
not killed him, he would have made her disgraced
before the world. Do thou then, O king, take
profit by the tale ; beware, spare not this foolish
youth, but kill him; else thou shalt be repentant."
When the king heard this story from the lady
he said, " To-morrow will I kill him." And they
went to bed.

When it was morning and the sun had appeared,
like as appeared the kindness shown by the
king's daughter to the butcher's apprentice, and
the world was illumined with light, the king
passed and sat upon his throne, and he caused
the youth to be brought and commanded the

executioner, " Smite off his head." The Nine-
teenth Vezir came forward and said, " O king,
beware, hurry not in this matter, look to the
thought of the Hereafter and the way of the
Law. The Apostle (peace on him !) saith,
' God Most High maketh wise in the Truth him
to whom He wisheth to do good.' According to
this Sacred Tradition, what is befitting the king
is this, that he transgress not the bounds of God.
The truth is this, that in this matter the prince
is sinless. O king, when can one obtain a son ?
Slay not thy prince, or grief for thy son will be
full hard, and in the end thou shalt be unable
to endure it. There is a story suitable to this ;
if the king grant leave I will relate it." The
king said, " Relate it, let us hear." Quoth the
vezir,

THE NINETEENTH VEZIR'S STORY.

" Hasan of Basra* (the mercy of God on
him !) was in his first estate a seller of jewels.
One day he rose up to trade, and came before a
king and transacted business, and then he transacted business with the vezir. The vezir said,
' To-day we go to a pageant at a certain

---

* Hasan of Basra was a very pious and learned man. He
died in 110 (A.D. 728).

place ; wilt thou come with us ?' Hasan
answered, ' Yea, I shall go.' When the vezir
and the king had mounted their steeds, they
brought a horse for Hasan likewise, and they
all went out of the gate and came to a plain.
Hasan saw that in the middle of that plain was
a white pavilion, the dome of which reared its
head into the air.   Then they went up close to
that pavilion and all of them alighted.   From
another side came a procession of people ;
Hasan of Basra saw that it was a party of
doctors and holy men who were carrying their
lecterns and copies of the Sacred Volume.
They came and entered that pavilion and recited
the Koran with sweet voice ; then they came
and walked three times round that dome, and
then stood at the door and said, ' O prince,
what can we ? were there release to thy sweet
soul by reading of the Koran, we would, all of
us, cease not therefrom day or night ; but it is
the decree of that Almighty King ; there is no
avail for His command save acquiescence and
patience.' And they went away.   After them
came white-bearded elders and devotees reciting
chants, and they walked three times round that
dome, and then stood at the door and said, ' O
prince, what can we ? were there release to thy
sweet soul by chant and prayer, we would, all

of us, devote ourselves to chant and prayer ; but
what profit ? it is the decree of that Almighty
King ; there is no avail therefor save resignation.' And they went away. After them came
many moon-faced damsels, in the hand of each
of whom was a golden dish filled full of all
manner of jewels, and they walked three times
round that dome, and then stood at the door and
said, ' O prince, what can we ? were there
release to thy sweet soul by the giving of
riches, we would give all these jewels, and
we ourselves would become slaves ; but what
avail ? it is the decree of that Almighty
King, and He hath no need of such things ;
there is no help for His decree save patience.'
And they went away. After them came an
innumerable army which surrounded that dome,
rank on rank, and they said, 'O prince, were
there release to thy sweet soul by battle, night
and day would we, all of us, do battle in thy cause ;
but what avail ? it is the decree of that Almighty
King ; there is no help therefor but patience and
resignation.' And they went away. After them
came the king the father of that prince, and the
vezirs and the nobles, and they walked three times
round that dome, and then stood at the door, and
the king said, ' O light of my eyes, darling of
my heart, were there release to thy sweet soul

to be found by science, I had found it by means
of the learned ; or were it by gifts and bounties,
I had assembled all my army and made war and
attained it ; but what avail ? decree is God's. He
is in want of nought ; there is no help save
patience and acquiescence in His judgment.'
And he wept full bitterly, and all the nobles and
vezirs wept likewise. When Hasan of Basra saw
these things he asked the vezir, ' What plight is
this plight ? '   The vezir said, ' O Hasan, our
king had a son : he was in beauty a second
Joseph ; and in writing, reading, chivalry, and
all accomplishments he had no rival ; and as he
was the king's only child he loved him very
much.   One day Death spared him not, and he
passed to the Abiding Home. After the wailing
and dismay, as there was no help save patience
under the heavenly decree, they brought him
and buried him in this dome.   And once every
year they come and thus visit the tomb.' When
Hasan of Basra heard these words from the
vezir and saw these things with his eyes, wealth
and riches went forth from his eye and heart ;
and he abandoned the whole of them and turned
dervish and donned the khirqa * ; and now,
when his name is mentioned, they add, ' The
mercy of God on him ! ' " .

* The dervish's cloak.

" Now, O king, I have told this story for that
the king may know that grief for children is
full bitter.   As yet thou hast not felt it, and may
God Most High not show it thee thus through
him.   O king, slay not the prince, else afterward thou shalt be repentant and shalt sigh
and groan until thou die." And he made intercession for the prince for that day. When the
king heard this story from the vezir compassion
came into his heart, and he sent the youth to the
prison and went himself to the chase.

When it was evening the king returned from
the chase and came to the palace, and again the
lady rose to greet him, and she sat with the
king.   After the repast the lady asked for news
of the youth. The king said, "To-day likewise such an one of my vezirs made intercession
for him, and I have sent him again to the
prison." The lady said, "O king, why dost thou
leave my counsel and act according to thine
own understanding? Hast not thou heard these
words they have said concerning the heedless:
'Whoso is presumptuous through reason is
abased.' And the sages have said that eight
things bring disgrace upon a man: the first is
going to dine at a place without invitation,
the second is interfering between another and
his wife, the third is giving ear to every one's

words, the fourth is slighting the king, the fifth is setting one's self above a great man, the sixth is speaking to those who listen not to one's words, the seventh is begging a favour of an avaricious and indifferent person, and the eighth is going to the enemies' gate.   Now, O king, those vezirs interfere between thee and me. Beware, act not according to their words.   They have said that he who acts according to a stranger's word will divorce his wife.   Their words are many ; and they are forty vezirs, and each one of them for this long time is planning wiles.   Mayhap my king has not heard the story of the old gardener and his son."   The king said, " Tell on, let us hear."   Quoth the lady,

The Lady's Nineteenth Story.

" In the by-gone time an old gardener had mounted his son upon an ass and was proceeding to the garden, himself on foot.   They met some men who said, ' See this old pederast, how he has mounted the boy upon the ass ; and is himself running alongside.'   Whenever the old man heard this he made the boy alight and mounted himself.   Again they met some other folk, these likewise said, ' Look at this heartless old man, he rides the ass himself and makes the poor

child go on foot.' Whenever the old man heard
this he **took** his **son** up in **front of** him. Then
some **people saw them** and said, ' **See** this old
pederast, how he has **taken the boy up in front of**
him.' The old man **heard this,** and he **put his
son up** behind him. Again certain **folks** saw
them and **said,** ' See this old **catamite, how he**
has taken **the boy up behind him.' The old man**
knew not what to **do, so he** put his **son down**
and alighted **himself** and drove the **ass before**
them. **The garden was near, and both of them**
were on **foot, and** they reached the **garden**
before meeting **with any** others."

"Now, O king, I have told this story **that thou**
mayst know that no one in **the world can escape**
the tongue of the **folk.** Each **one says a**
different thing. **It is even as when a boil came**
out on the foot of a **certain king who showed it**
to **someone** and said, ' **Come, look at this boil ;
is** it ripe **or unripe ?** ' He looked **and said,** ' **It is
ripe.'** Then he showed **it to** another **person,**
and he said, ' **It is unripe.' Then the** king said,
' We cannot **get sure** information concerning
even one foot.' **Do thou too, O king,** go by no
one's **word,** lose **not the** opportunity ; **no** good
will come to thee from this youth." When the
king heard **this story from the lady he said,** " **To-**
morrow will **I kill him." And they went to bed.**

When it was morning the king came and sat upon his throne, and he caused the youth to be brought and ordered the executioner, " Smite off his head." The Twentieth Vezir came forward and said, " O king of the world, I will speak a good word to thee : all these vezirs who have spoken these many words are well-wishers to thee. The Holy Apostle of God hath said, ' Whoso hath believed in God and the Last Day ; when he witnesseth to aught, let him speak with good or let him be silent.' Now, what is best for thee in this thy affair is this, as all thy vezirs say, ' Slay not the prince,' I too say, have patience, else the end of this will be care and sorrow. Mayhap the king has not heard the story of a certain king." The king said, " Tell on, let us hear." Quoth the vezir,

The Twentieth Vezir's Story.

" Of old time there was a great king. One day, when returning from the chase, he saw a dervish sitting by the way, crying, ' I have a piece of advice ; to him who will give me a thousand sequins I will tell it.' When the king heard these words of the dervish he drew in his horse's head and halted, and he said to the dervish, ' What is thy counsel ?' The dervish replied, ' Bring the sequins and give me them

that I may tell my counsel.' The king ordered
that they counted a thousand sequins into the
dervish's lap. The dervish said, 'O king, my
advice to thee is this, whenever thou art about
to do a deed, consider the end of that deed, and
then act.' The nobles who were present
laughed together at these words and said, 'Anyone knows that.' But the king rewarded that
poor man. He was greatly pleased with the
words of the dervish and commanded that they
wrote them on the palace gate and other places.
Now that king had an enemy, a great king; and
this hostile king was ever watching his opportunity; but he could find no way save this, he
said in himself, 'Let me go and promise the
king's barber some worldly good and give him a
poisoned lancet; some day when the king is sick
he can bleed him with that lancet.' So he
disguised himself, and went and gave the
barber a poisoned lancet and ten thousand
sequins. And the barber was covetous and
undertook to bleed the king with that lancet
what time it should be needful. One day the
king was sick, and he sent word to the barber to
come and bleed him. Thereupon the barber
took that poisoned lancet with him and went.
The attendants prepared the basin, and the
barber saw written on the rim of the basin,

'Whenever thou art about to perform a deed, think on the end thereof.' When the barber saw this he said in himself, ' I am now about to bleed the king with this lancet and doubtless he will perish, then they will not leave me alive, but will inevitably kill me ; after I am dead what use will these sequins be to me?' And he took up that lancet and put it in its place and drew out another lancet that he might bleed the king. When he took his arm a second time, the king said, ' Why didst thou not bleed me with the first lancet ?' The barber answered, ' O king, there was some dust on its point.' Then the king said, ' I saw it, it is not the treasury lancet ; there is some secret here, quick, tell it, else I will slay thee.' When the barber saw this importunity, he related the story from beginning to end and how he had seen the writing on the basin and changed his intention. The king put a robe of honour on the barber and let him keep the sequins which his enemy had given him. And the king said, ' The dervish's counsel is worth not one thousand sequins but a hundred thousand sequins.' "

" Now, O king, I have told this story for that the king may know that it is as when the dervish said, ' Whatsoever deed thou doest, consider the end thereof, then act.' If thou slay the prince, at last thou shalt be repentant. The rest the king knows." And he made intercession for the prince. When the king heard these words from the vezir he sent the prince to the prison and himself mounted for the chase.

When it was evening the king returned from the chase and came to the palace, and the lady rose to greet him, and they sat down. After the repast the lady again asked for news of the youth. The king said, " To-day such an one of my vezirs made intercession for him and I sent him to the prison." The lady said, " O king, it is related of the Khalif Ma'mūn* that he said, ' Four things are hurtful to kings ; the first is the nobles being negligent, the second is the ministers being envious, the third is the mean being bold, and the fourth is the vezirs being treacherous.' And the Moorish sages say, ' In nobles there is no friendship, in liars there is no fidelity, in the envious there is no peace, in the indifferent there is no generosity, and in the evil-natured there is no greatness.' .O king, these thy vezirs are, like thy traitor son, liars and evil-natured. Thou believest the words of these. The story of thee and this youth altogether resembles the story of those

---

* El-Ma'mūn, the son of Hārūn-er-Rashīd, was proclaimed khalif in 198 (A.D. 813) ; he died in 218 (A.D. 833).

Turkman children." The king said, " Tell
that story, let us hear it." Quoth the lady,

The Lady's Twentieth Story.

" Certain Turkmans from an encampment
went one day into a city. When they were
returning from the city to the encampment they
were an hungered, and when they were come
near they ate some bread and onions at a
spring-head. The juice of the onions went
into the Turkmans' eyes, and the tears came
forth from their eyes. Now the children of the
Turkmans had gone out to meet them, and they
saw that the tears were streaming from their
fathers' eyes and they thought that some one of
them had died in the city. So without asking
and without knowing, they ran back and came
to the encampment and said to their mothers,
' One of ours is dead in the city, our fathers are
coming weeping.' All the women and children
of that encampment came forth to meet them,
weeping together. The Turkmans who were
coming from the city thought that one of theirs
had died in the encampment ; so were they without knowledge one of the other, and they raised
a weeping and crying together such that it cannot be described. At length the elders of the
camp stood up in the midst and said, 'May all

ye remain whole ; the command is God's, there
is none other help than patience.' And they
questioned them. The Turkmans who were
coming from the city asked, 'Who is dead in
the encampment?' The others said, 'No one
is dead in the encampment; who has died in
the city?' Those coming from the city answered, 'No one has died in the city.' They
said, 'Then for whom are we wailing and
lamenting?' At length they perceived that all
this tumult arose from their thus trusting the
words of children."

"Now, O king, I have told this story for
that the king may know that confusion like to
that is brought about by youths. What I know
is this, if thou slay not the youth he will slay
thee." When the king heard these words from
the lady he said, "To-morrow will I kill him."
And they went to bed.

When it was morning the king came and sat
upon his throne, and he caused the youth to be
brought and ordered the executioner, "Smite off
his head." The Twenty-First Vezir came forward and said, "O king of the world, yesterday,
when reading in a book, I saw that they had
written that there was a great king in the land
of Hindustan, and in his time there was a work
on wisdom; and they laded three camels with

Q

it and brought it to him. One day the king said to the sages, ' Abridge this book for me, that I may study it.' Then all the sages of Hind came together and collected the necessary words from that work and made a book. When the king read it he was pleased. And the words that they wrote were these: ' O king, be not presumptuous, being deceived by the world; for the world showeth itself like a fair woman and fondleth men in its bosom ; and when they are asleep and heedless, of a sudden it woundeth and slayeth them. Knowing of a surety that it is thus, have care if it offer itself to thee, that thou keep thyself from it, so that thou be prosperous. And expend what thou gainest of wealth in the way of God Most High, and guard against iniquity, and show forth thy name through generosity, and abandon avarice. O king, the light of the world is darkness, and its newness is oldness, and its being is non-being. O king, strive that thou save thyself from it ; and incline not to the amassing of unlawful wealth, for it will pass from thy hand and be a woe to thee. Strive to collect wealth lawfully, and expend it on good works, and show thyself just among the folk to the utmost of thy power, that all the people of the world may love thee, and that thou be secured against the punishment of God Most High. And guard thy Faith for the Hereafter. And love not women and tell not them thy secrets. O king, be not deceived by womankind; for in body are they weak, but in guile are they strong.' Now, O king, these counsels are exceeding good counsels, and it behoves the king to keep them; and their saying is true that women are weak in body but strong in guile. Mayhap the king has not heard what befell a certain king with a woman." The king said, "Relate it, let us hear." Quoth the vezir,

THE TWENTY-FIRST VEZIR'S STORY.

"There was in the palace of the world a great king, and he had a beautiful wife, such that many a soul dangled in the tresses on her cheek. That lady had a secret affair with a youth, and she used to hide the youth in a chest in the palace. One day that youth said to the lady, 'If the king were aware of this our work, he would slay the two of us.' The lady said, 'Leave that thought, I can do so that I shall hide thee in the chest and say to the king, "Lo, my lover is lying in this chest;" and then, when the king is about to kill thee, I shall make him repentant by one word.' While the youth and the lady were saying these words, the king came, and the lady straightway put the youth into the chest and locked it. The king said, 'Why lockest thou that chest thus hastily? What is in the chest?' The lady answered, 'By God, it is my lover; I saw thee coming and I put him into the chest and locked it.' Then was the king wroth, and he bared his sword and thought to slay him who was in the chest, when the lady said, 'O king, art thou mad, where is gone thine understanding? Am I mad that I should advance a strange man to thy couch and then say to thee, "Lo, he is in the chest?" In truth, I wondered if thou were sincere in thy trust of me, and I tried thee, and now I know that thou thinkest evil concerning me.' And she ceased and sat in a corner. Then did the king repent him of what he had done; and he begged and besought of his wife, saying, 'Forgive me.' And he gave her many things, and craved pardon for his fault. When the king had gone out from the harem into the palace the lady took that youth forth of the chest and said, 'Didst thou see what a trick I played the king?' And they gave themselves up to mirth and merriment."

"Now, O king, I have told this story for that the king may know that guile and trickery such as this abound in women. O king, be-

ware, slay not the prince on the woman's word,
else afterward thou shalt be repentant, and
too late repentance profits not." And he made
intercession for the prince for that day. When
the king heard this story from the vezir he
sent the prince to the prison and himself
mounted for the chase.

When it was evening the king returned from
the chase and came to the palace, and the lady
rose to greet him, and they sat down. After
the repast the lady again began to speak about
the youth. The king said, "To-day too such an
one of my vezirs made intercession for him and
I sent him to the prison." The lady said, "O
king, this youth is ignoble. It is even as when
God Most High told Noah (peace on him!) of
the impurity of his son : said God Most High,
'He is not of thy family ; verily, it is a work
that is not right.' * Then it is known that if a
person follow not the way of his father, and be
not endowed with the nature of his father,
he cannot be called a lawful son. Therefore, when the wise see a fault in others they
hinder and cover it, and if they see that fault in
themselves they strive to banish it far from
them. There is no help for the ignoble that he

---

* Koran, xi. 48.

should follow the path of the noble. Mayhap the king has not heard the story of a certain abdal and a king." The king said, " Tell on, let us hear." Quoth the lady,

THE LADY'S TWENTY-FIRST STORY.

" There was of old time a great king, and there was by him an abdal. One day the king mounted for the chase, and the abdal said, 'O king, I am able for soldiering and hunting ; give me too horse and gear and bird, that I may go forth with thee to ride about and hunt.' So the king gave the abdal a horse and gear, and gave him a falcon on his wrist, and took him along with him to the chase, and they went off. While they were riding, the king saw a bird go into a bush, and he said to the abdal, ' Go, cast the falcon at the bird.' And the king stood to look on. The abdal went up close to the bush with the falcon, and a man stirred the bush, and the bird came out and flew off. The king said to the abdal, ' The bird is away, throw off the falcon.' And the abdal threw off the falcon from his wrist without slipping the leash, and he swung it round and round his head. The king shouted, ' Out on thee ! throw off the falcon !' The abdal said, ' O king, I have thrown it off, what am I to do ?'

But he left not to swing the falcon round his head. The king shouted, 'Out on thee! let the falcon go!' And the abdal let go the leash; but the falcon's eyes were darkened from its having been turned round, and it could not fly, and fell to the ground. And the king was angry and ill-pleased. Then the abdal said, 'O king, wherefore art thou angry? thou saidest, "Throw off the falcon," and I threw it off; then thou saidest, "Let it go," and I let it go; this falcon knows not how to fly: what fault is mine?' These words of the abdal were pleasant to the king and he fainted from laughing; and he perceived how no good comes from anything ignoble." *

"Now, O king, I have told this story for that the king may know that no good comes from the ignoble man who follows not the path of his father and mother. Beware, O king, be not negligent in the affair of this youth, or in the end some hurt will befall thee from him; the rest thou knowest." When the king heard this story from the lady he said, "On the morrow will I kill the youth." And they went to bed.

---

* The point of this story is lost in the translation. To let fly a falcon at game, is, in Turkish, to swing a falcon; the king says to the abdal, "Swing the falcon," meaning, let it fly at the bird; but the abdal understands him literally, and swings the falcon round his head.

When it was morning the king came and sat upon his throne, and he caused the youth to be brought and commanded the executioner, "Smite off his head." The Twenty-Second Vezir came forward and said, "O king of the world, the Holy Apostle of God (God Most High bless and save him!) hath said, 'Verily, God is with the prince so long as he acteth justly; but when he oppresseth, He maketh him over to his lust, then He letteth loose upon him Satan.' And the Apostle (peace on him!) hath likewise said, 'O ye: and tyranny, verily, it ruineth your hearts.' Now, O king, in compliance with these Traditions guard thee well against tyranny. A man does many deeds which he knows not to be tyranny till on the Resurrection-Day they appear before him like mountains, and he shall repent, crying, 'Woe! Alas!' Perchance in this world heedlessness may have bound up his eyes so that he has not seen it; even as they have said in this couplet:

> At length, when the dust clears away, thou shalt see
> If horse 'tis, or ass, that is ridden by thee.

Now, O king, there is a fable for this, the story of a king who would not believe until he saw the Gathering and the Resurrection in a vision." The king said, "Tell that story, let me hear it." Quoth the vezir,

THE TWENTY-SECOND VEZIR'S STORY.

" There was of old time a great king, and he
had a fair son, such that those who looked on
his face were bewildered and confounded, and
many persons were known to have love of him.
By reason thereof the prince went about with a
veil ; and whensoever he went to walk sergeants
would scatter the folk who were within eye-
shot, and in that way they shed the guiltless
blood of many lovers and cast them like moths
into the flame. And the king's headsman
would march alongside the prince, and whoso
looked at the prince and sighed or looked long
at his face, him they killed without mercy.
Now there was an abdal who loved the prince
from his heart, and every time the prince went
out to walk the abdal would run before him.
They cried to the abdal, 'Stop! go not!' and
they would ever strike him and say, ' We will
kill thee.'   But the abdal heeded not ; and they
slew him not, saying, ' He is a dervish.'   One
day in the week the prince went out into the
square and played ball on horseback ; and he
rode so swiftly that the beholders were amazed.
And the folk stood rank on rank at the distance
of a bowshot from the square and looked at the

prince playing with ball and mall, and wondered
at his fleetness and beauty. That abdal
entered the square and rolled like a ball in
front of the prince's horse, and they cursed him
and beat him, but he would not go away. They
told the king of this matter, and the king
said, 'Hang ye him.' Now the king's vezir
was present there, and he said, 'Thou hast spilt
this much blood unjustly ; to-morrow, on the
Resurrection-Day, when God Most High is
Judge and asks thee of these sins, what answer
wilt thou give ?' Quoth the king, ' O vezir,
who knows ? who has gone thither and seen
with his eyes and come back ? It is but a
word that they say and then cease.' And he
denied the Resurrection. And he laid his head
upon his pillow and slept, and forthwith he saw
in his dream that the Resurrection was come,
and the Bridge of Es-Sirāt* was raised, and the
gates of Paradise were opened, and the fires of
Hell were burning and were become red-hot,
and mankind was in troops, some of which they
led to Paradise and some to Hell. And they
of Paradise were in Paradise with the houris

---

* Es-Sirāt = 'The Path.' The allegorical Bridge by which
admittance is gained to Heaven is so called ; the Path, of course,
being the True Faith and the righteous life that it demands ;
but here taken as a literal bridge.

and the youths in the midst of gardens, and in
their hands was pure wine, and on the banks of
streams ripened all manner of fruits, and whatsoever fruit a man desired, a branch thereof came
and bent before him, and he took it, and a fruit
grew at the place where he was about to eat, and
the damsels and youths of Paradise left not to
give them of the wines of Paradise ; and the
king saw them of Paradise rejoicing in this
fashion. And the demons laid hold of them of
Hell and threw them into boiling pitch and
tormented them so that it cannot be described,
and their wailing and lamenting rose to the
Empyrean. Their hearts were on fire, and
when they besought a draught of water, in
place of water they gave them of the zaqqûm,*
which when they swallowed, all their entrails and
the flesh of their faces were torn in pieces; and
the king saw them tormented in this fashion, and
would have fled from himself by reason of his
fear. Then they brought the king too into the
presence of God Most High and they weighed
his good deeds and his sins, and his good deeds
showed little and his sins much ; and they sent
him to Hell. While the king was going to

---

* Ez-zaqqûm is the name of a foreign tree with a very bitter
fruit, and is metaphorically used in the Koran to denote the
food of the wicked in Hell.

Hell, a voice cried behind him, ‘ If in the world thou had had compassion on those that loved Us, would We now have had mercy upon thee.’ When they took the king to Hell a demon came before him and laid hold of the king and said, ‘Art not thou he who denied Heaven and Hell, and would not believe ?’ And he plunged him into a cauldron of pitch, so that the king thought they flayed him, and with the pain thereof he awoke. The vezir was by him, and the king told him one by one all these signs which he had seen, and said, ‘Quick, go fetch that abdal.’ And he sent the prince too after him. Now when the executioners brought the hapless abdal to the gallows he said, ‘ For the love of God give me a moment's grace that I may make the ablution and perform the two-bow prayer ; then whatsoever ye will do, do.’ So they gave him grace, and he made a fair ablution and performed the two-bow prayer, and he rubbed his face upon the ground and said, ‘My God, Thou art the Knower of the Unseen ; I am without sin in this matter ; needful was it either not to have given the king's son this much fair beauty, or not to have given me this love. Now Thou hast given to the prince fair beauty and to me love ; and lo, they are about to slay me for that I love the

beauty Thou **hast** created. O my God, **free-**
will placed **not** the love of the prince in me ;
at least show me once again his fair beauty,
then take my soul.' **And the** abdal rubbed his
face **in** the dust **and** prayed at the **Court of**
God (glorified and exalted be He !) While he
was in this plight the vezir **and the** prince
arrived, and when the vezir saw **the** dervish in
such case he pitied him and said **to** the prince,
' Go, raise the **captive** of the love **of** thee from
the earth, and take his head upon thy knee,
and **with** thy handkerchief wipe the tears **from**
his **eyes** and the dust **from** his face.' Then the
prince dismounted **from his horse** and took the
abdal's head upon his knee, and, saying, ' **Weep**
not, abdal,' **he** wiped with his handkerchief the
tears from his eyes and **the** dust **from** his face.
When the abdal looked **on the** face of him **who**
was wiping away his tears and saw that he was
the prince, he sighed once and groaned and gave
up his soul to God. Then the vezir and the
prince marvelled at this thing, and they told
the king. And when the king heard their words,
exceeding great pity came upon him, and he
attended the funeral of the abdal and buried him
by the side of his **own** tomb, and he wrote this
upon the stone : ' This **is a** martyr of love : he
died for love of us, **so he is of us.'** Thereafter

the king said nothing to the lovers of his son the
prince ; and the prince began to deal kindly with
those who were captives of the love of him."

" O king, I have told this story for that the
king may know that there will be a going
before God Most High with neck bound like a
prisoner, and may reflect and guard against
tyranny ; and that he may know that whoso
does good deeds shall enjoy eternal delight in
Paradise, and that whoso does evil deeds shall
go to Hell ; and that he may act accordingly.
For the life of this world is but as an hour ;
dispossess not thyself of eternal delight for the
sake of an hour. It is even as saith the
Apostle (peace on him !), ' The world is an
hour ; pass it in worship.' " And he kissed the
ground and made intercession for the prince.
When the king heard this story from the vezir
he sent the prince to the prison and went himself to the chase.

When it was evening the king returned from
the chase and came to the palace, and the lady
rose to greet him, and she sat with the king.
After the repast the lady asked for news of the
youth. The king said, " To-day too such an
one of my vezirs made intercession for him and
I sent him to the prison." The lady said,
" Well have they said that Fortune must be

blamed, but the fault must not be blamed. It is even as they have said :

> 'We ever blame our fortune, yet the blame with us doth lie ;
> It is not from our fortune—the blame that comes us nigh.'

Now, O king, the signs of good are not in thy vezirs ; their works are ever evil and treachery, and they are men of pride and avarice and envy. And the treachery they work against thee doth not suffice them, by me too they deal treacherously, and they envy me ; for they see that if the king were to follow my words and slay the youth, I should be honoured before the king, and that by reason of my truthfulness the king would ever take counsel of me, and that they would remain unhonoured ; therefore do they envy me. O king, God Most High doth bring things right. Mayhap the king has not heard the story of the courtier of a certain king." The king said, "Tell on, let us hear." Quoth the lady,

THE LADY'S TWENTY-SECOND STORY.

" There was of old time a great king, and there was one by him who ever said, 'O king, whatsoever thou doest, thou doest for thyself ; be it good or be it evil.' And the king loved him much, and he ever grew in esteem before the king. Now one day one of the envious

went before the king and said, 'O king, thou
thus much honourest and favourest such an one,
but he is an ingrate toward the king; he says
(God forefend the listeners!) that the king has
the disease of leprosy.   If the king believe me
not, let him call him to-morrow, and when he
comes near the king's breath, let him see how
he avoids the king.'   When it was morning
that envious man cooked a Tartar pie seasoned
with garlic; and he went and found that man
and took him to his house and set before him
that Tartar pie seasoned with garlic, and sundry
other foods all seasoned with garlic.   They ate
together and afterward went to the king's
divan.   The envious man said to the courtier,
'If the king speak to thee a word in private,
take care that thou let him not perceive the
smell of the garlic; for the king likes it not.
And if he call thee to his side, hold thy sleeve
to thy mouth that the smell come not forth
from thy mouth.'   Then they went and stood
in the divan, and the king beckoned to the
courtier, and called him to him, and said, 'Come,
I have somewhat to whisper in thine ear.'
When the courtier came near the king, he held
his sleeve to his mouth and stood a little way
off that the smell might not reach the king.
The king said in his heart, 'What they said

about this **man** is **then** true.' As for the
courtier, **he said in his** heart, 'God grant the
smell **of** the garlic **may not reach** the king.'
So **they** were both **of them without** knowledge
one of the other. **Thereupon** the king wrote an
order and gave it into the hand of that courtier
and said, '**Take** this note and carry **it to the**
chief magistrate, **and** keep whatever gift **he**
bestows on thee.' So the courtier took **the**
note and **went out; when he** met that **envious**
man. **The** envious man asked, 'Whither goest
thou ?' **The** courtier answered, ' The king
gave **me a** note **and said,** "Go take it to the
chief magistrate and keep whatever gift he
bestows on thee."' Quoth that envious man,
'**Thou** wilt always merit the king's favours ;
but he never asks **for us ;** do thou at least give
me this note ; and shall **not it be that we will**
recompense thee ?' **So the** courtier reflected
and said in himself, 'This **man** gave us **a**
dinner, doubtless he looks **for** something from
us.' And **he** presented **that** envious man with
the note and said, 'Take this note and go to
the chief magistrate and to thy luck.' The
envious man took **the** note and went to the
chief **magistrate, and the** latter took the note
and read **it. And the** king had written, 'Seize
him who gives this **note into thy** hand, and

R

spare him not, but flay him alive and stuff his
skin with grass and set it up on my road, that
when I pass now I may see it there.'   Straightway the chief magistrate commanded his
servants, 'Seize this wretch and slay him.'
Then the envious man saw how the matter was
and he began to cry out, 'The king did not
give this note to me, he gave it to another man;
I am come by mistake.'   But it was no avail;
the servants flayed him alive and stuffed his
skin with grass and set it up on the king's road.
An hour afterward the king disguised himself
and went out, and as he was walking he came
there, and he saw that it was not the skin of
the courtier as he had commanded, but that of
the man who had defamed the courtier to him.
Thereupon he wondered and passed on, and he
ordered them to bring the courtier; and they
straightway found him and brought him.   The
king said, 'I called thee to my side this day
and desired to say somewhat in thine ear, and
thou didst hold thy sleeve to thy mouth and
didst stand a little way off; what was the
reason?'   The courtier answered, 'Such and
such a noble had made a feast for me and
given me to eat food seasoned with garlic; and
I covered my mouth with my sleeve and stood
a little way off lest the smell might annoy thee.'

Then was he silent. The king said, 'What didst thou with that note I gave thee?' The courtier replied, 'O king, when I took that note and went out I met that man, and he questioned me, and I said that it was a letter with a gift for an answer from my king to the chief magistrate. And that man begged it of me much, and I was ashamed by reason of the garlic feast, and gave it him; if thou believe not, let him be brought, and ask him.' When the king heard these words from the courtier he said, 'Whatsoever a person does he does for himself; true then is their saying, "The wicked has found his due." Go thou and be at ease.'"

"Now, O king, I have told this story for that the king may know that they thus envy every hapless one, but I take refuge in God Most High. Lo, thou shalt see how God Most High will tread them under foot. Ah, beware, O king, be not heedless of the youth; for they have said that the heedless head looks well at the cantle." * When the king heard this tale from the lady he said, "To-morrow will I slay him." And they went to bed.

When it was morning the king came and sat

---

* *i.e.* When it is cut off and fastened by the enemy to his saddle.

upon his throne, and he caused the executioner
to bring the youth and commanded him,
" Smite off his head." The Twenty-Third
Vezir came forward and said, " O king of the
world, the Holy Apostle (peace on him!) hath
said, ' One hour of doing justice is better than
the worship of seventy years, and one hour of
acting cruelly undoeth the worship of seventy
years.' O king, despise not the Law, that on
the Resurrection-Day thou mayst be of the
host of the just kings. And countenance not
women, for in them guile and craft abound.
Mayhap the king has not heard the story of
that khoja and his son." The king said, " Tell
on, let us hear." Quoth the vezir,

The Twenty-Third Vezir's Story.

" There was of old time a great merchant,
and he had a son. One day he took his son
and went to a house and said, ' O son, I have a
charge to thee.' The youth said, ' On head and
eye!' * The khoja continued, ' O son, after I
am dead, if thou waste not the wealth I leave,
so long as thou livest thou shalt enjoy happiness
and delight with heart at ease ; but if thou
waste it, see that thou go not and beg of any-

---

* *i.e.* I am ready to obey.

one, but get a rope and hang thyself from this wooden ring.' The youth swore to obey. After a time the merchant was received into Mercy. And the youth in a short time wasted the wealth with flatterers, and he stood in need of a red florin. First of all, the flatterers turned from him, and whenever they saw him they said, 'Fool!' and reviled him. At last the youth grew weary of life, and one day, while he was sitting idle, his father's charge came into his mind. Thereupon he went and got a rope and came and entered that house, and he fastened one end of the rope to the wooden ring his father had spoken of, and tied the other end round his neck, and he had put a stool under his feet, and he threw himself from that stool. When he did this, the ring gave way and a piece of the boarding came down and the youth fell to the ground. Now that place had been filled full of gold and jewels, and these poured down. Then the youth knew that his father's charge to hang himself was because of this wealth. So he gathered together his senses and repented of what he had done, and he again devoted himself to commerce. One day he meant to go out into the plain, and he went forth from the city, and while he was going along he met with a snake-charmer, who

had gathered a number of snakes, and was
playing. Now among these was a white snake,
very gentle and sad ; and he bought that
snake, and got from the man the charm that the
snake might do him no hurt. And he took it
to his house, and he would ever divert himself
with it. One day that snake shook itself and
became a fair girl ; and when the youth saw
this he wondered and asked of the girl, 'What
is this plight ?' The girl answered, 'I am
the king's daughter of the jinn ; in the early
spring, while I was wandering about in the
meadows, that snake-charmer met me and pronounced a spell over me and blew upon me,
and I had no power to move or resume my
original form. Now is that snake-charmer
dead, and his magic is impotent ; and I have
resumed my own form. Come, take me to my
city and sell me to my father and mother. If
they say to thee, " What price shall we give
thee ?" ask for the Chinese mirror. They will
offer thee something else ; but say thou to
them, " If ye will give me that mirror, there is
your daughter, take her ; if not, lo, I shall go
away." And they will of necessity give thee
that mirror and take me from thee.' The youth
said, 'What is the virtue of that mirror ?' The
girl answered, 'Its virtue is this, that if thou

take that mirror in thy hand and say, " O
mirror, by the Names of God that are upon
thee, take me to such and such a place;" and
shut thine eyes, thou wilt find thyself in that
place when thou openest them.' Then the girl
said to the youth, ' Shut thine eyes;' and after
a time she said, ' Open thine eyes;' and he
opened them and saw himself upon a mountain.
In the plain below that mountain he saw a
mighty city, the pinnacles of the towers and
battlements whereof were even with the clouds;
and when the youth saw the city he marvelled.
Then the youth and the girl went to that city,
and he sent the girl to her mother. When
the girl's mother saw her she began to weep
and asked of her circumstances; and the girl
related the whole of them one by one. Then
the mother wished to take the girl and go to
their house, but the girl said, ' I promised the
youth, saying, " Take me to my mother, and
she will buy me from thee for a price;" if I
now go with thee, the youth will be displeased.'
The girl's mother asked the youth, ' O youth,
what wishest thou for this girl?' The youth
answered, ' I wish the Chinese mirror.' The
woman went and said to the girl's father, ' A
youth has brought our daughter; but he wishes
the mirror as her price.' Thereupon the father

took the mirror and came, and he gave it to the youth and took the girl. The youth said, ' O mirror, by the Names of God that are upon thee, take me to my own house.' And he shut his eyes; and when he opened them again he found himself in his own house. Now the king of that land had a fair daughter, and this youth had fallen in love with her without having seen her, having heard of her beauty. One night he took down the mirror and gave the oath and said, ' Take me before the king's daughter;' and he closed his eyes. He opened them again and found himself before the girl. They saluted each other, and the girl said, ' My father will find out, and he will spare nor thee nor me.' The youth answered, ' Shut thine eyes, I will send thee away.' Quoth the girl, ' Do thou too come with me.' Thereupon they both shut their eyes, and he gave the oath to the mirror, and they found themselves upon the bed in the girl's room. The girl said, ' Who art thou ? ' The youth told her that he was a merchant's son. After some time the girl said, 'Let us go to thy house.' Thereupon they gave the oath to the mirror and shut their eyes and they found themselves in the youth's house; and they made merry in that house. When it was morning the girl's father was told that she **had** disappeared, and for **a** time, sighing and lamenting, he searched **all** about and around, **but found her not.** After a time, he found some crafty witches, **and** related the affair to them **and sent** them in every direction; and each one of them devoted herself to search and quest in **a** different **quarter. Now** one of the witches came to the city where **the** girl was, and **while** she was going through **all** the **houses** and examining them, **of a** sudden **she** looked **from a** window and saw the girl, **and she knew her to be the** king's daughter. When **it** was night she entered that house through her **magic** power; **now the** youth **had** hung up the **Chinese** mirror on the **wall, she saw it and knew** its virtue through **her magic power, and she** took it and went **to the girl's** side **and gave** the oath **to** the Chinese mirror **and said,** 'Quick, take me **and** this girl **to the** king's palace.' **As to** the youth, **he** was asleep. **The** sorceress shut her eyes and opened them again and **found** herself **and the** girl in the palace; and she gave **the girl** and the mirror to the king. The king **placed the** mirror **in his** treasury and sent the **girl to the harem, and he** sent those witches as spies **to seize the youth. We go to the youth:** When **it was morning he arose** from sleep and found **not the girl by his** side, and the mirror

too was not in its place, and he said in himself,
' This trick cannot be the girl's; for she herself
desired me; it must be that a witch has come
from her father and done these deeds.'   Having
no other resource, sighing and wailing, he set out
for the city.   One day he entered the city, and
one of the witches, while prowling about spying,
met him.   Thereupon she ran to the king and
informed him.   And the king sent men who
found the youth and seized him, and brought
him into the presence of the king.   The king
said, ' Out on thee, degenerate youth, what
work is this work thou hast done?   I am a
king, and thou doest so by me; I will slay thee
with a torment such that thou shalt be an
example.'   Now the king had a deep pit, and
he used to put those with whom he was very
wroth into that deep pit, so that at length they
perished therein.   Then he commanded that
they should imprison him in that pit, and give
him no bread, that he might perish of hunger
therein.   Now the youth had a little cat and a
little dog; and these had come with him.
And when the men were gone the little dog
scraped and scraped till he made a hole, and
the little cat went down through that hole and
came before the youth.   Now the inside of
that pit was all full of mice, so that they ate up

the men who fell therein. As soon as they
saw the youth they rushed upon him, and the
little cat saw this thing, and it straightway slew
some of them. The mice saw that the cat
gave them no mercy, but killed them, and they
could not resist and took to flight ; and not a
mouse did dare so much as show its head out
of its hole. Then the mice informed their
nobles of these things, and the nobles said,
' Go and ask, and give that man whatever he
wants that he may take away that brute from
over us.' The mice came and said so to the
youth; and by command of the youth they dug
a tunnel, large enough for a man to pass
through, up to the king's palace. Then they
told the youth, and he arose and went to the
palace and found the girl and asked for the
mirror. The girl told him it was in the treasury; then he ordered the mice that they opened
a tunnel to the treasury also; and the youth went
in and took the mirror and came back to the
girl, and they went to his country. Early on
the morrow the slave-girls looked and saw not
the girl, and they told their lady ; and the lady
sent word to the king. The king forthwith
called the witches and said, ' In the evening the
youth again stole the mirror and my daughter
and is fled ; go, and where ye find him this

time, there slay him, and bring me my daughter and the mirror.' The witches hastened and found the youth and slew him; and they took the girl and the mirror and brought them and made them over to the king. So that in the end that youth lost his life through women."

"Now, O king, I have told this story for that the king may know that sorcery and witchcraft like to this abound in women. Beware, go not by the woman's word, slay not the prince who is fair even as the moon, that afterward thou suffer not regret and remorse." And he kissed the ground and made intercession for the prince. When the king heard this story from the vezir he sent the prince to the prison and himself mounted for the chase.

When it was evening the king returned from the chase and came to the palace, and the lady rose to greet him, and they sat down. After the repast the lady again began to speak about the youth. The king said, "To-day too such an one of my vezirs made intercession for him, and I sent him to the prison." The lady said, "O king, dost thou know that this youth will slay thee, for he has learned craft from his master, and with craft and magic he will bind thy mouth and tongue, and ever watch his opportunity; and thy affair will be like the story of

the geomancer and his apprentice ; mayhap my
king has not heard **it.**" The king said, " Tell
on, let **us** hear." **Quoth the** lady,

THE LADY'S TWENTY-THIRD STORY.

" **It** is related, that there was a **woman in the**
city of Cairo, and that woman **had a** worthless
son, who, no matter **to** what trade **she put** him,
did no good. One day the woman said to **the**
youth, ' My son, what trade shall I give thee ? '
The youth replied, ' Take me along with thee,
let us go ; and whatever trade I like, to that **do**
thou give me.' And that woman and her son
went to the bazaar, and while they **were** walking
about they saw a geomancer, and the youth observed that geomancer and liked **him.** There-
upon the woman made him over to him, and **the**
geomancer took **the** youth **and** began **to show**
him the principles of geomancy. After some
days the master said **to the** youth, ' To-morrow
I will become a ram ; sell me, but take heed and
give **not my** rope.' The youth said, ' Very good.'
The master became a ram, and the youth took
him and **led** him **to** the bazaar **and** sold him for
a thousand aspres ; **but** he gave not the rope,
but took it away with him, and returned. When
it was evening his master appeared. After some
days the **master** said, ' Now, youth, to-morrow

I will become a horse ; take and sell me, but
take heed and give not my headstall.' And he
became a horse, and the youth took him and
sold him but gave not the headstall ; and he
took the money and went to his own house.
When it was evening his master came to his
house and saw the youth was not there, and he
said, ' He will come in the morning,' and went
to bed. On the other hand, the youth went to
his mother and said, ' O mother, to-morrow I
will become a dove ; sell me, but take heed and
give not my key.' And he became a dove without peer ; and the woman put the dove up to
auction, and the bidders began to raise their
bids at the rate of five piastres. But this dove
which spake in the language of the people of
that city acquired such fame as cannot be described. Now as every one was speaking of
the qualities of this dove, his master heard and
came, and as soon as he saw him he knew him
to be the youth, and he said, ' Out on thee, mis-
begotten wretch, thou doest a deed like this and
I whole, now see what I will do to thee.' And
he went and bought him from the woman. The
woman said, ' I will not give the key.' Quoth
the master, ' Take fifty piastres more, and go
and buy another key such as thou pleasest.'
And he gave her the whole sum ; and the woman

was greedy and took it, and drew the key **from**
her girdle **and threw it on the** ground. As soon
as the key fell, it became a pigeon and began to
fly, and the master became **a** hawk and pursued
the pigeon. While these were flying along, the
king was seated in the plain taking his pleasure ;
and the youth looked and saw **no** escape, **and**
he became a red rose and fell in **front of the**
king. And the king wondered and said, 'What
means **a rose out of** season ?' and he took **it in
his hand. Then** the master became a minstrel,
and he came to the king's party with a mandolin
in his hand **and sang a stave** with a sweet voice.
And the king marvelled and said to the minstrel,
' What desirest thou from me ? ' The minstrel
answered, ' What I desire from **thee is the** rose
that is in thy hand.' **The** king said, ' **The rose**
came to me from God ; **ask** something **else.'**
The minstrel was **silent ;** then **he sang** another
stave, and again the king said, ' What desirest
thou from me ? ' Again **the** minstrel asked the
rose ; and this time the king stretched out his
hand **to** give it him, whereupon the rose fell to
the ground **and** became millet. Then the
minstrel became a **cock, and** began to pick up
the millet. One grain **of** the millet was hidden
under **the** king's **knee ; and that grain** became a
man and seized the cock and tore off its head.

And the king and the nobles wondered, and they asked the youth of these matters, and he explained them to them."

" Now, O king, I have told this story for that thou mayst know that even as that youth slew his master, so will this degenerate youth slay thee. And after thee he will never show me a good day; sooth, without thee the world were unlawful for me, thou art my care ; be thou but well, then let me be thy sacrifice." When the king heard this story from the lady he said, " On the morrow will I slay him." And they went to bed.

When it was morning the king came and sat upon his throne, and he caused the youth to be brought and ordered the executioner, " Smite off his head." Whereupon the Twenty-Fourth Vezir came forward and said, " O king of the world, obey not the lust of the flesh and incline not to women and slay not thy darling, but have mercy. Let not dust alight on your glorious heart through the words I have spoken; Our Lord the Holy Apostle hath said, ' Speak the truth even though it be bitter.' O king, the stories of the guile and craft of women are many ; mayhap my king has not heard the story of Della the Crafty." The king said, " Relate, let us hear." Quoth the vezir,

THE TWENTY-FOURTH VEZIR'S STORY.

" There was of old time, in the city of Cairo, a cunning woman called Della the Crafty.* And that woman had two husbands, each of whom thought the woman was his. And for a long time the woman had been wife to both of them; but neither of these two men was aware of the circumstance of the other. And one of them was by profession a sharper, and the other was a thief; and they were both pupils of the woman. One day the thief took some stuff he had stolen to the bazaar and there sold it. The man to whom he had given it met the rightful owner of the stuff, who cried, ' Praise be to God! the clue has appeared, the rest of my stuff is with thee; quick, tell me.' The man replied, ' Know the words thou utterest and then speak, I bought this stuff with money; while thou, by thus speaking, wouldst have this stuff from me.' The thief saw these and hastened to his house and said to his wife, ' Wife, my thieving has been found out; give me some bread that I may go to another place till this disturbance has quieted down.' The woman brought a pie and

---

* Perhaps a reminiscence of Delilah the Crafty in the Thousand and One Nights: see the Villon Society's Translation, vol. vi. p. 234.

S

a sheep tail, and cut the pie in halves and the
tail in halves,* and gave a half of each to the
thief.   The thief took them and started.   After
a time the sharper came suddenly in and said,
‘ Wife, to-day my sharping has been found out ;
give me some bread, for I may not be seen.
here for a few days, but must go to another
place.’   So the woman gave the sharper the
remaining halves of the thief's pie and tail ; and
he took them and started.   Now the thief, who
had gone first, reached a pleasant spring and a
pleasant shade, and he sat down by that pleasant
fountain-head and took out the pie and the tail
and thought to eat them.   Thereupon the
sharper too suddenly appeared ; and he likewise seated himself by the edge of the spring
and took out his pie and tail to eat them.   The
thief said, ‘ Brother, come, let us eat together.’
So the sharper came, and he looked at his own
pie and he looked at the thief's pie, and he saw
that they resembled one another ; and they
laid them together, and they were one pie.
And they laid the two pieces of tail together
likewise, and they saw it to be one tail.   And
the sharper wondered and said, ‘ Brother, be
there no shame in asking ; whence comest thou ?’

---

* Some of the Asiatic sheep have enormous tails.

The robber answered, 'I come from Cairo.'
Quoth the sharper, 'Where is your house?'
The thief replied, ' In Cairo; my house is the
house of Della the Crafty, and that woman is
my wife.' The sharper said, 'That house is
my house and that woman is my wife, and I
dwell there these many years; why liest thou
now?' The thief said, 'Out on thee, man, art
thou mad or art thou jesting? she is my wedded
wife these many years.' And the quarrel increased between them. Then said the sharper,
' There is no use of quarrelling here; come, let
us go to the woman and ask her which of us it
is; then will it be known and clear.' So they
both arose and went to the woman. As soon
as the woman saw them she knew what had
happened; and she showed each of them a
place, and sat down opposite them. The
sharper said, 'Out on thee, woman, whose wife
art thou?' The woman answered, 'By God,
till now was I the wife of both of you; but
henceforth he of you whose feats are the greater
shall be my husband. I have taught many feats
to each of you; and to whichever of you performs the greater feat will I be true wife.' And
they both agreed to this proposal. The sharper
said, ' To-day will I go a-sharping; afterward
do thou perform thy feat.' Then the sharper

and the thief arose and went to the bazaar.
The sharper saw that a Frank put a thousand
sequins into a purse, put the purse into his
bosom, and went to the bazaar. Forthwith the
sharper followed the Frank, and in the midst
of the bazaar he went close up to him and
cunningly stole his money from his breast.
Then he went to a hidden place, and took out
nine of the sequins, and drew from his finger a
silver ring on which his name was written and
put it into the purse, and came and put it back
into the Frank's breast. And the thief saw all
these deeds. Then the sharper went round and
came before the Frank and laid hold of him and
struck him several times and cried, ' Out on
thee, accursed, why didst thou take my purse
with my gold ?' The Frank cried, ' Off to
thine own business, begone, leave me, who art
thou ? I do not even know thee.' The sharper
said, ' It is not needful for thee to know me ;
come, let us go to the tribunal.' The Frank
consented and they went together ; and the
sharper made his complaint, and the cadi asked
the Frank, ' How many are thy sequins ?' The
Frank replied, ' There are a thousand sequins.'
Then he asked the sharper, ' How many were
thy sequins ?' He answered, ' There are nine
hundred and ninety-one sequins, and my silver

ring with my name engraved thereon is likewise
in the purse.' The cadi took the purse and
counted, and there were exactly nine hundred
and ninety-one sequins in it, and the ring too
was in it. Then they smote the Frank some
blows and gave the sequins to the sharper.
And the sharper took them and went with the
thief to the woman, and the woman said, ' Lo,
the sharper has performed a feat the like of
which no one has heard till this moment.'
When it was night the thief took a lasso and
went with the sharper to the king's palace.
The thief threw the lasso and scaled the wall
by means of it, and then pulled up the sharper.
Then they got down and went to the treasury
and the thief pulled out many different keys,
and he opened the door and entered the treasury
and said to the sharper, ' Load thyself with
as much gold as thou canst carry.' So the
sharper, loaded himself and they came out.
Then they went to the goose-house, and the
thief caught a goose and cut its throat and lit a
fire and thrust it on a spit and he said to the
sharper, ' Turn it.' And he himself made
straight for the king's bed-chamber. The
sharper said, ' What doest thou ? ' The thief
replied, ' I am going to lay before the king thy
feat and mine, and we shall see which of our

feats is the greater, and whether the woman becomes me or becomes thee.' The sharper said, 'Come, for the love of God let us go ; I give up the woman, let her be thine.' The thief replied, 'Thou sayest so now, but to-morrow thou wilt repent; but when the King has given judgment then thou wilt assent.' And he went and hid himself behind the door, and he saw a slave rubbing the king's feet and chewing a piece of mastic in his mouth and now he slept and now he woke. Very gently the thief hid himself below the bed, and he pushed the end of a horse's hair into the boy's mouth, and the youth chewed the hair along with the mastic. When he was yawning and his mouth was open, the thief pulled the hair and filched the mastic from his mouth. The boy opened his eyes and looked for the mastic on this side and that side, but found it not. When a little time had passed the boy fell asleep and the thief held a strong drug to his nose, and the boy was altogether bereft of his senses. Then the thief took him and hung him up by the girdle from the ceiling, like a lamp, and he began himself to rub the king's feet. And the sharper saw these things from the door. The king stirred and the thief said very gently, 'My king, if thou desire, I will relate a story.'

The king said, ' Tell on, let us hear.' The
thief began and recounted all that had happened
between himself and the sharper; and every now
and then he said to the sharper, who sat outside
and was roasting the goose, ' Turn away, the
goose is burning.' And he recounted how he
had entered his treasury with the sharper, and
how the sharper sat without roasting the goose,
and how he had himself by a trick filched the
mastic from the boy's mouth ; brief, he detailed
all that had happened, whatever it was. And as
he was speaking the sharper was trembling and
making signs to say, ' Come, let us go ;' but
the thief said to him, ' Turn away, the goose is
burning.' Then he looked to the king and
said, ' O king, is the feat of the sharper greater,
or is that of the robber greater ; and which of
them is the woman becoming ?' The king
said, ' The feat of the thief is the greater, and
the woman is his.' Then the thief rubbed the
king's feet a little more, and when the king
was asleep he rose very gently and came to the
sharper and said, ' Didst thou hear how the
king said, "The woman is the thief's ?"' The
sharper answered, ' I heard.' Then said the
thief, ' Whose is the woman ?' The sharper
replied, ' She is thine.' The thief said, ' Thou
liest ; I shall go and ask the king again.' The

sharper said, ' By God, let it be; come, let us go;
if thou wish, not the woman only, but I myself
will be thy slave.' Then they arose and brought
the wealth to the woman and recounted to her
these things. The woman applauded them and
chose the thief for her husband. Now, ' turn
away, the goose is burning,' has remained
famous in the language. When it was morning
the king arose from sleep and called the boy,
but there was no one ; he waited a while and
saw that no one came, and he was wroth and
rose from the bed and his eye fell upon the boy
hanging from the ceiling. He took him down
and saw that his senses were gone, and he called
the attendants and they restored the boy to his
senses. He questioned the boy, but he knew
nothing ; then he said in himself, ' That then
was the robber who told me the story and
rubbed my feet.' And he went and sat upon
his throne, and he said, ' Summon the vezirs
and emirs that they come.' Thereupon were
they summoned and straightway they assembled,
and the king related to them the events of the
night. And they all wondered, and they turned
and said to the king, ' This thief must be found.'
Straightway the king commanded and they
caused the criers to proclaim in the city, ' Let
him who has done this deed come before me,

and, by the truth of God, there shall be to him nor hurt nor harm from me; and the wealth which he has taken from my treasury shall be lawful for him, and I will give him as much again.' The thief gave ear and saw that the king had sworn, and he trusted him and came forward; and the criers took the thief and came into the king's presence. And they told the king, and the king questioned the thief, and the thief said, 'O king, whether thou kill or whether thou pardon; I have done this deed.' The king said, 'What is the cause of thy doing thus?' And the thief related the cause from its beginning to its end. The king applauded the thief and granted him the wealth he had taken, and also appointed him an allowance and ordained that the woman should be his. As the thief had thus attained the royal favour and bounty he vowed repentance from heart and soul, and married that woman, and was for a long time a servant in the king's service."

" Now, O king, I have told this story for that the king may know that wiles such as this abound in women; beware, slay not thy child on the woman's word, else thou shalt be repentant, and too late repentance profits not." And he made intercession for the prince for that day. When the king heard this story

from the vezir he sent the youth to the prison
and went himself to the chase.

When it was evening the king returned from
the chase and came to the palace, and the lady
rose to greet him, and they sat down.   After
the repast the lady again asked for news of the
youth.   The king said, " To-day also such an
one of my vezirs made intercession for him
and I sent him to the prison."   The lady said,
" Thus do the vezirs divert thee ; and thou too
takest the seeming for the real, and delayest ;
while they watch their opportunity.   Take
heed, be not negligent, these are many, thou art
but one, and I am a woman who speaks the
truth of it.   Now there is a story suitable to
this; if there be permission from my king I will
tell it."   The king said, " Tell on, what is it ? "
Quoth the lady,

The Lady's Twenty-Fourth Story.

" My king, thus relate they : Once upon a
time there was a king, and that king had a
courtier.   One day the king, by way of jest,
gave him a note and ordered him thus, ' Give
this note to the chief magistrate and take whatever he gives thee.'   Now, as it was winter
then, the weather was very cold.   So the
courtier took the note and went out, and he

gave it to someone and made him open and
read it. There was written in it, 'Thou shalt
give the courtier six loads of snow.' The
courtier hid the note and delivered it not, and
he returned and came into the king's presence.
The king asked the courtier, 'Hast thou taken
the charge I ordered to the chief magistrate?'
The courtier replied, 'I take it in the days of
the king's fortune;' and passed on to other
subjects. The courtier waited till the days of
summer came, when he took the note and gave
it to the chief magistrate. He read it and
there was written, 'Thou shalt give the
courtier six loads of snow.' The chief magistrate said, 'Whence can I give this much snow
in such a season?' The courtier said, 'The
king has thus commanded; though the snow
cannot be found, its price can be found.' The
chief magistrate consented, and he counted out
and made over to him the whole of the price of
it. Then he laid it before the king, and the
king applauded the courtier, and it seemed
right good to him, and he bestowed many gifts
on the courtier."

"Now, O king, I have told this story for
that thou mayst know that as that courtier
waited for his opportunity, so does this degenerate youth wait for his. Be not negligent,

slay him, else his slaying thee is certain." And
she was silent. And the king said, "To-
morrow will I slay him." And they went to
bed.

When it was morning the king came and sat
upon his throne, and he caused the youth to be
brought and ordered the executioner, " Smite
off his head." The Twenty-Fifth Vezir came
forward and said, "O king of the world,
now are the prince's hands bound and is his
heart wounded, and yet he guiltless, under thy
authority. So it beseems thee not to abandon
generosity and moderation and to withdraw from
the fear of God and destroy the prince. It is
even as when one day they asked the Holy
Apostle, 'What is the root of the Faith, and
what is its head, and what is its life, and what
is its heart, and what is its seed, and what is its
leaf, and what is its place, and what is its
fruit ?' The Apostle (peace on him!) replied,
'The root of the Faith is the grace of God,
and its head is the Word of the Profession, and
its life is the Koran, and its heart is sincerity,
and its place is the believer's heart, and its
seed is knowledge, and its leaf is piety, and its
branch is the fear of God, and its core is
modesty and generosity, and its fruit is thanking
God ; even as He saith in His Glorious Word,

" If ye render thanks, surely indeed will I give
you increase."' * O king, be thankful for the
glory and empire which God Most High has
given thee, and act with moderation and
generosity ; for moderation and generosity are
half the Faith, and they are the bark of the
tree of the Faith, so that yon monk through
his acting with generosity and moderation
was decked with the robe of honour of the
Faith, and his end was well in Either World ;
mayhap my king has not heard it." The
king said, " Tell on, let us hear." Quoth the
vezir,

The Twenty-Fifth Vezir's Story.

" It has come down in the records that when
the Apostle (peace on him !) was returning from
the Holy War against the Greeks, while he was
proceeding on the way with the Noble Companions, they lighted at a certain place. Khālid
ibn-Walīd † had gone off on some business, and
when he returned the Apostle (peace on him !)
had removed thence with his host and gone
away. So Khālid ibn-Walīd came and found
not the host. Thereabout the road lost itself ;

---

* Koran, xiv. 7.
† The famous general of Muhammed, who was surnamed, by
reason of his valour, the Sword of God.

so he ascended a high hill, and he saw behind
that hill many people assembled, and in their
midst they had raised a pulpit. So Khālid came
down and went up to them, and asked them,
saying, 'What people are ye, and of what tribe
are ye, and what number of warriors are ye, and
what is your meaning in being gathered here
together ?' They replied, 'We are of such and
such a tribe, and our multitude is now seventy
thousand persons, and our purpose in being
gathered here is, that there is a monk of ours in
a cave in this hill, and he preaches to us and
exhorts us once in the year, and we go away
sufficiently exhorted by his exhortation till the
next year; to-day is the year complete, and he
will surely come forth now and preach to us.'
Khālid said in his heart, 'This were right, that
I go not until I have seen this monk.' And he
got down from his beast. After a time a man
came forth in black garments, and all that people
humbled themselves, and he ascended the pulpit
and sat down. Then he said, 'O people, I will
not preach to you this day.' They said, 'Wherefore ?' He answered, 'For this, that there is
among you a man of the People of Muhammed.'
They all looked one at the other. No one re-
cognized Khālid, for he had on clothes like their
clothes, and he knew their language. The monk

said, 'Do ye remain in your places ; I will find him.' And they all sat down. And the monk said, 'O man, we know not where thou art seated, but God Most High knoweth ; for the sake of that Faith thou holdest and if thou love Muhammed, wheresoever thou art, stand upon thy feet that I may see thee.' Khālid thought, 'If I rise now, these will tear me in pieces.' The monk repeated his words. Then Khālid said in himself, 'If I had a thousand lives, they should all be a sacrifice in the way of the Faith and the cause of Muhammed (peace on him !)' And he stood upon his feet in the place where he was. The multitude saw him and knew he was of the People of Muhammed, and they rushed upon him to kill him. The monk cried out, 'Sit still in your places ; it were not gene-rosity or moderation to kill one man surrounded by seventy thousand.' And as soon as he had spoken this, the people sat still in their places. The monk said, 'Come near.' And Khālid went to the foot of the pulpit. The monk said, 'Art thou of the great of the Companions of the Messenger, or art thou of the least ?' Khālid answered, 'I am not merely of these great ones, there is none higher than I ; and I am not merely of these least ones, there is none lower than I.' The monk said, 'What knowest thou

of learning?' Khālid replied, 'I know that
which will suffice me.' The monk said, 'If I
ask thee a thing wilt thou answer?' Khālid
said, 'If I know what thou askest I will answer.'
The monk said, 'And if thou knowest not?'
Khālid replied, 'If I know not, there were no
shame.' Quoth the monk, 'I have heard that
your Muhammed says that of whatever God
Most High has created in Paradise, He has
created the like in the world. I believe not
this. There is a tree in Paradise which they
call the Tūbā, its roots are above in the air, and
there is not a place in Paradise where its
branches are not. What is its like in the
world?' Khālid replied, 'Its like in the world
is the sun, which is itself in the sky, yet when
it is midway in the heaven there remains not a
house or hill, but in all places are its rays.' The
monk said, 'Fair answer hast thou given.'
Again the monk asked, 'Your Muhammed says
that there are four rivers in Paradise, one of
wine, one of honey, one of milk, and one of
water; and that all of these come forth from
one channel and flow on and yet are not mixed.
What is the like of that in the world?' Khālid
said, 'Dost thou not see? God Most High has
created four different waters in the bodies of the
children of Adam in the space of a span, and

they come forth yet mix not one with the other ;
one is the water of the ear which is bitter, and
one is the water of the eye which is salt, and one
is the water of the nose which smells, and one is
the water that runs from the mouth, and it is
sweet.'   The monk said, 'Well hast thou done !
fair answer hast thou given !'   Again the monk
asked, 'Your Muhammed says there is a throne
in Paradise, the height of which is a five hundred
years' journey ; and whenever a saint would
mount upon it, that throne bows down and that
man mounts, and then it rises again.   What is
its like in the world ?'   Khālid replied, 'Its like
in the world is the camel ; dost thou not see
that while the camel is thus great, when a child
takes hold of its headstall and pulls its head
down and gets upon its neck, as the camel raises
up its head again, he mounts upon its back ?'
The monk said, 'Good answer hast thou given.'*
And he made to ask him another question, when
Khālid said, 'Act with moderation ; thou hast
asked me these questions ; I too have a question
to ask of thee.'   The monk said, 'Ask what

---

* The original has in addition the following question and
answer : *Rāhib eyder,* '*Muhammediniz,* "*Jennetde ekl u shurb
var, tebevvul u taghavvut yoq dir :*" *derimish, Dunyāde anin
misli ne dir ?*' *dedi. Khālid eytdi,* '*Ana rahmindaki chojuq
dir ; ana rahminda jānlu ekl u shurb ider, tebevvul u taghavvut
itmez ; eger itse, anasi helāk olur :*' *dedi. Rāhib,* '*Guzel jewāb
verdin :*' *dedi.*

T

thou wilt.'   Khālid said, 'What is the Key of
Paradise ? tell me.'   The monk replied, 'To believe in Jesus (peace on him!)'   Khālid said,
'By the God of Jesus, speak the truth of it.'
When he had thus sworn, the monk turned and
said to the people, 'O people, what time we
sware to this man he feared us, therefore was
his oath not binding on him.   Now has he likewise sworn to us, and he wishes from us the
truth, yet we have no fear of him.   Now it were
beseeming generosity to give this man a true
answer ; I would that ye follow me now.'   They
cried, 'We all are followers of thee.'   Then the
monk said, 'O people, one true word is better
than a thousand lies ; I have seen and read in
our books that the Key of Paradise is, "There is
no god save God : Muhammed is the Apostle
of God ;" that is, whoso pronounces in the world
the Word of the Profession will enter Paradise.'
And he turned and said, 'O people, be ye witnesses that I have believed in the Faith of
Muhammed.'   And he said, 'I testify that there
is no god save God, and I testify that Muhammed is His Servant and His Apostle.'   When
the people heard this they all entered the Truth,
and went with Khālid to the presence of the
Apostle ; and they enjoyed great happiness,
serving the Apostle of God."

"Now, O king, I have told this story for
that the king may know that if there be not
generosity in a man, it is an indication of the
imperfectness of his Faith. What were beseeming the king's generosity is this, that he slay
not the prince, who as yet has not eaten of the
fruit of the orchard of life, and whose eyes have
not yet rested on the pleasure-ground of the
world." And he made intercession with the
king for the prince for that day. When the
king heard this story from the vezir he sent the
prince to the prison and himself mounted for
the chase.

When it was evening the king returned from
the chase and came to the palace, and the lady
rose to greet him, and they sat down. After the
repast the lady again asked for news of the
youth. The king said, "To-day too such an
one of my vezirs made intercession for him and
I let him off." The lady said, "O king, many
people will indeed be brought to shame through
this youth ; it is even as the story of that man
of Khorāsān ; mayhap my king has not heard
it." The king said, "Tell on, let us hear."
Quoth the lady,

THE LADY'S TWENTY-FIFTH STORY.

"Once upon a time there was a man of Khorāsān who was poor, and who, when conversing with his neighbours, used to boast and brag and say, 'I did this thing and I did that thing to them of Khorāsān.' So the neighbours saw that he was a boastful braggart, and they would make him talk and divert themselves. Early one day this man of Khorāsān rose from his place, took a piece of bread, rubbed some grease on it, and ate it; and that grease made greasy his moustachios. He arose and came up to the khojas of the neighbours, wiping his moustachios and cleaning his teeth with a toothpick, and sat down. The khojas said to him, 'To-day thou hast had some new kind of savoury dish.' The man of Khorāsān replied, 'To-day they prepared no sweetmeats but such and such a thing, and no meat save some fritters; I ate them; lo, these are all the savoury dishes I have had.' And he began to brag, and said, 'To-day my soul is weary, I shall go and mount the gray horse, and go out of the city and make the horse gallop a bit, that my spirits may recover.' Just then his son came in at the door, and said to his father, 'To-day the cat has eaten the grease in that spoon wherewith

thou greasest thy moustachios every day.' The
man of Khorāsān said, 'Go, take some more
from the jar.' The boy said, 'I know of no
grease in our house save that in the spoon ;
where is even a jug, let alone a jar ?' The
man of Khorāsān said, 'Hast thou watered the
gray horse ?' The boy answered, 'I have
come to this age and have never seen even an ass
in our house ; where is the horse ?' And he left.
And the man of Khorāsān arose in confusion
from that party and went away; and the khojas
began to smile behind him. And when the
man of Khorāsān got to his house he reviled
his son and scolded him."

"Now, O king, I have told this story for
that my king may know that there is no polite-
ness or modesty in youths, and may learn that in
some way or other they bring about disgrace,
and that he may bear in mind this story.
There is no remedy save the killing of this
youth, or one day he will indeed bring thee to
shame and will slay thee. Ah! I speak to my
king as I know and understand ; the rest my
king knows." When the king heard this
story from the lady he said, "To-morrow will
I slay him." And they arose and went to
bed.

When it was morning the king came and sat

upon his throne, and he caused them to bring the youth and ordered the executioner, " Smite off his head." The Twenty-Sixth Vezir came forward and said, " O king of the world, the word of this woman is not better than the word of these vezirs. If the king put aside the word of these many vezirs, men of understanding, and go by the word of the woman, my fear is that he will be of the rebels against God Most High. O king, if thou respect not these vezirs, at least respect their learning, that God Most High shut thee not out from respect in the world and in the Hereafter. Mayhap the king has not heard the story of Nu'mān." The king said, " Tell on, let us hear." Quoth the vezir,

THE TWENTY-SIXTH VEZIR'S STORY.

" There was of old time in the city of Cairo a man called Nu'mān, and he had a son. One day when this boy's time to learn to read was fully come he took him to a school and gave to a teacher. This Nu'mān was exceeding poor, so that he followed the calling of a water-seller, and in this way he supported his wife and child. When the teacher had made the boy read through the Koran, he told the boy to fetch him his present. So the boy came and told his father. His father said, 'O son, the Koran is the Word of God Most High, we have nothing worthy of it; there is our camel with which I follow my trade of water-seller, take it at least and give it to thy teacher.' The boy took the camel and brought it to his teacher. But that day his father could gain no money, and that night his wife and his son and himself remained hungry. Now his wife was a great scold, and when she saw this thing she said, 'Out on thee, husband, art thou mad? Where are thy senses gone? Thou hadst a camel, and by means of it we made shift to live, and now thou hast taken and given it in a present; would that that boy had not been born, or that thou hadst not sent him to read; what is he and what his reading?' And she made so much noise and clamour that it cannot be described. Nu'mān saw this thing, and he bowed down his head, and from the greatness of his distress he fell asleep. In his dream a radiant elder, white-bearded and clad in white raiment, came and said, 'O Nu'mān, thy portion is in Damascus; go, take it.' Just then Nu'mān awoke and he saw no one, and he arose and said, 'Is the vision Divine or is it Satanic?' While saying this, he again fell asleep, and again he saw it. Brief, the elder appeared three times to him that night in his dream and said, 'Indeed is thy provision in Damascus; delay not, go to Damascus and take it.' When it was morning Nu'mān spake to his wife of the vision; his wife said, ' Thou gavest away our camel and didst leave us hungry, and now thou canst not abide our complaints and wishest to run off; I fear thou wilt leave thy child and me here and go off.' Nu'mān said, ' My life, I will not run off.' Quoth the woman, ' I will not bide, I will not bide; where thou goest I too will go with thee.' Nu'mān sware that he would not run off, and the woman was persuaded and let him go. So Nu'mān went forth; and one day he entered Damascus, and he went in through the gate of the Amawī Mosque. That day someone had baked bread in an oven and was taking it to his house; when he saw Nu'mān opposite him and knew him to be a stranger, he gave him a loaf. Nu'mān took it and ate it, and lay down through fatigue and fell asleep. That elder again came to him in his vision and said, ' O Nu'mān, thou hast received thy provision; delay not, go back to thy house.' Nu'mān awoke and was amazed and said, ' Then our bearing this much trouble and weariness was for a loaf.' And he returned. One day he

entered his house, and the woman looked and
saw there was nothing in his hand; and
Nu'mān told her. When the woman learned
that Nu'mān had brought nothing, she turned
and said, 'Out on thee, husband, thou art
become mad, thou art a worthless man; had
thy senses been in thy head, thou hadst not
given away our camel, the source of our
support, and left us thus friendless and hungry
and thirsty; not a day but thou doest some
mad thing.' And she complained much. And
Nu'mān's heart was broken by the weariness of
the road and the complaining of the woman,
and he fell asleep. Again in his vision that
elder came and said, 'O Nu'mān, delay not,
arise, dig close by thee, thy provision is there,
take it.' But Nu'mān heeded not. Three
times the elder appeared to him in his dream
and said, 'Thy provision is indeed close by
thee; arise, take it.' So Nu'mān, unable to
resist, arose and took a pick-axe and shovel
and began to dig where his head had lain.
The woman made mock of Nu'mān and said,
'Out on thee, man; the half of the treasure
revealed to thee is mine.' Nu'mān replied,
'So be it; but I am weary, come thou and dig
a bit that I may take breath a little.' The
woman said, 'Thou art not weary now; when

thou art weary I will help.' Nu'mān went on ;
and when he had dug as deep as half the
height of a man, a marble slab appeared. The
woman saw the marble and, saying in herself,
'This is not empty,' she asked the pick-axe
from Nu'mān. Nu'mān said, 'Have patience a
little longer.' The woman said, 'Thou art
weary.' Nu'mān replied, 'Now am I rested.'
Quoth the woman, 'I am sorry for thee, thou
dost not know kindness.' While thus talking
they saw that one side of that marble was
pierced and that there was a hole. Thereupon
grew Nu'mān eager, and he pulled the marble
from its place, and below it was a well and a
ladder. He caught hold of the ladder and
went down and saw a royal vase filled full with
red gold, and he called out to the woman,
'Come here.' Thereupon the woman descended
likewise and saw the vase of gold, and she
threw her arms round Nu'mān's neck and said,
'O my noble little husband! Blessed be God,
for thy luck and thy fortune.' Nu'mān took up
some of these sequins, and the woman said,
'What wilt thou do?' Nu'mān replied, 'I
shall take these to our king and tell him that
there is a vase full of them, and that an elder
came to me in my dream and told me, and I
shall say, "Take them all ; and, if thou wilt,

bestow on me a few of them that I and my wife
may eat and drink, and in our comfort may
bless and praise thee." ' Quoth the woman,
' My life, husband, speak not to our king now,
so that all of them may remain ours and we
shall have ease of heart.' Nu'mān listened not,
but took them and laid them before the king.
The king said, ' What is this ? ' Nu'mān
answered, ' O king, I found them in thy
ground.' And he told of the elder's coming
in his dream and of there being a vase full of
them, and said, ' O king, send a slave of thine,
and he will return ; and I shall accept the
king's alms, whatever it may be.' The king
said to a scribe, ' Come, read this, let us see
from whose time it has remained.' When the
scribe took the sequin into his hand he saw
that there was written on the one side of it,
' This is an alms from before God to Nu'mān.'
Then the scribe turned over the other side and
saw that it was thus written on that side, ' By
reason of his respect toward the Koran.'
When the scribe had read the inscriptions to
the king, the king said, ' What is thy name ? '
He replied, ' My name is Nu'mān.' The king
caused all these sequins to be read, and the
writing on the whole of them was the same.
The king said, ' Go ye and bring some from

the bottom of the vase.' And they went and brought some from the bottom of the vase, and they read them, and they all bore the inscription of the first. And the king wondered and said, 'Go, poor man, God Most High has given it thee, on my part too be it lawful for thee; come, take these sequins also.' So Nu'mān took them and went to his house, and he took out the sequins that were in the vase ; and he enjoyed delight in the world until he died, and in the Hereafter he attained a lofty station. And all this felicity was for his respect to the glorious Koran."

"O king, I have told this story for that the king may know that God Most High respects him who respects learning and the learned. So it is incumbent on the king that he respect the learning of the prince—for he is of the learned —and the learning of these vezirs, that he may gain the respect of God Most High in the world and in the Hereafter." And he made interces- sion for the prince for that day. When the king heard this story from the vezir he sent the prince to the prison and went himself to the chase.

When it was evening the king returned from the chase and came to the palace, and the lady rose to greet him, and they sat down. After the repast the lady asked for news of the youth.

The king said, " To-day too such an one of my vezirs made intercession for him and I sent him to the prison." The lady said, "O king, my words have no effect on thee ; and hast thou not heard that when the Holy Apostle (peace on him !) would draw forth his head from the ocean of the mysteries of God, and come from flight in the world of the Godhead to the world of humanity, he would call to Saint 'Ayisha, saying, 'O Humayrá !'* that is to say, 'Speak to me, O 'Ayisha ;' and would find such pleasure in the sight of her and in her words ? He who was the Seal of the Prophets thus respected his wife and yearned to hear her voice ; and thou art of his People, O king, yet these my words go in at thy one ear and come out at thy other. The affair of this youth resembles the story of the son and daughter of those two merchants ; mayhap my king has not heard it." The king said, " Tell on, let us hear." Quoth the lady,

The Lady's Twenty-Sixth Story.

" In Damascus the Noble there was a great merchant, and he had a son, a second Joseph.

---

* Humayrá means Rosina,—*little rosy-cheeks.* Muhammed used so to address his youthful wife, 'Ayisha ; his tenderness in doing so is often alluded to by Muslim writers, *e.g.* Dr. Redhouse's *Mesnevi,* p. 144.

One day, while the boy was passing through a
certain quarter, he of a sudden passed before
the door of another great merchant, and he
looked up to the windows and saw a girl who
brought to mind the moon of fourteen nights, a
distracter of the world, a second Zuleykhá; and
she was looking down from above upon the
merchant's son. When their eyes met each
other, they both of them fell in love one with
the other, from heart and soul. Thereupon the
girl threw down an apple from above, and the
merchant's son caught it in his hands and let it
not touch the ground. Now the girl's mother
was gone to the bath, and as the girl was alone
in the house she had got wearied, and the fancy
to be like a bride had come into her mind, and
she had put on whatever she possessed of costly
dresses and jewels; and as they met each other
when she was thus covered with gold and ornaments, they loved each the other forthwith.
Saying in herself, 'When will such an opportunity occur?' the girl came down and opened
the door and took the boy in and quickly shut
the door behind him, and snatched some kisses,
and then they went upstairs. On both sides
the fires of love flamed forth and they gave
themselves up to enjoyment. Of a sudden the
girl's father arrived and knocked at the door.

Then the boy's senses came into his head and
he said, 'Mercy, my lamb, what shall I do now?'
The girl said, 'There is a cellar in the garden;
go and hide in that cellar for the present.' So
the boy went off. Now one descended into
that cellar by a flight of forty steps; and in that
the boy was senseless and without discretion,
he was going down hurriedly, when his foot
slipped, and he fell down the forty steps and
was killed."

Now, O king, this thy son is likewise without
sense; and from him without sense comes no
good either to himself or to others, his works
are ever evil. Beware, be not negligent, kill this
youth, else he will slay thee." When the king
heard this story from the lady he said, "On the
morrow will I kill him." And they went to
bed.

When it was morning the king sat upon his
throne, and he caused the youth to be brought
and ordered the executioner, "Smite off his
head." The Twenty-Seventh Vezir came forward and said, "O king of the world, it is incumbent on kings to be not ashamed to ask of
things they know not; for he who is forward in
gaining knowledge will enter Paradise. A wise
man is he who asks another even of what he
knows, so that they may make him know what

he knows not.   And a foolish man is he who knows not and finds not one who does know and is ashamed to ask.   O king, thou believest not in us ; in thy city are many wise men and learned, ask them, and if this deed be not sin, we will speak no more.   Otherwise, beware of going by the woman's word and slaying thy son.   All fly, being weak, from the wiles and wickedness of women.   Mayhap my king has not heard the story of that woodman."   The king said, " Tell on, let us hear."   Quoth the vezir,

The Twenty-Seventh Vezir's Story.

There was of old time in a city a young woodman, and he had a wild scolding wife. This woman always took from the woodman whatever he earned, so that there never remained an aspre in his hand.   Sometimes at night his food was salt and he would say, ' The food thou hast cooked to-night is salt.'   Then the next night she would put no salt in the food, and cook it without salt ; and if he said, ' This has no salt,' she put in much salt, so that he could not eat.   One day the woodman concealed a little money from his wife that he might buy a rope ; and when it was night the woman found the money in the woodman's breast and said, 'Thou hast a secret doxy other than me; thou **art** taking money **to** give her.' The youth sware, **but the woman** would not believe. The woodman said, '**O my life, I** kept it to buy a rope.' The woman answered, '**May** they hang thee with that rope.' **The** woodman said, 'Why dost thou thus curse **me?**' **She** replied, 'The curse **I** have uttered against thee is but little.' Brief, they had a great quarrel, and the **woodman beat the woman.** That night passed somehow, **and** when **it was** morning **the wood- man arose and took** one of the beasts, and **was** setting **out for the** mountain, when he said to **the woman, '** Have care that thou **take not the** other beast to come after **me.'** Thereupon the **woman ran and** mounted **the other** beast **and** went to the mountain behind **her** husband **and** said, 'When thou **art** without **me who knows** what **thou** doest?' **The** woodman saw that the woman **was** coming **but he** said nothing **and** went **to the** mountain, **and the** woman **went with** him. **The** woodman began **to** cut wood; **and** when **the woman** was roaming about the moun- tain she came **to the** mouth **of a** pit. **The** woodman **saw that the** woman was looking **at** the **mouth of the pit and** he **cried out,'** Take care, come back **from the pit** mouth.' But **the woman** went nearer **it.** Again the **woodman cried out,**

' I tell thee to come back, and thou goest nearer ;
come away back.' The woman said, ' I shall
go yet nearer.' And she took a step forward
and put down her foot. Now the stone beneath
her was not fast, and she slipped and fell into
the pit. As the woodman could do nothing he
paid no heed, but laded the beasts and went to
his house. That night passed and on the morrow he again took the beasts and went to the
mountain. Saying, ' Let me go and see this
woman,' he went to the pit mouth and looked,
but the woman was not visible. His heart was
pained and he let down the rope and cried, ' O
wife, seize this rope that I may pull thee up.'
He felt the rope heavy and, taking courage,
pulled, and he saw an 'ifrīt* had caught hold of
the rope. The woodman was afraid, but the
'ifrīt said, ' Fear not, may God Most High be
pleased with thee ; thou hast rescued me from
a torment from which I could not have come of
myself till the Resurrection.' The woodman
said, ' In what manner of torment wast thou ?'
The 'ifrīt replied, ' For a long time this pit has
been my dwelling ; yesterday a scolding ill-
starred woman fell upon me, she got upon my
head and held me fast by the ears and left

---

* A kind of demon.

me not till now. But now thou didst come and let
down the rope and cry, "Seize the rope ;"and she
let me go, but caught not the rope. Praise be to
God! I have escaped and am saved. Now I
would reward thee for the kindness thou hast done
me.' And he pulled forth three leaves and gave
them to the youth and said,' Now I will go and
possess the daughter of the king of this land and,
whatsoever remedy they apply, I will not leave
her till thou come, and put one of these leaves
in water and rub that water on the girl's face ;
then will I go, and the king will confer many
favours on thee.' So the youth took these leaves
from the 'ifrīt's hand and, paying no heed to the
woman, went to his house. Our story goes to the
'ifrīt : The 'ifrīt went straight thence to the palace
of the king, and possessed his daughter. They
sent word to the king, saying, ' The girl has lost
her senses, and is lying sighing and wailing, crying, "O my head !" ' The king came and saw that
his daughter was seized with a pain in her head
and was sighing and crying, and he forthwith appointed a physician ; but the physician did no
good. He appointed another physician, he too
did no good. Brief, there were some ten physicians, but they did no good. When the girl saw
her father she cried, ' Mercy, father, my head !'
The father said, 'My child, when thou criest, say-

ing, " My head!" my head and my heart suffer
more than thine ; but what can I do ? I will get an
astrologer for thee.'   And he began to summon
those skilled in astrology, and many such came
and busied themselves with various treatments
and occult cures.   Our story goes to the young
woodman : The 'ifrīt had given the youth those
leaves and instructed him as to what should
happen, but the youth did not believe him and
paid no heed.   One day a man came from the
king's city and brought an imperial order, and
it was thus : ' My daughter is ill ; I have appointed these many physicians and these many
astrologers, but without avail.   To whatever
skilful master comes and cures her, if he be a
Muslim, I will give my daughter, if she but
recover ; and if he be an infidel, I will give a
world of gifts.'   And it was signed.   Thereupon the woodman came and said, ' I will go
and, with the permission of God, will treat her
that she recover.'   So they straightway gave
over the young woodman to the man who had
come ; and they set out at once.   One day they
entered the king's domains ; and they gave the
king word and he ordered, saying, ' Let him
come quickly.'   So they took him before him,
and the king ordered that they brought the girl,
and the young woodman acted according to the

'ifrīt's instructions, and the girl recovered. So
the king gave him his daughter and made him
his son-in-law. Now this king had a friend,
another king ; and that 'ifrīt loved his daughter,
and he ever annoyed the girl. When that king
heard that this other king's daughter had got
well, he sent a man and begged for the king's
son-in-law that he might cure his daughter. So
the king sent him, and he went before the girl
and saw that the demon was there. When the
demon saw the youth he said, ' See, I did thee
a kindness ; I love this girl ; art thou come to take
her too from my hand ? Lo, I will go and take
that girl from thy hand.' And he was exceeding angry. The youth was bewildered through
fear of him and said, ' I am not come here for the
girl ; but that woman in the pit was my wife, I
left her in the pit that I might escape from her,
but she has now got out and, go where I will,
she will not leave me. I have fled from her and
am come hither to thee ; she too is coming in
now.' As soon as the demon heard him say the
words, ' She too is coming in now,' he said, ' Mercy,
has she come here too ? This place is no longer
lawful for me.' And he left the king's daughter and
went away ; and the king's daughter recovered."

" Now, O king, I have told this story for
that the king may know that even a demon is

powerless against the iniquity and evil deeds of women, and flies away ; where then were the prince ? For these many days have the king and the prince, and high and low, been powerless in the hands of a woman ; one must judge by this what a woman can do." And he made intercession with the king for the prince for that day. When the king heard this story from the vezir he sent the prince to the prison and went himself to the chase.

When it was evening the king returned from the chase and came to the palace, and the lady rose to greet him, and they sat down. After the repast the lady again asked for news of the youth. The king said, " To-day such an one of my vezirs made intercession for him, and he led me astray, little remained but I blasphemed ; and for that I am ashamed among the vezirs, my countenance fell to the ground ; till I had let off the youth this day I escaped not from their hands." The lady said, " O king, this youth knows much ; all the vezirs are his faithful friends. Take care, some hurt will befall thee from the youth. Mayhap the king has not heard the story of those fleas and the scant-beard." The king said, " Tell on, let us hear." Quoth the lady,

THE LADY'S TWENTY-SEVENTH STORY.

"One day the fleas came together and said, 'The sons of Adam catch us and rub us between their fingers and kill us; why do they thus torture us by rub rubbing, and kill us? Let us go to Saint Solomon the Messenger and complain, and say, "Let them kill us as they do lice."' So they agreed to this and chose some from among them to send before Solomon as complainants; and they warned these much, saying, 'If there be a scant-bearded man in the presence of Solomon (peace on him!), take care and make not the complaint; for scant-beards know much and would make him give judgment contrary to our complaint.' So these fleas set out and came into the presence of Saint Solomon, and passed their eyes over the companions who were standing there. There was there a person with the appearance of a youth, and they, thinking him a youth, said in themselves, 'There is no scant-beard in this assembly.' Then they said to Saint Solomon, 'O Prophet of God, when the sons of Adam catch lice they do not rub them between their fingers, but kill them forthwith; why when they catch us do they first rub us between their fingers and then kill us? Henceforth, even as they kill lice, so

let them kill us.' Then Saint Solomon looked
to those who were present in the assembly,
whereupon that youth arose from his place and
said, ' O Prophet of God, when we find lice they
do not move but remain stock-still, therefore do
we kill them between our nails without rubbing ;
but when we find fleas they jump from here to
there and from there to here, so that even one
of them is caught with difficulty; for that they
annoy us twice, do we inflict on them an additional torment.' Then quoth Saint Solomon to
the fleas, ' What say ye ?' The fleas replied,
' We too will remain stock-still like lice ; only
let them kill us also without rubbing.' Saint
Solomon said to the youth, ' Lo, these are about
to remain stock-still like lice.' Quoth the
youth, ' Very good ; let them give a surety.'
Said Saint Solomon to the fleas, ' Give a surety.'
The fleas answered, ' Our glory is to jump ; we
shall become surety to no man.' Saint Solomon
said, ' Since ye will not give a surety, even as
they killed you heretofore, so let them kill you
still.' Then the fleas went out, and they asked,
' Is that a youth ?' They answered the fleas,
' That is not a youth, but a scant-beard.' So
they came and told their party of these things ;
and they all agreed that until the Resurrection
they should go about and wander in search of

scant-beards, and, where they found them, press upon them and eat them and drink their blood and kill them. And from that time have they continued to seek out scant-bearded men and eat them ; and the cause of this hatred was that scant-beard with the appearance of a youth."

" Now, O king, I have told this story for that the king may know that this youth too is in form a youth but in nature a scant-beard ; so be prepared lest thou fall into a maze like the fleas." When the king heard this story from the lady he said, " On the morrow will I see to his affair." And they went to bed.

When it was morning the king went and sat upon his throne, and he caused the youth to be brought and ordered the executioner, " Smite off his head." The Twenty-Eighth Vezir came forward and said, " O king of the world, go not by the woman's word, for the Holy Apostle hath thus said, ' Whoso loveth one with a perfect love shall rise along with him to-morrow on the Resurrection-Day.' This is beseeming the king, that he love the learned and these many vezirs ; for from the learned and the accomplished vezirs comes no evil. Mayhap my king has not heard the story of the devotee and the thief." The king said, " Tell on, let us hear." Quoth the vezir,

THE TWENTY-EIGHTH VEZIR'S STORY.

" They relate that there was in the city of
Baghdad a devotee, and this devotee had a cell
where he was always occupied in worship. One
day someone, when passing by there, called out
the devotee and gave him some money.   The
devotee accepted it ; and he took that money
and went to the bazaar and bought a little honey
and gave away the rest of the money to the
poor.   Now a thief watched him and said in
his heart, 'There must be much money with
this devotee.'   And he followed behind the
devotee, and the devotee entered his cell.   The
thief too slipped in and hid himself in a corner.
When it was evening the devotee lit his lamp
and occupied himself with worship ; and the
thief watched in his place, saying, 'The devotee
will go to sleep.'   But as to the devotee, his
intention was not to fall asleep, and the thief
became repentant of his ever having come, and
said, ' I see this devotee is the favourite of God
Most High ; if this time I escape from him, I
shall repent and thieve no more.'   After a time
someone came and knocked at the door, and
the devotee rose and went to the door, and the
thief stood ready to slip out and run off when
the door was opened.   But the devotee opened

the door so little that a man could scarce squeeze through, and he asked that person. That person said, 'The **Forty*** have sent me; they salute thee. This night one of us has gone to the mercy of God Most High, and they would seat thee in his place.' The devotee said, 'Let them excuse me; there is a man here in my stead, take him and let them accept him.' Thereupon he laid hold of the thief and made him over to that person and said, 'Lo, take him in my stead.' And forthwith the thief repented and sought pardon. So through his passing one night in the cell of that devotee he became of the Forty."

"Now, O king, I have told this story for that the king may know that the advantage of staying and abiding with the righteous, and likewise with the learned, is great. Since these many learned men say that the prince is guiltless, spare thou the prince's life for this day." When the king heard this story from the vezir he sent the prince to the prison and went himself to the chase.

That day, too, when it was evening, he came to the palace, and the lady rose to greet him,

---

* That is the *Rijāl-i Ghayb*, "The Unseen Ones," a set of forty mysterious and devout beings who wander over the earth ready to impart spiritual aid to those who seek it.

and they sat down. After the repast the lady
again began to speak about the youth. The
king said, " To-day too such an one of my
vezirs made intercession for him and I have
again sent him to the prison." The lady said,
" O king, that youth made free with me ; I tell
it thee and thou shuttest thine eyes to it and
listenest not; what means this ? Had I been
an evil woman, ere now were thy body lying in
the earth. Since I have been thus true to thee,
this beseems thee, that thou see to my right.
Thou favourest this youth now and sendest
him to the prison, but in the end shalt thou
repent even as repented that king who would
not accept the counsel of Avicenna."* The
king said, " Relate that story, let us hear."
Quoth the lady,

The Lady's Twenty-Eighth Story.

" In the city of Aleppo there was a king.
As mice abounded in that city the people complained of them every day. One day, while
the king was conversing with Avicenna, they
touched upon the mice. The king said, ' O
Avicenna, everyone complains of these mice ;

---

* This famous philosopher was born in Bukhārā in 373 (A.D.
983), and died at Hamadān in 427 (A.D. 1036).

would that we could find some remedy for them
that everyone might be at ease.' Avicenna
answered, 'I will do that to them that not a
single one of them remain in this city; but with
this condition, that thou stand at the city gate,
and beware, whatever wonder thou see, that
thou laugh not.' The king consented and was
glad. Straightway he ordered that they prepared his horse, and he mounted and went to
the gate. Avicenna, on his part, stood in a
street and repeated a charm and called the
mice. One of the mice came, and he caught it
and killed it and put it in a coffin and made
four mice bear that coffin, while he repeated
the charm and began to strike his hands one
against the other; and these four mice began to
march slowly along. And all the mice that
were in the city attended that funeral, so that
the streets were filled full of them. They came
to the gate where the king was standing, some
of them before the coffin and some of them
behind. And while the king was looking on,
he saw these mice with the coffin on their
shoulders, and, unable to resist, he laughed.
Thereupon, as soon as he laughed, as many of
the mice as were without the gate did all die,
but as many as were within the gate did all
disperse and run off inside. Avicenna said,

'O king, if thou had kept my counsel and not laughed, not a single mouse would have remained in this city, but they would all of them have gone out and died ; and everyone would have been at ease.' And the king repented of his having laughed ; but what could he do ? Too late repentance profits not."

"Now, O king, thou art about to forgive what this degenerate youth has done to us ; but he will not forgive thee, but will surely hurt thee and me and many poor creatures." When the king heard these beguiling words of the lady he said, "To-morrow will I see to him." And they arose and went to bed.

When it was morning the king arose and sat upon his throne, and he caused the youth to be brought and ordered the executioner, "Smite off his head." The Twenty-Ninth Vezir came forward and said, "O king of the world, one of the kings of Hind, when he laid his head on the pillow of death, said to his son, 'O darling of my heart, I will give thee a letter of charges ; act according to its injunctions.' And he drew forth a packet of written papers and gave it to his son and said, 'O my son, I have proved these much, and have passed my earthly life with comfort, and I hope from God Most High that my Hereafter may be happy also. If the world and the Hereafter be needful for thee likewise, act according to these counsels.' So the youth took and read them, and there was written : ' Do good to him who doth good to thee ; do good to him too who doth evil to thee ; supply the need of him who asketh a need of thee ; love the folk as much as in thee lieth ; take heed that thou cast no one's fault in his face ; speak not the word which will grieve ; if thy neighbour be sick, ask after him ; think of others what thou thinkest of thyself ; be not treacherous ; let thy love be alway with the good ; never interrupt a person and speak to others ; talk not with him who loveth thee not ; when with a great man speak not before he doth ; ever guard thee against hypocrites and evil women, and trust them not.' If thou do the contrary to these, thy story will resemble the story of that miserable wretch. But may-hap my king has not heard that story." The king said, " Tell on, let us hear." Quoth the vezir,

The Twenty-Ninth Vezir's Story.

" There was in the palace of the world a grocer, and he had a wife, a beauty of the age ; and that woman had a leman. One day this woman's leman said, ' If thy husband found us

out, he would not leave either of us sound.'
The woman said, 'I am able to manage that I
shall make merry with thee before my husband's
eyes.' The youth said, 'Such a thing cannot
be.' The woman replied, 'In such and such a
place there is a great tree, to-morrow I will go
a-pleasuring with my husband to the foot of
that tree; do thou hide thyself in a secret place
near that tree, and when I make a sign to thee,
come.' As her leman went off, her husband
came. The woman said, 'Fellow, my soul
would go a-pleasuring with thee to-morrow
to such and such a tree.' The fellow replied,
'So be it.' When it was morning the woman
and her husband went to that tree. The
woman said, 'They say that he who eats this
sweetmeat sees single things as though they
were double.' And she ate some and gave her
husband some to eat. Half-an-hour afterward
the woman climbed up the tree and turned and
looked down and began, 'May thou be blind!
may thou get the like from God! fellow, what
deed is this deed thou doest? Is there anyone
who has ever done this deed? Thou makest
merry with a strange woman under the eyes of
thy wife; quick, divorce me.' And she cried
out. Her husband said, 'Out on thee, woman,
hast thou turned mad? there is no one by me.'

Quoth the woman, 'Be silent, unblushing, shameless fellow ; lo, the woman is with thee, and thou deniest.' Her husband said, 'Come down.' She replied, 'I will not come down so long as that woman is with thee.' Her husband began to swear protesting, and the woman came down and said to him, 'Where is that harlot ? quick, show her me, else thou shalt know.' Again the fellow sware, and the woman said, 'Can it then be the work of the sweetmeat ?' The fellow said, 'May be.' Quoth the woman, 'Do thou too go up and look down on me, and let us see.' Her husband clutched the tree and, while he was climbing, the woman signed to her leman. The fellow looked down and saw the woman making merry with a youth. This time the fellow cried out, 'Away with thee, out on thee, shameless youth.' The woman said, 'Thou liest.' But the fellow could not endure it and began to come down, and the youth ran off."

"Now, O king, know that such tricks abound in women ; rule by a woman's word is not lawful." And he kissed the ground and made intercession for the prince. When the king heard this story from the vezir he sent the youth to the prison and went himself to the chase.

That day, too, he found the evening draw in

x

and he returned from the chase and came to the palace, and the lady rose to greet him, and they sat down. After the repast the lady began to speak about the youth. The king said, " To-day too such an one of my vezirs made intercession for him and I sent him to the prison." The lady said, " O king, thou delayest much the affair of this unworthy youth; what is thy desire in this much compassionating him ? What I know is that this youth is of the set of that youth whom Khizr (peace on him !) killed ; but mayhap my king has not heard." The king said, " Tell on, let us hear." Quoth the lady,

The Lady's Twenty-Ninth Story.

" One day when Saint Moses (peace on him !) was exhorting and preaching to his people, they said to him, ' Who among all this assembly of beings is the wisest ? ' Saint Moses answered, ' I am the wisest.' For that he said not, ' God Most High is the wisest,' a voice cried to him, ' O Moses, at the Confluence of the Two Seas is a servant of Mine who is wiser than thou : go, see him.' Thus God Most High reproved him. Then Saint Moses prayed, saying, ' My God, how shall I find that Thy servant ? ' God Most High said, ' Take a fish, and wherever it becomes alive and goes into the water, there find him.' So Saints Moses and Joshua the son of Nun took a fish and set out; and at the Confluence of the Two Seas they found a stone; and they made that stone their pillow, and lay down. And the fish became alive and went into the sea. When they awoke, Joshua saw that the fish had become alive and gone into the water; but it came not into his mind to tell Saint Moses. So they arose from thence and went on that day and that night. Then Saint Moses grew weary, and he sat down in a place and said to Joshua the son of Nun, 'Bring the mid-day meal and let us eat.' Joshua said, 'At that place where we lay, the fish became alive and went into the water; and Satan caused me to forget to tell thee.' And Moses (peace on him!) marvelled, and they arose from thence and returned and came to that stone, and they saw a man sitting there. Saint Moses went forward and saluted that man, and Khizr (peace on him!) returned the salutation, and turned and said to Moses (peace on him!), 'Who art thou?' Moses (peace on him!) replied, 'I am Moses, and I am come that I may learn wisdom of thee.' Khizr (peace on him!) said, 'Thou wilt be unable to have patience with my dealings.' Moses (peace on him!) answered, 'If it please

God, I shall have patience.' Khizr (peace on
him!) said, 'If thou wilt be my companion, ask
nothing of me.' Moses (peace on him!) said,
'I shall not.' Then they both arose and set out,
and they came to the sea-shore and entered a
ship. While on the way, Khizr (peace on him!)
tore up a plank of that ship ; and Moses (peace
on him!) said, 'O Khizr, these took nothing
from us and carried us in their ship, now thou
makest a hole in their ship ; wishest thou to
sink it ?' Khizr (peace on him!) said, 'O
Moses, did I not say to thee that thou couldst
not have patience ?' Moses (peace on him!)
replied, 'O Khizr, hold me excused ; I will not
speak again.' While they were thus talking, a
little sparrow came and took up some water
from the sea in his beak, and Khizr (peace on
him!) said, 'O Moses, thy knowledge and my
knowledge are not as much in the sight of God
Most High as the water this sparrow has taken
from the sea in his beak.' Then they came
forth from the ship and went to a village ; and
they saw some children playing. And Khizr
(peace on him!) went and smote one of them
and slew him. Moses (peace on him!) said, 'O
Khizr, wherefore didst thou slay that child unjustly ?' Khizr (peace on him!) replied, 'O
Moses, did I not say to thee that thou couldst

not have patience?' Moses (peace on him!)
said, 'Hold me excused; it passed from my
mind; if I ask again, bear me no longer company.' They passed and came to another
village; and in that village they would give
them no food. While they were going along
they saw in a street a bowing wall which was
like to fall down. Khizr (peace on him!) took
and built up that wall. And Moses (peace
on him!) said, 'O Khizr, in this village they
would give us neither lodging nor bread; yet
thou hast built up their wall without hire.'
Khizr (peace on him!) said, 'Now is our part-
ing with thee; but I will explain these questions
to thee. The owners of that ship to which I
did damage are poor friendless men; and there
is a king who is seizing upon all ships, but
because a plank of that one is broken he will
not seize upon it, so its owners will be able to
support themselves.* The two parents of the
boy whom I slew are believers; had the boy
grown up, he would have become a rebel against
God Most High, so I slew him that his evil
might not touch his father and his mother and
many others, and that he might not die in
unbelief. And beneath this wall which I have

---

* They could easily repair the slight damage.

built up is a buried treasure, its owners are two orphans ; had it fallen down now, that treasure would have been lost to them ; but when these orphans are grown up, the wall will fall down, and while they are building it they will find that treasure ; therefore did I build it up.' And Khizr (peace on him !) went in one direction, and Moses (peace on him !) went in another."*

" Now, O king, even as Khizr (peace on him !) slew that youth that he might not rebel and his evil touch his father and his mother and many poor creatures, so do thou kill this tyrant youth, else thou shalt be repentant." When the king heard these beguiling words of the lady he said, " To morrow will I slay him." And they went to bed.

When it was morning the king came and sat upon his throne, and he caused the youth to be brought and ordered the executioner, " Smite off his head." The Thirtieth Vezir came forward and said, " O king of the world, beware and beware, hurry not in this work, for hurry is the work of Satan. Our Lord the Apostle of God hath said that even as the blood courseth in a man's veins, so courseth Satan. This is

---

* All this story is an amplification of a passage in the eighteenth chapter of the Koran.

incumbent on my king, that he hasten not in this affair, for women are devils; and they have said that many heads were cut off in the two tribes by reason of a woman; but mayhap my king has not heard it." The king said, "Tell on, let us hear." Quoth the vezir,

THE THIRTIETH VEZIR'S STORY.

"It is thus related: An Arab of the tribe of the Benī-'Aqīl took a goat to a city with the purpose of selling it. An Arab of the tribe of the Benī-Nefīr wished to buy that goat. The owner of the goat wanted eight baghdādīs as the price, the purchaser offered six. The owner of the goat sware he would divorce his wife if he gave it for an aspre less than eight baghdādīs, and the purchaser sware he would divorce his if he gave an aspre more than six. Then the two of them began to quarrel. The Arab who wished to buy took up a stone and threw it at the owner of the goat; it hit his head which broke like a rotten gourd. His kinsfolk heard this and they came and smote that other man, and killed the killer. As a man of each tribe had been slain, they fell one upon the other. Every one came on his horse with his arms to the field, and they began to fight with each other, so that hills of slain arose and blood

flowed in streams. At length the tribe of the
Benī-'Aqīl was victorious, and put to flight the
tribe of the Benī-Nefīr. That tribe went to
the prince of the Abyssinians and asked help.
So the prince of Abyssinia gave them two
hundred horsemen ; and the Nefīr prince again
fell upon the 'Aqīl prince, and they began to
fight one with another. At length the fortune
of the 'Aqīl prince was changed into disaster,
and the Benī-Nefīr army returned with victory
and triumph."

" Now, O king, be it known to thee that for
that an Arab mentioned the divorcing of his
wife heads went off and the wealth and lives of
many were lost ; and the two lands were ruined
because of women. And this day I, thy slave,
make intercession for the prince." And he
kissed the ground. And the king sent the
prince to the prison and himself mounted for
the chase.

When it was evening he returned and came
to the palace, and the lady rose to greet him,
and they sat down. After the repast the lady
again asked of the youth. The king said, " To-
day too such an one of my vezirs made intercession for him, and I sent him to the prison."
The lady said, " O king, deem not those vezirs
friends to thee ; they watch their opportunity.

Thy **story** is like **the** story of that king and **the** vezir." The king **said**, "Relate that **story, let** us hear it." Quoth the lady,

The **Lady's** Thirtieth Story.

" In the palace of the world there was **a king.** One day **a** dervish came before **that** king **and** said, '**O** king, I **know** a charm **on** repeating which I can enter **into** whatever body **I** please.' **The king** forthwith ordered that they brought **a** goose, and **he** turned and said to the dervish, ' Canst thou **enter the** body of this goose ? ' The dervish repeated the charm and entered **the** body **of** that **goose,** and the dervish's body remained lifeless. **When** the king **saw that thing he** wondered. Then the dervish repeated that charm, and he again entered **his** own frame. **And** the king learned that charm from the dervish. One **day the** king **went** to the chase with the vezir ; they had taken **a** deer, when the king who was by the vezir's side repeated that charm and entered the body of the deer, and he frisked about **for a** time ; and his **own** frame remained lifeless. The king again repeated **the** charm **and** re-entered his frame. The vezir **saw these things and** marvelled, and he asked the king, **saying, 'Where** learnedst thou this ? ' The king **replied, 'I** learned it from a dervish.'

The vezir begged and entreated the king, saying,
'Teach me that charm.' As the king was in
the most generous humour he taught the vezir
that charm; and when the vezir had learned
that charm from the king he began to watch his
opportunity. One day the king and the vezir
went out in disguise, and while they were walking about they saw a dead parrot lying at the
foot of a tree. Quoth the vezir, 'O king, canst
thou enter the body of this parrot?' The king
forthwith recited that charm and entered the
body of the parrot, and he flew off and perched
upon a tree. Then the vezir forthwith repeated
that charm and entered the king's body, and he
taught that charm to a slave of his and made
him go into his body. And the king remained
in the parrot's body on that tree, and as soon
as he saw the vezir thus, he repented of his
having taught him the charm; but what avail,
what could he do? Now the king had a great
garden, and he flew off and went to that garden,
and sad and sorrowful perched on the branch of
a tree and sat pondering. Our story goes to
the vezir. When the vezir entered the king's
body he pushed on and went into the harem;
and when he went up to the queen he desired
to make merry with her. The lady looked, this
was the king, but he had not a trace of the airs

or love-tricks or manners of the king ; and she wondered and feigned to be sick ; and she would not let the king near her couch.* So the vezir waited, saying in himself, ' I shall have patience for to-day and to-night ; she will get well, then shall I make merry.' When the night was turned to morning the lady saw that there was not in him a trace of the king's nature, and she said in herself, ' By God, this is not the king.' And she feigned to be yet more sick and began to watch how it would end. Our story goes to the king. The king said, ' There is no profit in brooding sadly here ;' and he said with eloquent speech to the gardener, ' O gardener, take me and carry me to the bazaar and sell me, and may my price be lawful for thee, only give me not for less than a thousand sequins.' The gardener put the parrot in a cage and took it to the city, and every one saw that it was a sagacious parrot ; and they all wondered at the eloquence of the parrot. Now there was in that city a woman who received a thousand sequins from every person who passed a night with her. One night that woman saw in a dream that she was making merry till the morning with a mer-

---

* In Belletête's text the lady, while wondering at the alteration in the king's manner, complies at once with the vezir's wishes.

chant. When it was morning she awoke, and she arose and went to that merchant and said, 'O merchant, this night I made merry with thee in my dream till morning ; a night's intercourse with me is a thousand sequins ; now fetch and give me the thousand sequins.' Quoth the merchant, 'Why should I give them ?' The woman said, 'For that I made merry with thee.' The merchant said, 'Thou didst not.' And the woman began a great quarrel and summoned the merchant to the tribunal. So they arose, and while they were going to the tribunal they met the parrot. The parrot gave ear and heard their quarrel and said, 'Come here, let us see, what is your quarrel ?' So they came up to the parrot, and many people were present there, and they recounted all the events one by one. The parrot listened and turned to the merchant and said, 'Go, bring a thousand sequins and a mirror.' The merchant went and brought a thousand sequins in a purse and a mirror. The parrot placed the purse with the sequins opposite the mirror so that the reflection of the purse was seen in the mirror. All those who were present looked on. The parrot said to that woman, 'What wantest thou of the merchant ?' She replied, 'I want my due, a thousand sequins.' The parrot said, 'Come, take the thousand

sequins that are in the mirror.' The woman
said, 'How? There are no sequins in the
mirror.' The parrot said, 'These are they in
the rouleau.' The woman replied, 'That rouleau
is the reflection of the rouleau outside.' The
parrot said, 'The due of thy making merry with
the merchant in thy dream is as that which is
seen in the mirror; if thou are content with thy
due, take it; if not, thou hast no further due.'
All those who were present applauded this
judgment of the parrot; and the lady was
ashamed and went away. Then said they who
were present to the merchant, 'Buy thou this
parrot for ten sequins of full weight.' And the
merchant asked the gardener, and the gardener
wished a thousand sequins. So this story
reached the king's chief lady, and she said, 'Can
a parrot like this be found?' And she sent the
thousand sequins and bought the parrot and
hung up the cage before the palace. In the
evening the vezir entered the harem, and he
came up to the chief lady and said, 'Till now I
have been without thee, for thou wast sick; but
art thou not yet well?' The lady answered, 'I
am not going to get better; off, begone.' So
the vezir went and made merry with the other
girls; but the chief lady would not let him near
her. As for the parrot, he sighed and wailed.

One day the vezir said to the chief lady, ' I
know a charm which when I repeat I can enter
whatever body I please.' The chief lady said.
' Enter the body of one of the slave-girls that
are here.' The vezir answered, ' It cannot be a
living one, it must be a lifeless form.' The lady
said, ' There is a slaughtered goose in the
kitchen ; let them bring that, and enter it that I
may see.' So she called out and they brought
it. The vezir repeated that charm and entered
the body of the goose and walked about crying,
' Quack ! quack !' And the king's body remained empty. Forthwith the parrot repeated
that charm and entered the king's body, and
straightway he seized the goose by the neck
and dashed it against the wall and killed it.
And the lady marvelled and saw that it was the
king himself, and she asked him of these things.
And the king explained to her the whole of
them."

" Now, O king, I have told this story for
that the king may know that there is no trusting
in vezirs ; they have not found an opportunity
and so seem weak. Be thou ready, what time
they look for the youth it is in their hands to
slay thee. O king, kill this youth that this evil
touch not thee and me, else the very opposite is
certain." When the king heard this story from

the lady dread fell upon his heart and he said,
"O lady, what am I ?   Neither does my heart
approve the acts of these ; on the morrow I will
kill the youth."   And they went to bed.

When it was morning the king went and sat
upon his throne, and he caused the youth to be
brought and ordered the executioner, " Smite
off his head."   The Thirty-First Vezir came
forward and said, "O king of the world, go not
by the woman's word ; it is a calumny against
the prince.   Mayhap the king has not heard
the story of the blind man and the khalif."
The king said, " Tell on, let us hear."   Quoth
the vezir,

The Thirty-First Vezir's Story.

" In the time of the Khalif Reshid there was
a blind man, and if anyone lost anything he
would find it.   One day a box belonging to the
khalif was lost, and it was filled full inside with
rubies and turkises.   They told the khalif of
this blind man ; and he said, ' Bring him.'   So
they brought him.   The khalif said, ' A thing
of ours is lost, find it then ; and say what is the
thing that is lost.'   The blind man pondered a
little, then he felt about him with his hands, and
a date-stone came into his hand.   He said, ' O
king, what is lost is then a box ; and so there

are a few pearls and a few turkises and a few rubies in it.' The khalif said, 'Who has taken it?' The blind man answered, 'It is the groom.' The khalif asked, 'Where has he put it?' The blind man said, 'He has laid it in the well.' Now there was a well in the khalif's palace; and they made a man go down the well, and he brought up the box from the well. The khalif wondered at the blind man's thus knowing, and he said, 'O sheykh, how marvellously hast thou known of this lost thing!' The blind man said, 'I knew it by inference; when thou saidest to me that a thing was lost, I felt about me and found a date-stone, and I knew therefrom that a box would be of that form; the flowers of the date resemble pearls, I knew therefrom that there were pearls in the box; its leaves resemble turkises,* these too were there; and its fruit is sometimes yellow and sometimes red, but it is mostly red, rubies were there. And when thou askedst me who was the thief, a horse neighed below, and I knew that he was the groom. And when thou askedst me where he had put it, someone cried out, "He has brought the water from the well," and from

---

* Blue and green being regarded as variations of one colour.

that I knew that he had laid it in the well.'
The khalif greatly applauded and admired the
sagacity of the blind man."

"Now, O king, these many vezirs of thine
speak not their words idly. Slay not the prince, or
at last the fire thereof shall not leave thy heart,
and night and day thou shalt burn in the fire of
sighs." And he kissed the ground and made
intercession for the prince. When the king
heard this story from the vezir he sent the youth
to the prison and himself mounted for the chase.

When it was evening he returned from the
chase and came to the palace, and the lady rose
to greet him, and they sat down. After the
repast the lady again began to speak about the
youth. The king said, "To-day too such an
one of my vezirs made intercession for him, and
I again sent him to the prison." The lady
said, "O king, this youth has trodden under
foot the honour of many, and has given thy
dignity and worth to the tongue of reproach.
Mayhap my king has not heard the story of
that cadi." The king said, "Tell on, let us
hear." Quoth the lady,

THE LADY'S THIRTY-FIRST STORY.

"In the city of Cesarea were two cadis; and
they loved not one another, but were ever at

enmity. One day certain people said to the king of that country, ' Cadi Such-an-one is a lover of thy son ; day and night he watches his opportunity and says, " Would that I could see him alone." ' The king was wroth, and ordered that they banished that cadi. Straightway they told the other cadi, ' To-day of a sudden the king grew wroth with that cadi, thine adversary, and deposed and banished him.'   Forthwith this cadi mounted his horse and went before the king, he performed the ceremonies of salutation and asked permission of the king and said, ' My king, give me leave that I may go from this city.'   The king said, ' Why wouldst thou go ? What has happened to thee ? '   The cadi replied, ' I have heard that they said to the king that Cadi Such-an-one is a lover of the prince and watches his opportunity; and that slanderers caused my king to be wroth and made him depose and banish him. Now I am a lover of the king and I am also a lover of the prince ; to-morrow slanderers will come and say this and that concerning me, and cause my king to be wroth, and he will depose and banish me too. So now, ere thou art wroth with me, I would go.'   The king said, ' With what would thy heart now be pleased ? '   Straightway the cadi kissed the ground and said, ' It would be very pleased did thou pardon that cadi and appoint him again to his place.' So the king pardoned the cadi and appointed him again to his place."

"Now, O king, know that a wise foe is better than a foolish friend. This youth is a foolish youth, and by reason of that is my honour thus gone. I may not look on the blessed beauty of my king because of my shame. Each one of the vezirs says some different thing. God Most High knows that I am my king's friend; I would not that a calamity should come down on thee. Knowing this much, I have spoken these words without selfish aim. Slay the youth, else afterward he will slay thee without mercy." When the king heard these beguiling words of the lady he said, "To-morrow will I see to him." And they went to bed.

When it was morning the king came and sat upon his throne, and he caused the youth to be brought, and ordered the executioner, "Smite off his head." The Thirty-Second Vezir came forward and said.

THE THIRTY-SECOND VEZIR'S STORY.

"One day while the Sultan of Egypt was sitting with his vezirs and nobles in the place of the divan, his fancy led him to talk of womankind. He asked one of his nobles, 'How art thou with thy wife?' The noble answered, 'O king, of whatsoever gifts and bounties I receive from my king every year, I spend the half on my wife, yet, when all is done, she complains, saying, "What hast thou spent on me these many years?"' Then he asked his vezir, 'And ye; how are ye?' The vezir said, 'Whatsoever wealth I gain under your royal shadow, it all passes through her hands; she keeps what she wishes and gives away what she wishes not; yet, when all is done, she complains, saying, "What good have I seen from thee?"' Then he asked all his vezirs, and each one of them complained in some manner of his wife. The king said, 'I used to think my wife alone in this matter, but they seem then all the same; my lady is in lack of nothing, yet, when all is done, she complains, saying, "What have I?"'"

"Now, O king, know that no one is satisfied with a woman; do not thou then slay the youth on the woman's word. Make not a woman ruler over thee, destroy not thine own comfort, act not that thou shalt continue in wailing and lamentation." And he made intercession for the prince. When this story was heard from the vezir the king sent the youth to the prison and went himself to the chase.

When it was evening the king returned from the chase, and the lady rose to greet him, and they sat down. After the repast the lady began to speak about the youth. The king said, "To-day such an one of my vezirs made intercession for him, and I sent him to the prison." The lady said, "O king of the world, tear from thy heart the love of the youth that the love of God Most High may come therein, and that kingship may be secured to thee in the world and the Hereafter. Mayhap the king has not heard the story of Fuzayl."* The king said, "Tell on, let us hear." Quoth the lady,

THE LADY'S THIRTY-SECOND STORY.

"One day Fuzayl (the mercy of God on him!) took his son upon his knee, and while he was fondling him, the boy looked in his father's face and said, 'Father, lovest thou me?' Fuzayl answered, 'My son, I love thee.' Then the boy said, 'Lovest thou God?' Fuzayl answered, 'Son, I love Him.' The boy said, 'Father, can two loves be contained in one heart?' When Fuzayl heard these words from the boy he knew that they were not merely the boy's words, but

---

* Fuzayl was a pious Muslim who received his education from the Imām Ja'fer-i Sādiq ; he died at Mekka in 187 (A.D. 803).

an inspiration from before God. Straightway he put his son from his knee on to the ground, and he tore from his heart his love for his son, and filled it with the love of God Most High. And now, whenever his name is mentioned, they say, 'The mercy of God on him!'"

"Now, O king, until thou too likewise tear from thy heart love for the youth, thou canst not love God Most High. If thou wish to be king in the world and the Hereafter, kill this unworthy youth." When the king heard this tale from the lady he said, "To-morrow will I kill him." And they went to bed.

When it was morning the king came and sat upon his throne, and he caused the youth to be brought and ordered the executioner, "Smite off his head." The Thirty-Third Vezir came forward and said, "O king of the world, the cruelty toward the prince has been great; if it be as punishment to the prince, it will suffice. Beware, go not by the woman's word, slay not the prince, or in the end thou shalt be repentant. And through the wiles of women have many of the people of Paradise become deserving of Hell. If the king grant leave I will relate a story suitable to this." The king said, "Tell on, let us hear." Quoth the vezir,

The Thirty-Third Vezir's Story.

" In the olden time **there** was a youth, and they told him that in a certain city was **a** wondrous fair woman who **had no like** in beauty in **any** place. The youth fell in love with **her** without having seen her, and he set **out for** the **city** where the woman was. While he was journeying on the road, he saw some folk sowing wheat ; and after **an hour** that **seed** ripened and **was cut,** whereupon they burned it with fire. And **the** youth wondered **at** them. He went **on further and saw a** man grasping **a** stone and trying **to** lift **it, but he could not lift it ;** then he **put** another stone on the top **of that** stone, and **he was** able to lift them **a** little ; **then he** put **yet** another stone on that, and this time, when he had laid the three stones together, **he lifted them up** and **bare** them **off. And he** wondered **at this** too. **He went on** further and saw some people mounted on a sheep, and there was one mounted above them, and there were some others who sought **to** mount but could not. And the youth **marvelled at** these also. **And he** passed on and came **to the** city where **that** woman was ; **and he saw an** elder seated **at the** gate **of** that city. The youth saluted **him,** and he returned the salutation **and** asked, saying, 'Wherefore art

thou come here?' The youth replied, 'They
say that in this city is a beautiful woman ; I am
come to see her.' The elder said, 'What hast
thou seen of wonders on the road thou camest?'
He replied, ' I have seen many wonders, things
greatly to be marvelled at.' The elder said,
' Tell them that I may hear.' So the youth related all that he had seen. He asked, ' Knowest
thou what those were ?' The youth said, ' Nay.'
The elder said, ' They who sowed the seed and,
when it had reached perfection, burned it, are
those persons who perform a good deed and
then go and act with hypocrisy and say to the
passers-by, " Now have I done a good deed ;"
and so burn it with their tongues and make it
nought. And that man who could not carry the
stone and put two other stones on it and then
carried them, is he who commits a sin ; at first
it feels very heavy ; he does it again, then it feels
lighter than the first time ; he does it yet again,
and this time he gets used to it and it feels not
heavy at all, whereupon he takes it and bears it
wheresoever he will. And those people mounted
on the sheep, and the man over them, and those
others who sought to mount but were unable :
that sheep is the world, and those mounted on
that sheep are the rich men, and he mounted
over them is their prince, and those who were

unable to mount are the poor.' When the youth
heard **these** words from the elder he applauded
them much and said, ' O elder, since thou hast
thus known these, thou must **know of** that
woman ; tell me wherever she be.' The elder
said, ' Thou hast got **all** these my counsels and
seen these many examples yet **thou hast** not
awakened from heedlessness and hast asked for
an unlawful woman.' And he smote him a blow
on the face, and straightway the youth's senses
left him. After a time he opened **his** eyes and
he found himself **in** Hell."

" **Now, O** king, **I have** told this story for that
the king **may** know that there are many youths
whose faces will be black before God Most
High by reason of women. O king, beware,
slay not the **prince** on the woman's word, **or**
afterward thou **shalt** suffer remorse." And he
made intercession **for the** prince for that day.
And the king yielded to him and sent the
prince **to the prison and went** himself to the
chase.

When it was evening the king returned from
the chase and came to the palace, and the lady
rose to greet him, and they **sat** down. After
the **repast the lady** began to speak about the
youth. The king said, " To-day too such an
one of **my** vezirs made intercession for him and

I sent him to the prison." The lady said, "O king, in some among youths devilry and evil-nature abound, and there is a story suitable to this ; mayhap my king has not heard it." The king said, " Tell on, let us hear." Quoth the lady,

The Lady's Thirty-Third Story.

"Once upon a time a certain man had a naughty son who would ever cry for the least thing, and whenever they cooked food and gave it him he would cry and say, ' Ye have given me too little ; I am not filled.' They cooked a large pot of food and filled a great dish with it and gave it to the boy. Whereupon the boy kicked it with his foot and spilt it, and went and sat down. His mother said, ' Out on thee, that shouldst eat poison ; when I give thee sufficient quantity thou sayest it is too little, and if I give thee much thou sayest it is too much ; why hast thou now spilt all this food ?' Thereupon the boy lay down on the ground and rolled and began to cry. At length his father and mother were helpless with him, and cursed him, saying, ' Son, may God take thy life !' "

" Now, O king, since thou wilt not slay this youth, may God take his life and may all the world escape from his wickedness." When the king heard this story from the lady he said, "To-morrow will I see to him." And they went to bed.

When it was morning the king went and sat upon his throne, and he caused the youth to be brought, and ordered the executioner, "Smite off his head." The Thirty-Fourth Vezir came forward and said, "O king of the world, kings are shepherds on the earth, the rest are the sheep; slay not now thy son on the woman's word, or to-morrow, on the Resurrection-Day, when the Owner of the sheep will ask of thee the plight of the lambs, thou wilt find it hard to answer. And it is well known that the treachery and wickedness of women are great. Mayhap the king has not heard the story of the Persian and his wife." The king said, "Tell on, let us hear." Quoth the vezir,

THE THIRTY-FOURTH VEZIR'S STORY.

"In the land of Persia there was a merchant, and that merchant's wealth was exceeding great. One night a guest came to the merchant's house and lodged there. The merchant brought some food and they sat down. The guest saw in a corner a dog and a fair woman eating out of one dish; and he wondered exceedingly and asked the merchant. The merchant said, ' Their plight is not spoken of.' But the guest entreated and begged him to tell. Then the merchant said, ' This woman is my slave-girl whom I bought with my money. I made her my wife and loved her as my life, so that all I had was in her hands. I had a black slave. Now these struck up a friendship ; and as to me, I knew not of it. One day they agreed to slay me. One day the woman said to me, " Come, I would go with thee to a certain place ; there is a matter, we will see to it." And she took me and brought me to a quiet place where they had pitched a tent. Now that slave was therein ; and he came out suddenly, and they bore me down that they might kill me. I had always fed this dog, and he followed me and was come along with me, and when he saw me in this plight he ran and seized that slave from behind and pulled him and drew him off me. I too found strength and opportunity, and I made to seize the woman, but she fled off. I killed the slave, but, as my love was with the woman, I could not bring myself to kill her. For that this dog was the cause of my safety do I thus honour him ; and to disgrace and abase the woman do I thus keep the two of them together and feed them.'"

"Now, O king, the learned have said that there is no trusting in three things; the first is a woman, the second is a horse, and the third is a sword. Beware, O king, slay not the prince on the woman's word, else afterward thou wilt be repentant. And grant to me, your slave, the prince's life for to-day." When the king heard this story from the vezir he sent the youth to the prison and went himself to the chase.

When it was evening he returned and came to the palace, and the lady rose to greet him, and they sat down. After the repast the lady began to speak about the youth. The king said, "To-day such an one of my vezirs made intercession for him and I sent him to the prison." The lady said, "I am from heart and soul my king's sincere friend. What is beseeming the king is this, that he impute not my words to selfish interest, but accomplish them; and there is a story suitable to this, if there be permission I will relate it." The king said, "Relate, let us hear." Quoth the lady,

The Lady's Thirty-Fourth Story.

"There was in the palace of the world a king, and that king had a falcon, which, whenever he launched it at a quarry, used to take

two animals at once. There was a noble of
that country, and his name was Emir Sārim.
He heard of this accomplishment of that falcon,
and he arose to see it, and came to that city and
went before the king. And the king honoured
that noble in the highest degree. After some
days that noble brought about a fitting opportunity, and told how they praised the falcon and
how he longed to see it. The king ordered
that on the morrow they went forth to the,
chase ; and he launched the falcon several times,
and on each occasion it took two animals at
once ; and Emir Sārim wondered exceedingly.
Then quoth the king to that noble, ' Is the falcon
deserving of the praise ? ' Emir Sārim replied,
' Yea, and of greater.' The king said, ' Take
this falcon, I have given it to thee, let it be
thine.' So Emir Sārim rejoiced and accepted
it. And he bowed down his head and pondered,
and after a while he raised his head and said,
' O king, I cannot find anything worthy to give
my king in return for this falcon ; but I have
twelve sons and a thousand valiant and famous
warriors, let them all be my king's.' And in
this way did the worth of the falcon increase ;
for at first it used to catch two birds, but now
it caught twelve youths and a thousand valiant
warriors. And these words came pleasant to

the king, and he bestowed much wealth on Emir Sârim."

" Now, O king, what is befitting kings is this, that they accomplish the words of those that wish them well ; and I love my king from heart and soul. It is needful then to see to that unworthy youth." When the king heard this story from the lady, he said, " Do not thou be troubled, to-morrow I will slay him." And they went to bed.

When it was morning the king went forth and sat upon his throne, and he said, " Where is the youth and where the executioner ? " When they had brought the youth and the executioner, the Thirty-Fifth Vezir came forward and said, " O king, mercy, by thy head and by God, thou hast sinned. I would read and expound the Koran before the king ; if the king give me not leave, he will sin ; and if he listen not to my reading and follow not its meaning, it will be error itself." Then the king said, " I ask pardon of God ; we hear and obey." Quoth the vezir, " God Most High saith in His ancient Word, 'Say: If ye love God, then follow me : God will love you and forgive you your sins ; for God is Forgiving, Merciful.'* O

---

* Koran, iii. 29.

king, the reason of the revelation of this verse
was this, the hypocrites came and said to the
Apostle, 'O Apostle of God, we love thee, thou
art the true Apostle of God.' And when they
went forth they said, 'God forbid! again God
forbid! he is a mighty liar and a sorcerer and a
soothsayer and a madman.' And God Most
High thus addressed His Beloved, 'O Beloved,
say to them: If ye really love God follow me;
and God Most High will love you too and
forgive your sins; for God Most High is Forgiving, Merciful.' O king, that man who is a
believer and an unitarian must love God Most
High and follow His Apostle; and to follow
him is to observe whatever he said or did.
Now the Apostle saith concerning women,
'They are lacking in understanding and
religion;' so it beseems not the king to act
contrary to the Apostle's word and go by the
word of the woman. And the Apostle also
saith, 'Consult them and do the contrary.' O
king, the wise man is he who in compliance with
this Sacred Tradition never trusts the love and
friendship of women or acts according to their
words. And there is a story suitable to this;
if the king grant leave I will relate it." The
king said, "Relate, let us hear." Quoth the
vezir,

The Thirty-Fifth Vezir's Story.

" Once upon a time a man went on to the roof
of his house and repaired it, and when he was
about to come down he called to his wife, ' Ho!
wife, how shall I come down?' The woman
answered, ' The roof is free, what would happen? thou art a young man, jump down.' The
youth jumped down, and his ankle was put out
of joint, and for a whole year he was bedridden,
and his ankle came not back to its place. The
next year the youth again went on to the roof
and repaired it; then he turned and called to his
wife, ' Ho! wife, how shall I come down?' The
woman said, ' Jump not, thine ankle has not yet
come to its place; come down gently.' The
youth said, ' The other time, for that I followed
thy words and not those of the Apostle, was my
ankle put out of joint and it has not yet come to
its place; now shall I follow the words of the
Apostle and do the contrary to what thou sayest.'
And he jumped down, and straightway his ankle
came to its place."

And he kissed the ground and made intercession for the prince. When the king heard this
story from the vezir he sent the youth to the
prison and went himself to the chase.

When it was evening he returned and came to

z

the palace, and the lady rose to greet him, and
they sat down.   After the repast the lady began
to speak about the youth.   The king said, " To-
day too such an one of my vezirs made intercession for him and I sent him to the prison."   The
lady said, "O king, why didst thou not kill the
youth to-day?   When youths take a thing into
their heads their hearts are never at rest until they
accomplish it.   Mayhap my king has not heard
the story of a certain king's son."   The king
said, " Tell on, let us hear."   Quoth the lady,

The Lady's Thirty-Fifth Story.

" In the palace of the world there was a king,
and he had a son, who read the Koran and lessons in a school and whose intelligence pleased
his master.   One day the boy could not do his
lesson; the teacher did not give him another
lesson, but said, ' Go, study thy lesson.'   It was
the same on the second day and the third day.
When the master saw this he told his father,
and his father said, ' O son, why wilt not thou
study thy lesson?'   The boy replied, ' One day
I passed through the bazaar and saw hung up in
a shop very many lamps, row upon row ; and
this came into my heart : if they were to give me
a stick into my hand and I were to strike once
at those lamps with all my might, I wonder how

many I should break. Since that time I have
not learned my lesson, for my mind has been
always at the breaking of the lamps.' The king
gave him a stick and sent him and a teacher and
a servant to the shop, and ordered that they
should pay for as many lamps as were destroyed.
So they went off and came to that shop and said
to the prince, ' Now, strike, letus see.' And the
prince struck a blow with the stick at those
lamps with all his might and he destroyed many
lamps, and those present cried, ' The blessing
of God on the prince ; he has broken these many
lamps!'* Then they satisfied the shopkeeper.
As the prince's longing was gone and his whim
gratified, he again began to read and study his
lessons as heretofore."

"O king, I have told this story for that the
king may know that a youth must needs accomplish that whereon he resolves. And there is
an evil resolve in the heart of this youth, he
has determined on the king's throne and life.
O king, beware, be not negligent, or this youth
will slay thee in the end, know thou that for
certain." When the king heard this story from
the lady he said, " To-morrow will I kill him."
And they went to bed.

---

* He is so clever to break such a number at one stroke.

When it was morning the king went and sat upon his throne, and he caused the youth to be brought and ordered the executioner, " Smite off his head." The Thirty-Sixth Vezir came forward and said, "O king of the world, slay not the prince according to the woman's word; for the craft and mischief of women are great, and it is needful ever to guard against their mischief. Mayhap my king has not heard the story of a certain merchant youth." The king said, " Tell on, let us hear." Quoth the vezir,

THE THIRTY-SIXTH VEZIR'S STORY.

"Of old time there was a dervish who, while he was wandering about, slept a night at a certain village. In the morning the villagers said to the dervish, 'O dervish, there are robbers on the road which leads from the right side of the village; take heed and go not by that road, but go by the left.' When the morn was high the dervish went that road where the robbers were; he said, 'I am a dervish; what of mine can they take?' When it was near afternoon he came to a certain place and saw a palace, and he opened the gate and went inside, and he saw that there was no one there, and he waited till the evening. There was no one coming or going on any side, so he went and lay down. When it was midnight a noise arose and the dervish was afraid. There was some horse dung in a corner, and he buried himself in that, **so** that he was all covered, save that his two **eyes** could see. The door opened and the dervish saw forty mounted men, and one by them whose hands were bound **and** round whose neck they had fastened **a** rope and whom they were **thus** dragging. They said, ' Has then anyone come this day?' And they went through the palace but saw **no one.** They tied that bound youth to a pillar, and lit a fire, and cooked **food and** took it and ate and drank; and when they were drunk they lay down and **slept.** The dervish **arose from the** place where **he was** and asked of the youth whose hands were bound concerning these things. The youth replied, ' Dervish, this is no time **for** questions; deliver me from this.' So the dervish delivered that youth. Thereupon **the** youth went and took a dagger in his hand and slew all of those thieves. Then he took a candle and put it into a lantern and gave **it into** the dervish's hand and said, ' Take this lantern, but cover it with thy **cloak** that it may not give light without.' So the dervish took **it and** hid it and they went forth thence and **came to** a ruined city, and they went to **the fire-room of a bath** and entered it through **a** certain **place. There** was there a beautiful room, and the youth said to the dervish, 'Bring out the lantern that our eyes may see.' The dervish displayed the lantern and they saw a girl sleeping with a youth, and the other youth smote him who was lying with the girl and slew him. The girl awoke from sleep and said to that youth, 'Now thou hast slain him; what answer wilt thou give his comrades to-morrow?' The youth answered, 'Be at ease, I have slain them too.' Then the youth took the dervish and they entered the treasury of those robbers, and the dervish saw that on one side of that treasury lay heaped-up gold and on one side white silver. The youth said, 'Dervish, go, get two of those robbers' horses and lade them with this money, and take it off and go.' The dervish said, 'Youth, what deed is this deed thou hast done?' The youth answered, 'There is a farm of mine at four leagues' distance from this place; and these were forty-one robbers, and every year they came upon me, seeking to seize me; but with the leave of God Most High I used to scatter the whole of them. While they were prowling about yesterday I, having gone apart from my own men, had come to a meadow, when sleep overcame me and I lay down, and while my men were waiting, these discovered me and seized me while asleep and bound me

and took me and brought me to that palace.
Now, praise be to God! thou art the means;
thou didst deliver me; and I slew the whole of
them and am delivered from their evil.' And he
gave the dervish much wealth and said, 'Take
this wealth and these horses, be all of them
thine; and go to a thousand such places. Now
do my men seek me, go and tell them that they
come and find me here.' So the dervish mounted
and set off. As the youth had been without
sleep during the night he said to the girl, 'Make
ready food,' and he lay down to sleep. The
girl said in her heart, 'Wretch, mayst thou be
hanged by thy neck! Thou hast slain my husband and all these his comrades; I fear nought
from thee.' And she put a drug into the food.
The youth awoke from sleep and found the food
ready, and he ate it and he passed from himself
and became senseless. The girl took and
dragged him and threw him into a pit and
covered up the mouth of it. The dervish went
and found that youth's men and told them, and
these men thanked him. And they said to the
dervish, 'Come, let us go, show us our master.'
The dervish turned back and took these men
and went, and they saw the girl seated but the
youth was not there. These asked the woman,
'Where is our master?' The woman replied,

' He mounted in the morning and went forth to hunt and has not returned.' They waited a while and saw that their master came not, and they again asked the woman. She again replied, ' I know not, he has not come back.' Then they seized the woman and bound her firmly and tortured her ; and she said, ' I imprisoned him,' and showed them the pit. They drew the youth out of the pit and said, ' Why didst thou put him into the pit ? ' The woman answered, ' I have a youthful leman ; when my first lord went out to rob, that youth would come and be with me, if he were my lord all were well with me ; I saw only this man as a hindrance and I sought to slay him, for I wished to take my young leman and this wealth and go to another place and give myself up to pleasure.' All who were standing there cursed that woman and then they committed her soul to Hell. So because there was not truth in her did she fall a prey to this retribution."

" Now, O king, I have related this story for that the king may know that there is no generosity or piety in women. They are lust-worshippers and traitors ; and in a thousand of them there is not one true. O king, beware, slay not the prince on the woman's word, or afterward thou shalt be repentant ; and too late repentance profits **not**, and the cut-off head grows **not** again." And he made intercession for **the** prince **for** that day. When the king heard this story **from the** vezir he sent the youth to the prison and went himself **to** the chase.

When **it was** evening he returned **and** came to the palace, and **the** lady rose **to** greet him, and they sat down. After the repast **the lady asked about the youth.** The **king** said, "**To-**day **too such an** one of my vezirs made intercession **for** him, and I sent him to the prison." The lady said, "**O** king, be not negligent, there is no trusting youths ; one day **will it** be that he will **slay** thee, **and** secure the throne. **Mayhap my** king **has not heard the** story of **Sultan** 'Alā-ud-Dīn." * **The king** said, "Tell on, let us hear."** Quoth** the lady,

THE LADY'S THIRTY-SIXTH STORY.

"**There was in Qonya a** king whose name **was** 'Alā-ud-Dīn. **One** day **he** went alone to **the** madhouse **to** learn the state **of** the madmen **who were there.** While he **was** going round, a **youth from among them** saw the king, and said,

---

* 'Alā-ud-Dīn Key-Qubād the Seljūqī, Sultan of Rūm, died in 636 (A.D. 1238-9).

'Welcome, O king of the world; I came a
stranger to this city, my father and my mother
are in such and such a town. To-day it is twenty-
three days that I am here; each one of the
comers and the goers says something. What can
I do? The keeper of the madhouse coveted me,
and has imprisoned me here, and will not give
me leave to go to my father and mother. For
the love of God and the Apostle, deliver me
from this!' When the youth spake these
sensible words to the king, the latter said, 'See,
such deeds occur in my day, and they oppress
the poor.' And he wept, and freed the youth.
When the youth was freed, he looked, and saw
a knife by the king's side, and he said to the
king. 'My king, I am a master cutler, show me
that knife, let me examine it; I shall make thee
a knife as an offering.' So the king drew the
knife from its sheath, and gave it to the youth.
When the youth got the knife, he stood at the
door of the madhouse, and cried, 'Out on thee,
wretch, is it right thou shouldst imprison a set
of poor creatures here, saying they are mad?
And every day comes another wretch who
beats the whole of them? Now, quick, throw
out this filth with thine own hands, or I will
rip thee open.' The king's senses well nigh
left him, and he straightway began to throw

that filth out of the window. While he was
throwing it out, the keeper of the madhouse
came in ; and as soon as the youth saw him, he
threw the knife from his hand, and ran and
came up to the king, and said, ' O king, for
God's sake leave me not, the man who always
beats us has come ; lo, this is he.' When the
keeper saw the king he was confounded, and
asked of the circumstances ; and the king told
him all that had happened. The keeper quickly
bound the youth, and brought water for the
king, who washed his hands and face, and went
out, and vowed never again to go alone to the
madhouse, or follow the words of a madman."

" Now, O king, this youth too is mad, it is
needful to guard against him ; be it not that
any hurt reach thee from him." When the
king heard these insinuating words from the
lady, he said, " To-morrow will I slay him."
And they went to bed.

When it was morning, the king came and sat
upon his throne, and he caused the youth to be
brought, and ordered the executioner, " Kill ! "
The Thirty-Seventh Vezir came forward and
said, " O king of the world, hurry not in this
matter. Satan mixes himself up with men ;
now he has entered into thy heart, and tempted
thee. Mayhap my king has not heard the

story of Eve and Satan." The king said, " Tell on, let us hear." Quoth the vezir,

The Thirty-Seventh Vezir's Story.

" From that time when Satan was cursed and driven from Paradise by reason of Adam (peace on him!) he pursued him with hatred, and sought to take vengeance. He had a son named Khannās;* and he made him assume the form of a kid, and took him before our mother Eve, and said, ' Let this kid remain by thee; I shall come now and fetch it.' Eve said, ' By reason of thee have we come forth from Paradise; art thou come now again?' Satan replied, ' If they drove you from Paradise, they have driven me thence too; one must pass from the past.' And he left the kid, and went off. Saint Adam came and saw the kid, and he said, ' Whose kid is this?' Eve answered, ' Satan has left it, and gone off; he said, " I will come now and fetch it."' Saint Adam (peace on him!) was wroth, and he killed the kid, and threw it into the desert, and went away. Satan came and said, ' Where is the kid?' Eve said, ' Adam came and killed the kid, and threw it into the desert.' Satan cried

---

* The word khannās means "tempting to backslide."

out, 'Khannās!' The kid said, 'Here I am, father.' And it became alive, and went up to him. Again Satan left it, and went off; for though Eve entreated him, saying, 'Take it, and go,' he would not take it. Saint Adam came and saw the kid, and asked about it, and Eve told him what had happened. Adam said, 'Why didst thou keep that accursed one's kid?' And he was angry with Eve; and he cut the kid into many pieces, and threw each piece in a different direction, and went away. Again Satan came and asked, and Eve told him what had happened. Again Satan cried, 'O Khannās!' And it answered, 'Here I am, father.' And it became alive, and went up to him. Again Satan left it, and went off; and though Eve said many times, 'Leave it not,' it was no avail, for Satan vanished. Again Adam came and saw the kid, and this time he smote Eve: and people have beaten their wives since that time. Adam seized the kid, and cut its throat, and cooked it, and he and Eve ate it; then he went away. Again Satan came and asked, 'Where is the kid?' Eve said, 'This time was Adam wroth, and he cut its throat, and cooked it, and we both of us ate it.' Satan again cried, 'O Khannās!' This time it answered from Eve's belly, 'Here I am, father.'

Satan said, ' My son, thou hast found thy best place ; let us tempt the sons of Adam, thou from within, and I from without, till the Resurrection, and urge them to many sins, and make them deserving of Hell.' "

" Now, O king, be it known to thee that even as the blood runs in the body and veins of man, so runs Satan tempting him. Till thorough enquiry have been made, slay not the youth, else afterward thou shalt burn in the fire of remorse." When the king heard this story from the vezir he sent the prince to the prison and went himself to the chase.

When it was evening he returned and came to the palace, and the lady rose to greet him, and they sat down. After the repast the lady asked about the youth. The king said, " To-day too such an one of my vezirs made intercession for him and I sent him to the prison." The lady said, " O king, trust not the words of the vezirs ; if thou do so, many a poor one will be abased and degraded through their vengeance. Mayhap my king has not heard the story of a certain king." The king said, " Tell on, let us hear." Quoth the lady,

THE LADY'S THIRTY-SEVENTH STORY.

" In the palace of the world there was a king, and that king had three vezirs; but there was rivalry between these. Two of them day and night incited the king against the third, saying, ' He is a traitor.' But the king believed them not. At length they promised the pages much gold and instructed them thus : ' When the king has lain down, ere he has yet fallen asleep, do ye feign to think him asleep and, while talking with each other, say at a fitting time, " I have heard from such an one that yon vezir says this and that concerning the king, and that he hates him ; many people say that vezir is an enemy to our king." ' So they did thus ; and when the king heard them he said in his heart, ' What those vezirs said is then true ; lo, the very pages have heard somewhat ; it must indeed have some foundation ; till now I believed not the vezirs, but it is then true.' And the king executed that hapless vezir. The vezirs were glad and they gave the pages the gold they had promised. So these took it and went to a private place and, while they were dividing it, one of them said, ' I spake the first ; I want more.' The other said, ' If I had not said he was an enemy to our king, the king would not

have killed him ; I shall take more.' And while
they were quarrelling with one another, the
king passed by there and he listened attentively
to their words, and when he learned of the
matters he said, ' Dost thou see ? they have by
a trick made us kill that hapless vezir.' And he
was repentant."

"Now, O king, these thy vezirs are leagued
likewise; we shall see what that unworthy
youth has promised them. Now if thou slay
him not to-morrow, he will slay thee" When
the king heard this story from the lady he said,
" To-morrow will I kill him." And they went
to bed.

When it was morning the king went and sat
upon his throne, and he caused the youth to be
brought and ordered the executioner, " Smite
off his head." The Thirty-Eighth Vezir came
forward and said, " O king of the world, be it
not that a grief come to the heart of my king
through our counsel ; for the Holy Apostle of
God hath said, ' If one see any of you do aught
reprovable, assuredly let him hinder him ; if it
be possible by the tongue, but if that be powerless, let him hinder him with the heart.' Now,
to act according to this Tradition is incumbent
upon all of us ; so let us counsel the king and
hinder as much as in us lies the wickedness of

Satan. Beware, slay not the prince on the word of the woman, for in such guile and craft abound. Mayhap my king has not heard the story of a certain merchant and his slave-girl." The king said, "Tell on, let us hear." Quoth the vezir,

THE THIRTY-EIGHTH VEZIR'S STORY.*

"*Shuyle riwayet iderler ki: Misr shehrinde bir bazirgan var idi. Bir gun bir jariye satun alub khanesine geturdi. Khanesinde bir may-muni var idi; geturub, jariyeye chekdi. Jariye eyder, 'Bazirgan, bu ne hal dir?' Bazirgan eyder, 'Buna bir gez ram ol, seni azad ideyim.' Jariye dakhi na-char muqayyed olmadi; hamile qaldi. Vaqti geldikde, bir oghlan doghurdi, jemi' a'zasi adam shekllu, illa maymun gibi bir qoyrughi var idi. Bazirgan ve jariye bu oghlanin terbiyesine meshghul oldilar. Oghlan besh alti ayliq oldi. Bir gun bazirgan bir biyuk qazghan sud doldirub, altina muhkem atesh yaqub; qayna-diqda, ol oghlani tutub qazghanin ichine braqdi. Jariye feryade bashladi; bazirgan eyder, 'Sus, feryad itme; var, malimdan azad ol.' deyub, chiqardi. Jariyeye bir miqdar altun dakhi verdi.*

---

* For reasons stated in the Preface this story is left untranslated.

A A

Dunub, qazghani uyle qaynatdi ki hich kemugi
dakhi qalmadi. Jariye bu tarafdan gunlinden
bazirgana wafir kin eyleyub, 'Jigerim nasl
yaqdin ise, ben dakhi seni yaqarim:' deyub,
fursat guzetmege bashladi. Bazirgan qazghani
indirub, bir biri uzrine yedi tas qoyub, qazghanin
uzrine gelen kefi alub, yedi tasdan suzub, yedinji
tasda olan kefi alub, bir shishe ichine qoyub,
braqdi. Jariyeye, 'Yemek hazir eyle:' deyub,
tashra chiqdi. Jariye dakhi yemek pishirub, bir
qab ichine ol zehirden qarishdirub, hazir eyledi.
Bazirgan geldi, unune geturub, siniyi qoyub, kendi
bir bujagha chekilub, oturdi. Bazirgan ol
ta'amdan bir qashiq alub aghzina qoydighi gibi,
zehir oldighin bilub, jariyeye elindeki qashighi
firlatdi. Qashiqdan bir nokhud qader zehirli
ta'am jariyenin eline doqinub, doqindighi yer
siyah eyledi. Bazirgan bu tarafda sim siyah
olub, shishdi, tulum gibi oldi ve helak oldi. Jariye
dakhi 'ilaj idub iyu oldi; baqi qalan zehiri
saqlayub, talib olanlara bey' eyledi."

"Now, O king, such guile and craft abound
in women; it is needful ever to guard against
their fraud." And he made intercession for the
prince. When the king heard this story from
the vezir he sent the youth to the prison and
went himself to the chase.

When it was evening the king returned and

came to the palace, and the lady rose to greet him, and they sat down. After the repast the lady began to speak about the youth. The king said, " To-day too such an one of my vezirs made intercession for him, and I sent him to the prison." The lady said, " O king of the world, take care, go by no one's word ; for this youth is a depraved youth. Mayhap my king has not heard the story of the Messenger Noah's son." The king said, " Tell on, let us hear." Quoth the lady,

The Lady's Thirty-Eighth Story.

" The great commentators thus comment on the glorious Koran of God Most High. They relate that when God Most High addressed Saint Noah, he went to his people and ever called his people to the Faith, saying, ' I am the Apostle of God Most High ; own me for Apostle and serve God and abandon iniquity, else God Most High will visit you with bitter torment and send the Flood.' But they accepted him not and listened not to his words. Then Saint Noah complained to God Most High. And God Most High said, ' O Noah, fit thou out a ship, and put the people of thy house into that ship ; for I will surely send the Flood.' And Gabriel (peace on him !) came and taught

him, and they built the ship, and it was finished.
Noah (peace on him!) sought to take his family
into the ship, when the unbelievers came and
filled the ship with filth, and God Most High
sent upon them an itch, and they could not
become whole.   At length one of these unbelievers went to the ship and the filth touched
a part of him, and it was made whole of the itch.
And he took and rubbed it on all his limbs, and
that ailment left him.   He forthwith told the
rest of the unbelievers, and they all came and
cleansed the ship of the filth ; and, according to
one account seven times, and according to another seventy times, did they wash themselves
with it ; and they rubbed the water of it on their
boils and they were made whole.   Then Saint
Noah put his family into the ship, and he put in
of every animal a pair.   And Saint Noah had
three sons ; one was Ham and one was Shem
and one was Japheth ; and two of them entered
the ship and one of them entered not, but turned
to the unbelievers.   And that son asked Saint
Noah; and he learned how the Flood was to be,
and he went and built a dome of glass, and took
there a sufficient quantity of bread and water,
and entered and sat down.   Forty days was
the Flood; and the water stood forty cubits
above the highest mountain.   At length it

abated ; but that rebel youth was drowned in
the glass building."*

"O king, when the son of a Messenger was
thus, how should be the plight of others ? And
thy son is such a rebel ; overthrow him, or at
last thou shalt be repentant." When the king
heard this story from the lady he said, "To-
morrow will I slay the youth." And they went
to bed.

When it was morning the king went and sat
upon his throne, and he caused the youth to be
brought and ordered the executioner, " Smite
off his head." The Thirty-Ninth Vezir came
foward and said, " O king of the world, it is
incumbent to act with deliberation and consultation in this matter ; for God Most High
hath enjoined consultation in His glorious
Koran. If the king will hearken to the words
of these his slaves, my word is this, slay not the
prince on the woman's word that afterward thou
be not repentant. And there is a story suitable
to this, if my king grant leave I will relate it."
The king said, " Relate, let us hear." Quoth
the vezir,

* The part of this story about Noah's son is an amplification
of a passage in the eleventh chapter of the Koran.

THE THIRTY-NINTH VEZIR'S STORY.

"There was of old time a great king, and he
had a shepherd who was exceeding leal and
upright and truthful of speech, so that his qualities were ever spoken of before the king. And
by reason thereof the king at length took that
shepherd to his side and clad him in a robe of
honour and made him master of the horse. The
other vezirs envied him, and they tried him
many times, but found not in him aught save
truthfulness. Now one night when the grand
vezir was speaking of this thing in his harem,
his daughter said, ' If I get that shepherd to tell
a lie before the king, what will ye say ?' Quoth
the vezir, 'There is leave for thee; see and
make him lie somehow.' Now the girl was
exceeding crafty and cunning, and she was also
exceeding fair. And she arose and dressed
herself and girt herself so that she was covered
with pearls and jewels, and she rubbed surma
and antimony on her eyelids and eyelashes,
so that she became like the moon of fourteen
nights. And whoso saw her was bewildered,
and had an infidel seen her he would have
turned Muslim. And she went forth and came
to the room of the master of the horse and
knocked at the door. The master of the horse

said, 'Who art thou?' The girl answered,
'Come, open the door, out on thee, cruel!'
And the master of the horse opened the door
and looked, and when he saw the girl his senses
well nigh forsook him, and he knew not what
he did, and he forthwith embraced the girl and
took her in. So the girl began with all manner
of airs and graces, and the hapless shepherd
sought to make merry with her. The girl said,
'My soul longs for horse's flesh.' The master
of the horse said, 'Can such thing be? I will
give thee fattened horse to eat.' Quoth the girl,
'My desire is to try thee; let me see, lovest
thou me?' The master of the horse answered,
'When I saw thee my senses left me, I am mad
for love of thee; if thou wish I will give thee
my life.' The girl said, 'What know I? I
believe it not.' Quoth the master of the horse,
'By God, I love thee.' The girl asked, 'Dost
thou now love me?' The master of the horse
replied, 'I love thee.' The girl said, 'For my
sake cut the throat of that bay horse.' The
master of the horse answered, 'That horse is
the king's most favourite horse; what answer
shall I give afterward?' The girl arose and
clung to the neck of the master of the horse
and said, 'My life, my master, do what I ask
thee, kill him now; if the king question thee,

thou canst say he turned sick and died.' The
free-will of the master of the horse passed from
his hand, and he went and slew the horse, and
came back and made merry with the girl. And
he said, 'Stay here.' The girl answered, 'To-
morrow will my father seek me.' He asked,
'Who is thy father?' The girl said, 'He is
the grand vezir.' The master of the horse said,
'O what shall we do?' The girl replied, 'Be
thou but well, I will come to thee every night.'
So the master of the horse agreed, and the girl
went away. When it was morning the master
of the horse was distraught, on the one hand
by love for the girl, and on the other by fear of
the king, and he said in himself, 'This secret
must be divulged to no one, still is it needful to
take counsel thereon; let me take counsel of
my cap.' And he pulled his cap from his head
and set it on the ground, and made believe it
was the king, and went out. Then he turned
and came in politely, and even as he would
salute the king, so saluted he his cap, and he
remained standing on his feet. He said, as
from the king, 'O master of the horse, saddle
that bay horse, to-day I go to the chase.' He
turned and said, as from himself, 'In the evening
the bay horse turned sick and ate not his feed,
but left not to lie down and rise up, and about

midnight he became restive and died.' Then
he turned again, and said, as from the king,
'What sayest thou? Only yesterday that horse
was sound; is he dead to-day already? Let
them look if there be any knife-wound.' And
they went and saw that the horse's throat had
been cut, and came and told. As it was clear
he would be put to shame, this way pleased not
the master of the horse. He said, 'This time
let me speak the truth, and see how it would
be.' And he went out and came in again, and
said, as from the king, 'Master of the horse,
go saddle the bay horse, to-day I would go
forth to the chase.' Then he turned and said,
as from himself, 'O king, this night when I was
in my room, a fair girl like the moon of fourteen
nights came and clung to my neck, and said to
me, "Kill that bay horse for my sake, and I
will submit to thee." And I had never seen one
thus lovely in my life, and my choice and free-
will passed from my hands, and I went and
killed the bay horse.' Then he said, as from
the king, 'What girl was that girl? Does any
one so ungratefully by his benefactor for a girl?'
He turned and said, as from himself, 'She clung
to my neck, and caressed me with many pretty
airs, and my power left me; but it came into
my mind, and I asked her with pain whose

daughter she was, and she said she was the
daughter of the grand vezir. If she had asked
my life then, I would have given it ; where then
was the bay horse ? ' And he sprang from the
ground, and said, ' Here my head, here the
sword ! ' And he thought that it was clear there
were here either death or protection, and it
pleased him. And he went forth and came to
the king, and that day he asked about the
horses ; and he told the king the truth of it.
And it came pleasant to the king, and he said,
' Out on thee ; had it been I, I too had given
not only the bay horse, but my life.' And he
was exceeding pleased at his having spoken the
truth, and he put on him a robe of honour,
and got for him the vezir's daughter. So by
reason of his speaking true and straightforward
his face was white and his work was right before
the king, and he became son-in-law to the vezir,
and at length was he vezir himself. Now the
well known proverb has remained, in case when
there is none of whom to take counsel: ' Place
before thee the cap that is on thy head, and
take counsel of it.' "

" O king, I have told this story for that the
king may know that counsel is incumbent.
Accepting the words of the wise points the way
to eternal felicity. To go by the words of the

woman would be to be like that grand vezir, a plotter." And he kissed the ground, and made intercession for the prince for that day. When the king heard this story from the vezir, he sent the youth to the prison, and went himself to the chase.

When it was evening the king returned, and came to the palace, and the lady rose to greet him, and they sat down. After the repast, the lady began to speak about the youth. The king said, " To-day such an one of my vezirs made intercession for him, and I sent him to the prison." The lady said, " O king, I see thee very fickle ; now thou turnest to the vezirs ; thou abidest not by one speech ; thou art ever changing. Such is great shame to kings. One must go steadfastly by the words of one person ; they have said, ' Be at war or be at peace.' So, O king, do not thou be always changing. There is not one worthy among these vezirs. Mayhap my king has not heard the story of a certain king." The king said, " Tell on, let us hear." Quoth the lady,

The Lady's Thirty-Ninth Story.

" There was of old time a king, and there was in his city a wise elder, and that elder had an ass, and he would ever say, ' My ass is wiser

than the king's vezirs.' One day these words
reached the king's ears, and he caused that
elder to be brought, and said, 'Why utterest
thou thus meaningless a speech, O unworthy
elder?' And he was angry. The elder said,
'O king, I have greatly tried the meaning of
this speech; if the king give leave I will speak
it.' The king said, 'Speak on.' The elder
said, 'O king, one day I was crossing a bridge
with my ass, when suddenly the ass's foot went
into a hole, and he fell, and with a thousand
difficulties I delivered him. Ever since, when
he comes to that bridge, he goes not near that
hole, but passes it at a distance. O king, though
thou ever seizest thy vezirs, and takest their
wealth, and dismissest them, and killest some of
them, still they never draw their feet from the
hole of thy fury and displeasure, and are overthrown. So thou seest they fear not at all, and
those who come after them fall into that hole,
and are bound in the prison of the king's anger.
My ass learned by once falling, and never again
has gone near that hole; but thy vezirs will not
take warning by one another, and they throw
themselves into the hole of danger. In such
circumstances, is my ass wiser than thy vezirs,
or is he not?' When the king and the nobles
heard these words of the elder they all deemed

them true, and they gave him a robe of honour, and sent him back to his house."

"O king, I have told this story for that the king may know that it does not follow of necessity that vezirs are wise; it is a favour of God Most High who giveth it; otherwise, how should they be wise? Beware, O king, go not by the words of the vezirs; let not the opportunity slip from thy hand." When the king heard these enticing and beguiling words of the lady, he said, "Surely on the morrow will I kill him." And they went to bed.

When it was morning, the king came and sat upon his throne, and he caused the youth to be brought, and ordered the executioner, "Smite off his head." The Fortieth Vezir came forward and said, "O king of the world, they have said that by four things are works accomplished : the first is, associating with the able; the second is, guarding against enemies ; the third is, taking counsel of the wise ; and the fourth is, getting help from friends. Now it is incumbent on the king that he take counsel of the wise, and gain the friendship of them. O king, we have heard or seen no evil thing from the prince's mouth or deeds; while the wiles and lies of women are notorious, and they are lust-worshippers. Mayhap my king has not heard

the story of that tailor's wife." The king said,
" Tell on, let us hear." Quoth the vezir,

THE FORTIETH VEZIR'S STORY.*

" *Zeman-i sabiqda bir terzinin bir mahbuba
'avreti var idi. Bir gun 'avret jariyesin pamuq
atdirmaq ichun hallaja gunderdi. Jariye hallaj
dukkanine vardi, qaftani pamuq atdirmagha
verdi. Hallaj atariken jariyeye zekerin gusterdi.
Jariye utanub beru yanindan ute yanina gechdi.
Bu dolaninja, hallaj dakhi zekerin ol yana
gechurdi; jariye ol yaninda dakhi uyle gurdi.
Gelub, qadinina eytdi, ' Ol vardighim hallajin
iki zekeri var :' dedi. Khatun eytdi, ' Var, ol
hallaja suyle, " Seni qadinim ister, geje gelsun,"
deyu, suyle :' dedi. Jariye gelub, ol khaberi
hallaja suyledi. Hallaj dakhi, geje olinja, ol
ma'hud olan mahalla gelub, hazir oldi. 'Avret
tashra chiqdi, hallaj ile bulishub, eytdi, 'Ben
qojamla yatarken, gel, benimle bulish :' dedi.
Chun geje yarusi oldi, hallaj varub, 'avreti
uyandirdi. 'Avret qolay yatdi; hallaj ise meshghul oldi. 'Avret gurdi ki kenduye dakhil olan
zeker bir dir, ' Hay, janim hallaj, ikisi ile eyle :'
dedi. Aheste aheste suylerken, eri uyandi;
' " Ikisi ile" dedigin ne dir ?' deyub, 'avretin*

---

ferjine **el** *eyledi. Hallajin zekeri eline geldi ;*
hallaj geru chekindi, zekeri herifin elinden sirildi,
chiqdi. Heman **hallaj** *qachdi. Herif eytdi,*
'Bre 'avret ! ol "**Ikisi** *ile" dedigin* **ne idi ?**'
dedi. 'Avret eytdi, ' **Ey** *qoja, dushimde gurdim*
sen bir denize dushmishsin, bir elinle yuzersin,
" Meded ! boghuldim !" **deyu,** *chaghirirsin ;* **ben**
kenarden, " Ikisi **ile yuz !**" *deyu chaghirdim ;*
sen dakhi iki elinle yuzmege bashladin :' dedi.
Andan *qojasi* **eytdi,** '*'Avret, ben dakhi kendumi*
deryada *oldighim* **shundan** *bildim ki, elime* **bir**
yash *baliq* **geldi, sonra** *sirilub, chiqdi, qachdi ;*
sen gerchek *suylersin :*' *deyub, 'avretina evvel-*
kinden ziyade muhabbet *eyledi."*

"Now, O king, I have told this story for
that the king may know that tricks like to these
and all manner of craftiness abound in women.
Beware, slay not the prince on the woman's
word, or afterward thou shalt be repentant."
And he kissed the ground, and made intercession for the prince for that day. And the
king granted it, and sent the youth to the
prison, and went himself to the chase.

When it was evening the king returned from
the chase and came to the palace, and the lady
rose to greet him, and they sat down. After
the repast the lady asked for news of the
youth. The king said, "To-day too such an one

of my vezirs made intercession for him and I
sent him to the prison." The lady said, "O
king, be it known that not one of those vezirs
is thy friend; God knows what pact they have
with the youth. Mayhap the king has not heard
what befel between the Sultan of Egypt and his
vezirs." The king said, "Tell on, let us hear."
Quoth the lady,

The Lady's Fortieth Story.

"There was of old time in the city of Cairo
a great Sultan, and he had a youthful son.
And that youth made a pact with the vezirs,
saying, 'If ye make me Sultan, I will give you
leave to do whatever ye may please.' When
they had agreed to this, he sowed enmity
between the king and the vezirs and nobles;
and each of them rose in revolt in a different
quarter, and they took the youth for their
chief, and waged war and did battle with the
king. The king could not overcome them,
and at length they made the youth king.
They began to feast with the new king every
day, and to accomplish their desires. And the
king's father saw that the purpose of the
vezirs and the youth was evil, and he called
a confidant, and one night they fled in disguise
and entered a cave; and for seven days and

seven nights **the** king went not forth from that cave. The new king heard **of** his father having fled, and **he** and the vezirs began to seek him and to send **out** criers, who proclaimed, 'Whoso seizes **my** father and brings him to me, him will I honour.' **And the** old king and his courtier went forth from the cave and came to a village, and were guests of an old woman in that village; **and** that old **woman sowed** seed. And **she** bestirred herself to entertain them, **and** brought them a mat, and they **sat down.** The king was hungry, and **he** pulled **out a** sequin and gave **it to** the old woman, **and** said, **'Mother, go,** fetch us food **that we** may **eat.'** The woman said, 'What will ye **do** with a sequin's **worth of food?'** The king replied, 'No harm, fetch **it.' And** the **woman** went and brought all manner of delicacies **and set them before the** king. And they sat **down and ate.** After the repast **they** began to talk **with** the woman; **and the** woman said, 'What youths **be ye?'** The king said, **'We are of the servants** of the fugitive king; **we are** seeking **our** master.' **The** woman said, **'I** fear that **ye too are** followers **of that** unworthy youth, **and** would seize the king **and** take him.' The king **asked,** 'Does **that** unworthy youth seek his father?' The woman replied, 'Does

he seek him ? what means that ? Those traitor
vezirs and nobles every day cause criers to
proclaim, " To him who seizes and brings that
fugitive Sultan we will give the lordship of
whatever place he may wish ; but of him who
conceals him, or in whose house he is found, are
the head and family gone." ' When the king
heard these words from the woman his soul was
troubled, and he said to her, ' And are the nobles
also submissive to the youth ? ' The woman
answered, ' He has deposed many nobles, and
appointed other nobles ; these new nobles are
all of them submissive to him.' The king said,
' Is there any of those old nobles whom thou
knowest ? ' The woman replied, ' There is a
vezir who was deposed by the fugitive Sultan ;
I go about his house on business—I know him.'
As soon as the king heard this he turned and
said to his confidant, ' What sayest thou, shall I
tell this woman that I am the Sultan ? ' The
confidant replied, ' Command is the king's.' The
Sultan turned and said to the woman, ' O
mother, I have a secret ; if I tell it thee, canst
thou keep it ? ' The woman said, ' I will give
my head, but I will not give your secret.' The
king made the woman swear, and then said, ' O
mother, dost thou know me who I am ? ' She
answered, ' Nay.' Then the king said, ' Lo, I

am the fugitive Sultan ; **be** it not that this word
escape thy mouth.' When the woman heard
this **the** blood went **from** her face, and she fell
at the king's feet. **The** king said, ' Hast thou
son or daughter ? ' She replied, ' I have **a** son.'
The king **said,** ' If God Most High seat me on
my throne, I will give thy son whatever **lordship** he please.' The woman bowed down and
fell at the king's **feet.** Then the king said to
her, ' **Go now to the** house of **that** vezir, and
call him to **a** private place and salute him from
me, and say, '' **The king** is now seated in my
house and wants **thee,** be it not that thou
flinchest and comest not." ' When it was evening
the woman **went** to the vezir's house, and took
the vezir to a private **place,** and **gave** him **the
king's** greeting, and **told** him all and **how** that
he was sitting **in her** house. **The** vezir was
glad, **and he** said, ' **Do thou** now **be** off, I too
will come now ; ' **and** he sent **her** away. The
woman came and **told** these things **to** the king.
After a little he saw the vezir in the dress of
an Arab, **and he** came and fell **at the** king's
feet and **mourned and wept.** The king said,
' **O vezir, I** wronged thee and **took** thy wealth
and **deposed thee ;.** ah ! the past **is** past, the
gone is gone. Befriend me as much as in thee
lies, and **if** God Most **High** raise **me to my**

throne, I know the honour I will do thee.'
The vezir said, 'O king, if thou tookest my
wealth, it was thine own wealth ; if thou didst
depose me, I was thy slave and had done
wrong ; thou didst weil.   Now this is the way,
that thou follow my words and lay aside kingship till our plan be accomplished ; if afterward
thou art wroth with me, then command ; now
let us work.'   The king said, 'Do what thou
wilt ; now is not the time for words.'   The
vezir said, 'O king, arise and take my lamp in
thine hand, and go on through the desert before
thee till thou comest to my house ; if any one
see thee he will think thee my man and recog-
nise thee not.'   The king took the vezir's lamp
in his hand, and they went on and passed
through the bazaars of Cairo, and came to the
vezir's house ; and the vezir prepared a private
room for the king.   The king remained there
some days, and the vezir secretly sent word to
all the great nobles who had been deposed, and
assembled them.   And one night he brought
them to the king and reconciled them, and said,
'On the morrow be ye ready and show zeal
each one of you for his estate.'   That night they
gathered together all the disbanded soldiers who
were there ; and when it was morning they beat
the kettledrums on every side, and ere those

traitor nobles and vezirs had arisen they put
many of them to the sword; and they seized
the king's son and all the rest of his vezirs, and
brought them before the king. And the king
executed the whole of them, slaying each of
them with a different torment. Thenceforth
he sat upon his throne with tranquillity of
heart, and enjoyed happiness and delight."

"Now, O king, I have told this story for
that the king may know that vezirs are not to
be altogether trusted; and be thou ready, for
these vezirs purpose evil against the king, and
the like of this story shall befall thee. I have
watched for my king and told him. And I know
of a surety that they have made a pact if left
till the morrow to seat the youth upon the
throne, and to seize thee and to give thee into
the youth's hands. God knows what will happen
to ill-fortuned me. Woe is me!" And she wept
full bitterly. When the king heard this story
from the lady, and beheld this plight, he believed
the lady's words, and held them to be true; and
fear for his life fell upon the king. He said, "O
lady, weep not; on the morrow will I seize the
whole of the vezirs, and, after I have put the
youth to death, I will give to each of them, one
by one, his due." When the lady heard these
words from the king she was glad, and said, "O

king, when thou hast slain the whole of them,
appoint nobles vezirs in their stead, and then lean
thy back against the wall of retirement, and give
thyself up to mirth and merriment : till thou hast
done thus thou shalt not be at ease." And
the king consented to this proposal, and they
passed that night till the morning conversing.

When it was morning the king was wrathful
and he came and sat upon his throne, and he said,
"Where is the youth ? let him come." They
brought him, and the king said, "Ask ye him
if he confesses to the charge of his mother."
Thereupon the grand vezir said, "Let him come
before you and be asked, and it will be well ;
bring him, let us ask him." The king commanded that they brought him, and he said,
"Youth, speak ; how hast thou done by thy
mother ?" The youth was silent. The king
turned and said, "Be not silent, there is leave
to thee, speak." The youth was silent. Again
the grand vezir said, "Perchance his governor
might make him tell." Straightway the king
commanded that they should bring his governor ;
and they sought him but found him not, and
came and told the king. The king said, "This
day it is needful to make manifest my justice :
let the executioner come." He came ; and the

king commanded, saying, "Take the youth and
all those vezirs ; and kill them." And they took
the whole of them from the presence of the
king ; and they made clean the judgment-square
and sprinkled it with sand. And they made
the vezirs sit down by tens, and they brought
the youth too. Then the executioner set the
prince upon his knees and bound his eyes, and
he drew his sword from its scabbard and bared
it, and said, "Is there leave, O king? In thy
glory is my arm strong and my sword keen.
The cut-off head grows not again, and too late
repentance profits not." And he went twice
round the divan and asked leave of the king ;
and the king commanded him, saying, "Smite
off his head." The executioner went round the
divan once more, and as he was again asking
leave of the king, the bearer of glad tidings
came, crying, "The prince's governor comes!"
The king said, "Quick, seize and bring him."
Forthwith the slaves brought the governor, not
letting his feet touch the ground. When the
king saw the governor he was wroth, and said,
"Kill him!" The governor said, "O king,
wherefore art thou angry? If it be thy desire
to make the youth speak, bring him and let him
speak." Quoth the king, "Is it thou who saidest
to the youth, 'Speak not'?" The governor

answered, "Yea." The king said, "Why?"
The governor said, "O king of the world, I
saw the prince's ruling star in the astrolabe that
for forty days it was in evil aspect, such evil
aspect that if he uttered the least word he
should perish, but that if he spake not he should
escape. I taught him a Name, and charged him
straitly that he should not speak the least word.
Now is the time accomplished, and I am come;
command that they bring him, and I shall give
him leave to speak." The king commanded
that they brought the youth, and the governor
said, "My prince, be my life a ransom for thy
father and for thee! Praise be to God! the
evil aspect of thy star is accomplished; loose
thy nightingale tongue and speak; what is this
plight?" Straightway the youth said, "In the
name of God!" And he related what befel him
with the lady from its beginning to its end; and
then he fell upon the ground and began to
weep. And the king put his finger to his
mouth and wondered. And the members of
the divan marvelled at this deed of the woman,
and they said, "The prince's words are with
reason and truth, and such like trickery comes
from womankind." Then the king asked the
slave-girls, and they bare witness that they had
been behind the wall and had heard the thing,

and that the prince spake truly. And the king saw that the right was the prince's, and he repented him of what he had done. And he besought pardon, and kissed the prince's two eyes, and pressed him to his heart and wept full bitterly. And straightway he commanded that they brought the vezirs; and the king made many excuses to them, and clad each of them in sumptuous robes, and bestowed boundless gifts and favours upon them, and begged forgiveness of all of them. And the vezirs said, " My king, whatsoever cruelty and injustice thou hast done us, be it all forgiven thee; our fear was lest thou should slay the prince, acting on the woman's word; for our vezirship is by the health and safety of our king and our prince; and their existence is a mercy to the world; after they were perished the perishing of the whole of us were a thing assured." And they all kissed the ground together, and asked for retribution on the woman. And the king commanded that they brought a wild ass; and they took the lady to the square of judgment and set her upon that ass, and bound her fast to his tail and legs, and took her forth to the desert. And they smote the ass with a whip, and the ass began to gallop and the woman fell from his back to the ground; and the wild ass

looked, and when he saw the woman behind him
he shied and ran off. And the woman was torn
into pieces small even as her ear, and left upon
the shrubs and stones.   Thus that which she
had purposed against the prince befel herself.
The sires say, " Wish good that good may come
to thee : if thou dig a pit for another, dig it
deep ; for it is like thou shalt fall therein thyself ;
then thou needest not trouble trying to get out."
And from that time has the saying been
among the folk, " May I see thee on the ass !"
After that the king summoned all the vezirs and
the nobles and the commonalty, and he made a
great feast with all manner of minstrels and
music, and for forty days and forty nights they
feasted and made merry gratefully.   And then
they lived for many years, and did justice and
dealt with equity.

May God Most High associate all of us with
the good and true, and keep us safe from the
guile of crafty women.   Amen.

As his object in writing these example-fraught
stories, and presenting and offering them to the
view of the public, is to draw down benedic-
tions on himself, it is prayed and entreated that
the author be remembered with a blessing.

THE END.

APPENDIX A.

Stories occurring in other Texts than that from which the foregoing Translation has been made.

FROM BELLETÊTE'S VOLUME OF EXTRACTS.

THE NINTH VEZIR'S STORY.

THEY have told that while a certain Turkman was ploughing, his ploughshare of a sudden caught in something, so that though the oxen pulled, they were unable to drag it up. So the Turkman turned up the earth with the point of his goad, and saw that the ploughshare had caught in a ring. He loosed his oxen, and fetched from the house a hoe and shovel, and dug, and saw that that ring was fastened with lead to a marble slab. Then putting forth his strength, he raised the slab, and saw that underneath a flight of seven steps led down. So he went down these steps, and saw forty royal jars standing in a row, the lid of each of which was of gold. On the lids of some were ruby sheep with their lambs, on those of others swine with their pigs, and on those of others peafowl with their chicks. On each one was something, and in the mouth of everything was a jewel, like a lamp at night. So the Turkman went and opened the lid of each one, and he saw them all to be filled full of Diocletian

florins ; * and he searched those forty jars from top to bottom
and he saw that they stood bound round with chains of gold.
When the Turkman saw all this, he was amazed and bewildered.
Then he came out and put the slab back into its place, and
arranged the earth so that it was not noticeable.   Then he stood
and thought, ' How shall I spend all this, and to whom shall I
tell this secret ?   If I tell it to my wife, will she be able to keep
it ?'   Then he said, ' Ah ! I shall first try her, and see.'   He
went to the house, and said, ' Ha, wife, something has happened to me to-day !   I shall tell thee, but see thou tell it to
no one.'   His wife said, ' May it be good ; I shall tell no one.'
Quoth the Turkman, ' While I was ploughing in the field, I was
ware of something, and I looked down and a crow rose up and
flew away ; I know not what it may portend.'   His wife said,
' May it be good ! '   That day passed, and the next day the
ploughman heard the folk saying that ten crows had flown out
of such and such an one ; and on the day following he heard that
it was a hundred crows ; and he knew that there was no telling
his secret to his wife.   And he said, ' If I tell her of the treasure,
one will become a hundred on the stranger's tongue ; and the
treasure and my head will both go from me.'   So he told it not
to his wife, but said in himself, ' Some craft is needful here.'   So
he went and took three tiles of gold from the treasure and
carried them to the smith, and said, ' Fashion me a ploughshare
of this iron and give it me.'   When the smith saw it he was
glad, and the Turkman went away.   After some days he came
back and asked for the iron ; the smith gave him a ploughshare
fashioned of black iron.   The Turkman said, ' My iron was
yellow, while this is black ;' and they quarrelled, till at length
they haled both of them before the king.   They laid before the
Turkman iron, copper, silver and gold, and said, ' Which of
these was it like ?'   The Turkman pointed out the gold and
said, ' My iron was like this.'   Then the king upbraided the smith,
and they put him to the torture, so that at length he was com-

---

* Any ancient gold coin was called *Daqyanos altuni* = Diocletian
sequin, or, as here, *Daqyanos filuri.*

pelled to give the gold to the king. The king gave one tile to the Turkman. Therefore the Turkman for a long time kept the treasure hidden from his household, till **at** length, through fear of **his wife, he was** unable to enjoy any rest, and he died ; and the treasure still remains **in its place."**

THE TENTH VEZIR'S STORY.

" They have told that there was **once an** aged gardener who was also an ass-driver. One Friday he found **it was** necessary to water his garden, on that day too he had grain in **the** mill and it was his turn to grind **it,** and on that day too the turn for the Friday-worship * came round ; so that that man was bewil- **dered** and **confounded, and** he knew not which of these things **he ought to do. At length,** having remembered that the Apostle, **whenever he was in doubt about** a matter, used to do that of it which bare most on the Hereafter, he left the other things and **went to the mosque. When** he arose from worship and came **to his house, he saw that** his ass was standing ready harnessed. **He went** to his garden, and he saw that some one else had been watering his own garden, and that the water had trickled through **and** watered his garden. He went to the mill, and saw his flour **ground. He** asked, ' Who ground this **flour ?'** The miller said, ' A man, thinking it **was** his own grain, ground it, then he **saw** that it was thine, then he ground his own ; take thou thy flour and **go.'** Then that man knew of a surety that whoso strives in the **way of God will not be** shut out from **the** world or the Hereafter."

THE ELEVENTH VEZIR'S STORY.

" **They have told that in** the palace of the world was **a** great king who **had a** daughter rare of beauty, such that the fame of her beauty **had gone forth to** all lands. One day that girl of a sudden fell in love with a youth from among the king's servants, so that **she was** night and day without rest for the love of him. Love for the youth grew ever more **and** more masterful in the **girl, so that she left off to eat** and drink and sleep, **and her**

---

* It **is** scarcely necessary to remind the reader that Friday is the Muhammedan Sabbath.

tulip-hued face was turned to saffron, and her occupation was
ever sighing and wailing. Every day her nurse said, ' Daughter,
art thou not well? What ails thee? For thine occupation is
ever sighing; what secret hast thou? Hide it not from me;
belike I could find a remedy.' But the girl answered nothing.
One day, unable to bear the fire of love, she said, ' O nurse, why
should we hide it from thee? I love such and such a servant
of my father; if thou canst not bring me to union with him, I
shall die.' So that night the nurse put on trousers like the
night watchman, and with this disguise entered the sleeping-
chamber of the youth; and she gave him an intoxicating drug,
and took him and brought him to the girl. So the girl got
ready all things needful for a carouse, and spread beds of silk
and satin, and put down embroidered cushions, and then laid
the youth on them. And she fetched strong vinegar and dropped
it on his face. The youth sneezed and sat up, and looked and
saw seated by his side a beauty whose like he had never seen
in the world. And he saw the palace, the beds and the cushions,
such as he had never seen in his life. Quoth the youth, ' Seest
thou, I have died and they have borne me away and laid me in
Paradise.' Then the girl put her arm round the youth's neck
and said, ' O my life, master, for this long time have I been
without rest for the love of thee.' When the youth heard these
words from the girl, he said, ' O life of my life, what place is
this, and thou, whose soul art thou?' The girl said, ' Eat the
fruit and ask not of the tree.' So the youth loved the girl with
a thousand hearts and souls, and he put his arms round her neck
and they began to kiss and clip one another. Then the nurse
went out and watched the door.* The girl fetched wine of the
hue of the Judas-tree, and put a cup into the youth's hand, and
the youth quaffed it to the girl's love, then he filled it and handed
it to her. First he snatched a kiss from the girl, then she from
him. Then the girl quaffed the cup to the youth's love. After
they had sat playing thus for a while, they both stripped naked,

---

* Before going out she gives her young mistress the prudent advice,
' *Muhrin saqla.*'

like **pearls,** and **went into** the bed, and the girl took the youth **to her bosom,** and the youth took the girl in his arms, and thus **were they lip** to lip and **breast** to breast, as though the two **of them were but one soul.** Now the girl **would** suck, like the **parrot,** the sugared sherbet **of the** youth's lips, **and** now the **youth** would drink, like Khizr, the water **of** life from **the** girl's. **All** that night **till dawn the girl cooled her** liver, burnt by her longing for **the** youth, with the water of union.* When morning was near they slept a little, and straightway the nurse came in and gave the youth the drug, and carried him back again to his **own** place. When the youth awoke he found **himself in** his **own** place, and he knew **not** whether what he had **seen were a dream. And the king's daughter in a** little while regained **her health."**

THE LADY'S EIGHTEENTH STORY.

" **They** have told **that** in bygone times there was a king, and **he had a** skilful minstrel. One day a certain person gave to the **latter a little boy that he** might teach him the science of music. **The boy abode a long** time by **him, and,** though the master **instructed him, he** succeeded not **in** learning; and **the** master **could make** nothing of **him. He** arranged **a** scale and said, **' Whatsoever** thou sayest to me, say in this scale.' So whatsoever the boy said, he used to say in that scale; **and** the master likewise **answered him** in that scale. Now one day a spark of fire fell on **the master's turban. The** boy saw it and chanted, **' O master, I see something, shall I say it or no ?' and he** went over the **whole scale. Then the** master chanted, **' O** boy, **what dost** thou **see, speak ?' and** he too went **over** all that the boy had gone **over. Then the turn came to the boy, and** he chanted, **' O master, a spark has** fallen on thy turban and **it is** burning.' The **master** straightway tore off his turban and cast it on the ground, **and saw that it was burning.** He blew out **the** fire on this side **and that, and took it in his hand, and** said to the boy, **' What time for chanting is this !** everything is good **in** its own place;' **and he admonished him."**

---

* As **with the** Elizabethan poets, the liver **was** supposed to be the seat of passion.

FROM THE INDIA OFFICE MS.

THE LADY'S FIRST STORY.

"They have told that there was in the palace of the world a
great king, and that king had a son who was feeble of understanding. Now the king found a cunning master who was learned
in all the sciences, and he caused him to be brought before him,
and, telling him of his son's case, asked of him a remedy for the
evil. The sage said, 'O king, this is an easy matter ; in a little
time will I make him a master of discretion.' The king was
glad, and bestowed gifts and favours on the sage, and made over
to him his son. Now the sage taught him for a season, and instructed him in knowledge ; and he made the boy familiar with
every science. And the boy grew learned and accomplished,
so that all the world marvelled at his words. One day his
master took him, and brought him before the king, and said,
'O king of the world, lo, I have made thy son to excel in every
science.' And the king his father was glad and said, 'O my
son, were I to hold a certain thing hidden in my hand, couldst
thou guess what it was ?' He replied, 'Yea, I could.' Then
the king secretly took his ring from his finger, and held it in his
hand, and said, 'What is it that I have in my hand ?' The boy
thought for a little while, then said, 'O father, that thing in its
first estate was in the hills.' The king said in his heart, 'Aye,
he knows ; the mines are in the hills.' The boy continued, 'It
is a round flat thing. It must be a mill-stone.' Then was the
king ashamed before the nobles and the lords, and he said, 'O
son, could a mill-stone be hidden in any man's hand ?' And
saying to the master, 'Take him away and teach him,' he sent
him off."

THE SECOND VEZIR'S STORY.

"One day the Apostle (peace on him !) was seated in the
mosque, expounding the chapter, 'Verily, We have sent it down,'*
when he came to the story of the Messenger Samson. Quoth

---

* Koran, xcvii. 1. Samson is never mentioned in the Koran.

the **Apostle (peace on** him !), ' They say that Samson **was a** Messenger who **warred** for a thousand months in the cause of God **Most** High. **He had** his dwelling in a high hill ; and in the **daytime he would come** down from the hill and war, and when it was evening **he** would return **to** the hill and sleep beside his wife. The misbelievers were powerless against Samson ; and they agreed among themselves, **saying,** " Let us give money to his wife, that she may bind him and deliver **him** to us." So they took a dish filled with **gold, and** went **to** his wife, and said, "Bind thy husband with **this** rope, and deliver him to us, and this dish with the gold therein shall be thine." When the woman saw **so** much money, she **coveted** it, and said, " So be it ; " and **she took** the **rope.** Samson came back from **fighting ; and he was** weary, and he lay down and slept. And **the woman came and bound** fast his hands with that rope ; and **she said in herself, " This** man is a Messenger, belike he may **break this rope : " and,** wishing to try if it **were** so, she wakened **Samson.** He, seeing **that his** hands were bound, said, " Who **bound** my hands ? " **His wife answered, " I** bound them ; **but what matter ?** thou art a Messenger, pull and break the rope." **So Samson put** forth his strength, and strained and strained, **and the rope** brake ; and he lay down again and slept. And **the** woman went and said to the misbelievers, " He has broken **the** rope." So they gave her chains, and again she bound him and wakened him to try him. Samson saw that his hands were bound again, and he said, " Who has bound me ? " She replied, " I **bound thee** to try thee." Samson again put forth his strength, **and the chains were** broken in pieces. And the woman was **amazed,** and said, " O Prophet of God, with what must one bind **thee ? "** Samson answered, " Nought but thy hair can avail." **Now the woman had two tresses** of hair ; these she cut off and **bound round his** hands, and then wakened him again. Samson **saw that his hands were** bound, and he said, " Who has bound **me again ? "** The woman answered, " She who has ever bound **thee has bound thee ;** pull, strain." Then she let these misbelievers, **who were lying** hidden, know ; and they came forth and seized **Samson and bare** him **to** their **city.** And **they**

C C

cut off his two hands and his two feet, and left him in a certain
place, and went away. And Samson (peace on him!) said,
" My God, give me again my hands and my feet, that I may war
in Thy cause." Then Gabriel (peace on him!) came and touched
him with his wing, and Samson was made whole again. The
palace of their king was supported by a single column; and
that palace was filled full of misbelievers. And Samson went
and pulled down that column, and the palace fell to the ground,
and as many misbelievers as were therein were killed. And
Samson began again to war, and he ceased not from warring
until that he was martyred.' Then did the Companions of the
Prophet (peace on him!) envy the Messenger Samson his warring for a thousand months; so God (glorified and exalted be
He!) sent down this verse, ' The Night of Power is better than
a thousand months;'* that is to say, that the merit of doing
worship all the Night of Power until the dawn is greater than
that of warring for a thousand months."

The Lady's Third Story. ·

" They have told that there was once a witch, and she had a
little boy. One day, while the witch was working witchery, her
little boy was playing beside her in a river. The water caught
the boy and swept him into a hole. When the witch saw her
boy in this plight, she threw herself after him into the river.
The stream swept her likewise into that hole; so that they both
perished." †

The Seventh Vezir's Story.

" They have told that there was in the city of Cairo a crafty
woman. One day she made a broidered gown into a bundle and

---

* Koran, xcvii. 3. The 'Night of Power' is the most excellent night
in all the year; on it the divine decrees for the ensuing twelvemonth
are issued to the executive angels; but unfortunately there is some
doubt as to when it really falls; it is, however, generally believed to be
one of the nights towards the close of Ramazán.

† This somewhat feeble tale, which is designed to show how a too
fond parent may lose his life through the frowardness of his son, is one
of the very few stories belonging to the Sindibád cycle that occur in the
Forty Vezirs. See Mr. Clouston's Book of Sindibád, pp. 37 and 144.

gave it into the hands of one of her slave-girls, whom she made
follow her to the bazaar, where she got into the shop of a merchant, and there seated herself. The merchant said, ' My lady,
what is thy need ? ' Then the lady took the gown and laid it
before the merchant, and when the merchant had opened the
bundle and seen the gown, she said, ' Let this gown remain with
thee in pledge, and do thou give me such and such a sum, and
when our matters are arranged I shall bring back the money and
get away the gown.' The merchant turned not from the words
of the woman, neither could he withstand her fashions, so he
straightway gave her such and such a sum, and, taking the
gown, laid it by. The woman took the money and went away,
but after a little she came back and said, ' Give me the gown
and take the money, that there be no trouble to thee.' So the
merchant gave her the bundle with the gown, and took the
money and laid it by him. The woman took the gown and went
to a place apart ; there she took that gown out of the bundle
and put in its place another gown not worth an aspre. Then she
tied up her bundle and went again before the merchant and said,
' O merchant, we have troubled thee much ; the money has
again become needful ; pray, give it ; here is the gown.' And
she laid the bundle before the merchant, who took it without
opening or looking at it, and gave the woman the money. And
the woman took the money and went to her house, and she
made merry, feasting. On his part the merchant saw that
one month passed, that two months passed, and yet the lady
came not ; and disquiet increased within him, and he spake of
this matter to one of his friends. That man said, ' Fetch the
gown and let me see it.' When they opened the bundle they
saw that the gown was not worth an aspre, and the merchant
perceived that the woman was a trickstress. And he arose and
went before the governor and told all that had befallen him.
The governor said, ' That woman has played a trick on thee ;
but this is the city of Cairo, and here tricks are many. Now I
too will teach thee a trick ; and if she be not found by this trick,
then is there no help.' ' Grace, my lord,' quoth the merchant,
clasping the knees of the governor. The latter said, ' Go to-

night and carry to thy house whatever thou hast in thy shop, and tear up some of the boards about thy shop ; and early on the morrow go to thy shop, and begin to cry and lament, saying, "Last night have they broken into my shop and taken away whatever was therein ; that vexed me not, but there was in my shop a costly gown belonging to a lady, that too have they taken, and now if the lady come and bring the money and ask her gown, how shall I answer her ?"' So the merchant went and did this.   And it was noised abroad in the city of Cairo that they had that night broken into the shop of such and such a merchant and stolen all his goods, but that he was not grieved because of his own property, but because of a costly gown he had in pledge that belonged to a lady, which also they had taken and gone off. ' God give them their due !' said the folk.   That lady heard this news, and she was glad, and she took the sum she had received from the merchant, and said to her handmaids, ' Get ready, let us go to the merchant, and give him the money, and ask back the gown. If he say, "The gown has been stolen, I will give its value," we shall say the gown was worth ten times a hundred thousand aspres ; and we shall get at least four or five hundred thousand aspres.' So they went straight to that merchant, and she saluted him, and beckoned to her slave-girls, and one of them produced the money and laid it before the merchant. The lady said, ' O merchant, see, I have brought the money ; give me my gown.' The merchant answered, ' I have let the gown be stolen ; what am I to do?' Quoth the woman, ' I know nought of that ; I want the gown.' Then the merchants and neighbours came about them and said, ' O lady, the gown has been lost ; name its value : take a portion of it and remit a portion of it.' The lady answered, ' O merchants, ye saw not the gown ; I bought that gown, and I gave for it not less than ten times a hundred thousand aspres ; think on that, and judge ; let him give the gown, or let him give its price.' When the merchants had besought her, the lady said, ' One hundred thousand of them, two hundred thousand of them, yea, five hundred thousand of them have I forgiven him for your sakes ; let him give the rest.' Then they arose and went before the governor of the city ; **and the** merchant said, 'My lord, this **woman came and** left a gown with me in pledge, and got such and such **a** sum, and went away. For some months she came not. Now have they plundered my shop, and the gown has been lost with my **own possessions.** No lie can be spoken in thy noble presence. **Order and** command **are** thine.' Then the woman began to cry out, 'I want my gown **or its** worth in money.' **The** governor said, 'O lady, look at **this poor** wretch ; this is a **case** for ruth.' **And** he made a sign to the merchant, who went out and fetched the gown, and came back, saying, 'Good **news, my** lord ; I have found the gown ;' and he laid it before **the governor. The** latter opened the bundle, and **seeing** that **the gown was** worth nothing, exclaimed, 'Out on **thee, whore of the age,** thou **settest** the city **of** Cairo in an **uproar !' And he** straightway commanded that they stripped **the woman, and tied a stone** about her neck ; and he sent her **to turn fish in the river Nile."**

THE LADY'S SEVENTH STORY.

"**They have told** that there **was in the** palace of **the world a king, and** he had by him a master carpenter, who was such **a** master that there was not his equal in the world. He had an unworthy apprentice, who one day went before the king and said, '**I am greater** than my master ; it **were** beseeming the king **that he honour me** as he honours him.' Then the king called the master and the apprentice together into his presence **to prove them.** The master said, 'O king, I have a plan ; **let each of us take a piece** of wood and go into a dark place ; **and the skill of** whichever of **us cut the** wood will then be known.' **They agreed thereto.** So the master took an adze and a piece **of wood, and went into** that dark place. And he struck, and he **struck again, and he struck yet** again, and then he **came** out, **and all the folk saw (what he** had done) and applauded and commended him. **Then** the apprentice struck, but at his second stroke **he** cut all his fingers ; **and so was he** put to shame before the king and the **people."**

The Ninth Vezir's Story.

" They have told that Kay-Qubād * had a devout and pious
wife, who was so modest that she could not endure the mention
of men, but ever spake of their uncleanness. The king was
an-angered by her words, and he sought to make trial of her.
Now the king had a fair young slave-boy who was exceeding
ready at service.   One day the king gave this boy to his wife.
Now he had said to the boy, ' If, when alone with this lady, thou
canst lead her astray by sweet and witty speeches, I will give
thee whatsoever thou mayst desire.'   So the boy served for some
days before the lady, till one day he said some witty thing.
The woman said nothing.   Some days afterward the boy again
made a jest.   When the lady smiled at these words of the boy,
he knew that love had entered into her heart.   One day he
pressed the lady's hand and laid his own upon her arm.   The
woman said, ' Out on thee, boy, dost thou really love me ? '
The boy answered, ' Dost thou doubt it?   I await thy bidding
with heart and soul.'   The lady said, ' Be it not that thou tell
this secret to anyone ; if thou lovest me, I love thee a thousand
times more.'   Whenever the boy heard these words of the lady,
he let go her arm and embraced her neck and began to kiss
her ; and the lady likewise began to kiss him.   Then they
parted, and the boy ran and told these secrets to the king.   The
king said, ' It is not true ; I believe it not.'   The boy answered,
' I will show thee this thing before thine own eyes.'   The king
asked, ' If it be so, what is thy plan ? '   The boy replied, ' I
shall now hide thee in the closet, and thou shalt see with thine
eyes and believe.'   So he hid the king in the closet.   And the
lady came again and embraced the boy, and while they were
kissing and clipping, the king came forth from the closet, and
said, ' Out on thee, modest whore ! '   And the woman was put
to shame."

---

* The first sovereign of the Kayānī (Achæmenian) dynasty, the
second line of pre-Muhammedan Persian kings.   The Dejoces of Greek
writers is thought to represent this prince.

THE LADY'S NINTH STORY.

"They have told that a rogue went to the Ka'ba,* and as he was going about among the pilgrims, he said in himself, 'How may I show off my roguery in this place?' Just then he came before the Zemzem well,† and he saw that some of the pilgrims were drinking of it, and some were making the ablution at it. As soon as the rogue saw this, he tucked up his skirt and ran forward, crying, 'Ho, men, a camel polluted this well to-night; the ablution cannot be made at this well.'‡ So the pilgrims drew back their hands from the well; and the rogue said in himself, 'I have accomplished my affair;' and he went away."

THE THIRTEENTH VEZIR'S STORY.

"It has come down in the Commentaries that when God Most High said, (as it is written in His Ancient Word,) 'Ye cannot attain to righteousnsss until ye give away of what ye love;'§ the Messenger Abraham heard this saying, and sacrificed to God very many camels and sheep. But God Most High said, 'Give what thou lovest.' And Abraham answered, 'My God, what I love is my son Ishmael.' And he desired to sacrifice him to God Most High;‖ and he went before his mother and said, 'O lady, to-day they have bidden me to a wedding-feast; stain Ishmael's hands and feet and hair with hinna,¶ that I may take him with me to-morrow when I go.' So that night his mother stained his hands and feet and hair with hinna, and on the morrow she decked him out like a flower, and gave him over to his father. And the Messenger Ishmael

---

* The Sacred Temple at Mekka, see p. 122.

† The sacred well in the Temple at Mekka, said to be that which appeared to Hagar. For a description of it, see Sir R. F. Burton's *Pilgrimage*, vol. iii.

‡ Pure water being, of course, required.

§ Koran, iii. 86.

‖ That Ishmael, and not Isaac, was Abraham's intended victim, is the general Muslim belief; but the point is disputed.

¶ As is done on state occasions in the East.

(peace on him !) ran before his father, playing as they went along ; and the tears flowed like a stream from the eyes of Abraham (peace on him !) ; and his heart was torn in pieces. Unable to bear it, he said, ' O son, walk behind me.' So Ishmael (peace on him !) walked behind ; and Satan (a curse on him !) came before him and said, ' O Ishmael, whither goest thou ?' Ishmael answered, ' I go with my father to a wedding.' Satan said, 'What a wedding ! thy father is taking thee to cut thy throat.' Ishmael replied, ' Begone, O accursed, what have I done to my father that he should slay me ?' And he took a stone in his hand and cast it at Satan, and Satan fled. But he went about and came by another way and said, ' O Ishmael, thou art a little boy, and I have pity for thee ; know of a surety that thy father is taking thee to slay thee.' And again Ishmael took a stone and cast it at Satan, saying, ' Begone, O accursed ;' and Satan fled. But he came again by yet another way and said, ' By God, thy father is taking thee to slay thee.' Ishmael (peace on him !) answered, ' O accursed, what have I done to my father ? why should he cut my throat ?' Satan replied, ' God Most High desired thee of thy father in sacrifice.' Ishmael answered, ' Since I am worthy to be a sacrifice to God, ought not I to be content ?' And he smote Satan with a stone, and struck out one of his eyes. When they reached the place, Abraham (peace on him !) said, ' O son, knowest thou wherefore I have brought thee hither ?' Ishmael (peace on him !) answered, ' I know, father ; I have a charge to thee, which do thou fulfil, and then accomplish what thou pleasest. O father, bind fast my two hands, lest in the bitterness of death my hands should clutch at thee, and thou, unable to proceed, should not draw down the knife, and so we should both be guilty. And bind my two eyes, lest when my eyes meet thy eyes thou strike not fair with the knife.' So Abraham observed these charges ; and he took the knife in his hand, and the tears were running from his eyes, and he said, ' My God, I gave my wealth and my flocks to Thee, and they were not accepted ; lo, I have brought Ishmael, the darling of my heart, to sacrifice him to Thee ; do Thou accept him.' Then saying, ' In the name of God,' he pressed the knife

against Ishmael's throat. Saying, 'God is greatest,' he sought
to draw it down, but the knife would not cut Ishmael's throat.
He marvelled at this, and pressed it down again, and again **it**
would not cut. Saying, 'Knife, wilt not thou cut?' he tried it
on his hand, and saw it to be like **a** diamond. Again **he** pressed
it down, but **it** cut **not. Then** was Abraham (peace on him!)
wroth. There **was** there a marble rock; he struck **the** knife
against that, and the knife sank into that rock, as it had been
puff-paste. When the Messenger Abraham saw this, he marvelled and said, 'O blessed knife, thou canst not cut that tender
throat of Ishmael; how cuttest thou this hard rock?' God
Most High gave a heart to that knife, and it said, 'O Abraham,
wherefore dost **thou rage?** God Most High said to me, "Be it
not that thou cut a single hair of Ishmael, else shall I never
deliver thee from hell."' Then God Most High said, 'O Abra-
ham, thou hast verified **the** vision;' * and He gave him a ram
from Heaven, and set Ishmael the Messenger free."†

THE LADY'S FIFTEENTH STORY.

"**They** relate that **there was a** devotee **in the** province of
Fárs,‡ and that this devotee **had a** friend who **loved** him exceedingly. And that man was by trade a grocer, and sold oil and
honey; and every day he gave the devotee **a** sufficient quantity
of oil **and** honey. The devotee ate a little of it and put the rest
into **a** jar, and kept that **jar in a corner of** his house. One day
the jar became full, **and the** devotee said in himself, 'Now shall
I take this oil and honey **and** sell it; and I shall buy five head
of sheep with the money; and these sheep with their lambs will
in time become a flock **; and** I shall grow very rich, and wear
new clothes, and marry **a** virgin; and I shall have a son by her,
and I shall teach him all things polite.' § Then he took his
staff in his hand, and put the jar on his head, and went to the
bazaar; but as he was leaning his staff against the wall he

---

* Koran, xxxvii. 105. † See Koran, xxxvii. 97-111.
‡ A province in the south of Persia.
§ The word *adeb* means alike polite manners and polite learning.

forgot the jar, and it struck against the wall, so that it was broken, and all that oil and honey ran down his beard."

THE SIXTEENTH VEZIR'S STORY.

" They relate that there was a carpenter, and he had a beautiful wife ; and that woman was a harlot. And the carpenter misdoubted of his wife, and from time to time he would watch her, but he could never learn anything for certain. One day her husband the carpenter said to her, ' I go to such and such a place ; to-night I shall remain there ; do thou keep well the house.' And he mounted his horse and went away. And the woman was glad, and she sent word to her lover, and that night the two of them met together and made merry, and then went to bed. When it was midnight the carpenter returned to his house, and he went in and saw his wife in this case. Then he went softly and hid himself under the bedstead, that he might hear how they should converse together. But the woman knew that her husband was come, and she said to the youth in a low voice, ' My husband is come and is lying under the bedstead ; it has now become needful to find some shift, otherwise he will slay the two of us. Now do thou ask me aloud whether I love my husband or thyself the better.' So the youth asked her. And the woman said, ' Leave these words ; they are not worthy of thee.' The youth repeated them through his fear. The woman answered, ' Women do these deeds through the stress of lust ; but when their lust is passed, they regard as strangers those persons with whom they may have made merry. If not, then may that woman see no good who loves not her husband a thousand-fold better than herself, and would not sacrifice her life for him !' When the carpenter heard this answer, his esteem for his wife increased, and the wretch said in himself, ' I have been disquieted through my own evil thoughts, imagining she did not love me.' At length the youth arose from his place and went away, and the carpenter came softly and laid himself there, and the woman looked on the ground, as it were for shame. And the carpenter said, ' I should now have hewn that youth in pieces, but I knew that thy love for me was steadfast, and I had ruth on thee, for I knew thee worthy of me ; so pray for me, for I have been grievously troubled concerning thee.' Thus did the woman accomplish all her affairs."

THE LADY'S SIXTEENTH STORY.

" It is related that a certain **man had** four **sons. One** day the mother **of** these died. **And** the funeral assembly came together. And they sent one son for the **shroud, and one** for the bier, and one for the grave-digger, **and one to** point out the grave. And the folk sat awaiting them. **But** each of the boys who had been sent began to play where he had gone, and each forgot his father's message. After the people had waited a long **time** they became weary, and began to look in the face of **that man. Then** the father of these boys raised up his hand, and **cursed them,** saying, **'May** God Most High never bring you **again** from that business whereunto ye went !' And for that **they honoured not their** father, but played, God Most High **changed their** forms, and turned him who had gone for the **shroud into** a spider, and him who had gone to point out the **grave into a** blind mole, and him who had gone for the bier into **a** woodpecker, and him who had gone for **the** grave-digger **into a** gnat. And all this for honouring **not** their father, but playing."

THE NINETEENTH VEZIR'S STORY.

" It is related that when our mother Eve bare Cain and Abel, she bare a daughter along with **each.** God Most High com- **manded** the Messenger Adam, saying, 'For the sake of their offspring, **give** to Cain the girl born with Abel, and give to Abel the girl born with Cain.' The Messenger Adam did so. **Now** the girl born **with Cain was** exceeding fair ; and Cain said, ' O **father, let the** girl **born** with him be his, and let the girl born **with me** be mine.' **Adam** answered, ' God Most High com- manded otherwise.' **But Cain** loved that girl exceedingly ; so **he went and** slew **Abel.** Thus because of a woman was blood first shed upon the ground." *

---

* This traditional story does not occur in the Koran.

THE TWENTY-THIRD VEZIR'S STORY.

" They have told that there was in the time of the Messenger
David a noble named Uriah. And that noble had a beautiful
wife. And the Messenger David loved that woman ; but he
feared her husband. One day the Messenger David sent that
noble to a perilous fight ; and by the divine decree Uriah was
there martyred. The Messenger David sought to take that
woman, though he had already ninety-nine wives. And God
Most High sent to him two angels in the likeness of men. And
these angels came before the Messenger David, and one of them
said, ' O Prophet of God, this is my brother, and he has ninety-
nine sheep, and I have but one sheep, and he seeks to take that
one sheep from me by force.' The Messenger David answered,
' Assuredly he does thee wrong in coveting thy one sheep while
he has these many.' Then he said to the elder brother, 'Wherefore seekest thou to take his one sheep, coveting it ? now will I
give thee thy due.' Then that angel said to him, ' O thou,
though thou hast ninety-nine wives, yet didst thou send Uriah
into the front of the battle and cause him to be martyred, and
now thou seekest to take his wife.' Then straightway the Messenger David knew these to be angels, and he was ashamed, for
he knew that though he had ninety-nine wives he yet sought to
take the wife of Uriah. And he bowed his face to the ground
and wept, so that by reason of his tears the grass grew in the
place where he lay. And he lamented. And he raised not his
head, but wept, until God commanded him to raise his head."*

THE LADY'S TWENTY-NINTH STORY.

" They have told that there was a king, who one day went
out to ride, and while he was going along, he saw a youth
whose stature was that of a man and whose favour was right
goodly. He said in his heart, ' Where shall I find a youth like
this ? He is indeed a man to fight the foe. I shall give him
horse and harness, and appoint him a wage ; maybe sometime

---

* See Koran, xxxviii. 20-24.

he will be profitable to us.' So he gave him horse and harness, and appointed **him a wage ;** and he was ever by the king, and whithersoever the king went he went with him. It chanced that an enemy arose ; so **the** king called up his army and went against him, and they had **a** great battle. But the youth abode still on his horse **by the king's** side. The king said **to** him, 'Charge thou likewise, and go into the battle.' The youth answered, 'O king, in my one hand I **hold** the bridle, in my other I hold my gear ; with what hand could I fight the foe ?' These words seemed right pleasant to **the** king ; and he saw that manhood comes not with beard and whiskers."

THE **LADY'S** THIRTY-FIRST **STORY.**

"**They relate that in the** city of Tabriz was a khoja, and **he** had exceeding great riches and many possessions ; and he was a mighty player **at the** chess. One day a Frank came, and he likewise had much wealth, and he likewise played at the chess. The Frank said to the khoja, 'Let us play for gold.' The khoja consented, and they played for gold, and that day the Frank won **many** sequins. On the morrow the khoja won many **sequins.** And thus, now the khoja, and **now** the Frank, would **win** great victories one of the other. At length **the** Frank, **having** many times **won** the **game of the** khoja, got all his **wealth.** Now the khoja **had** a slave-girl named Dil-árám, who **wrote** a fair hand and knew well the chess. The Frank said to **the** khoja, 'O khoja, **lo, I have overcome** thee, **and** all **of** thy wealth have **I won** at thy hands ; **come, let us** play yet another **game ;** lo, **I have in** my pocket five thousand sequins, do thou **stake** thy slave-girl Dil-árám ;* and let us see which is the **winner.'** The **khoja** agreed to this and they set out the chess things ; and they began to play, moving the pawns one against **the** other. Now Dil-árám came and watched their game from **the window.** This time the Frank drove the khoja into a **corner and shut up all the ways,** so that no place was left where

---

* The MS. has "do thou stake five thousand sequins ;" but the above, from Behrnauer, is doubtless the true reading.

he might move, for had he moved never so little he would have
been checkmated; and he was confounded and bewildered.
Dil-árám saw the combination from the window and how that
by sacrificing two pieces her master could checkmate the Frank.
But the khoja saw it not, and sought to give up the game. And
Dil-árám saw this from over against them, and straightway she
turned her face from the window and cried, 'Stay and checkmate.' And the khoja pondered, and he saw the combination
and checkmated the Frank. Thereafter was the khoja suc-
cessful at the play, and he won all that the Frank had, so that
the Frank fled back empty-handed to Frankland."

The Thirty-Second Vezir's Story.

"They relate that a certain man in the city of Cairo had
charge over a garden. One day he caught a thief in the garden,
and sought to beat him. The thief said to him, 'Come, beat
me not; one day I shall be profitable to thee; for the great
have said, "Cast a good deed on the sea, and one day it shall
be profitable to thee."'* So the gardener beat him not, but let
him go. One day the gardener went into the city, and as he
was walking about, a woman came and said to him, 'Come
along.' So the gardener followed her. And the woman went
on till she entered a house, when she said to the gardener,
'Come in.' And the woman turned and locked the door, and
they passed through three or four doors, and again she turned
and locked these doors. When they had gone through yet
another door, the gardener beheld some ten or fifteen young
robbers seated eating and drinking. Their chief said to one of
them, 'Go, kill the fellow.' So he arose from his place and
drew his sword that he might kill him, when he looked and saw
that he was the youth who had seized him in the garden, but
had not beaten him. And he was an-angered with that woman,
and said, 'I have but one friend in the world; wherefore hast
thou brought him?' Then he turned and said to the gardener,

---

* *cf.* Cast thy bread upon the waters; for thou shalt find it after
many days.—Ecclesiastes, ii. 1.

' Hadst thou beaten me with thy stick, I had now smitten thee with my sword.' And he set the gardener free, and sent him away."

THE THIRTY-FOURTH VEZIR'S STORY.

"They have told that there was once a sheep-owner who had many sheep. Among these was one very gentle ewe which lambed before any of the others. Every year the owner of the sheep took her lamb as a gift to the ruler; and as he was greedy of money, he ever took from that ewe her lambkin before its time. So one year she lambed, and the fellow took from her her lamb as before. And the ewe saw that her lamb was going, and she bleated and followed after it. They beat her back, but could not drive her from her little one; so the owner of the sheep seized her and bound her, and cut the lamb's throat, and then let the ewe loose. The poor ewe ran away, and went and cast herself from a high rock, and was dashed in pieces. And they went and cut her open, and they saw that her liver * was all pierced with holes; that for every lamb there was a hole in her vitals."

THE LADY'S THIRTY-FOURTH STORY.†

"*Naql iderler ki bir khoja var* **idi**. *Ghayet ile mahbub* **bir oghli var** *idi, shuyle guzel idi* **ki** *guren kishi hayran olurdi.* **Bu khoja** *oghlini ghayet saqlardi;* **bir** *yere chiqarmazdi, ve doninin baghini muhrlerdi. Qachan bir minarede ezan oqumishlar, ' Nichun buyle chaghirirlar ?' deyu, soraridi. Khoja dakhi dedi ki, 'Bir adam ulmish, ani defn iderler,' deridi. Oghlan dakhi bu suze inanurdi. Bu oghlanin husni 'Ajemde suylenurdi; ve 'Ajemden bir khoja bu oghlanin 'ashqina mal ve eshyasi ile Baghdada gelub, bu oghlanin babasi ile dost olub, da'ima oghlanin yuzine baqub, nerede durdughin tefettush iderdi. Chun*

---

* The liver was regarded by old writers as the seat of the passions, see p. 383.

† For reasons stated in the Preface this story is left untranslated.

khoja bildi kim ol khass khazinede oghlan saqlu durur, ayda bir kerre yuzin gurmek mushkil dir. Bir gun khoja oghlanin babasina eytdi, 'Ben filan yere gidejek oldum; benim bir sandughim var dir, neqadar qimetlu nesnem var ise, jumle ol sanduq ichine qoyub, sana gundereyim; sen dakhi alub, ani oghlunun oldughi khazinede saqla,' dedikde, khoja dakhi, 'Bash uzrine,' deyub, ichine kendi girejegi qader bir sanduq yapdirdi. Andan ichine sherab kebab bezm alati tamam dukdi. Andan khidmetkarina eytdi, 'Var, bir hammal getur, bu sandughi filan khojanin qonaghina getur; "Efendim gunderdi, sizde emanet dursun," deyub, buraghub, gel; yine ertesi, "Efendim sandughi ister," deyub, al, gel,' dedi. Pes khidmetkar hammala gitdi; khoja kendini sanduq ichine pinhan eyledi; oghlan sandughi hammala yukledub, khojanin khanesine geturub, buraghub, gitdi. Chun geje oldu, khoja sanduqdan tashra chiqdi, gurdi ki oghlanin bashi ujinde shem'edan ile mum yanar, bir mah-peyker jame-i kh‚ab ichinde yatub; khoja buni gurinje, hayran olub, 'Fe-tabareka 'llahu ahsenu 'l khaliqin' dedi. Pes khoja sherab kebab mejlisi hazir eyledi; aheste varub, oghlani uyandirdi. Oghlan yerinden durub, suhbete araste idub, eytdi, 'Bunda neye geldin?' deyu, sordi. Khoja fi 'l hal qadehi doldirub, oghlana sondi, 'Buni sana kim oldughim bildireyim,' deyub, oghlana yalvarub, unine altun dukdi. Oghlan dakhi qadehi alub, ichdi. Chun uch durt qadeh oghlana ichirdi, oghlanin ruyi lale-reng olub, mest olub, khoja ile suhbete bashladi. Ol geje khoja sabaha degin beraber 'ishret idub, her ne muradi var ise, hasil eyledi. Chun sabah oldi, khoja yine sandugha girdi; khidmetkar gelub, sandughi hammala yukledub, khanesine geturdi. Oghlanin babasi ertesi otururken yine muezzin ezan verdi. Fi 'l hal oghlan eytdi, 'Behey baba, yuf 'allenen oghlan ulur, anin ichun bu harif buraya chiqar baghirir; bu geje beni yuf‘allediler, nichun ben ulmedim?' dedikde, babasi oghlanin aghizina wurub 'Buyle suz suyleme, 'ayb dir,' dedi. Andan sandughin nichun geldigin bildi."*

---

* Koran, xxiii. 14.

The **Thirty-Sixth** Vezir's Second Story.

'They have **told that one** day a smooth-faced youth was **going** along **a** road **with a** book in his hand. A woman was looking from **a** window, and her heart was taken with that youth, and she said to him, 'What **is that** in thy hand?' The youth answered, 'This **book is** called *The Wiles of Women.*' The beauty replied, 'I never heard **the name thou sayest ;** but, my **lord,** might not it be that thou tarry a little while, **that** we may converse together? **Our** house is empty, and all is ready for a carouse.' Now the youth was a mighty wencher, so he **inclined to her** and **said,** 'I obey thy bidding.' So the lady **sent a slave-girl who opened** the **door ; and** the youth entered **and went upstairs and** beheld **a room** furnished with all things **needful for a carouse.** And the lady came forward to greet him, **and she took him to her** side, and they sat down. Then the **beauty said to the youth,** 'Welcome, and fair welcome !' and she **played all** manner **of love-tricks.** And she took a goblet of rosy **wine in her hand and presented it to** the youth, and he took it **and drank it, and** they began **to make merry.** After **a** time **some one knocked at** the door ; **one of the** slave-girls ran **to open it, and** straightway she **came back,** crying, '**Alas ! the master has** come.' **The** lady **said, 'What** shall we **do !** If he **come,** welcome **to** him, **let** him come.' Then **turning to** the **youth,** she said, '**My** life, my husband, the **master of the** house, **has come ;** do thou go into this closet, and **rest there for** a little **time ; he** will sit here for a short space and then **go** away.' **The youth** consented, and entered the closet and lay down, and **his senses** forsook him **for fear.** Then **the** husband came in **and he saw** all things needful **for a carouse** spread out, **and many** dainties **on** the table, and **he** addressed to his wife **mocking words like** these, 'Lady, what mean these preparations **that thou hast** spread here without fear? For whom are these? **Or is there some** stranger here?—for **if so, I** will go away and **leave you to** enjoy yourselves.' The lady answered, 'My **honoured lord, the** truth **of** the **affair is** this : **I,** thy handmaid, **was seated at the** window, looking **out, when a** youth passed

with a book in his hand, which he was reading as he went along.
And I put my head out of the window and asked him, saying,
" My lord, what is that in .thy hand ? " The youth answered,
" This is called *The Wiles of Women.*" And my heart inclined
to him, and I sent one to bring him in. And he consented, and
raised us from the dust,* and honoured our house by his
entrance. And I, thy handmaid, was bold, and I set out the
things needful for a carouse. And I welcomed him and took
him to my side, and he drank a goblet or two of wine at my
hand, and gladdened my heart. And when we had begun to
make merry thou camest with all honour ; but the youth was
abashed as soon as he beheld thee, and, unable to abide because
of his shame, he went into this closet, where he is now lying.'
The youth heard these words from within and he gave up hope
of his life. And the husband heard these words of the woman,
and he knew not what to do unto her, and cried in wrath, 'Out
on thee, accursed, what words are these thou thus speakest
without fear ? Dost thou commit this lewdness in my house ?'
And he arose and went up to the lady to beat her. And straightway the woman took the key of the closet from her pocket and
gave it into her husband's hand, and said, ' *Yad-est.*'† Now the
night before they had eaten a fowl, and they had taken a *yad-est*
over the merry-thought. So the husband straightway laid down
the key, and said, ' Out on thee, cruel, with how strange a trick
hast thou deceived me !' And he was ashamed and went away ;
and she cried out after him, 'I know not the half of what I
shall do to thee.'‡ Then she opened the closet and saw the
youth lying senseless, and she sprinkled rose-water on his face

---

* *i.e.* honoured us by accepting our invitation.

† In the Turkish *yad-est,* a kind of game which has much in common
with our Philopena, the merry-thought of a fowl takes the place of the
two-kerneled almond ; neither player must accept anything from the
other without immediately saying *yad-est* (=it is remembered) ; should
he forget to do so, the other, on repeating these words, becomes
entitled to some sort of forfeit. Here the husband, who has taken a
yad-est with his wife, is led by the latter to imagine that she has made
those preparations and invented that story in order to take him by sur-
prise, and so win the forfeit.

‡ *i.e.* I am going to think upon some heavy forfeit to make thee pay.

and brought him to himself. And the youth opened his eyes, and said, ' Out on thee, cruel, how strange a work hast thou wrought ; thou hast well-nigh taken my head.' The lady answered, ' What ails thee ? There is nothing ; come, let us make merry.' The youth replied, ' Mercy, if thou lovest God, be gracious ; this much suffices ; give me leave to go away.' The woman saw that the youth could not abide for fear, so she said, ' O youth, when thou art gone, pray write this story on the margins of that book thou callest *The Wiles of Women.'* *

THE LADY'S THIRTY-SEVENTH STORY.

" Thus relate they : A certain vezir had an unworthy son, whose parents were powerless to restrain his wickedness. And this vezir had a fair slave-girl whom he loved exceedingly. And the boy likewise was in love with that slave-girl, and he would ever give her money and clothes ; but she would in no wise obey him ; and he saw that she would not yield to him. One day he watched and found an opportunity, and urged the slave-girl. He saw that she would not obey him, so he straightway drew a knife and slew her. And his father got word, but he could not bring himself to kill the boy. And the slave-girl went from the world guiltless."

FROM BEHRNAUER'S GERMAN TRANSLATION.†

THE LADY'S SECOND STORY.

" There was of old time a king who gathered the learned about him. He said to them, ' What manner of work must I do in this world that I may find it for myself in the World to come ?' The learned answered, ' From a place whence nought can be taken, take nought ; and in a place where nought can be

---

* This tale bears some resemblance to the Twenty-First Vezir's Story, p. 227.

† Not having seen any of the following stories (except the second) in Turkish, I have had to content myself with translating from Behrnauer's German.

given, give nought; and let not the favourable opportunity
escape thee; that is, do a good and righteous work when it is
in thy power and the opportunity therefor is in thy hands.
Life keeps troth with no man.' The king said, 'Who can do
that?' The learned answered, 'That man can, who strives after
the grace of God, and shuns anger.'"

THE LADY'S FIFTEENTH STORY (PART II.)*

"O king, thy plight is likewise even as that which I shall
relate to thee of those four opium-eaters.

"At the foot of a mountain, by the side of a great river, these
seated themselves and began to eat. Of a sudden one of them
conceived a quaint fancy, and said, 'What if this flowing stream
were oil!' Another said, 'What if this hill were rice!' A third
said, 'What if the two of them were cooked! Then should we
eat them!' When the fourth heard these words, he said, 'Ye
have begun to eat without saying to me, "Stretch forth."† Is
that good-fellowship?' And he left the food and arose, and
was aggrieved, and went away. When the other opium-eaters
heard this speech, they said, 'A curse on opium-eating!' And
they were sorrowful."

THE LADY'S SEVENTEENTH STORY.

"It is related that one day there were young fledgelings in
the nest of a little water-ousel. She always rejoiced exceedingly
when she looked upon them; for she had for a long while
patiently borne pain and want, waiting and watching over her
eggs, thinking on these, like a woman in childbed. One day
while she was twittering with her little ones and playing herself
with them, a dragon set his jaws against her nest. When the
little ones saw him they were troubled and clung fast to their
parents. These parents would have flown away, but they could
not abandon their nest. They went against the snake, that he

---

* This story is given by Belletéte as well; in translating I have
followed sometimes him, sometimes Behrnauer.
† That is: Stretch forth thy hand to the food and help thyself.

might not devour their little ones. But the snake first devoured
them, and afterwards their nestlings."

THE THIRTY-SECOND VEZIR'S STORY.

" It **is** related that there was of old time a king from whose
foot there issued a wasting sweat, such that no remedy could be
found therefor. The physicians came together and agreed that
the body of an Indian boy must be split open and the king's foot
thrust therein ; ' Such,' they declared, ' is the only remedy for this
evil.' They sought long, but no such boy could be found ; until
at length they went to an Indian wedded pair who **dwelt** in the
city, and they discovered **the** sought-for boy with them. The
king caused the parents to come before **him,** and offered them
gold, **and said, '** Sell **me your boy.'** They answered, ' O king,
what can we do? We need it sore to-day, for we have nought ;
well, we shall take the gold and leave **the** boy to **thee ;** God
will surely give us another boy.' Therewith they made over the
boy to the king, took the gold, and went away. The boy was
brought before the king that his body might be split open. Then
began the boy to laugh. They asked him, ' Why in all the
world laughest thou who shouldest weep?' **He** answered,
' Why should not I **now** laugh? When a boy falls into need
or danger, he flies to his father ; **if that** avails not, he flies
to his mother ; if that avails not, he **flies** to the magistrate ;
if that too avails not, he flies to the **great** and mighty autho-
rities and kings. Now, indeed, **my parents sell** me to the
king, and he is about to kill me **for** the healing of his pain,
so that thereby he may be delivered **in** this present life ;
but what will he say in that other **World** in his justification
before the Majesty of the **Most** High? Now, have I found
no tenderness in my mother, nor any affection in my father,
nor yet any justice or equity in **the** king ; whom then shall
I **implore?** I fly for refuge to that God who is **an** almighty
Avenger : for all the injustice wrought against me, He will
surely take me in charge, and cause to be bestowed on me my
full right !' When the king heard this, fear fell upon him, so
that love for the boy was kindled **in** his soul, and **he** set him

free.   Through strong emotion he shed warm tears, whereof
the physicians took and rubbed upon the sore on his foot.   And
straightway God Most High vouchsafed to him recovery, and
he was made whole again."

The Lady's Thirty-Second Story.

"It is related that there was of old time a rich merchant who
was very niggard.   He had an exceeding good wife who was
truly devoted to him, and was, at the same time, very generous.
Though he would always command her, saying, 'Give no one
anything from my house, and do no one aught of good,' she
paid no heed thereto, and ever gave a mite to the poor.   One day
the merchant swore that he would repudiate her, saying, 'If
thou bestow any alms from my house, I will divorce thee from
me for ever.'   Once there befell a great famine.   A beggar came
to the door ; the woman brought out three little butter-cakes
and gave them to the beggar, who took the cakes and went
away.   The merchant saw him when he was leaving the house,
and went after him, and asked, 'Ho beggar, whence hast thou
these three cakes?'   The beggar answered, 'They gave me
them at that house there,' and he pointed to the merchant's
house.   The merchant opened the door, rushed angrily in, and
struck his wife so that he broke her arm.   As the divorce was
now accomplished, they parted from one another.   The woman
went forth from the city and journeyed to another place.   There
she abode for a long time as a widow,* then she married again.
As a punishment for his niggardise, her first husband, the niggard merchant, lost all his money and his substance, and became
very poor.   Ashamed by reason of his disgrace, he journeyed
forth from the city, and came begging to the door of his first
wife, and begged, saying, 'An alms ; may God repay it you.'
The woman asked her husband, 'Shall I give him some bread?'
The man answered, 'No, he is a stranger beggar ; we shall
make him come in that he may eat with us.'   Forthwith they
made him come in, and he seated himself by the edge of the

---

* So the German has it : als Wittwe.

table. The woman looked at him, drew back her hand, and ate not. **The** man asked, 'What ails thee?' The woman answered, 'The beggar who is seated here was erewhile my husband.' The man asked, 'How was the case between you?' The woman answered, 'He was then a merchant **and had** much money and substance; but he was niggard, and swore **that he** would surely divorce me if ever I bestowed **aught from our** house in alms. Now one day I gave three **little butter-cakes to** a beggar, who took them and went away. **Soon afterwards came** this man in wrath into the house, and he struck me and broke my arm, and drove me forth from the house. I came into this city. It **was** my lot **to** marry thee.' The man said, 'O wife, thy **story is wonderful;** but my story **is yet more** wonderful than thine.' **The** woman asked, '**How so?**' Her husband **answered,** 'That beggar who then came to thy door, and to **whom** thou gavest the three little butter-cakes, was I; at that time **I was poor and** needy, but yet generous. It was my wont to share what I had gathered with the poor and the orphans. Thou art not suited to him, but to me; therefore has God freed thee from him and given thee to me. He so ordered it, **that I** should stand in need of thy help; and so I **then went a beggar** to thy door. When a man's wife **is good and truly devoted to her** husband, she avails to the preserving **of his abiding** happiness, if he but follow her words.'"

THE THIRTY-THIRD VEZIR'S STORY.

"It is related that there was of **old time a** great merchant who was very sagacious **and** clear-sighted, and who had journeyed through the world as **a** trader and **had** looked at it heedfully. At length he determined to fix his dwelling in the place which should **please him best. So** he went one day into a city, **the** people, customs, water **and** air whereof were agreeable to him, **in order** to take up his abode therein. **He** thought in himself, '**How** shall I set about it, that there be **in** this city no greater or more learned man **than myself, so** that the folk **here** may obey me?' Thereupon he sent a public crier through the city, whom he bade proclaim as follows : ' Let every poor and needy one who is without substance go to such and such a merchant and get for himself money.' When the folk heard this, they went, and the merchant dealt out money among them, and he wrote bonds for them, thus : ' When the king of this city dies, give me back my money.' Thereon was the fame of this spread abroad, and it reached the king's ears. He learned that a merchant was come who had distributed money among the folk and set the king's decease as the time for repayment. When the king heard this, it pleased him not, and he was wroth and caused that merchant to be straightway dragged before him. When they had brought him, the king asked him, ' Why hast thou set my death as the time for the repayment of thy money ? ' The merchant answered, ' Long be the king's reign ! For that I love thee have I so done.' The king asked, ' How so ? ' The merchant answered, ' My lord and king, God Most High has created the soul of man greedy ; its inborn nature is niggardise and covetousness ; fain would it ever take, but never give. Therefore did I say, " Give me back my money when the king dies." So now will the folk pray God, saying, " O Lord, lengthen our king's life ! Long may he live ! " And God Most High will hear and grant this pious wish of every one of them, and the king's life will be long, and I shall have offered up my substance in a work well pleasing unto God.' When the king heard this, he let give the merchant a sheep, and said, ' Go, fodder this sheep ; give him richest fodder and water, and deny him nought. Forty days long let him gorge and guzzle in full delight. From day to day will the flesh of the sheep melt away and be lost in fat, yet for all that will he devour his fodder and gulp his water.' Having said these words, he appointed forty men to watch the merchant ; of whom twenty were to keep watch by day, and twenty by night, lest the merchant should beat or cudgel that sheep, or should leave him hungry or thirsty. The merchant took the sheep, led him to his house, placed him there in an underground chamber, and bound him fast by one foot with a rope to a strong pole. And he brought thither a wolf which he had bought, and bound him up in another corner of the cellar ; **and they were** separated by but a thin partition. **When he had** given **the** sheep fodder to gorge and water **to guzzle for the** whole **tale of** days, he took away the partition. As soon as the wolf **beheld** the sheep, he rushed toward him, seeking to devour him. **The poor** sheep dashed himself hither and thither for fear **of the wolf ;** gorging and guzzling **profited** him not, and daily his flesh shrank, until **at length, when forty** days were past, he was grown all lean **and could no more stir** from his place. They now took the **sheep to** the king, and he asked those men whom he had appointed as **watch,** ' What has the merchant done to the sheep ? ' They **told** the **story of the** sheep and the wolf. **Then the** king perceived the **sagacity of the merchant, and he put on him** a robe of honour, and made **him his grand vezir.** He performed the duties of this office **with great integrity** and justice, and after the death of the king **he ascended the throne, and** all the princes and feudatories swore fealty to him."

FROM THE QUARITCH MS. NO. II.

THE THIRTIETH VEZIR'S STORY.

" In the ranks of the sheykhs there **was** a sheykh **who had** about him a company of disciples **clad in rags. One day,** while seated **in his** convent talking **with his** disciples, the sheykh said, ' I purpose to go on **a two or three days'** journey, **and I** seek a dervish who will **come and serve me and** bear **me** company.' A dervish arose **and said, '** O sheykh, if thou will accept me, I shall gird up my loins.' Quoth the sheykh, ' **After** what fashion wouldst thou serve me by the way ? ' He answered, ' I should carry thine ewer and thy **prayer-mat,** and bear thee **company.'** Quoth the sheykh, ' Sit down, I need no companion **like to thee.'** Then the dervish sat down in his place. **Again quoth the** sheykh, ' Ho dervishes, I desire one to come **and bear me company.'** So another dervish arose **and** said, ' O sheykh, **I shall bear thee company.'** Quoth the sheykh, ' After **what fashion** wouldst thou bear **me** company?' He answered, ' **I should carry** thy staff, and when thou lightest I should **spread** thy **rug.'** Quoth

the sheykh, 'Sit down, neither canst thou bear me company.'
Again the sheykh said, 'O cherishers of the aged, I seek one to
bear me company on this journey.' Then an abdal took his
crook in his hand and came forward and said, 'O sheykh, I
shall bear thee company.' Quoth the sheykh, 'After what
fashion wouldst thou bear me company?' He answered, 'O
sheykh, when I see thee stray from the path, I shall with this
hook draw thee back into the way.' Quoth the sheykh, 'I have
indeed found my companion; this is indeed the companion that
I sought. Gird up thy loins and let us go.'"

THE THIRTY-THIRD VEZIR'S STORY.

"They have told that in Tartary the chiliarch Sheykh Ahmed
(the mercy of God on him!) had ninety thousand times ten
thousand families.* Among his disciples this was, it is said, a
custom: If a dervish traveller became the guest of one of them,
they would entreat him kindly, and when night was come,
would send to his side a maid or matron with her bed and
pillow. If that dervish heeded her not, they would hold him
for a saint (and retain him); but if he played any love-trick
with her, they would give him a piece of clothing and send him
off. To whatever convent he might go, they would do thus to
that dervish; for that Sheykh Ahmed Yeseví had said to them,
'Every dervish who eateth not of that your morsel, know ye
that he is I, know ye my words; and that dervish who eateth
thereof, he is no dervish.' Thus had he said. Therefore did
they so, until that dervish came to their chief convent, and they
would there see the clothes that he had on. When morning
was come, after worship, they would take him and would
publicly deliver him to God.† Until one night the sheykh
appeared to them in a dream, and forbade them this practice,
and said, 'Feast him not with a spoon, neither put out his eye
with the handle thereof.'"

---

* *i.e.* convents of dervishes of his order.
† This probably means that they would strangle him.

APPENDIX B.

VARIATIONS OCCURRING IN THE TRANSLATION BY PETIS DE LA CROIX.

[The edition of the text from which Petis **de la Croix** made his incomplete translation of this Romance **appears to have** differed considerably from any of those **that have come under** my notice. For while **there** is but little **difference** between the versions of a single story found in the Constantinople Text, the India Office MS., Belletête, or Behrnauer, the same story often appears in **De la** Croix with many important **variations and** amplifications, **and,** occasionally, **with** lengthy additions. **Consequently, the** variations mentioned **in** the following notes **are to be understood as** being peculiar to the **Translation of De la Croix, none of the** other versions bearing the **least trace of them.** Although I have thought it advisable **to indicate all** the **important** points wherein the stories **as rendered by the** old **French** orientalist **differ from** the **same** tales as given elsewhere, **it** would **not perhaps be very safe to** lay any great stress on these variations, **with Galland's Mille et** Une Nuits before us, **as** an example of **the manner in which the** translators **of** those days thought themselves **at liberty to deal** with the texts they took in hand. **I may say that the** king to whom the stories are told is **by De la Croix named** Hafikin ; * by Belletête, Shāh Hāfiqīn ; by **the Constantinople Text** and the India Office MS., Shāh Khānqīn. **These forms are** all meaningless, and Behrnauer is **doubtless correct in** writing the name Shāh-i-Khāfiqayn=King of **the Two** Horizons, *i.e.* East and West, *i.e.* **the whole** world. **The** wicked step-mother and the silent prince, who are nameless in **all the** other versions, **are** called by De la Croix, Canzada (for Khān-zāda=Khan-born, *i.e.* **Child** of the Khan) **and** Nourgehan (for Nūr-i-Jihān=Light **o' the World), respectively.**]

* In the English translation of De la **Croix's work, this appears as** Hasikin, the printer having mistaken the f for **a long s.**

NOTE I. (The First Vezir's Story [1].) The conclusion of this story is very different in Petis de la Croix ; according to his version, when the men come in to kill the sheykh they are seized with terror at beholding him whirling round with the lighted candles in his hands, and, fancying he is about to work some fatal spell, rush out. The sheykh thereon bolts the door, gets some water, performs the ablution, and so regains his powers. He immediately takes the form of the woman and makes her assume his, then summoning back the men, he gets them to arrest the woman whom they imagine to be the sheykh himself. They are then carried before the governor who, under the same mistake, causes the woman to be beheaded, whereon the sheykh again performs the double transformation, and, having upbraided the governor for his servility and cruelty, disappears.

NOTE II. (The Third Vezir's Story [5].) In De la Croix's version, this story, which figures there as that of the Fourth Vezir, ends with [5 *a*] the recognition of the youngest prince as king in his father's stead ; [5 *b*] all that portion dealing with the old king having his own obsequies performed before his death being tacked on to the beginning of what is in the Const. Text the Lady's Eighth Story [16] (see Note VII.)

NOTE III. (The Fourth Vezir's Story [7].) This story which is the Lady's Seventh in De la Croix, ends there with [7 *a*] the victory of Moses over Og ; [7 *b*] the portion about Balaam being omitted.

NOTE IV. (The Lady's Fourth Story [8].) An incident, omitted in the other versions, is given by De la Croix at the beginning of this story. The poor man (here called a Sūfī, *i.e.* a mystic philosopher or devotee,) goes to the palace of the king (here said to be Hārūn-er-Reshīd) and demands a present of a thousand sequins. Being called into the royal presence and asked what he means by making such a demand, he says that he is a very poor man, destitute of the means of life, and that last night he complained to God of His injustice in heaping all manner of good things on the king who was no better than his neighbours, while such as he were denied the barest necessities. A voice from heaven, he adds, rebuked him for decrying the king and told him to go and put the royal generosity to the proof, when he would find the sovereign as superior to other men in liberality as he was in fortune. Hârûn, pleased with his wit, gives him the thousand sequins ; and it is after all this money is spent that he promises to show Khizr to the king for three years' keep.

NOTE V. (The Lady's Fifth Story [10].) In De la Croix, the youth does not wish to play the magician false, but is constrained by his mother-in-law to enter into a plot which she and her husband have formed for his murder. Before carrying out their design, they all three descend into the hoard and load themselves with treasures ; but as they turn to come back, the youth remembers that though he has learned the charms for gaining entrance into the vault, he has not acquired those necessary for getting out again, whereon the negro and the dragons rush forward and tear the three would-be murderers in pieces.

NOTE VI. (The Lady's Seventh Story [14].) The version of this story given by De la Croix differs widely from that in the present translation. The following is an epitome of the former : Solomon has at his court a bird whose beautiful gridelin feathers and many accomplishments have quite won his heart. One day this bird leaves the court and goes to the wood where his mate resides. As soon as the latter sees him, she begins to upbraid him for his devotion to the court and long-continued absence, and in her rage she dashes at her own eggs and destroys all except one, which the male bird manages to protect till her fury is appeased. In due time a little bird is born who is even more beautiful than his father, having a yellow head, a blue neck, a white body, violet wings, and a red tail. Meanwhile Solomon grows anxious for Gridelin's return, and sends two red birds of the same sort to fetch him. After a while these birds find him and try to induce him to accompany them by a feigned tale to the effect that Solomon, annoyed at his absence, has begun to use the birds unkindly and drive them from court, so that the condition of his fellows can only be bettered by his return. Gridelin replies that freedom is better than service at a court, and advises them to remain away from the prophet. The messengers, seeing their fiction has no effect, confess that Solomon has sent them, whereon Gridelin is much grieved as the king has shown him many favours; but he cannot return, having promised his mate to remain with her. He resolves to send his son Violet to make his apology, who, returning with the red birds, is well received; but as he has not Gridelin's wit, Solomon is not satisfied and threatens him with perpetual imprisonment unless he brings his father back. He agrees to do so, and goes off and tells his father that Solomon is very angry and is sending his fowlers to take him, at the same time he offers to lead him to a place of safety. Gridelin goes with his son who takes him straight to where Solomon's people are lying in wait to secure him. "Hence, O king," quoth the lady, "thou mayst learn the treachery of sons."

NOTE VII. (The Lady's Eighth Story [16].) As already stated (Note II.) [5 *b*] the account of the aged king having his own obsequies performed while he is yet alive, which in the other versions forms the latter portion of the Third Vezir's Story [5], is in De la Croix prefixed to [16] the tale of the Three Princes and the Stolen Jewels, it being there said to be the father of those youths who conceives and carries out that strange fancy.

NOTE VIII. (The Tenth Vezir's Story [19].) De la Croix's version of this story gives a great deal of additional matter. Some time after he has fallen heir to the khoja's belongings, the prince is amazed on returning home one evening to find his house empty and all his wife's treasures gone. The cadi, suspecting him of having murdered his wife, throws him into prison, whence he is not delivered until he has given up all his remaining possessions. Thus finding himself once more destitute, he returns to the service of the tailor in whose employment he had formerly been. One day he meets in the street a man whom he recognises as a tailor he had known in Cairo. This man falls at his feet and salutes him as King of Egypt, telling him that his brother is dead, that the people desire him as their sovereign, and that he himself has come forth to seek him. The prince accompanies the man back to Cairo, where he is made king; his first desire is to appoint the tailor grand vezir, but this honour the latter prudently declines, asking to be made court tailor instead. One day the cadi comes to the king and says that he has got three murderers, one of whom declares that he is innocent and yet deserves to die. The king orders this man to be brought, and as soon as he sees him, knows him to be one of the slaves who had served him in Baghdad. On being asked by the king what he means by saying that he is innocent and yet deserves to die, the prisoner answers that he had a good master in Baghdad whose wife fell in love with him, and induced him to elope with her one day when her husband was out and when she had sent all the other slaves away on different errands. While they were journeying towards Basra, they alighted near a castle, the lord of which, who was nephew to the King of Basra, happening to pass by, was smitten by the lady's charms, and carried her off, giving his attendants orders to beat away the slave should he prove importunate. So the latter came to Cairo where he saw a murder committed, and the two assassins running towards him just as the watch came up, all three were taken together. "And so," he adds, "though I am innocent of the murder, I deserve to die for my treachery towards my master." The king, however, pardons him because of his repentance. One evening, some little time after, when the king is going in disguise through the streets, he hears the shrieks of a woman issuing from one of the houses. He and his attendants force their way in and find a woman lying naked on the floor with two slaves whipping her and a young man looking on. The king at once recognises in her the khoja's wife whom he had married, but feigning not to know her, asks the young man why he is treating the woman so cruelly. He, having been told who the speaker is, says that he is the King of Basra's nephew, and that the woman is his wife whom he found in the desert attended by a slave, when she told him she was flying from an aged man whom her father had forced her to marry, and besought him to slay the attendant slave. He, however, merely drove the latter away, and then married the lady whom he treated with all kindness ; but he had just learned that she had proposed to one of his slaves to kill him and then marry her. The slave, however, being faithful, had informed him, and he was determined to punish her by thus whipping her every night. But the king says that this punishment is not sufficient and orders her to be thrown into the Nile.

NOTE IX. (The Thirteenth Vezir's Story [25].) There are considerable differences in this story as given by De la Croix, the most noteworthy of which is the much more prominent part assigned to the lady whom the prince meets in the sepulchral pit. She is called Dil-ārām, the Princess of Georgia, and tells her story to the prince—who is styled the Prince of Carizme (for Khārezm)—while they are sitting outside the enchanted palace, to the effect that she was betrothed to a foreign king, but while voyaging to his dominions, suffered shipwreck upon the shores of the people who bury the living survivor with the dead consort (here called the Samsard * and said to be a race of dog-headed men), where she had to marry a husband on whose death she had shared the usual fate of widows and widowers. On making their way into the palace, instead of finding a coffin and inscription, they discover an aged man seated on a sofa with a crown of emeralds on his head. This old man, who receives them kindly, tells them that he was the Emperor of China, that he is a great philosopher and magician, and, having discovered the philosopher's stone, which is the elixir of life, he caused the jinn to build him this palace where he intends to live for ever. They reside with him for a time, and the princess has two sons by the prince ; but at length she grows tired of the monotonous life and desires to depart. The prince consents ; and when they tell the old emperor that they

---

* Perhaps for Sumatra : describing the islands near Java, Sir John Maundeville says, "Aftre this Yle, men gon be See to another Yle, that is clept Calonak : and it is a fair Lond and a plentifous of Godes. . . . . And zif a man, that is maryed, dye in that Contree, men buryen his Wyf with him alle quyk."

are about to leave, but will return again, the latter, knowing that they will not keep their promise, is so grieved that he employs his magic power to bring about his own death. No sooner is he dead than the palace vanishes; and the prince and princess embark with their sons in the boat in which they had come; but they are captured by pirates who, putting the prince ashore on an island, sail away with his wife and children. The prince here finds himself among a headless people whose mouths are in their breasts and whose eyes are in their shoulders; these, being at war with a neighbouring race who have birds' heads, make the prince commander of their armies. He gains a complete victory over the bird-headed men, who are all either slain or captured and eaten by their headless enemies. As a reward, the headless king compels the prince to marry his daughter; but on the nuptial night a jinn, who is enamoured of the bride, carries both her and her husband off, and leaves the latter on a neighbouring island. He there finds an old man who turns out to be one of the astrologers who had cast his horoscope, and who tells him that his father is dead and is succeeded by a new king whose ill-feeling towards the wise men has caused the latter to leave his dominions. He himself had settled in that island, attracted by the fame of the just and good government of its queen. He takes the prince to introduce him to this sovereign whom he finds to be his wife Dil-ārām, the piratical vessel which she was on board having been wrecked in a storm, though she herself and her two sons had managed to reach the shore of an island. The king, an old man of ninety, had been much pleased with her, formally married her, and at his death bequeathed to her his kingdom. Thus the prince is at last happily reunited with his wife and children, the thirty years during which his star was afflicted being now past.

E E

APPENDIX C.

COMPARATIVE TABLE SHOWING THE STORIES FOUND IN THE DIFFERENT TEXTS AND THE ORDER IN WHICH THEY OCCUR.

[The Figures indicate the Stories as numbered in the Table of Contents. Where no Figure is given, no Story occurs in the Text.]

STORIES.	Const. Text.	Ind. Office MS.	Behrnauer.	Quaritch MS. No. I.	Quaritch MS. No. II.	Belletête.	P. de la Croix.
First Vezir	1	3	1	1	Lacuna	1	1
Lady's First	2	85	2	2	do.	2	2
Second Vezir	3	86	3	3	do.	3	77
Lady's Second	4	4	105		4	6	12
Third Vezir	5 a, b	1	5 a, b	5 a, b	5 a, b	5 a, b	11
Lady's Third	6	87	6	6	6	8	14
Fourth Vezir	7 a, b	27	7 a, b	7 a, b	7 a, b	9	5 a
Lady's Fourth	8	30	8	8	8	12	18 a, b
Fifth Vezir	9	41	9	9	9	13	19
Lady's Fifth	10	18 a	10	10	10	16	23
Sixth Vezir	11	77	11	11	11	17	22
Lady's Sixth	12	58	12	12	12	18 a, b	8
Seventh Vezir	13	88	13	13	13	19	21
Lady's Seventh	14	89	14	14	14	77	7 a
Eighth Vezir	15	7 a, b	15	15	15	23	10
Lady's Eighth	16	10	16	16	16	24	5 b, 16
Ninth Vezir	17	90	17	17	17	81	25
Lady's Ninth	18 a, b	91	18 a, b	18 a, b	18 a, b	26	26
Tenth Vezir	19	19	88	88	88	82	39*
Lady's Tenth	20	50	77	77	77	28. 106	
Eleventh Vezir	21	83	19	19	19	83	
Lady's Eleventh	22	20	20	20		36	
Twelfth Vezir	23	21	21	21	1	31	

* Petis de la Croix's Translation breaks off at the end of the Tenth Vezir's Story.

Stories.	Const. Text.	Ind. Office MS.	Behrnauer.	Quaritch MS. No. I.	Quaritch MS. No. II.	Belletête.	P. de la Croix.
Lady's Twelfth - -	24	22	22	22	2.20	38	
Thirteenth Vezir - -	25	92	23	23		35 *a,b*	
Lady's Thirteenth -	26	46	24	24		40	
Fourteenth Vezir- -	27	59	25	25		41	
Lady's Fourteenth -	28	29	26	26		42	
Fifteenth Vezir - -	29	23	79	79	23	47	
Lady's Fifteenth - -	30	93	28.106	28.106	93	44	
Sixteenth Vezir - -	31	94	49	49	94	53	
Lady's Sixteenth - -	32	95	56	56	95	70	
Seventeenth Vezir -	33	31	81	81	31	57	
Lady's Seventeenth -	34	62	107	107	62	78	
Eighteenth Vezir- -	35 *a,b*	33	82	82	33	61	
Lady's Eighteenth -	36	34	46	46	34	84	
Nineteenth Vezir- -	37	96	83	83	96	65	
Lady's Nineteenth -	38	76	29	29	76	60	
Twentieth Vezir - -	39	73	31	31	73	63	
Lady's Twentieth -	40	36	32	32	36	80*	
Twenty-first Vezir -	41	37	33	33	37		
Lady's Twenty-first -	42	38	34	34	38		
Twenty-second Vezir -	43	39	35 *a,b*	35 *a,b*	39		
Lady's Twenty-second-	44	40	36	36	40		
Twenty-third Vezir -	45	97	37	27	97		
Lady's Twenty-third -	46	72	38	30	72		
Twenty-fourth Vezir -	47.	79	39	92	79		
Lady's Twenty-fourth -	48	28	40	95	28		
Twenty-fifth Vezir -	49	49	41	37	49		
Lady's Twenty-fifth -	50	42	42	38	42		
Twenty-sixth Vezir -	51	55	43	39	55		
Lady's Twenty-sixth -	52	56	44	40	56		
Twenty-seventh Vezir -	53	81	45	41	81		

* Belletête's selection of Stories ends with what he makes the Lady's Twentieth; he adds, however, the Conclusion of the Romance.

Stories.	Const. Text.	Ind. Office MS.	Behrnauer.	Quaritch MS. No. I.	Quaritch MS. No. II.	Belletête.	P. de la Croix.
Lady's Twenty-seventh	54	70	70	42	107		
Twenty-eighth Vezir -	55	47	47	43	75		
Lady's Twenty-eighth -	56	78	78	44	44		
Twenty-ninth Vezir -	57	51	51	45	45		
Lady's Twenty-ninth -	58	98	98	70	70		
Thirtieth Vezir - -	59	53	53	47	111		
Lady's Thirtieth - -	60	48	84	78	48		
Thirty-first Vezir -	61	57	57	51	47		
Lady's Thirty-first -	62	99	99	98	68		
Thirty-second Vezir -	63	100	108	53	100		
Lady's Thirty-second -	64	66	109	84	66		
Thirty-third Vezir -	65		110	57	112		
Lady's Thirty-third -	66			99	99		
Thirty-fourth Vezir -	67	101					
Lady's Thirty-fourth -	68	102	54	54	54		
Thirty-fifth Vezir - -	69		101	101	101		
Lady's Thirty-fifth -	70		102	102	102		
Thirty-sixth Vezir -	71	57,103	61	61	61		
Lady's Thirty-sixth -	72	64	64	64	64		
Thirty-seventh Vezir -	73	65	65	65	65		
Lady's Thirty-seventh -	74	104	104	104	104		
Thirty-eighth Vezir -	75	71	71	71	71		
Lady's Thirty-eighth -	76	60	60	60	60		
Thirty-ninth Vezir -	77	67	67	67	67		
Lady's Thirty-ninth -	78	74	74	74	74		
Fortieth Vezir - -	79	63	63	63	63		
Lady's Fortieth - -	80	80	80	80	80		

In the Quaritch MS. No. I, between the Lady's Twenty-fourth Story and the Twenty-fifth Vezir's, are inserted the following eight stories, attributed to " a certain one from among the Vezirs " and the lady alternately: **73, 76,** 58, 89, 90, 50, 59, 62. Similarly, in the Quaritch MS. No. II, between the Lady's Twelfth Story and the Fifteenth Vezir's, appear the undermentioned eighteen tales, likewise attributed to an undefined Vezir and the lady alternately: **21, 22, 82,** 46, **83, 29, 35** *a, b,* **32,** 41, 42, 43, 78, 51, 98, 53, 84, 57, 24.